SERPENTINE

ADVANCED PRAISE FOR SERPENTINE

Wow! Another great read! I think I read this one in record time (one and a half days). I couldn't put it down. Again, highlights the abuse of power that exists south of the border! As with many of your books, this would make for a great movie. Well done Pete and Alison. Already looking forward to the next one. ~ **Jim Fielding**

A real page turner with something for everyone, action, romance, suspense and detective work! I can't wait to read another of Peter and Alison's books! ~ **Adelle Saul**

Pete Parkin has done it again with his new mystery thriller 'Serpentine'. I am smart now so I put my seat-belt on before starting one of his books and I don't take it off until the last word on the last page has been read. ~ **David Bradley**

Peter Parkin and Alison Darby do it again! I was on the edge of my seat on more than one occasion. As usual, the characters are unforgettable and story lineunique and interesting. I highly recommend Serpentine! ~ **Linda Seder**

The book is thrilling from start to end, and it is a great pleasure to read it. The characters stay true until the end, and their strength to stand up for the truth is what made the book such a captivating read. It is not just for thrill-seeking fans, Serpentine is a book for anyone who wants to read about conspiracy and how doing the right thing can mean more than just bringing justice for those who deserves it. Serpentine is well written and I enjoyed the journey with all the characters. 5/5 stars.
~ **Ailyn K, Penny for my Thoughts**

Suspend your disbelief for a little while and enjoy a real page-turner. 5/5 stars.
~ **MartyAnne Kowalski**

With SERPENTINE, readers revel not only in a champion suspenseful thriller/mystery, but conspiracy theory too. 5/5 stars. ~ **Mallory Anne-Marie Forbes**

A good ole fashioned suspense thriller. 4/5 stars. ~ **Annette Stauffer**

OTHER BOOKS

Headhunter

For executive Jeff Kavanaugh, the most horrifying day of his life begins with an eerie premonition. He doesn't understand the signs, but something is ominously different. His world seems off. Out of place, out of order. Weird symbols are dancing in front of his eyes.

Jeff has a gift that he can't control and he's been conditioned for most of his young life to avoid it rather than embrace it. But the courage he is forced to summon that fateful day changes his life forever. Will Jeff finally see his gift as a true blessing… or, instead, as a curse?

Skeleton

One sudden and violent incident triggers an awakening. A mind that has been shrouded for years by Alzheimer's disease becomes lucid for a few precious moments—just long enough to open the doors to a secret that has been buried for over thirty years.

Dennis Chambers, Chief of Detectives for the city of Washington, D. C., can't forget the words that were uttered. He is obsessed with trying to unlock his mother's mind at least one more time. For just a few more words. As he doggedly pursues the elusive and horrifying secret, deadly forces are at work determined to keep it buried forever.

MetroCafe

Mike Baxter, along with his three best friends and colleagues, are enjoying their annual golfing vacation in Florida with their wives when tragedy strikes, turning their all too comfortable world upside down. The four friends are now down to three and they quickly become embroiled in an apparent embezzlement scheme that their dead friend seems to have engineered. The company that bears Mike's name is in the thick of it and the friends desperately attempt to buy time before being forced to disclose the deception.

Was it simple embezzlement? Or was it something far more sinister and horrifying?

Check out more of Peter & Alison's books at
http://www.sandspress.com

sands press

A division of 3244601 Canada Inc.
300 Central Avenue West
Brockville, Ontario
K6V 5V2

Toll Free 1-800-563-0911 or 613-498-2398
http://www.sandspress.com

ISBN 978-0-9936753-8-6

Cover Concept by DigiWriting
Formatting by Kevin Davidson
Associate Publisher Kristine Barker, Sands Press
Agent Sparks Literary Consultants, Calgary

For information on bulk purchases of this book or any book published by Sands Press, please call 1.800.563.0911 or email sales@sandspress.com

1st Printing May 2016

To book an author for your live event, please call: 1.800.563.0911

sands press
Brockville, Ontario

SERPENTINE

PETER PARKIN

&

ALISON DARBY

sands press
Brockville, Ontario

"The world is a dangerous place to live, not because of the people who are evil, but because of the people who don't do anything about it." Albert Einstein

CHAPTER 1

It reached majestically upward into the glorious Virginia sky. Undulating through the curves, serpent-like in its demeanor. Then the thing dove violently downward at a pitch that defied science, from a 400-foot height guaranteed to cause stomachs to rise to a point in the human body where they were never meant to be. It nosed upwards once again, cresting at a height only slightly less than the first. And down once more, almost straight down this time.

Then, mysteriously, it just disappeared.

From its dizzying height it was as if it had been swallowed up by some sinister force that never wanted it to see the light of day again.

It was swallowed up all right—by the earth itself. Into the tunnel it went, destined to careen along for almost a full two miles. Propelled at first merely by the powerful gravity from the death drop—but once that Kinetic energy was exhausted, the electromagnets kicked in, designed to slam human skulls back against their protective headrests for the entire 100 mph ride through the tunnel.

If there were actual humans sitting in this abomination not one head would be able to move forward to gaze around, due to the extreme G-forces at work. Eyeballs would have to do all the work. But there wasn't much work for the eyes to do either because it was pitch black in the seemingly endless tunnel. They would frantically attempt to do their work anyway, trying desperately to find some essence of light, some reassurance that the nightmare would end.

The monster flew through the tunnel at a breakneck pace, slithering and sliding its way through the curves, curves that were designed to do nothing less than thrill, scare and confuse the living hell out of any human who had been brave enough to pay the thirty dollars price of admission for a near-death experience.

But at that moment there was no one onboard. The thing was on its final test run on this, its 'opening day.'

This was the 'Black Mamba.' The newest, scariest, most horrifying rollercoaster in the world. Named after the world's most dangerous snake, a snake that possessed enough venom at any one time—without re-charging—to kill twenty men in one measly hour. A snake that was one of the fastest in the world, able to slither at a speed of twenty kilometers per hour. Most people couldn't outrun such a creature—a creature that also commonly grew to over eight feet in length.

So, when Nathan Morrell named his new creation, he couldn't resist 'Black Mamba. It suited his design perfectly.

In fact, he had named all of his rollercoasters after deadly snakes. There was the Cameroon Racer down in Johannesburg, the Copperhead in Honolulu, the Bushmaster in Dallas, the Constrictor way 'down under' in Sydney, and the Boomslang in Tokyo.

Nathan—or Nate, as most people called him—was fascinated by snakes. And obsessed with rollercoasters.

Or was he just fascinated with fear?

Many people had asked Nate that question over the years and he himself had actually wondered about it too. Was it the mechanics and sheer genius of rollercoasters that fascinated him? Or was it the frenzied effect that these contraptions had on people? The screams, rapid heartbeats, sweats and palpitations? And the contrast with the sheer relief they felt when they staggered out of their seats when the experience was over?

Or was it that he had the innate ability to design these things and create the terror?

It wasn't that Nate loved scaring people—he just loved giving them what they wanted, and then some. He relished seeing the faces of riders when they disembarked, enjoyed hearing their sighs of relief. Just as much as he enjoyed hearing their screams when they toppled forward off that first big hill, seeing the ground rush up at them.

That was one of the things Nate had become known for. He was known as being "beyond the first hill." He knew that the 'big one' was always the absolute thrill with most rollercoasters—and riders knew that, too. After that hill was over, it was generally anti-climactic for the rest of the ride.

But that wasn't the case with a coaster designed by Nathan Morrell's company, 'Flying Machines Inc.' Nate and his team had reached world prominence by pushing the envelope and creating coaster experiences that were above and beyond "the first hill." Coasters from Flying Machines Inc. had twists and turns that made the first hill seem like a mere toboggan ride. Each of Nate's coasters also refused to rely solely on gravity and Kinetic energy to power the beast. At different points along the ride—unexpected points—engineered electromagnetism took over and propelled the train forward just when it was starting to get exhausted. To the absolute glee and terror of the riders.

And Nate knew full well that 'glee' and 'terror' were one and the same when in a safe, controlled environment.

Safety was paramount—Nate's coasters were off the charts in terms of the terror element, but they were also hailed as the safest in the world.

Even when it came to safety restraints, Nate balanced safety with the experience itself. Most new coasters used shoulder harnesses—they pulled down from above the rider's head and snapped in place around the crotch area. Nate hated these restraints and so did most riders. They were uncomfortable and really restricted the natural movement of the rider. Some riders referred to them as "head bangers." But, these restraints were absolutely essential for coasters that had inversions. If you were upside down for part of the ride, you absolutely had no choice but to use a shoulder harness.

Nate didn't believe in inversions. None of his coasters had that feature. In fact, in his opinion, inversions had been overused in the last two decades—kind of boring. Nate was a traditionalist—rollercoasters were meant to be ridden with eyes forward and upright. Upside down was a farce.

So, he went against the grain. Instead, he concentrated on downhill thrills and speed elements. Electromagnetics made the extreme speeds possible, at any time in the ride, and when the riders least expected them. They always expected speed when rocketing down a steep hill, but they sure didn't expect it riding through a lateral tunnel, or on other straightaways along the course.

Because Flying Machines coasters had no inversions, there was no need for cumbersome shoulder harnesses. All they needed were secure lap bars, which were padded and automatically adjustable to the size of each rider. The advantage of lap bars, which most coaster enthusiasts would swear by, was the enhanced feeling of danger. Not being enveloped by a cumbersome shoulder harness accentuated the feeling of being vulnerable and unprotected. And wasn't that the point of a good coaster ride? To have that sudden feeling of being totally in danger of losing your life—but knowing deep down inside that you were actually as snug as a bug in a rug?

The lap bars were state of the art. They unlocked automatically once the train re-entered the station and came to a stop. They could also be operated manually, or by remote control at any point along the course if riders needed to be retrieved due to a malfunction. They consisted of a simple, but secure, ratchet mechanism. Tried and true, through decades of safe excitement.

The Black Mamba had the most avant-garde of Nate's ideas—the long dark tunnel. It twisted and turned, shuddered and shook, and was magnetically propelled at a terrifying pace through absolute claustrophobic darkness. The only thing Nate didn't like about the tunnel was that he wouldn't be able to hear the screams of the riders as they raced through it. The 'scream factor' was an important measurement for a coaster designer. It was similar to a singer receiving a standing ovation at a concert. The applause was a rush to the singer. The screams were a rush for Nate.

In the fifteen years that Nate's company had been in existence, it had risen to a position of prominence that was unrivalled by any other designer. Flying Machines Inc. was in such demand it couldn't keep up. Nate had taken the amusement park world by storm with his daring innovativeness and almost obsessive attention to detail. That was Nate's nature.

Nathan Morrell was a 'savant.'

Not only was he the most prominent thrill designer in the world, he was also the most hated. He had enemies, he knew. Particularly his former employer, the one who had given him his start twenty-five years before—until Nate finally left in frustration and started his own company. Success in any business bred enemies—Nate knew this. It didn't bother him. In fact, it was probably the ultimate compliment. But he was putting competitors out of business. That was the part he didn't like—he wasn't in the business of hurting people. But he was indeed in the business of being the best. And if that caused casualties, he couldn't help that. It wasn't nice, but that was the way of the world. The strongest survived.

The Black Mamba was the latest addition to the gargantuan amusement park, 'Adventureland,' just on the outskirts of Alexandria, Virginia. Close enough to Washington, D.C.—only about six miles away—to attract all of the well-heeled political nerds who needed an adrenaline rush once in a while to break the awful monotony that was the Capitol region. It was a destination amusement park, complete with hotels, restaurants, and medical facilities. Some people didn't come just for the day—it was too large to do in a day. And Nate knew that most would ride his Black Mamba several times during their visit. Virginia was indeed a good market, and an affluent market.

Nate watched as the empty train came to a gentle rolling stop in the station. The test had gone well. Just as it had for the last few days, when he and his engineers had ridden the terror themselves. It worked like a charm, and even he had screamed his way through it. If he could scream, anyone could scream.

He turned around at the feel of a heavy hand on his shoulder.

"Well, boss, are you ready?"

Nate smiled at his friend and colleague.

Tom Foster, Nate's chief mechanical engineer, was always with him at 'opening days.'

"This is always such a big moment, isn't it, Tom? Exciting as hell!"

"It sure is. We're looking good, aren't we? This thing is the bomb of rollercoasters. The Press is here in droves—have you seen them all?"

Nate allowed his eyes to scan the midway. "Yeah, they're all waiting patiently." He glanced at his watch. "The first full capacity run is in ten minutes. I can see by the red jackets that they're already lining up."

Tom laughed. "Isn't that the ultimate test? The rollercoaster junkies get to ride first!"

Nate ran his fingers through his thick brown hair. It was June and already well into the warm Virginia weather. He needed a haircut badly. His hair always grew fast and it got so hot sometimes it was unbearable. But he hated having to sit still to get his hair cut. Nate wasn't one to sit still for very long.

Nate's company was based in Alexandria—he thought it was ironic that his very own city was the last to finally get one of his coasters. Well, better late than never. Hometown boy makes good and all that crap.

He watched as the red-jacketed riders moved through the turnstiles. And the Press crowded as close as they could get to the fenced perimeter, cameras clicking away at the people in line.

The red jackets were members of the world's most notorious rollercoaster maniacs: The Coaster Crazies. There were a total of 5,000 members, but usually only twenty or so toured at a time—taking in as many rollercoasters as they could in a two-week stretch. Some members actually never rode at all, but merely scared themselves silly, vicariously, by reading and watching online accounts of the ordeals of their fellow members.

Nate counted twenty-six in this particular group—and that was all his coaster could hold. A lot of coasters were set up with two separate trains running the same track—staggered by a safe distance. But Nate's designs were far too fast to allow that—he never succumbed to the pressure to incorporate two trains in his designs. The speeds and stress on the coaster superstructure were far too severe to take that chance. Also, the sporadic triggering of the electromagnets put incredible pressure on the integrity of the complicated edifice. Nate was a structural engineer—he knew these things.

So the Coaster Crazies had been granted the honor of being the sole initiators of the world's newest and most daring rollercoaster. This had been arranged months in advance, with a considerable amount of media hype. Good publicity—Nate had encouraged it. The media had interviewed each of the brave club members and some had even been invited on to late night talk shows. There was a certain fascination with people who stared death in the face. And there was always publicity when a new Flying Machines coaster opened up. These red jackets were the new media darlings.

It was quite the event. The governor of the state of Virginia was there, as was the mayor of Alexandria. It was a big thing for a relatively small city like Alexandria. Nate directed his blue eyes over in the direction of the VIP tent—he could see the various dignitaries already seated. He and Tom were supposed to be seated over there at this very moment, but Nate didn't pay much attention to ceremony.

Tom shook his shoulder again. "Hey, are we gonna grab a seat and a beer?"

"No, Tom, you go ahead without me. I have to be close by to watch this thing. It's like the birth of a child for me—although I don't know what that feels like yet."

Tom smiled knowingly. It was like this at every opening. He looked his friend in the eyes—eyes that were mesmerizingly blue, but also disarmingly weird. He knew that Nate had the ability, when he wanted to use it, of having each eye concentrate on two different things at once. He could read two pages of a book simultaneously. He could watch Tom with one eye and the roller coaster with the other. Which was exactly what he was doing right then.

"Okay, buddy. We'll celebrate after the red jackets disembark. Maybe then you can relax."

Nate laughed and shuffled his feet nervously. "I don't know if I can ever really relax. You know me well enough by now. This stuff is exciting—but also nerve-wracking as hell."

"Hey, that's why you have me. I can do the relaxing for you!"

Nate punched him in the shoulder. "Yes, you are indeed good at that, you lazy bum! See ya later."

Tom walked off to the tent. Nate watched him longingly—wishing he could be more like him; if truth were told, he was salivating for a cold beer. But he just couldn't allow himself. Not yet. There was more watching to do, and one intense eye was on the coaster that was now filled to capacity.

*****

Shelby Sutcliffe settled into her seat—the back seat, of course. Always the back seat for Shelby. She loved the whiplash effect and got high just watching the people in front of her experiencing the thrills milliseconds before she would experience them. Her seatmate, Cheryl Sanders, had ridden with her many times before. They both enjoyed the rear of the train and had become accustomed to each other as seat partners. They wore their red jackets proudly: ten-year members of the Coaster Crazies.

Shelby was pumped over this one. The most heralded coaster in the world by the most famous designers, Flying Machines. She couldn't believe her luck being chosen to be one of the twenty-six members to initiate this already infamous ride; infamous even before it had hosted a single paying customer. She was thrilled.

Shelby tucked her long blonde hair down into the back of her blouse and then she braced herself. She smiled over at Cheryl. "Are you ready, girl?"

"Gawd, yes! Hey, how come you still look so pretty even though you're about to be scared out of your mind?"

Shelby blushed. "I think being scared makes me look pretty. Otherwise, I'd probably just wither up."

Cheryl grinned. "Yeah, you may be right. It brings the life out in us. But… how come the prettiness only happens with you?"

Shelby leaned in closer to Cheryl, giggled, and whispered, "Don't tell anyone, but I think it's simply a dead giveaway that I'm about to have an orgasm."

"What?!" Cheryl shrieked.

Shelby couldn't hide her excitement. "It's true! I have one every time! Every time I go over the first hill it happens." She put her hands up to her mouth, slightly ashamed about what she'd just confessed. "Forgive me, Cheryl. I'm sorry if I've embarrassed you."

"Embarrassed me? Hell, no! It reminds me of that line from *When Harry Met Sally*. Something like, 'I'll have what she's having!'"

Both ladies laughed hard and Shelby could feel some of the tension release.

She was just about to say something else when they were shaken out of their nervous giggles. The train shuddered, groaned and began its journey down the track. They both grabbed onto the lap bar as tight as they could and grinned at each other. This was it, the initiation of the most famous new ride in the world.

Even something simple like the lap bar was one of the things they were both looking forward to about riding the Black Mamba. It was much more of a thrill than being shrouded by a shoulder harness, and neither of them really cared about being upside down anyway. They were both purists.

As she always did before an inaugural ride, Shelby whispered a silent prayer.

*****

Nate moved up closer to the fenced perimeter as the train left the station. He smiled as he watched the red jackets waving to the media, family and friends. There was a round of applause, laughter, and the sound of a cannon booming from the adjacent field. He felt proud. This was his baby. His best baby yet.

The train began its laborious climb to its first hill height of 400 feet. He knew that the drop sensation experienced by the riders was going to be an almost vertical one—the scariest drop ever designed. He'd experienced it already and he knew that the thrill would be beyond compare. Until, of course, they entered the tunnel. That was the ultimate.

Both his eyes were focused on the train, but his left eye suddenly picked up something unusual and it began to wander. A well-dressed man's outstretched arm. At first, Nate thought the guy was waving, but his eye picked up an anomaly. It looked like his hand was formed in a fist. Aiming upwards at the second hill of the track. Then the man turned and walked away.

Nate shrugged and focused both eyes back on the train, which was still in the early stages of its climb.

*****

Shelby held on tight as they reached the top of the hill. She looked over at Cheryl, who was as ashen as she always was on these junkets. Shelby took one hand off the bar and squeezed her friend's. "Don't worry. This is going to be a blast!"

Cheryl nodded without taking her eyes off the horror in front of them. Shelby looked straight ahead now herself and saw the front portion of the train disappear from view as it plummeted off the top of the first hill.

She could feel the pull as gravity began its dastardly deed. There was also a familiar flip in her stomach and dizziness in her head. Her cheeks suddenly felt flush—that was the final sign to her that the orgasm had started its incredible rush.

At that point in the ride she always felt the most vulnerable. There was nothing but openness on each side, and the train was still going slow enough to experience the unsettling feeling of having no protection whatsoever. At least when the ride sped up, her focus went off the scary open space surrounding her and concentrated more on the speed terror.

She held her breath as their rear portion of the car reached the precipice. Then the rush came quickly—earlier this time than usual—in waves that enveloped her entire body. Just as suddenly as it had happened, the orgasm was over. It was a short one. Now all that was left was fear.

The monster dove. Pulled over the edge and down into the abyss by unseen forces. In that instant, Shelby was taken by the fact that she had never, ever, in all of her hundreds of coaster rides, felt like she was going to fall straight down to her death.

But on this ride, on the edge of this hill, that was exactly what she was experiencing. She was scared out of her mind by how vertical the fall was—it took her breath away. She screamed. Then she laughed—a forced laugh, not a voluntary one. A laugh that was intended to make her feel better, feel safe, make her feel like she was just being silly being scared like this.

Her heart was pounding through her chest as the train, within just a couple of seconds, hit the bottom of the hill and shot back upwards at a speed that Shelby couldn't even imagine in her worst nightmares.

They were still climbing to the top of the second hill at a breakneck speed when Shelby was finally able to glance over at Cheryl. She was screaming—her mouth was wide open and her cheeks were glistening from tears.

Shelby didn't dare take her hand off the bar. She wanted so much to caress the back of Cheryl's head and say, "It's okay. We'll be fine."

She wanted so much to ask, "Isn't this fun?" But she couldn't do either of those things. Her hands felt like they were glued to the bar and, for the first time in her coastering career, she didn't believe this to be fun at all.

Shelby squeezed the protective foam of the bar as hard as she could, trying desperately to release the tension from the rest of her body.

She pulled on it. It moved! Up! The damn thing was unlocked!

Shelby raised her head, locking her eyes in stunned terror on the front section of the train as it careened now to the top of the second hill. She knew that after this hill they would plummet into the two-mile tunnel—the thing she'd been looking forward to the most. But not anymore. Shelby knew for a fact that she wouldn't survive this hill—the lap bar wouldn't hold her.

She screamed to no one in particular, "Stop the ride!" But she knew in her heart that what she was demanding was impossible, not just at this moment but at any moment in a coaster ride. Once you started, you were on until the end. And the end was coming, just not the one she'd planned.

She was so scared now that she wasn't sure her body could survive the fear itself, let alone the plummet. In an insane instant, she regretted being a daredevil. She'd finally pushed the envelope too far and the envelope was now pushing back.

Shelby shook her head to clear her eyes. They seemed to have turned kind of blurry all of a sudden because the people in the seats in front of her looked to be sliding sideways.

She shook her head again as their section of the train reached the top of the second hill. She heard screams from the people in the seats ahead of her. But not the usual screams of gleeful thrills—these were different screams.

Then the entire train lurched as the front of it appeared to jackknife.

The beast had a mind of its own. It had no choice, as it no longer seemed to have a track to ride on. It was airborne and all Shelby could see was space. Unprotected space. She glanced over at Cheryl, but instead of her friend there was just an empty forlorn seat, with its lap bar in the 'up' position.

Acting on pure survival instinct, Shelby pulled up hard on the useless lap bar. Then she placed both hands on the seat cushion and shoved herself up and out of the crippled train. She was free of the doomed machine, but all she could do was blindly reach out and flail around desperately with both arms. Hoping for something, anything that she could wrap her sweaty hands around.

CHAPTER 2

For just an instant, Nate thought his eyes were playing tricks on him. But he had uncanny vision, so he knew that that was highly unlikely.

So, was it perhaps the sun reflecting off the metal track?

Something else?

Or just his imagination?

He stared hard. The spot his eyes had picked up was right at the top of hill number two. It looked like a flash—a steady flash. Almost like the traditional sparklers set off on the fourth of July.

He walked closer to the perimeter fence, keeping his left eye focused on that spot, while his right eye watched the train swoop up from the bottom of the first hill. It was racing fast, powered by the energy from its steep descent, and would reach the top in about five seconds. The red jackets had their arms up in the air and he could hear their screams of joy as the Mamba swept them skyward.

The closer he got to the fence the less pronounced the flash was. He sighed with relief; convinced that it was indeed just the sun's reflection. The different angle he was positioned at must have changed his view.

The press people were in front of him, snapping and videotaping the ascent of The Black Mamba. Chattering excitedly, clearly blown away from witnessing the steep drop the machine had taken on the first hill. Nate looked around— pleased at the reaction of the crowd. The line-up for the next runs was already the length of a city block. He glanced back at the VIP tent and saw Tom raise his beer mug in a toast. Nate smiled. He was proud.

Then there was a gasp. Amidst all the laughter and the noise, Nate was still able to hear it. It was a soft gasp, probably from just one person, but different enough from the excited laughter that Nate could discern it quickly.

He whirled his head around to once again face the track. He saw it. So did everyone else. There was a collective gasp now, the most horrifying noise Nate had ever heard. Screams of terror didn't come close to scaring the shit out of him the way this gasp en masse did.

The train was airborne. It had left the track at the top of the second hill and was now beginning its death spiral. He could see that most people were still in the train, arms waving hopelessly in the air. But some of the seats were empty, and it looked as if those lap bars were in the up position.

Nate didn't know why in God's name a certain thought came into his mind at that moment, but it did—maybe because he had such an analytical brain. *'How could those bars be up? How is that possible?'* He realized how silly the question was— passengers in a coaster plummeting to the ground from a height of 250 feet weren't going to be saved by lap bars.

From the initial gasps there was now a profound silence in the crowd. Everything seemed to be moving in slow motion. The train tumbling through the air, bouncing off metal trestles, heads bobbing in their seats as the train somersaulted end over end—each collision with a trestle changing its direction.

There were no screams from the crowd—just a horrible silence. Nate just stood and stared, not quite believing what he was seeing. His feet seemed frozen to the ground as his eyes took in the macabre scene. No commands were coming from his brain—it was as if his mind had accepted that it was hopeless, that there was nothing to do.

His eyes followed the train right to the ground. When it hit the pavement of the inner concourse of the midway, it bounced and split into grotesque mangled fragments. Several bodies flew out of their seats on impact. Some were whole, while others were severed into pieces from the impacts with the trestles and the pavement. And others remained in their seats, contained by the twisted metal. Another thought entered Nate's mind: *'The lap bars were useless, but some of these people still held themselves in all the way down.'*

The shiny steel of the Black Mamba was mangled beyond recognition. It no longer resembled anything close to the sleek train that it had been just a few seconds ago. It was littered with red jackets—jackets that held the remnants of once living, breathing, happy people who were probably also beyond recognition.

The Black Mamba and The Coaster Crazies were joined forever as one.

Nate shook himself out of his trance. People were screaming and running in all directions. He whirled around to see if he could see any emergency personnel. There wasn't a white coat in sight. He could see an ambulance parked beside the VIP tent, but it seemed unmanned. He yelled, "We need help!"

He ran to the ambulance, jumped up on the running board and peered inside the cab. It was empty. Then he heard his name being called.

He jumped off the side of the ambulance and saw Tom running toward him. "Tom, where are the emergency people?"

Tom was breathing hard, sweat dripping down his face. "I don't know! This is terrible!"

"Yes, it is—but we have to do something! C'mon, jump in on the passenger side!"

Nate slid behind the wheel of the ambulance and sighed with relief when he saw the keys dangling. He cranked the engine and turned on the siren. Then he gunned the vehicle in the direction of The Black Mamba. He deftly wheeled around clusters of people who were staggering in shock at what they'd just seen. He crashed the ambulance through the perimeter fence, blasting it into pieces, and sped towards the rollercoaster superstructure, his eyes focused on what used to be the second hill.

He looked over at Tom, whose face was ashen. "Brace yourself, buddy. This ain't gonna be pretty."

Tom swallowed hard and struggled to speak through a mouth that felt like sandpaper. "Do you think we'll be able to do anything?"

Nate grimaced. "We're sure as fuck gonna try."

*****

Shelby felt like she was in suspended animation for a few seconds. Out of the corner of her eye, she saw the train tumbling away from her—down, down. She was aware of the awkward movements and screams of the passengers as the Black Mamba took them on the last thrill ride of their lives. And, strangely, she also noticed that it was a bright sunny day.

Then everything sped up. Shelby was falling in cadence with the train, and she felt the crushing panic as the ground began to rush up to meet her. Shelby knew this feeling well—she was an expert skydiver. But when she jumped out of planes, she had the security of a parachute, knowing she could pull the chord at any moment her heart desired. Knowing she could enjoy the thrill of a freefall while having the canopy as her savior once she'd had enough.

This time, there was no canopy. No savior.

She swung her arms wildly, banging into several pieces of metal as she began her fall. It hurt like hell, but she didn't have time to be in pain. In addition to being a skydiver, Shelby had also been a gymnast in college and she instinctively used both skills to her advantage right then. She twisted her body, stretched out and then sent herself into a tight tuck. The result was a forward somersault, which gave her some control as she fell parallel to the superstructure. She suddenly stopped the roll and stretched her arms out as far as she could. She collided with another piece of metal and bounced away from the trestle. Thinking on autopilot, she immediately created another somersault to bring herself back in the direction she wanted.

When Shelby ended the somersault she was on her back parallel to the ground, deciding to use her legs this time instead of her arms. She slammed into a vertical piece of steel, but just before bouncing away again she managed to wrap both strong legs around it. The rest of her body kept going—crashing down and backwards into the metal wall that was underneath the trestle.

She had stopped her descent, but was now upside down. Shelby strained with her thighs and abdomen and managed to pull herself up into a sitting position, legs still wrapped around the trestle. She quickly brought one hand up and grabbed onto the top part of it. The other hand couldn't make it—she could tell that her upper right arm was broken, probably at the shoulder joint. Must have happened on one of her collisions with the superstructure.

Shelby kept her legs wrapped tight and her left hand holding on for dear life. Her right arm dangled uselessly by her side and was starting to throb. Now that she was safe for the moment her brain was allowing her to experience pain. Up until then she had been experiencing only terror. There had been no room for pain.

Shelby started to think. Started to remember. And then she started to cry. Resting her head against the hot steel, she wondered if she would wake up in a few minutes. Surely this was a nightmare. This couldn't really have happened, could it?

She opened her eyes and allowed herself a glance downward. Then upward. She hadn't fallen very far—maybe only about 100 feet. There were another 150 or so feet below her.

Shelby was astounded at how silent it was. From the happy screams and shrieking laughter of just a few seconds ago, to the spooky stillness that existed now. The contrast was weird. It felt like death. Was she dead?

She could feel a slight breeze against her face, which was a nice relief from the stifling heat. She forced herself to look down again—this time to see where the train had landed.

She saw it—a crumpled mess of black steel, peppered with red jackets. A shudder ran through her body and she started to become lightheaded. A familiar feeling that she'd had many many times before. Oh, no, not now! Dear Lord, don't let me faint now!

She pulled herself in as close to the metal bar as she could and wrapped her arm completely around it. Grasped onto her crippled right shoulder with her left hand and locked herself in place as tightly as possible.

A second later she heard the ambulance siren. And, for the first time since the nightmare had begun, Shelby screamed. Like a banshee.

*****

Nate slammed on the brakes and shoved the ambulance into 'park.' He and Tom jumped out and ran over to the wreckage. Then they stopped dead in their tracks.

Nate started gagging and thrust his hand up in front of his mouth. Tom couldn't control it—he leaned over and retched.

Neither of them said anything for a few seconds. There was nothing to say.

Then Nate asked what seemed now to be a fruitless question. "Are you up to checking for pulses?"

Tom wiped his sleeve across his mouth, and whispered, "Is there any point?"

Nate shook his head. "Probably not. But we have to." He looked around and saw crowds of people up against the perimeter fence a quarter of a mile away. And he also saw cameras held aloft, lots of cameras. "Still no fucking paramedics! Where the hell are they?"

Tom started walking towards the bodies. "Okay, let's get started, Nate."

Nate followed. "Start with the ones who are still whole."

Tom nodded and bent down at the first body he came to. It was a woman, about forty years of age. She was lying face down on the cement, her face pancaked. Tom knew there was no hope, but he put his fingers to her wrist anyway.

Nate went to what once was the front seat section. It looked bent at the joint, buckled from the rest of the train. He made a mental note of this. There were two riders in the front seat, trapped by the lap bars that had been crunched into them on impact—impact with something, probably on the way down. Their torsos appeared to be almost severed by the crushing pressure of the bars. He knew it was a moot point, but he checked anyway for their pulses, and then sadly moved on to the next seat.

They checked them all one by one. Some bodies were scattered well away from the wreckage. No one was alive. That had been obvious just by looking at them before they'd even checked for signs of life, but they had forced themselves to go through the motions anyway.

Nate was kneeling beside the last body, that of a young man who looked no older than eighteen. He looked up and started scanning the mangled skeleton of hill number two.

"This is number twenty-five. There's one missing, Tom."

CHAPTER 3

Tom followed Nate's eyes. Lifted his hand above his forehead to shield his gaze from the strong afternoon sun.

"Maybe the person fell out earlier? Around the first hill?"

Nate scratched his forehead. "Maybe. Let's go check."

The two friends jogged over to the first hill of the structure and began scouring the area surrounding it. Nate heard sirens off in the distance.

He motioned for Tom to follow him along the base of the superstructure down towards the second hill. He looked from side to side. Suddenly, he held up his hand signaling Tom to stop.

"What did you…"

"Shh!"

Nate cocked his head in the direction of the structure. "Did you hear that?"

"No…I didn't hear anything."

"There! There it is again!"

Nate looked up. He felt a sudden surge of adrenaline through his body. "Jesus Christ, Tom! Look!" He pointed.

There she was, clinging to the trestle, about two-thirds of the way up the height of the second hill.

Tom just stared, not believing what he was seeing. Nate shook him by the shoulders. "We have to go up and get her!"

Tom paused before replying. "I hear the ambulances, Nate. Maybe we should wait for the pros."

She noticed them and started screaming again. Louder this time. Nate could see that she was hanging on with one arm, the other one dangling by her side.

Nate started running. "You can wait if you want. I'm going up there!"

Tom hesitated again and then reluctantly followed his friend. He yelled, "What's the plan?"

"Just follow me! We'll figure it out when we get to her!"

The coaster had steps along the side of the track for each of its hills. Totally unprotected, no railings—just narrow steps. Not great, but it was a way to get to the top in an emergency.

Nate started to climb. One step at a time, bent over in a hunch, hands in front for support on the steps ahead of him. Tom was right behind him. They were moving fast.

Nate's feet started to slip on the metal—the steps were narrow and he was wearing slippery-soled oxford dress shoes. He turned around slowly and eased himself down into a half-sitting position on the narrow gangway. They were already about fifty feet off the ground.

"Tom, it looks like you have the same type of shoes on as me. Take 'em off. We're going to slip to our deaths in these things."

The interruption caused Tom to cast his eyes to the ground. Then he slowly lowered himself onto his chest and started panting hard.

"Hey, what's wrong?"

Tom's breathing was getting more labored by the second. His hands grasped the sides of the gangway and clenched until his fingers were stone white.

"Tom!"

"I...can't...move."

"Why?"

Nate could see that his friend's face was soaked with sweat. It was hot in the afternoon sun...but not that hot. He started moving down towards him.

"No! Don't...touch...me!"

Nate looked up and off to the side, and could see that his objective was still clinging bravely to the side of the trestle. He turned his attention back to Tom.

"Is it your heart? Let me help you!"

"No! It's just...a...fear...of heights. I'll...be okay...in a few minutes."

"Christ! A fear of heights?!! You're fucking with me, right?!"

Tom looked up at him. "I thought...I could do it. Thought...I could...force myself. Go on...without me...Nate."

Nate threw his shoes into the air and cautiously twisted himself back around, facing upward again. "Tom, just hold on tight. Help will be here soon. If not, I'll see you on the way down."

He resumed his climb, one careful step at a time. This reminded him of when he was down in Mexico years ago, climbing the ancient Mayan pyramid at Chichen Itza. The narrow steps, the steep incline, the feeling that one false step could send him tumbling to a certain death. And he couldn't help thinking of the irony of his best friend, a rollercoaster designer, being afraid of heights.

*****

Shelby had never screamed so much in her life. Her frightened mind told her that no one would hear her, but she screamed anyway. It helped release the tension and, most importantly, she was convinced that it was keeping her from fainting. If she fainted way up here, she was doomed.

Fainting had been a problem for her since she was a young child. Sometimes, without any warning whatsoever, it happened. Not often, but usually at the worst times. And this was as worse a time as any. At other times, the lightheadedness was the only warning signal. She was determined that she would fight it off, and so far the screaming seemed to be working. The lightness in her head had disappeared and her mind was as sharp as a razor. She thought to herself that maybe this was the solution to her fainting—just start screaming. And then she thought that it was amazing she was even thinking of that at a time like this.

Her left arm was getting stiff and tired wrapped around the metal rod, but she knew that she couldn't make any adjustments. The right arm was useless right now, so it wasn't able to give her other arm relief. She glanced down at her bare thighs—she'd worn sexy little red shorts today to match her red jacket. But wished now that she hadn't. The skin on her legs was blistered and torn from the collisions with the trestle. Blood had also stained her white socks and cute little pink Adidas. She couldn't reach up and touch her forehead, but she knew it was bleeding too. She'd had to rub her eyes against her shoulders several times already to keep the blood from blinding her vision.

Shelby started screaming again. Would anyone hear her? Ever? Would they look up here? She heard more sirens and started screaming again. The metal that she was wrapped around was hot as hell—the afternoon sun was having its effect. It burned her skin, but she willed the pain away.

Then she saw them. One of the men was pointing at her. She could see through the metal braces of the trestle structure that there were two of them. They didn't look like paramedics—dressed too spiffy. Shelby didn't care who they were. She'd been seen! Help was on its way!

She watched them run to the lower section of the track and begin their climb up the gangway. *They're coming for me!* Shelby could feel the blood rush to her face and she started to cry. Then she screamed again. Raised her face to the sky and just let it rip. *There's no fucking way I'm going to allow myself to faint now!*

*****

Nate was totally on his own. He knew that it would have been easier to rescue the woman with Tom at his side, but he had no choice. He climbed as fast as he could along the metal gangway. The metal was hot and his socks were getting soaked with sweat. They were starting to bunch up under the soles of his feet and becoming almost as cumbersome as his shoes had been. They had to go.

He carefully lifted his right foot into the air and yanked off the sock. Then the other foot. He resumed his climb. The metal burned into the soles of his feet, but Nate gritted his teeth and focused on what he was doing. He glanced down the side of the gangway and saw the woman hanging on for dear life. He was close enough now that he could make out some of her features. She was blonde and slender, athletic looking—muscular in a feminine way; the finely toned muscles of her left arm were bulging under the strain of hanging onto the beam. Nate figured she was no older than thirty, which was a good thing. She'd be easier to rescue than someone in their senior years.

She looked straight at him. Even at a distance, he could see a pleading in her eyes. Then he saw her slip. Her left hand, which had been clasped to her right shoulder, lost its grip. It slipped back, but she caught herself at the last second and managed to grip her hand around the bar. She started to lean back and he could tell she was trying desperately to get her arm back to where it had been. She let go with her hand and flung her arm desperately around the bar—her hand grabbed onto her right shoulder once again, but it didn't hold.

Her upper torso fell backwards and her back slammed down against the metal wall. She was upside down now, with only her legs keeping her from plummeting to her death.

The steel wall extended from her prone figure all the way to the ground, a distance of about 170 feet. It was a unique feature of The Black Mamba. Each of the coaster's hills had these walls, which swooped up and down in their design in line with inclines and declines of the track. This particular wall actually followed the lines of the second hill right down to the underground tunnel's entrance.

Each wall was decorated with murals of the Black Mamba and, even though the trestle structure extended all the way to the anchors in the ground, the wall served to completely cover the exterior of the trestles for the lower two-thirds of the structure.

So, if the woman's legs lost their grip, she would face a certain death spiral because there were no remaining trestles accessible for her to grab onto.

Nate yelled. "Hold on! I'm coming!"

He felt panic in his heart. Nate needed to save this woman. Someone had to survive this disaster and she was his last hope.

He threw caution to the wind and ran up the gangway until he was right above the spot where she was hanging. Laid down on his chest and leaned his head over the edge. She was clinging to life only about eighty feet below him. Because she was upside down and vertical now, all he could see were her legs clinging to the bar. They were bloodstained and the muscles were clenched and pulsating. He could tell her strength was fading fast.

Nate called down to her. "Can you get yourself back up in position again?"

The woman responded by bending herself at the waist, with her left hand reaching desperately for the bar—she got halfway and then fell back again, banging her head on the metal wall. He could tell she was exhausted.

"Okay, okay—don't try that again! I'm coming down!" The way she tried to reach for the bar with just her left hand told Nate that her right arm was probably broken. Making things even more difficult for him.

No matter. He held on to the top of the gangway and swung his body over the edge, finding purchase on the trestle for his feet. This thing was like a ladder—vertical bars crossed with horizontal bars.

The hot metal burned into the skin of his feet as he worked his way down to her. Nate moved fast—he calculated that she couldn't hang on much longer with just her legs and the blood must be rushing down to her head in a torrent.

He eased over by crisscrossing several bars and then went down again until he was right next to her. He slid his right hand under her back and hoisted her up until she was able once more to grab onto the bar with her left hand. She was slow to react, but she managed to grab it.

She didn't say a word, but looked right into his eyes; her gaze saying much more than any words possibly could. He could see that her eyes were blue, just like his.

Suddenly, her eyeballs began to roll. Nate removed his right hand from behind her back and held onto the trestle bar. He brought his left hand around and slapped her hard across the face. Then again.

It worked. She shook her head and he could tell she was beginning to focus again.

"Listen to me carefully. Let go of the bar and wrap your left arm around my neck. I'm going to climb us back up."

She nodded.

"Are you sure you understand? When you let go of that bar you'll have to wrap around my neck fast, or you're going to be upside down again. We'll only get one shot at this."

She nodded again.

Nate smiled. "You're going to be okay. Don't worry—I have a strong neck."

She managed a thin smile and nodded once more.

"Okay, here we go. Do it!"

She made a swift move with her arm and he felt the pressure of it wrapping around his neck.

"Now, let go of your legs from around the bar!"

She did and he could feel the instant weight transfer. She was heavier than he figured. Nate didn't waste a second—he began to climb, one bar at a time. It was slow going, but he was confident they were going to make it.

At about forty feet from the top, he could feel her arm begin to loosen around his neck. He ignored it and kept going. Her weight was beginning to slow him down—each move of his feet to the next rung caused her body to swing, making him feel the weight even more.

Suddenly, her arm slipped from his neck completely! Nate held on tight to the rung with his right hand and whirled his body outward. She was falling! Left arm reaching up to him in desperation. Her beautiful blue eyes were wide with fear, her mouth a chasm trying to find the energy to scream.

Nate panicked. He swung his left hand down and was just able to catch her forearm before she disappeared from his reach. Using all of the strength he had left, he yanked her upward, violently, twisting her body so it would slam backwards against the trestle. Then he quickly slid his body in front of hers, feet planted on either side. His body was now pinning her to the superstructure, and they were face to face for the first time.

Nate caught his breath and eased his head back so he could see her more clearly.

Her eyes were closed. He checked the pulse in her neck. Strong. She was unconscious, but seemed fine otherwise.

Nate held on tight to the trestle and pressed his body forward as hard as he could, moving one knee over until it was positioned in her crotch. His strength was the only thing keeping both of them from certain death.

More sirens. Praying that one of those sirens was from a ladder truck.

CHAPTER 4

Voices were hushed. She could hear them, but knew that they were deliberately keeping their conversations on the down-low for her benefit. And she knew all the people who were talking. She just couldn't see them yet, because for some reason her eyes refused to open. She tried hard, but to no avail.

There were other sounds, too; sounds that were all too familiar to her. Beeping noises and the clang of metal objects. The squeaking of rubber soled shoes on tile. Announcements over a PA system. The steady drone of carts and beds being pushed down a hallway.

Shelby parted her lips to speak, but nothing happened. Her mouth was painfully dry and it felt like her tongue was stuck against her teeth. Suddenly, she felt something being shoved between her lips followed by a refreshing and welcome rush of ice water. A soft hand was on her forehead. She knew it was her mother's hand, knew just from the touch. A touch that hadn't changed its sensation since she'd been a child.

An excited whisper. "She's waking up!"

Another one. "Thank God!"

Shelby motioned towards her eyes with her left hand, and someone immediately responded by dabbing at them with a wet cloth. Her eyelids cooperated—they felt sticky, but they finally opened. Her mother rubbed gently around the rims of her eyes with the same wet cloth, wiping away the puss.

Shelby managed a smile. "You'd make a great nurse, Mom."

Her mother smiled back. "No, one nurse in the family's enough, I think."

She noticed that her younger sister, Laura, was standing behind their mom. She was smiling, too, but also crying. Shelby hoped she was crying out of joy and not about something she hadn't been told yet. She knew she was in a hospital and she recognized several décor items that told her it was her very own hospital. Shelby was a surgical nurse at Inova Alexandria Hospital, one of the finest care facilities in the entire country.

But what Shelby couldn't remember was what had happened to put her here. "Mom, why am I here?" She struggled with her right arm and tried to move it. She couldn't. She could tell that it was taped tightly to her body; she could feel the tape wrapped completely around her. "Why is my arm immobilized?"

"You were in an accident. Don't you remember?"

Shelby shook her head, while noticing her sister opening the door and motioning to someone.

One of the doctors rushed in—she recognized him as the senior orthopedic resident, Bill Butler.

His face was beaming. "So nice to see you awake! How is our special guest doing?"

Shelby didn't smile back. "Bill, why am I here? And what's wrong with me?"

"You're going to be just fine, don't you worry." He had a clipboard in his hand and glanced down at it as he was speaking to her. "We did x-rays—nothing's broken. We were worried about your shoulder, but all you have is a real bad bruise—some serious internal bleeding in the joint area and it's very swollen. Looks like a watermelon. You'll have very little movement for a while, so we immobilized it for you. Best you not move it for a couple of days—let the swelling come down. I've prescribed some anti-inflammatories for you."

Shelby was paying close attention. "Okay, what about the rest of me?"

"Lots of cuts and bruises, pretty much all over. You got banged up pretty good. We've treated all of the cuts and none of them needed stitches. Overall, you're very lucky."

"When did this happen?" She wasn't ready yet to ask what happened.

"This afternoon. It's 8:00 at night now."

"Why was I unconscious?"

"You came into the hospital that way. You fainted at the scene and didn't start to show signs of coming around until after the ambulance dropped you off." Bill paused. "You woke up and were quite distraught, so we gave you a strong sedative to put you to sleep and just calm you down. Looks like it worked."

Shelby braced herself, took a deep breath and then asked the question she'd been putting off. "What happened?"

Bill stepped forward at the same time as her mother and sister backed up. He sat on the edge of the bed and held onto her left hand, squeezing it gently. He lowered his voice to just above a whisper. "You were on a rollercoaster."

Shelby blinked twice—Bill was starting to look blurry. Then she felt her feet start to tingle, followed by a violent tremor that reverberated up her back and into the back of her head. The lightheadedness started to return—that familiar feeling again. She shook her head and then let out a scream—a scream that scared even her.

A nurse rushed into the room with a crash cart. Bill reached his hand out and pulled a needle off the top shelf. Held it up in the air and tested it. Then he clenched Shelby's forearm and pulled up her sleeve.

Shelby shoved his hand away. "No! Don't you dare drug me again!"

Bill's face bore a look of shock. "It's for your own good, Shelby."

"It's not! It's for your own good, so you people don't have to see or deal with me upset. I need to be upset! And…let me tell you this…I am recalling some images now. And one thing I recall is that I discovered on that damned ride that screaming stops the rush in my head—stops the dizziness. And I never knew that before. I know it now. So…leave me alone. I'm stronger than you think."

There was stunned silence for a good thirty seconds. It seemed like everyone in the room was afraid to even breathe. Then Bill slowly put the needle back into the tray on the crash cart, and motioned for the nurse to leave. She didn't need a second invitation—she was out of the room in a flash.

Bill turned his attention back to Shelby. "You may think you're strong, and I know you well enough to know that's partly true. On the other hand, you're a human being with real emotions—and what you've endured can only be described as a tremendous shock to the psyche. Memories are going to be painful as hell."

"Who else survived?"

"No one. You're it."

Shelby nodded her understanding and tears started rolling down her cheeks. She began twirling the bed sheet with her left hand and looked up at her mother, who at that moment was looking very "motherly." Laura was rubbing their mother's back while looking quizzically at Shelby. Everyone was awaiting her next words.

Shelby closed her eyes and summoned the images. She wanted those images, wanted to get them over with.

The first one came to her clearly: she could see her hands pulling up on the lap bar as the train approached the top of the second hill. She felt her body shudder as she re-lived the feeling of knowing the bar wouldn't hold her, and then the horror of watching the front of the train going airborne, knowing it was pulling the rear with it. A feeling of utter loneliness came over her as she recalled glancing to her right and seeing an empty seat where her friend Cheryl had been sitting only seconds before.

Then she was airborne herself, pushing herself up and out of the crippled Black Mamba. Spinning, smashing into metal bars—she could feel the pain all over again. Then Shelby saw herself go into a somersault, failing and then trying again in final desperation, knowing that the steel wall was coming up fast and she would no longer have anything to grab onto.

She shuddered again and felt Bill's strong hand on her left shoulder, squeezing it gently. Shelby screamed and could feel Bill's hand pull back fast. She kept her eyes closed as she summoned the next images. Crashing into the trestle with her legs outstretched. Grabbing on and squeezing her thighs together around the cruel hot steel as tightly as she could. Shelby screamed again.

Then she saw an image that warmed her heart: two men climbing up to her. Watching one of them stop and lie down on the track. Worried that the one in front would change his mind. But he hadn't. He kept coming, brave and fast. Talked to her from above, instructed her. Then flung himself over the edge and climbed down to her. Lifted her upside down body up and back into a sitting position.

Shelby smiled now and she could hear a gasp of relief from her mother and sister. But she didn't dare open her eyes yet—afraid the images would stop. She had to watch this through to the end. As a nurse, she knew how difficult and lengthy a process it was for people suffering from post-traumatic stress disorder. Locking away memories merely made it worse in the long run—and she was determined, after having survived this accident, not to prolong the pain. She wanted it over with and was determined to face her memories head-on, not lock them away for endless therapy to deal with.

The man was well dressed; she remembered that. That seemed out of place. And yet he was barefoot; she'd watched him remove his shoes on the way up and toss them to the ground. Remembered hearing him curse a couple of times about the hot metal on his feet when he was beside her on the trestle.

Then he was carrying her up. Her left arm clinging for life around his neck, her body swinging carelessly behind. Step by painful step, curse by ugly curse, the well-dressed man was climbing her to safety. She smiled again and heard another happy gasp from her mother.

The lightheadedness started returning again. Shelby screamed. It cleared. Then something horrifying replaced it. She could feel her left arm slipping from around the stranger's neck. The helpless feeling of having absolutely nothing to hang on to. The memory of this kicked her in the gut—it was even scarier than when she saw the train leaving the track. Because she'd had the chance to enjoy the feeling of being saved, only to have it stripped away.

She was falling now—away from him. Opened her mouth to scream, but nothing came out. Then one strong arm from above swung down at lightning speed. She could see the look of determination on his face as his big hand clasped onto her thin forearm.

She saw him grimace as he flung her upwards, towards him. Shelby felt herself twisting in the air. Astonished—not only had he pulled her up to safety, but he'd had the presence of mind to spin her backwards in mid-air so her face wouldn't smash into the trestle.

The last thing she remembered in her vision was the violent collision of the back of her head with the trestle. Then everything went black, blacker than the Black Mamba. The monster that had tried to kill her.

She opened her eyes. And all eyes were on her.

She said one thing and only one thing. "Find him."

CHAPTER 5

He'd endured two days of hell. There'd been no escape, and neither had Nate expected there would be. The media, the police, the amusement park operators, and the insurance companies—he'd spent time with them all and virtually everyone was puzzled over the horrifying accident. It didn't make sense.

The track at the top of the second hill had split clean through. And the lap bars had unlocked—although that was immaterial to the accident of course. But in Nate's mind it added to the puzzle. Two things went wrong at exactly the same time. And for the track to split like that—it was unthinkable. The engineering specs were extremely high on his coasters—the steel used was the strongest possible, going well beyond code requirements.

The Adventureland amusement park was closed indefinitely. And no access was being permitted to anyone unless authorized. Even Nate couldn't get in, couldn't get a look at his own structure. He and his team weren't allowed anywhere near the site. Which Nate found very frustrating—he felt responsible for what had happened and the guilt was eating him up. What had he missed? What had gone wrong?

The only survivor was that woman he'd saved. Nate had kept her pinned to the trestle until an aerial ladder was able to pluck them from their twelve storey perch. The woman had been unconscious the entire time; Nate assumed that the collision of her head with the trestle had knocked her out cold.

Once on the ground, the paramedics did a quick check of her vitals; then an ambulance rushed her to the hospital. Nate warned them to be careful with her shoulder; that it seemed to be broken. He was relieved when the paramedics gave him the thumbs up sign—indicating that her vitals all seemed strong. Nate desperately needed the woman to be okay.

Nate felt lost. He was accustomed to being able to take action, and it was his creation that had caused such a horrible massacre. 'Massacre' was the only word he could think of to describe the carnage. His rollercoaster had turned into a death machine—left its secure track and tumbled end over end in a 250-foot drop of doom. And he wasn't even being allowed to examine the track or the train.

Other experts had been called in to do that. And he understood this to a certain extent—-that it needed objective analysis. No one could expect him or the amusement park operators to be totally objective. He understood that. But he'd expected to be consulted, to at least be there when the outside experts began their investigation.

There was one thing he didn't understand though.

As Nate pondered that one thing, he stood up and started pacing the floor of his massive main living room. The scene of the accident had been cordoned off as if it was a crime scene. And he was told that the lead investigators of the accident were the National Transportation Safety Board. That didn't make any sense at all. The NTSB had no jurisdiction whatsoever with amusement parks. Their mandate was primarily trucking, highways, bridges, shipping, and aviation.

It had been a point of controversy for years that there was no federal body responsible for the safety of amusement parks in the United States. Everyone wanted it, including even coaster designers like Nate, but the Feds ignored it. They left it to the States and municipalities to self-govern and set their own standards. Whenever an accident happened at an amusement park it was the local police, fire department or state/municipal safety board that investigated.

So why in this case was the NTSB involved? It was now a federal government investigation, but there was no reason in the world why this would be different than any other accident. Sure, it was more severe than anything that had ever happened before, but despite that, there was just simply no jurisdiction for the Feds.

Nate wondered if it was because Alexandria was only six miles from Washington, D.C. And…he wondered if it was because the NTSB actually had their training facility right in Virginia—in a town called Ashburn. Nate knew that it famously housed the reconstructed 747 fuselage of TWA 800, which went down in the Atlantic in 1996. One of the most controversial plane crashes of all time—it just fell from the sky in flames. Witnesses vowed that they'd seen a missile rising up towards it from the surface of the sea shortly before it burst into flames. But, those accounts were debunked and basically ignored. The final 'official' cause of the crash was an exploding fuel tank, although there seemed to be little evidence to indicate that. Nate figured that was just a safer conclusion than the missile one.

Maybe his reconstructed rollercoaster would now be side by side with TWA 800 in the NTSB training facility?

He turned on the TV for a distraction. He didn't watch the local news because he knew what the headlines would be. Instead, he tuned in to CNN and watched the ongoing coverage of the conflict in Ukraine. The Americans accusing the Russians of imperialism after their annexation of the Crimea, and the Russians complaining about the usual U.S. interference in matters that didn't concern them.

Nate chuckled to himself—how could the Russians be that naïve? The billions of dollars that had been invested by U.S. oil companies in the Ukraine certainly gave the Americans a right to care what was going on. But—the name calling from both sides was getting ridiculous and dangerous. They were like a bunch of kids in a playground. The latest warnings now in the headlines hinted that the Ukraine was ready to explode into a full-fledged civil war.

That caused Nate to reflect on the similarities with his own country, and in particular where he lived. The American Civil War had torn the country apart for four years in the 1800s, and in his view it still hadn't recovered. That war killed over 600,000 soldiers, and caused divisions in families that took generations to heal. And all over something that could have been resolved by clear heads. Clear heads that could have just sat down and talked to each other. That's what worried him about Ukraine. The only talking that was going on was through the biased media.

And Nate thought that even though the American Civil War happened more than 160 years ago, it had a remarkable parallel to the events of today. The civil war in Syria had the rebels there hoping that the United States and other foreign powers would help them topple the Assad regime. That didn't happen.

And in Ukraine, the government there was now doing their damnedest to get the world behind their plight. Hoping that other countries would come running to their defense in a civil war that seemed inevitable. At this point, that rescue didn't seem likely either.

The parallel Nate thought was remarkable was that during the American Civil War, the Confederates had counted on foreign interference, too—they'd gambled on the idea that countries in Europe, particularly England, would come to their defense in their attempts to secede from the United States. They were convinced they would have foreign help because Europe was so dependent on the cotton that came from the southern states' slave-labored plantations. But help never came. Europe wisely chose to stay out of it. So, the Americans just proceeded to slaughter each other.

Nate's home had housed some Confederates during part of its grand history, as Virginia was one of the rebel states. It was built in 1750, over a hundred years before the civil war had even started. He loved the historical character of the house, and the fact that it probably played some kind of role during the most infamous war ever.

His address was 207 Jefferson Street, a street named after the first—and last—President of the Confederacy, Jefferson Davis. Nate had searched high and low in the attics and crawl spaces of his house, hoping to find some old Confederate currency. But no luck.

He and his wife, Stephanie, had bought this marvelous house five years before for a cool three million dollars. It was a large home—larger than they needed for just the two of them—at 5,400 square feet. The original wing was preserved in exactly the state that it was in when it was first built; pine floors, ostentatious crystal chandeliers, colonial fireplaces and ten-foot ceilings. Absolutely nothing had been replaced in that wing, and it was in pristine condition, exuding an elegant feel.

The second wing was an addition put on about fifty years before and it contained more casual living space. More laid back—beer and pretzels style. Nate felt most comfortable in the newer wing. The original wing was so elegant he was afraid to even set foot in there. It was more of a showpiece for anyone who really cared about that sort of thing. People like his wife. Stephanie reveled in the attention the house got, almost as much as she reveled in the attention *she* got.

There was a beautiful and bright conservatory room serving as the dividing point for the two wings, with French doors opening out into a completely walled and hedged backyard.

Nate's house was located in a beautiful neighborhood of Alexandria, referred to as Old Town. It was indeed old—and quaint. A free trolley rolled up and down King Street, allowing people to jump on and off to enjoy the stores, restaurants, art galleries and coffee houses. Nate's office was actually right on King Street, and he was able to walk to it on nice days—which in Virginia meant pretty much every single day. The history of Old Town was accentuated by the cobblestone streets and sidewalks—this section of Alexandria was one of the biggest tourist draws in Virginia. People were generally fascinated with Civil War architecture, and particularly so when it was a city that had been occupied by the rebel Confederates.

Nate's daydreaming was broken by a fresh headline on the TV. *His* headline. The anchor lady mentioned Flying Machines Inc. as the designers and manufacturers of The Black Mamba. Then she cited a statistic—the rate of serious injury on rollercoasters was only one person for every twenty-four million visitors. It was actually safer riding in a rollercoaster than riding in a baby stroller.

Nate quickly grabbed the remote and hit the 'off' button. That was a statistic he didn't need to hear, knowing that his coaster had just killed twenty-five people.

Even though he was doing his best to allow himself to drift off and daydream once in a while, try to think of other things, or distract himself with TV, he couldn't escape what had happened two days before. And he doubted he would ever be able to completely put it out of his mind, no matter how long he lived.

But he had to try—he had to be whole again. Nate had to put his talented brain to work, either to solve this mystery or move on to other things. He couldn't dwell on it or punish himself. He knew that. But much easier said than done, especially for a savant like Nate who had the ability to observe, think and analyze at a level way beyond the average human.

His brain was jerked out of its trance by the sound of the phone ringing in the next room. He heard Stephanie answer it—probably just another media outlet wanting some kind of statement from him and, after two days of that crap, he was sick of giving statements. He hoped she would just hang up. He knew she was sick of it all, too.

She sashayed into the room; phone in hand, looking like she didn't have a serious care in the world. And in her little cocoon, that was probably the case. She was dressed in her usual way—kind of a 'southern' way. A long flamboyant summer dress, bare shoulders and arms. Big hair and a face that was 'made up' as if she was ready to attend some kind of soiree. And maybe she was. Nate didn't care anymore.

"I took a message for you. Here's the phone if you want to call her back. Her name is Laura Morgan—says she has something important to ask you. She wanted me to emphasize to you that she's not from the Press. But if she's lying, could you please ask her if they could please quit staking out our house? I have a tennis lesson this afternoon and I'm afraid to walk out to the driveway."

Nate stood up and grabbed the phone out of her hand. "Steph, more than two dozen people died the other day. That's just a big inconvenience to you, huh?"

"Well, they're dead—there's nothing I can do about it. Life goes on."

Nate shook his head sadly. "Maybe one day you'll realize the world doesn't revolve around you. I hope so, for your sake."

"What do you mean by that?"

"Nothing. At least nothing that would register with you."

Stephanie turned on her heel and stomped back to the kitchen. Nate sighed and hit the memory button on the phone. Then he dialed the number for Laura Morgan.

"Hello?"

"Hi. Is this Laura Morgan?"

"Yes, it is. Can I help you?"

"I'm Nathan Morrell. You called me a few minutes ago."

"Oh, I'm so glad you called back. Are you the same Nathan Morrell from the rollercoaster accident?"

Nate paused, then said softly, "You told my wife that you weren't with the Press."

"No. No, I'm not with the Press. I'm the sister of the woman you saved."

Nate felt his face flush. "Oh, well, okay then. How is she doing?"

"She's doing really well. They're keeping her in the hospital for a few more days, just for observation. She was unconscious, as you know, and they're afraid of any post-traumatic stress symptoms. So, they'll be watching her closely."

"I'm so glad she's okay. Please give her my best wishes."

"Mr. Morrell, I wanted to thank you for what you did. It was so very brave of you. She wouldn't be alive, I'm sure, if it wasn't for you."

Nate could feel his mouth going dry.

"Mr. Morrell? Are you still there?"

"Yes, yes I'm here. Thanks for your kind words, Laura."

"I saw you on TV and in the newspapers. I know who you are, Mr. Morrell. You saved my sister, but you're also the CEO of the company that designed the Black Mamba."

"Yes, I am, Laura. I…don't know what else to say."

"Don't hang up. My sister wants to meet you. You probably don't even know her name—it's Shelby Sutcliffe. And she wants to thank you in person. Would you agree to come to the Inova Alexandria Hospital to meet her? Please?"

"Are you sure that's a good idea—now that you know who I am?"

"My sister has been sheltered away from the media; no interviews, newspapers or TV. We told her your name, but she has no idea yet who you are. Shelby's desperate to meet you—she remembers clearly what you did. It's very important to her. Will you do it?"

A part of Nate's brain wanted to say no. But the compassionate part of him wanted to see his lone survivor in person once again—in a safer venue. He wanted to see for himself that she did indeed survive the horror, that he had indeed done something worthwhile. And maybe he also needed to face the music—face whatever wrath was coming to him.

"I'll come by today, Laura."

CHAPTER 6

Nate donned his New York Mets baseball cap and a pair of sunglasses—not a great disguise, but better than nothing, he figured. He walked out to the driveway and hopped into his car. A few reporters were hanging around, but they respectfully gave way to him as he backed up and headed on down the street. It wasn't a long drive to Inova Hospital. It was located on Seminary Road, only about ten minutes away. He was nervous about seeing Shelby. Felt unworthy. She was going to thank him for saving her life, when his invention was what put her life in peril to begin with.

As he drove along, he started remembering back to the only time he'd ever been laid up in a hospital. It was a long time ago...

He got to his feet slowly, deliberately. A simple task like standing up, something that he'd taken for granted his whole life, was now an effort for him. He picked his helmet up off the field—at least he thought it was his helmet—and began the long walk back to the bench. There were players on either side of him trying hold him up straight—he was aware that he was teetering, but he didn't think it was serious. Thought he could easily make it back to the bench on his own.

The next thing he knew he was on the ground again, staring up at the beautiful blue sky. Just before the darkness smothered him. And it was a profound darkness—he tried to explain it later to his friends but it was impossible to describe properly. You had to be there.

His mother always warned him about football being a dangerous sport, but like most athletic boys his age he ignored her. He was a good athlete, strong, in excellent shape, could handle a lot of punishment. But of course he couldn't foresee that he was going to be clotheslined at the forty-yard line, then pounded from the side while he was still staggering from the first cowardly hit. He could still feel the impact—his helmet had been jarred loose and sent flying from the initial hit. The second hit came when his head was unprotected—butted by his opponent's helmet. He 'saw stars'—he had heard that expression many times, but didn't really believe that anyone really saw them. He found out firsthand that it was true.

He spent the night in the hospital. His coach and the rest of the team hung around as long as they could until his mother could get there. Then they left, but not until collectively signing the game ball and leaving it for him. He'd earned it—Nate had scored two touchdowns and they'd won the game. He had given them a big enough lead that they were able to hang on through the last quarter and win without him.

Even though he was the quarterback. The leader. The General on the field.

His back-up proved to be almost as good. He had to be, because Nate was out for the rest of the season.

After a few days rest at home with his mother fawning over him constantly, Nate went back to school. It was his senior year in high school, so he was well known to everyone. Not necessarily because he was a senior, but because he was a football star and President of the Student Council. So, when he wasn't there he was missed—when he came back, he was a hero.

Everyone who mattered had been at that game—had seen the double hit against their star quarterback. Gasped as they watched him crumple to the ground. Applauded when he crawled to his feet like the brave warrior he was. Then gasped once again when his legs gave out and he fell to the field unconscious. Watched in stunned silence as the trainers tended to him on the field, then clapped and cheered again as he was carried off the field on a stretcher.

There was a reception party waiting for him when he came through the front doors of the school. Lining both sides of the hallway, cheering and applauding once again. Nate remembered feeling embarrassed, but also feeling darn good.

The girls were all over him. They must have felt he needed mothering—so they did their darnedest to make him feel mothered. He loved it. Girls had always come easy to him, but this getting injured business made it a cakewalk.

So he came back a hero.

He also came back a genius.

Well, sort of.

He noticed that something was different a few days after the injury. Reading textbooks was a weird experience. When he put a book down and tried to recall what he'd just studied, he could see entire pages in his head. Word for word. Sentence by sentence. Paragraph by paragraph. He had instant recall, photographic recall.

At first, it freaked him out. He didn't tell his friends or even his family. He felt like a freak. And he knew in his gut that it had something to do with the head injury. It was too much of a coincidence. He thought that it might be just a temporary condition; that it would fade over time. But, as the weeks went by, he began to realize that what he had would most likely be with him for good.

The Principal was the first one to ask him about it. A few minutes before Nate had to make a speech in his role as Student Council President, the Principal handed him a two-page document and asked him to read it out to the students after he'd finished his speech. It had something to do with graduation arrangements. Anyway, Nate simply looked the pages over and recited the words verbatim during his speech without looking at the text. After the assembly, the Principal came up and asked him how he was able to do that. Nate just shrugged and walked away.

Then, at the Senior Prom, Nate, his girlfriend Vicky, and a bunch of his friends, were horsing around beside the piano during a break in the music. One of his buddies tried to one-

finger the tune to Guns 'N Roses' Welcome to the Jungle. Nate had already had a couple of drinks and was not totally on his guard—and, truth be told, probably wanted to show off a bit. He figured he could tap out the tune to that song easily, even though he'd never played a note on the piano in his life.

He didn't even realize himself what was going to happen. What started as a one-finger attempt resulted in a brilliant two-hand rendition of the song, just from the tune in his head. As soon as he sat down at the piano, his fingers just seemed to know what to do and where to go. It was like he was in a trance. All of his friends were speechless. They started shouting out other tunes and he obliged—he had no choice now, the jig was up. And he was actually enjoying this newfound talent. He thought it made the photographic memory seem like child's play. When he finally lifted himself off the piano bench, he'd played ten songs flawlessly, like a trained concert pianist. And his small group of friends around the piano had swelled to about eighty.

He stood up, did a mock bow, and then took Vicky out to his car for the best sex they'd ever had. She breathlessly whispered to him that she thought his brilliance was sexy. That came as a shock to a jock like Nate. He always thought that being an athlete made him appealing, but this brilliance stuff was now deemed sexy. He was a double-threat! At that moment he decided he would stop trying to hide it and just simply embrace whatever God had decided to bestow upon him. Including the great sex.

And he figured it was finally time to tell his mother. So he did. And she immediately booked an appointment with their family doctor, who then referred them to a neurologist.

Nate remembered sitting through a lot of gobbledygook, watching his mother nod respectfully and take notes, pretending to understand. A lot of it just went over her head, not because she wasn't smart, but because she was so distressed over the whole thing. Nate understood every word—or at least remembered every word. Such that he was able to explain it to his mom later once she'd calmed down.

In short, he had Savant Syndrome. His mom had a tough time getting past the word 'savant.' She thought that was synonymous with 'autistic.' Nate re-explained, after the doctor explained, that only fifty percent of savants are autistic. Put another way: not all savants are autistic, and not all autistics are savants.

People could be born with the syndrome or it could be triggered by a brain injury. His mother gasped at that, too. The doctor stressed that Savant Syndrome is not considered a mental disorder, whereas Autistic Savantism is.

Nate's concussion on the football field had apparently resulted in damage to his left anterior temporal lobe, which is where the damage has to occur to cause savantism. The neurologist said it was nothing to worry about—that Nate was lucky that he ended up getting "good brain damage" rather than "bad brain damage." His mom felt better after he put it in that context.

Savants generally excel at mathematics, art, memory, and music. Strangely, the musical talent with savants is almost always restricted to the piano. No one has yet been able to comprehend why that is—just another strange aspect to a syndrome that is still very much a mystery.

Nate's gifts included math—he was a good mathematician before the injury, but quite brilliant afterwards.

And of course his memory was now phenomenal, including being 'eidetic'—photographic. Not only that, he could read upside down; his mind could take a snapshot, and then flip it around in his head.

His powers of observation were also extremely acute—and photographic as well. If he concentrated on something, the image would never leave his mind. And he could telescope the image to make it larger—all it took was concentration. Which he had plenty of—much more so than before the accident.

One other talent he'd picked up was within his eyesight. He could focus each eye in separate directions and each was capable of 'taking a picture' in his mind. The eyes were able to work independently of each other. He thought this was a really freaky skill, and one that people could actually notice if he used it. Nate tried not to use this skill when he was in the company of others—but sometimes he couldn't resist. And sometimes it was just an amusing party trick.

Art was not a gift he was blessed with though. He had no talent whatsoever for art, not before the accident and not after.

Nate and his mother both did a lot of research on Savant Syndrome after their visit with the neurologist. He told them to just go live their lives, that there was nothing that could be done about this, and neither should they even want anything to be done. Nate was still the same boy—just exceptionally gifted now in some areas that he wasn't before. But he was still the same charming lad, the boy with the outgoing personality, the one who could be the life of the party, and the boy who had always had an overwhelming capacity for sensitivity, kindness and compassion.

Nate was still Nate. Just new and improved.

Nate parked his car in the hospital parking lot, paid for his ticket at the machine and left the stub on the dashboard of his BMW 735i. The car was only a year old and it was the first bimmer he'd ever bought. But he loved it—the way it cornered and accelerated. He'd never had a car like it before. As he walked away, he turned his head and took a moment to admire the gleaming emerald green machine. It stood out in the parking lot, for sure.

He saw his image reflecting back at him from the glass doors of the hospital as he approached the entrance. For a moment, he didn't recognize himself with the baseball cap and sunglasses on. Nor was he prepared to see his stilting gait—his feet still hurt like hell from the burning metal of the trestles and he was walking tentatively. But he didn't realize how frail he looked walking like that. He looked like an old man the way he was hobbling. And his shoulders seemed hunched—he wasn't standing erect in his usual confident way.

He knew the last couple of days had taken a lot out of him—he wasn't sleeping or eating right, and it was apparently starting to show. Nate wasn't accustomed to looking his age—he was forty-five now, but today he thought he looked twenty-five years older. And there were times since the accident when he'd felt like he was indeed seventy. He was tired, beat up, insecure and frustrated, and he knew he had to just shake it off. His problem was that he took everything that he had a hand in personally. Nate took responsibility seriously.

But while the accident had taken a toll on him, he had to remind himself that he was still alive. At least he hadn't suffered the horror that those poor victims and their families had suffered. However, knowing that he'd played a big role in their loss was weighing heavily on him. Had he missed something? Had he done something wrong in his design specifications? Or just the design itself? Had he been unknowingly reckless? He had to find out.

He checked in at the front desk and was directed down the hall to the elevators. Shelby was housed on the second floor in room twenty-one. Nate found his steps getting slower and slower the closer he got to her room. He had to face her, had to do this duty, but the coward part of him didn't want to. He had to, though, and he was glad that the hero part of him was winning the internal battle in his brain.

He knocked on the door to room twenty-one and heard a sweet singsong voice inviting him in.

He walked to the foot of the bed and turned on his charm. "Hi Shelby. I'm Nathan Morrell. We've met before."

She laughed. Smiled demurely at him. Then laughed again. "We have indeed met before. Can't recall where. Perhaps we were just hanging around somewhere?"

Nate chuckled. She had a good sense of humor. He liked that. And now that he was looking at her under better circumstances, he was impressed. Her eyes were a sparkling blue and her hair was blonde and long. He could tell she'd applied a bit of makeup, but not too much. He didn't like heavily made up women. She had a smile that would melt an igloo, and he really liked that about her too. Nate figured she was no older than thirty or so. He was thankful that he'd saved this lovely person. It was weird thinking that she came so close to dying that day—yet here she was, full of life and smiling her pretty smile. Seeing her alive meant so much to him; he was finally glad he came. Glad to be the hero.

She motioned with her left hand. "Come here to me. I want to give you a big kiss."

Nate walked over and leaned across the bed. She wrapped her arm around his neck and laughed again. "I think I've done this to you before, haven't I?"

"Yes, indeed you have. But not the kiss part."

"Well, that can be fixed." She pressed her lips against his cheek and held them there for a good five seconds.

She pulled her face back and studied him. Then she took off his hat. "It's not polite to wear a hat around a lady, especially one whose life you saved."

"You're right. Pardon my bad manners, dear lady."

She handed Nate his hat. "You don't know how happy I am that you came to see me. You saved my life—I can't believe what you did. I watched you climbing up, throwing away your shoes, hurling yourself over the top and coming down to me. I heard you cursing the hot steel on your feet as you dragged me up the trestle with my arm hanging around your neck. I remember all those things."

Nate felt his face turning red and he looked down at the floor. "You weren't that heavy and the steel wasn't that hot. I just get ornery when I haven't had my eighth cup of coffee."

Shelby laughed in a special way that Nate knew only she owned. "You're too modest." She reached out and held his hand. "But you know what I remember the most?"

"What?"

"When my arm slipped off your neck and I was falling, you thrust your hand down and grabbed my arm. When you pulled me up, you spun me so that the back of me would hit the trestle rather than the front. I can't believe you did that—and that you were able to think so fast to do that."

Nate shuffled his feet and looked down again. He didn't know what to say.

Suddenly, the door to Shelby's room opened, and a tornado of a man blew in—with a nurse following close behind. "Sir, you can't..."

The short, fat, and balding man rushed to the other side of Shelby's bed and tossed a business card onto the sheets. "I have to be quick—they don't want me here. But, you need to know I'm the lawyer who's launching the Class Action suit against Flying Machines Inc. and Adventureland. You're entitled to be part of this lawsuit and you're a key witness. Call me."

With that, the little man rushed past the flustered nurse and headed towards the door, giving Nate a quick glance as he passed him. Suddenly, he skidded to a stop and pointed. "You're...you're him!"

CHAPTER 7

Shelby sat upright in her bed. "That's him alright! This is the man who saved my life!"

The lawyer chuckled. "He's also the prick who almost killed you. But, don't worry—we'll make him pay."

Shelby looked from the lawyer to Nate, and back to the lawyer again. "What... what do you mean?"

The lawyer was just about to reply when another nurse came into the room, an older lady. "Sir, we have to ask you to leave. You didn't check in at the desk, and you're not on the list of invited guests."

The first nurse started sputtering, "I tried to tell him, Helen, but he..."

The second nurse, who seemed to have some authority, waved her hand at her colleague, silencing her. "Sir, please, get out of here now or I'll call Security."

He shuffled towards the door, then turned his head back to Shelby. "Just ask him, Ms. Sutcliffe, just ask him."

As soon as they'd left, she turned her head slowly towards Nate, and asked him in a soft voice, almost a whisper, "What did he mean?"

Nate swallowed hard and sat down on the edge of her bed. "I was one of the VIPs invited for the inaugural ride of the Black Mamba." He paused, trying to choose his words carefully, but he knew there was no other way to say it than to just say it. "I'm the CEO of Flying Machines Inc. I designed the Black Mamba."

Shelby just stared at him. No twinkle in her beautiful blue eyes. No expression on her pretty face. She slid down on the bed and pulled the sheets up to her chin. "Please leave."

Nate didn't want to leave just yet. He felt he needed to explain, to defend himself in some way. "Are you okay? Do you want me to call the nurse?"

Shelby closed her eyes and sighed. "I'm fine."

"Can we talk about this?"

With her eyes still closed, she replied, "Mr. Morrell, I asked you to leave. Please do that before I scream at you."

*****

Nate just drove—had no idea where he was going, although there really wasn't very far you could go in Alexandria. He headed to familiar territory almost by remote; Old Town was where he felt most comfortable. It was where he lived and where the sights had a calming effect on him.

He loved this city. It was where he'd been born, but despite that connection Alexandria had character that most American cities had to struggle to attain. It was founded in 1749 and was the birthplace of George Washington, the very first President of the United States. And at the other extreme it was where Jim Morrison of *The Doors* had been born.

It enjoyed a colorful history, and that history was just one of the things that made the city unique. During the Civil War, the Union soldiers had moved in and taken over from the Confederates, making it one of the largest supply centers for the war effort. And as a Confederate state, it was in itself a paradox—while it was home to one of the largest slave-trading operations in the United States, it was also a large 'free-black' community.

Nate parked his car in his reserved spot at his own office on King Street and started walking. He thought of dropping into the office for a bit, but decided against it. He hadn't been there since the accident and really wasn't in the mood to talk to anyone yet—even though his staff probably needed to see his face, hear his reassuring words. Nate himself needed to hear some reassuring words and wasn't in the right frame of mind yet to prop anyone else up. For the moment, his friend and partner, Tom, would have to carry the ball.

Nate knew that he'd be okay in a day or so. The shock of seeing the look on Shelby's face at that very moment when he told her who he was…well…it was a moment of shame that he'd never ever forget. He couldn't recall ever seeing anyone look at him that way before; a look that was a combination of disgust, anger and pity, all rolled up in an expressionless mask. Made even blanker when she'd laid her head back on the pillow and just closed her eyes. At that moment, she'd signaled finality; that she wanted nothing more to do with her 'hero.'

Nate concentrated on walking fast—the faster the better. He held his head up high and focused on keeping his shoulders erect. His feet still hurt like hell, but he pushed the pain out of his head and forced them to move. His eyes were wandering in different directions. Paranoid that people were looking at him, talking about him. But—everyone just seemed to be going about their business, unconcerned about the hero who had transformed into a goat. Nate took in some deep breaths as he walked—told himself that this feeling of vulnerability would pass.

He wandered into the Old Town Farmers Market on Market Square—he knew it was the oldest market of its kind in the entire nation. Packed with people, the smell of fresh produce was refreshing, almost intoxicating.

Nate found himself out on the street again, marveling at how there always seemed to be something to do in this small city. It had so many special events and parades: First Night Alexandria on New Year's Eve was something that he and Stephanie had never missed; the George Washington Birthday Parade in February attracted visitors from across the country; Saint Patrick's Day Parade in March was incredibly colorful and of course the pubs cooperated by staying open from morning until the next dawn; the USA and City Birthday celebration in July brought out the patriots; and the King Street Art Festival in September showcased talent from right across the country. And no one ever missed the Del Ray Turkey Trot in November—an event that was perfectly timed with Thanksgiving. Then, in December, there was the Scottish Christmas Walk and the Boat Parade of Lights down the Potomac River. There was always something to see and do in this little city and he had no desire to live anywhere else. The wonderful temperate climate was also hard to beat. He felt sorry for people who had to endure winter in all its fury. Winter in Virginia was similar to spring in most other areas of the world.

Nate had visited most of the world's major cities, but none of them captivated him as much as his own city. Maybe it was because he had been born in Alexandria, but he didn't think that was it. He knew a lot of people who absolutely hated the cities they were born and raised in; Nate had never felt that way about Alexandria. He loved that it was so scenic. It enjoyed the lushness that the state of Virginia was so famous for, but also had the big city feel of being right across the river from Washington. And being that close to the seat of power for the entire country was a feeling that was hard to describe.

He continued walking—his feet were starting to feel better now. Nate's talent for concentration was allowing the pain to recede. He hadn't yet chased the feeling of shame out of his head yet, but that would come in time. He had to rationalize the whole thing, had to understand what happened. He knew in his gut that he and his people hadn't made any mistakes—that something else had happened that they couldn't have anticipated. He didn't know what that was yet, but once he was allowed to examine the wreckage he'd be able to figure it out.

He glanced to his left and noticed the Alexandria Black History Museum, and he knew that just up ahead was the birthplace of George Washington. He thought that was kind of ironic; a museum celebrating black history in a state that had tried to separate from the United States during the Civil War primarily over the slavery issue. And doubly ironic that it was down the street from the ancestral home of a President who himself had owned slaves.

Nate chuckled at the paradox. The chuckle didn't last long—he realized that his situation was a paradox as well. The man who had designed the rollercoaster that killed twenty-five people was also the man who had personally saved the lone survivor.

His mind wandered again—he thought about his marriage to Stephanie. How they'd been together for ten years. No children. He'd wanted them, she hadn't. Of course, when they were dating she'd been all for it. After they'd tied the knot, her attitude changed. She seemed to get caught up in Nate's success—became this monster of materialism that Nate had never seen coming. Why hadn't he seen it coming? Was he that bad a judge of character? He—the one who could analyze virtually anything—wasn't able to analyze the one he thought he loved? She'd transformed into a posh and shallow little princess, who in a moment of anger—and perhaps in an attempt to hurt Nate—confessed to having more than one affair. Stephanie was someone who craved attention—she was more insecure than Nate had ever realized. It probably didn't take much more than a smile, a wink or a nod to get her into the sack. She needed to be desired—didn't seem to realize that most people told her just what they knew she wanted to hear. Women told her she was beautiful just to be in her company, to hob-knob with one of the wealthiest women in town. They gushed over her house so they could be invited to her lavish tea parties. And most men would say virtually anything to any woman just to get laid. Stephanie didn't seem to understand that she was just being used by everyone—but maybe she was just using them, too, in order to get her fleeting rushes of desirability.

Nate had turned around and was on his way back to his office parking lot. He was feeling a lot better. It was such a warm and sunny day, he removed his jacket and hat—he figured the hat wasn't a very good disguise anyway.

The divorce was going to be expensive. They were still living together, but that was as far as it went. He slept in the newer wing of the house and Stephanie slept in the original section. She felt more comfortable there anyway, with the posh ornateness surrounding her. That was what made her feel good—and every time she had the opportunity to show it all off to friends, she did just that. She had a special way about her of making people feel small, making them feel inadequate—actually seemed to enjoy watching them squirm.

His marriage had been an expensive mistake—but, like everything else in his life, Nate would move on. He would correct the situation and move on. Funny, the fact that his wife had had affairs didn't even bother him. Because he hadn't loved her for a long time now. He should have ended the marriage after the first two years, but his career had become so all-consuming he hadn't paid much attention to his personal life. He had known in his heart who she really was—what she had turned out to be. She was virtually 'unlovable.' There wasn't one quality he could think of that he loved about her. Maybe he was a bit guilty himself—guilty of putting up with things, keeping her in his life because she was the convenient 'trophy wife' for his business dealings and jet setting.

He didn't know. It could have been that—at least part of it. Who really knows why things happen the way they do, what motivates people to do the things they do in life? You'd have to have the ability to go back in time to truly understand what was going through your head. Even though his brain was one of the best analytical machines ever created, Nate wasn't capable of properly analyzing himself. Well, maybe it was more just a case of not being able to be objective about his personal life and the decisions he'd made. That was tough for anyone to do.

For now, it was just a marriage in transition—one that had already ended, but just needed the legal work to make it official. They were legally separated, but just sharing the same premises for the sake of convenience and economics. She wanted him to be the one to move out—because she couldn't bear to part with the house. Nate didn't care—he could live anywhere. But he hadn't had the time to look around yet, and with what just happened at Adventureland it would no doubt have to take a back seat for a little bit longer.

Nate was walking across the street to the carpark when he heard his name being called. He turned around to see his friend and colleague, Tom Foster, running toward him.

"Hey, buddy. I saw you through the window. You're not returning phone messages so I figured I'd just grab you."

Nate smiled at his friend. "Sorry, Tom. I've been on the phone for two days now with anyone and everyone. I should have called you back."

"No problem, Nate, I understand. How are you doing?"

"Well, not bad I guess. I just visited that woman I helped on the coaster. It was going okay until a little sleaze of a lawyer burst in and announced that he's launching a Class Action suit. And then, of course, I had to tell her who I was."

Tom squeezed Nate's shoulder. "That must have been tough. And I heard about the lawsuit—no surprise, of course. I've already talked to our lawyers and our liability insurers. Neither of them seem concerned. Told me that we should just hang tight while the investigation continues—once we have the results of that, we'll have something to discuss. A lawsuit was inevitable. And we've had those before. It's pretty much normal now to expect a lawsuit after even the most minor incident."

"Yeah, I understand all that. The lawsuit doesn't concern me. Once the NTSB finishes their report, we'll be vindicated—I have no doubt about that. We don't make mistakes. But—the look on that woman's face, Tom, when she realized who I was. I really felt bad."

"That's just a normal reaction, Nate. Put yourself in her shoes—she meets her hero and then finds out he's got warts. She'll get over it and realize that you risked your own life for hers. I sure couldn't have done what you did."

Nate laughed. "Yeah, what was that all about? You—afraid of heights? I never knew!"

"Well, it wasn't something I wanted to tell you. I've ridden our coasters with you many times, but it seems that it doesn't bother me as much when I'm securely in a car with a bar protecting me. On that track that day, totally exposed, open all around me, I panicked."

Nate patted him on the back. "It's okay. I won't tell anyone. Just another little surprise about my best friend that I'll have to absorb!"

Nate pulled his keys out of his pocket. "Have to go, Tom. I'll be in the office again in a couple of days."

"I hope so. The troops are asking about you. Anxious about how you're doing."

"Yeah, I expect they are. Tell them I'm doing fine."

Nate turned toward his car.

"Oh, Nate, before you go, I got a call from the NSPE organizers. They wanted to know if you still plan on speaking at the convention next week."

Nate had forgotten completely, and forgetting anything was a hard thing for Nate to do. "God, it slipped my mind." He paused. "Feels funny, giving a speech after what happened."

"I can fill in for you if you're not up to it."

Nate scratched his forehead and looked out at the street with one eye and at Tom with the other. "No, I committed to speak and that's what I'll do. After seeing Shelby's crestfallen face today, I know I can handle anything. The sooner I get back up on the horse, the easier it'll be for me to ride again. Tell them I'm coming."

"Great. They were quite worried. Ticket sales have increased fifty percent since the accident—I know you don't need to hear that, but they know the main reason for the jump in ticket sales is the publicity surrounding the Black Mamba."

Nate shook his head. "Human nature. Everyone loves sensationalism."

"Okay, Nate. I'm heading back into the trenches. I'll hold down the fort until you get back."

Nate got into his car and pulled out of the parking lot. And started thinking about next week's convention. It was the annual gathering of the National Society of Professional Engineers. Nate attended the convention every year, but this was the first time he'd been asked to speak. The notoriety of his company had gained worldwide attention over the last few years, so his speech was one that the organizers were looking forward to. His topic was 'The History of Rollercoasters.' And boy, was that going to be a topic of interest to everyone now. Nate wasn't surprised at all that ticket sales had increased so much in the last few days. He was sure that everyone would be sitting on pins and needles wondering if he was going to address the accident. He wouldn't. With a lawsuit pending, he wouldn't take the risk of saying anything about what had happened. The Press would be there and there was a Q & A scheduled after his speech. He would just have to be careful.

The convention was being held at the Walter E. Washington Convention Center across the river in Washington, D.C. Nate knew that the keynote speaker was a representative of AE911Truth, an organization of thousands of architects and engineers from around the world. That organization had been fighting for years to force a re-opening of the investigation into how the three World Trade Center towers had fallen on Sept. 11th, 2001. Nate himself was a member of that organization; primarily just to support his profession and his fellow engineers who belonged. Being a structural engineer, he knew full well that the official story about 911 was bunk. It was scientifically impossible for those three towers to have collapsed the way they had. Something was terribly wrong with that original investigation. Despite the gallant efforts of AE911Truth, he doubted that the case would ever be re-opened. And while his analytical brain told him that something terribly sinister—more sinister than mere terrorism—surrounded that horrible day in 2001, the proud American citizen inside of him didn't really want to know the truth.

So, Nate would indeed deliver his speech as planned. There was very little he and his engineering colleagues could do about what had happened thirteen years ago, but he certainly wasn't going to hide from what had happened two days ago. The sooner he confronted the big world again, the better his own little world would become.

But he had to admit he was a bit relieved that at least one other speech would be more controversial than his.

CHAPTER 8

"…and trying to define that sinking feeling in the stomach is a tough one for most people. They forget that their bodies are not completely solid. The human body is constructed of a bunch of loose parts, barely connected to each other. When the body accelerates in a rollercoaster those parts accelerate independently of each other.

"In normal everyday activity, gravity works to push all of the body parts against each other. That's a normal feeling that people are used to. But when the body goes into 'free fall,' all of that changes. There is virtually no net force. The various parts of the body stop pushing on each other. In essence, they are weightless, each falling all by themselves.

"This is what people describe as a 'sinking feeling' in their stomachs. The stomach is suddenly as light as a feather because there is much less force pressing on it. In a rollercoaster, the entire body feels the sensation—and visual tricks help achieve this. There are upside down curves on some coasters, twists and turns, perilous heights, near misses and structures whizzing by. This visual stuff is an important part of the entire experience because the human body can acutely detect acceleration, but not velocity. A rollercoaster designer's challenge is to create a ride that gives the illusion that the train is rocketing at out-of-control speeds, and all the visual stimuli along the way help create this illusion."

Nate paused for effect and took the opportunity to gaze out over the audience. There were a couple thousand in attendance in the huge ballroom, most of them engineers or architects, but some he knew were also members of the general public who had some connection with the engineering profession. He knew there were a lot of contractors in attendance, as well as developers. Those professionals had a serious interest in the latest engineering trends. The front rows were reserved for the Press and he was more than aware of the cameras aimed in his direction.

Nate had been talking for about half an hour and he could tell that he had everyone's rapt attention. It could be the content of his speech, or his dynamic delivery of it—but more likely it was his notoriety. Everyone was probably waiting with baited breath, wondering if he was going to mention the Black Mamba.

He looked down at his notes and continued. *"Rollercoasters have been with us for an awfully long time, long enough to now be an actual fabric of our civilization. Human beings love to be scared, but only if they're convinced it's an illusion. They like to be scared if they know they are still safe and secure. Because, simply put, being scared is exhilarating. It's fun. That special adrenaline rush is hard to define or duplicate.*

"I wonder if any of you are aware that rollercoasters actually began their ascendant rise as 'ice slides?' They were long, steep, made out of wood and completely covered in ice. This was way back in the 16th century in Russia. Daredevils would shoot down the slope in wooden sleds or even in carved-out blocks of ice, crashing at the bottom into a sand pile. There was no smooth braking system back then such as we have today.

"The ice slides evolved from there by the able assistance of the French. They were enamored with the concept—but the warmer climate in France tended to melt the darn things, so they decided to build waxed slides. That proved to be too slow, so they finally added wheels. In 1817, they invented the first coaster where the train was actually attached to the track—the axle fit nicely into a carved groove, allowing it to career down the slope while still staying under control by the guided groove in the track.

"Here in America, the first rollercoaster was the 'Mauch Chunk Switchback Railway,' which snaked its way around the Pennsylvania Mountains in the mid-1800s. Sorry, folks, even though we've been first in a lot of inventions, the Russians and the French actually beat us to the punch with rollercoasters. The 'Mauch' was actually built first as simply a track that could carry coal to a railway for shipment across the country. When that service was no longer needed, the track was reborn as a scenic tour that tourists could pay one dollar to ride. It was a leisurely ride up to the top of the mountain, but a wild and bumpy ride back down. This became a big hit with tourists and imitations popped up all over the country. And they got scarier and scarier, but also safer and safer.

"With the advent of the Great Depression and then World War Two, production of rollercoasters declined—no one had the money to spend on frivolous entertainment anymore. But the amusement park industry boomed once again in the 1970s and has continued unabated ever since. Rollercoasters became more innovative, as most of you are well aware. And most of you here will agree with me that education has certainly been the cause of this innovation. We know so much more now about physics—our schools are top-notch and engineers are learning techniques and principles that couldn't even have been imagined 100 years ago. The engineering profession has come a long way and the amusement industry has been a direct beneficiary of that."

Nate paused again. You could hear a pin drop in the audience. Of course, most of them were engineers and certainly must be enjoying a certain sense of pride in being reminded of how far their profession had come. But...he knew what they were really thinking. Probably some admired him for just showing his face today. Others, competitors of his, may even be enjoying his fall from grace. And yet, some were probably looking at him as some kind of curiosity. A man who had climbed the structure of a rollercoaster—his rollercoaster—to save a stranger. And they were probably wondering how he was able to sleep at night, knowing his invention had killed so many people.

Virtually every analytical brain in the audience—and there were a lot of them—was looking at him, listening to him, while at the same time trying to figure out in their own minds what could have possibly gone wrong. What could have caused the track to snap? What could have caused the lap bars to unlock? What colossal errors had occurred during the design and manufacturing processes of this deadly rollercoaster?

Nate took a deep breath that he hoped no one noticed and started speaking again.

"Engineers have taken us well beyond the wooden rollercoasters to the point where they're almost extinct now. Although they still exist and are actually still being erected in some parts of the world. They do give a different kind of thrill—the noise factor. The tracks are always steel, of course, but it's the wooden structure itself that rattles and crackles, giving the illusion to the rider that the thing is just going to fall apart. The tracks used in wooden coasters are almost identical to regular railway tracks. The range is very limited with wooden coasters though. The wooden track and superstructure are very cumbersome, and not flexible enough to accomplish complex twists and turns, and certainly can't handle an upside down ride. With these wooden coasters, the thrill is mainly an 'up and down' one.

"But, with the introduction of tubular steel tracks and steel superstructures in the 1950s, the world of rollercoasters changed forever. This introduced an era of inverted rides, along with twists and turns that only the flexibility of steel could accomplish. And steel brought to the amusement world a smoother ride as well. The wheels used on steel coasters are manufactured out of polyurethane or nylon, allowing the riders to enjoy a smooth ride while concentrating their fear instead on the steep drops, twists, turns, and being in inverted positions. No more rattling noises to contend with, or to be distracted by. Steel gives so much more flexibility to the rollercoaster designer, that the sky really is the limit. And the track works in conjunction with the wheels to give that super smooth ride—because, with a tubular steel coaster, all of the track pieces are welded perfectly together to give a safe and seamless ride.

"And no longer are some rollercoaster designs relying solely on gravity. Historically, coasters build up potential energy as a chain-drag system pulls the train up to the top of the first hill. At that point, potential energy converts to kinetic energy, as gravity forces the train to drop. From that point on, the coaster continues to run based only on this kinetic energy. Each hill gets progressively smaller, as on these subsequent hills there is no chain drag to pull the train up. It has to make it on kinetic energy alone. So, when it reaches the top of the second hill, kinetic energy is exhausted and converts back to potential energy again—until it drops a second time when kinetic takes over again. And this goes on and on for the rest of the ride and through progressively smaller hills, until the ride comes to an end.

"No more. We have electromagnetism at our disposal now and some designers are making full use of it. Acceleration can now occur at any time in the ride, and at the most unexpected times. And the hills no longer need to get progressively smaller—because magnets can get our trains up any hill height we design. It's a remarkable innovation that can only enhance the

enjoyment of rollercoaster enthusiasts in the years ahead.

"And I'm one of those enthusiasts. I enjoy what I do and I am extremely proud of our profession. Thank you, ladies and gentleman, for your kind attention. Enjoy the rest of the convention and, of course, the fascinating city of Washington."

Nate knew that a Q & A was supposed to be allowed after each speech. But there had been three speeches before his and only one of those speakers had to field any questions. So, Nate wasn't going to press his luck and invite questions. He just wanted to get off the podium as fast as he could. So, to the sound of applause, that's exactly what he did.

He turned away from the microphone and began walking across the stage to the wing at the rear. But then he heard his name being called. The Master of Ceremonies was at the podium and calling him back. He turned and saw that several people in the audience were already standing at the floor microphones that were stationed throughout.

Damn!

He walked back to the podium and pointed to a young lady in the front row.

"Thank you, Mr. Morrell. I enjoyed your speech. I'm Kate Sheridan with the Chicago Times. Could you please tell us the current status of the investigation into the accident that occurred last week at Adventureland?"

Nate leaned into the mike. "I'm sorry, I can't answer that. The investigation is being headed up by the NTSB and so far there are no findings that I'm aware of."

She nodded a thank you and took her seat. Nate pointed to an older gentleman in the fourth row.

"Mr. Morrell, my name is Clark Livingston—I own a consulting engineering company in Dallas. Do you think that rollercoaster designs are getting out of control—are they pushing the limits too far?"

Nate expected there would be a question like this. "No, I don't, Mr. Livingston. I think the designs over the last 200 years that I referred to in my speech reflected the knowledge, skill and education that existed at the time. So, 'pushing the limits' is a relative term—relative to what we know. A coaster manufactured 100 years ago was probably considered 'out of control' at that time—but it wasn't at all. It was in line with what knowledge the manufacturers had when it was built—very much the same as today. We know so much more now that cars, airplanes, rockets, weapons, ships…and yes, even rollercoasters, have evolved to a level that couldn't have been imagined decades ago. Well, maybe George Orwell imagined them, but he was probably the only one."

There were a few chuckles throughout the audience.

The Master of Ceremonies once again stepped forward to the mike. "Folks, this will be the last question. We still have a heavy program ahead of us today." He nodded at Nate to continue.

Nate pointed to an older lady near the back of the audience. But, before she had a chance to ask her question, a booming voice came from another mike. Nate's right eye picked him up right away, while his left eye was still watching the woman. He was hard to miss—about six and a half feet tall, well-tanned, and dressed in probably the most expensive suit in the house. Plus—Nate knew him well. It was his former boss, Andrew Wingate, the man who had given him his start after college, and the man who Nate handed in his resignation to fifteen years ago to start his own company.

"I'm sorry to interrupt, dear lady, but I needed to get the last question."

Nate wasn't surprised—Andrew was still the rude, arrogant bully that he'd always been.

The elderly lady nodded and sat down.

Nate nodded in Andrew's direction. "Go ahead with your question, Andrew. Then when you're finished I'm going to break the MC's rule and allow that polite lady to still have the last question."

Andrew smiled and shrugged his shoulders. "That's okay by me. So, Nate— you don't mind if I call you that, do you?"

"You already did—continue with your question, sir."

"Well, my question pertains to your use of electromagnets to power your rockets…er, I mean, coasters. Aren't you tampering with the element of fear to the extreme? It's terrifying enough for riders plunging down those steep hills that you design. Don't you think their nerves need a bit of a break in between sensations?"

"No, I think our use of electromagnets is cutting edge technology, and has been deemed perfectly safe through years of testing."

Nate raised his hand to point to the lady, but was interrupted by the booming voice once again.

"Excuse me. Did you say 'safe?' How many safety tests did you conduct on the welds used in that track that seemed to just mysteriously split in half?"

"Andrew, we conducted exhaustive tests on the track welds."

He was trying to keep his cool, but the man was annoying him—and he knew he was doing it deliberately. Nate pointed once again to the woman, but before she could get to her feet Andrew bellowed one more time. Nate could see now that the Press had their cameras pointed in Wingate's direction—he was no doubt loving this.

"Part three of my question. Why is the NTSB investigating the accident? I've been designing rollercoasters for forty-five years and I've never heard of such a thing before. They have no jurisdiction with amusement park rides at all." Nate heard a collective murmur from the audience.

"Your guess is as good as mine, Andrew." He wasn't going to let Andrew bait him or get under his skin. The man was obviously hoping for that, and hoping that the media would have something to quote in the morning papers that would be embarrassing or perhaps even incriminating for Nate and his company.

Nate nodded to the lady once more and she jumped to the floor mike before Andrew could interrupt again. "Mr. Morrell—I don't have a question, just a comment. I think you're a very brave man for saving that young lady. I know the accident must be weighing heavily on you, but I think what you did for her was remarkable. And...you coming here tonight to make this speech to us after the horrible thing that happened is just another example of your bravery."

Before she sat down, she glared over at Andrew Wingate to the sound of thunderous applause from the audience.

Nate smiled. The feisty old lady reminded him so much of his mother.

CHAPTER 9

Shelby was glad to be home—away from hospital food and the prying questions from nurses and doctors. She was tired of being reminded of what had happened to her. Feeling a lot better—the bruises and cuts were healing nicely—and she had regained almost full movement in her right shoulder.

Shelby just needed her soul to heal. She had no problem falling asleep at night, but it was the constant waking up that was getting to her. Every night, the same thing. Lurching up in bed, gasping in shock. Seeing the event over and over again. Watching the front of the train buckling as it rammed into the split in the track, the train lifting up in the air and flinging itself over the side.

She experienced the horror of being airborne, doing somersaults in the air—she could feel the impacts of the trestle against her body, bouncing off it on the way down. Then, finally, by some miracle, grasping onto the trestle with her legs, violently halting her fall to certain death.

Then her hero leaning over the top of the second hill, calling to her, reassuring her, then hurling himself over the edge and climbing down to her. Climbing back up with her arm wrapped around his neck. Then falling again, him flinging his arm down and grabbing her just before she was out of reach. Twisting her in the air and slamming her backwards against the trestle. Then…darkness.

She wondered how long these vivid nightmares would continue. It was getting to the point where Shelby was afraid to fall asleep—fearful that the same terrifying movie reel would start up again.

So…Nathan Morrell was the man who had designed and manufactured the Black Mamba. She was shocked at that moment when she had found out who he was. It was hard to understand how she felt—it brought it all close to home. What she'd suffered, the deaths of her fellow riders, and there she was sitting and chatting with the man who had somehow screwed up, causing unspeakable horror, death and suffering.

Maybe she just needed someone to blame. It was hard to blame a machine or just a mere Act of God. It was always better, she knew, if there was a real live person to blame. It made the anger and the blame more real. And more satisfying.

Shelby opened the back door from her kitchen and strolled out to the garden.

All the flowers she'd planted last year after she bought this house were starting to bloom in their colorful glory. She laid down on a chaise lounge and savored the soft fragrant breeze. Enjoying this last day of freedom was important to her—she was back to work at the hospital tomorrow. Back to dealing with other people's miseries and trying her damnedest to forget her own.

Her little house was at 210 Peacock Ave., just a couple of blocks from the hospital. She loved how close it was, because she could walk there every day and not have to incur the cost of parking. Plus, the exercise was good for her. A great way to start the day and a splendid way to end it. And the weather in Virginia was almost always wonderful, so walking to work was a joy.

Shelby was a surgical nurse—highly trained and extremely specialized. Heart surgeries were what she was called upon to assist with the most. She was thirty-two years old and had been a nurse for ten years. She loved her profession, because she just loved people. Loved nurturing them in their time of need, loved assisting the surgeons in saving their lives. She had to prep them beforehand, assist with the life saving techniques during the operations, then calm them down and reassure them afterwards in recovery. Nothing in life gave her more satisfaction.

Shelby's tiny little house was an old Georgian townhouse. Probably at least 100 years old, but in an excellent state of repair. She'd really had nothing to do except plant her garden, and gardening brought her a lot of joy. She loved seeing things grow, things that she herself had nurtured.

A voice called out to her from the backyard next door. She turned her head to look. It was her neighbor, an internal medicine resident at the hospital. A nice enough guy, they'd dated a few times, but nothing serious as far as she was concerned. He felt differently than her though.

"Hey, how are you feeling? I heard about the accident. Horrible!"

Shelby sat up in the chaise lounge and called back. "I'm doing better, thanks. It'll take some time, but I'll be okay."

"How about I take you out to dinner tonight? That might relax you a bit."

Shelby paused for a second or two as she thought about it. "No, I don't feel I'm up to socializing yet, Scott. A rain check, okay?"

She could tell by his face that he was a bit crestfallen. She'd put him off so many times that it was starting to weigh on him, she guessed.

"Oh, okay. I understand. Maybe I'll see you at the hospital, then?"

"Maybe." Shelby got up and went back inside to the relative safety of her abode, hoping the guy would finally get the message and stop asking her out. She just wasn't interested, nor did she want to lead him on. Saying 'no' was easy.

But she found herself thinking a lot about one other man. Nathan Morrell. She couldn't help it. The courage he had displayed in saving her, and also the sheer courage of just coming to see her. She knew he was hurt by her reaction, but she just couldn't help it at the time.

He was certainly an attractive man. Bright blue eyes, tall and dark, broad shoulders, and a confident air about him that she found alluring. His voice was also fabulous—like a broadcaster's. The kind of voice she could fall asleep listening to.

But her attraction to him was conflicted with her anger and confusion. If it hadn't been for him and whatever colossal errors he'd made, her 'Coaster Crazies' would still be alive, and she wouldn't be suffering nightmares.

Maybe she was attracted to him just out of the intense experience they'd gone through together. It brought them together in a strange way and she owed her life to his bravery. But…if it hadn't been for his faulty invention, he wouldn't have had to be brave for her in the first place. She would never have suffered the horror she did and they would never have met. She pondered that for a second. Fate?

No…she wasn't going to let his heroic act distort her thinking. She walked over to her purse and pulled out the business card for that fat little lawyer who had barged into her hospital room. Shelby picked up the phone and dialed.

CHAPTER 10

John Fletcher stared at the photographs on his desk, and then read over once again the report that he himself had written up. Then he looked at the other report—the report that he'd been ordered to sign. The report that ignored everything he had ascertained.

He stood up, went to his office window and gazed out over L'Enfant Plaza. This had been his home away from home for the last thirty-five years—the venerable head office of the National Transportation Safety Board. John was the Chief Investigator for the organization, an institution that had been charged by an act of Congress to investigate serious transportation accidents, including air, road and marine.

But…not rollercoasters.

That was the first thing that made him scratch his head in confusion a week ago. Why on earth was the NTSB investigating the Black Mamba accident, when it didn't fall within its jurisdiction? Didn't make sense. They had enough on their plate right now—a plane crash in Denver, a ship sinking off the coast of South Carolina, a bridge collapse in Florida, and a balloon explosion over Virginia. Amusement parks were a State and Municipal responsibility, not a Federal one.

His questioning fell on deaf ears. No one listened to him; no one gave him an explanation. He was told to just 'do it.' And, on top of all that, he was the most senior person in the investigations department—he didn't do fieldwork anymore. He had a large staff that did that. Why had he been asked to do this one personally?

Ignoring protocol as well. Normally, with any accident investigation, a 'Go Team' was assigned—usually three or four investigators working under an Investigator-In-Charge. The IIC oversaw every step of the process and assigned every member of the team to their individual specialized tasks. Then the report was compiled after considerable debate and consultation. For this accident, none of that was allowed to happen. No 'Go Team' was assigned and the only person permitted to examine the wreckage was John himself. This violated all of the protocols established for the NTSB.

The only other time he'd seen anything like this was with the TWA 800 incident back in 1996. The NTSB closed ranks and numerous protocols were broken. Resulting in the final official conclusion that a fuel tank explosion caused the jet to tumble into the Atlantic, killing all souls onboard. John had no choice but to live with that conclusion—he and many of his colleagues kept their opinions to themselves after having them ignored. To this day though, he would swear on his mother's grave that an exploding fuel tank did not bring that plane down.

So, John was starting to get that sinking feeling again. Was history repeating itself? He was sixty years old, just five years away from full retirement with benefits. But that really didn't matter—he wasn't going to make it that long anyway. All he wanted was to have his health benefits continue while he was still alive and have the life insurance proceeds passed along to his wife.

His son…well, he had no idea where he was, so he wasn't concerned with him. He had estranged himself from the family years ago and, despite John and Linda's best efforts, he was no longer in their lives. But Linda—he wanted her taken care of and he didn't want medical bills to exhaust their savings before he died. His radiation treatments were expensive.

He had a brain tumor. Inoperable. In fact, it was an unusual one, too—they referred to it as subject to 'vascularization.' A tumor that was not only in an inaccessible area of his brain, but also one that was so entangled with blood vessels that it would be too dangerous to the life and well-being of the patient to attempt to remove. He'd been living with it for two years—at least that was when it was discovered, but the oncologist said it had probably been growing in there for at least ten years. He recalled that's when the first persistent headaches had started and they'd gotten progressively worse every year since.

John had about a year to go.

The headaches were probably the only symptom that was debilitating at times for him. Sometimes, his eyes would get a bit blurry, and they'd "tunnel" a bit. Other than that, some nausea at unexpected moments.

But he'd been able to perform his job just fine. His brain and metallurgical skills were as sharp as ever. His bosses knew about his condition and had been supportive, allowing time off when needed and giving him space when the headaches made him irritable. John couldn't have expected better support than what they'd shown him.

This report on his desk that had been sent over to him to sign—he didn't know what to make of it. Someone must have received the wrong information and had overlooked what he'd already provided. There had to be some mistake. Going on that assumption, he'd asked for a meeting. He expected a knock on his office door any moment now. It would be his direct superior, Gary Tuttle. Somehow they'd sort this out together.

*****

"Are these photos still in your hard drive?"

John was perplexed. "Well, of course they are. Everything is stored on my computer."

"We'll need access to your computer. To clean the hard drive." This ominous statement came from a man John had never met before. He had no forewarning that the man would be attending this meeting along with Gary.

"I don't understand this at all. I've shown you the photos and I've let you read my report. And another thing I don't understand is why a senior official from the National Security Agency is even sitting here in my office."

John was starting to get agitated—no doubt noticed by Gary, who up until now had been fairly silent. He finally spoke. "John, essentially, we've lost control of this investigation. It's in the hands of the NSA now. I know about as much as you know."

John was wringing his hands while sensing that a headache was coming on. He looked at the NSA agent. "Do you have a business card?"

"No."

"Do you have a name?"

"No."

John couldn't resist. "Haven't you people learned anything from the Edward Snowden affair? He blew the whistle on your spying, Internet tampering, listening in on the phone calls of heads of state, let alone normal everyday Americans— and none of that surprises me with what you're telling me to do here today."

The well-dressed, bald-headed agent adorned with designer tinted prescription lenses, leaned forward in his chair, wearing a stern look that John guessed he probably practiced in the mirror each morning. "This is a national security issue. I can't stress that enough. We expect your cooperation."

"Do I get to understand why I'm cooperating?"

"No."

John pulled the photos back across the desk and pounded his index finger down on the images. "I don't understand why a rollercoaster accident would be a national security issue. But, from these photos, you can clearly see that the steel was melted right at the split. It didn't snap, it didn't break due to a faulty weld—it was melted. By what, I don't know—but I'm guessing military grade thermate. I'd have to check further for residue, but that's what it looks like to me. Which means there would have had to have been a fuse or fuses attached to the underside of the track. Set off by remote control. Which I suspect also caused the lap bars to unlock. The same remote could have caused both things to happen. Two presses of a button—first press for the fuses to light, second press for the bars to unlock. Easily done. And thermate burns fast and clean—wouldn't take long at all for that steel to burn through. It would have been a rapid intense burn."

Neither Gary nor the nameless agent said a word.

John was on fire now. He reached across the desk and picked up the report that the NSA wanted him to sign. "This report says there was a faulty weld at the point of the split. That is patently false! There was no weld in that section of steel—it was solid with no seams. The split happened in solid seamless steel!"

The agent spoke once again. "Mr. Fletcher, it won't help to raise your voice. I have told you this is a matter of national security and the report must read the way I have presented it to you. Some things are for the greater good and being self-righteous isn't always helpful. Again, we expect your cooperation."

The mysterious man's words were beginning to resonate in John's head. Along with a severe headache. He was not going to be swayed by anything John had to say and his boss, Gary Tuttle, wasn't taking John's side in the least. This whole affair was indeed starting to smell just like TWA 800. If nothing, John was a realist. He had to live to fight another day—or in his case, one year less a day. He had to at least give the impression of cooperation, because no one cared about the arguments he was making.

"Okay, you have it. I accept that there are things here that I'm just not meant to know."

The agent smiled for the first time. "Good."

John noticed that Gary crossed his legs and seemed to be relaxing more too.

"Can I ask a couple of logistical questions?"

"Absolutely."

"There's going to be a lawsuit. Are we going to allow this man to twist in the wind? He wasn't negligent—his company did nothing wrong. This was, pure and simple, sabotage—and a very professional version of it."

The agent crossed his legs, too, and leaned back in his chair. "If it's declared sabotage, the insurance companies won't be obligated to pay. And we need to have the families of the victims compensated. We can't allow any hint of sabotage. In Virginia, as well as in many other States, we have what is known within insurance law as 'Strict Liability.' There is no need for the plaintiffs to prove negligence—all they have to show is that something caused injury or death. In this case, it's clear that a rollercoaster caused death. So, it doesn't even matter whether or not we announce there was a faulty weld—the object caused death. Period. Ergo, the insurers will pay up. And we as the government will be happy that the victims' families are well taken care of."

John nodded. "I understand the principle of Strict Liability. But that hangs Flying Machines Inc. out to dry. The reputation of the company and its owners will be ruined forever—when they did nothing wrong."

"Yes. Probably. As I said, this is a national security issue, and when that's involved we have to worry about the greater good instead of individual harm."

John rubbed his forehead. "This could lead to a charge of criminal negligence against the CEO, Nathan Morrell."

"No, I can promise you that we won't let that happen. We do have influence with the courts, of course, and we would ensure that no Grand Jury would indict him. That's the least we can do for Mr. Morrell. We're not monsters."

John coughed at that remark. "Okay, I'm with you. Where do we go from here?"

The agent passed him a sheet of paper. "We want the Black Mamba dismantled completely within the next two days. We'll send our own crew to do that. We want your cooperation in arranging for as many tractor-trailer units as you estimate will be needed. Every piece, and I mean every single piece, of the track, superstructure, and the train itself will need to be covered and transported to the address on that sheet of paper."

John looked at the sheet. "This is way down in Key West, Florida."

"Yes, that's the Florida Keys Transfer Station. From there, the debris will be loaded onto a ship within a few days and dumped at sea."

John looked down at his hands and shook his head sadly. "I don't know what in hell is going on here, and maybe I really don't want to know. But what you're proposing is the taking and destroying of evidence and property that the owner and the insurance companies are entitled to see and have. It's their property."

The agent sighed in exasperation. "I'm sure you've heard of the terminology, 'Eminent Domain.' In simple terms, the Constitution allows governments to confiscate whatever it deems necessary for the greater good."

John protested. "Eminent Domain was never intended for something like this—that was established for essential utilities, precious resources, etc. Not for taking damaged property, property that the owner and the insurance company are entitled to the salvage of. And…the Constitution permits Eminent Domain, yes, but it also states quite clearly that the owners of the property are to be compensated."

"Then they'll be compensated. What's a wreck of a rollercoaster worth, John? You tell me, huh?"

John raised his head slowly and looked into the agent's eyes. "This was sabotage. We can't just let this go—we have to know who did this and why. It could be an act of terrorism and it could happen again. Shouldn't we alert other amusement parks—like, subtly, quietly?"

The agent shook his head. "No, we already have some leads on this, and trust me, we'll prosecute this in our own way. We won't let this go unpunished. And we know enough already to know that this won't recur with another park. You'll have to trust me on that, too."

John found it hard to hide his smirk. *Trust me. Yeah, right. Tell that to Edward*

Snowden.

Gary and the agent stood and started toward the door, but not before the agent picked up the photos and John's report. At the door, he turned to face John. "Within a few minutes one of our people will be here to clean your hard drive. You'll be asked to sign a confidentiality agreement about all of this, and swear out an avadavat that you have not told anyone else about your findings. Also, John, did you make copies of the photos?"

"No."

"Do you or your wife own a laptop?"

"No," John lied.

"You'll have to hand over your mobile phone to our man as well, okay? I'm sure the NTSB will get you a new one. Don't use it during the next few minutes until he gets here, for any phone calls, texts, or emails. Trust me, we'll know if you do."

John coughed once more. There was that 'trust' word again.

CHAPTER 11

It was another bright and sunny day. Kind of a waste going to a lawyer's office on a day like this, but it was her day off and she had to get this first visit over with eventually. So, today was as good a day as any.

Shelby hopped into her spiffy red Hyundai Elantra and headed south on S. Van Doron, then connected with the Capitol Beltway eastbound. This was the route she took whenever she wanted to have a jaunt over to Washington, D.C— the Beltway turned into the Woodrow Wilson Memorial Bridge which would take her across the Potomac River right into the Capitol. Once in a while she did that—not too often. It was far more pleasant right there in Alexandria, away from all the noise, crime and congestion that Washington was known for.

She had everything in Alexandria that she needed, right at her fingertips. Washington was fun once in a while though—for some of the museums, and whenever there was a public political event like an inauguration. For a woman, Shelby was a bit unusual—she did enjoy politics and was fascinated with the power plays that dominated the workings of government. The constant bickering between Democrats and Republicans annoyed most Americans, but to Shelby it was just an interesting study of human nature and massive egos at work. She thought it was funny most of the time—they were like big kids in a playground.

She would just love to be a fly on the wall in the Oval Office, to be able to hear what was really talked about before the perfectly sanitized versions reached the ears of the American people.

She turned off the Beltway onto S. Washington Street and went north. It then changed to N. Washington Street and she kept driving until she saw King Street—the lawyer said his office was on the northwest corner of N. Washington Street and King Street. Shelby pulled into a municipal parking lot, paid for her ticket and dropped it onto the dashboard.

Shelby took the elevator up to the fourth floor, gave her name to the receptionist and then took a seat in the opulent lobby. She waited for the short, fat and balding lawyer, whom she'd also formed an early opinion of—the man was obnoxious as hell. Accustomed to pushing his way into situations without asking permission. Without being respectful. His behavior that day last week in the hospital was despicable as far as she was concerned. But...she guessed he was in that category of lawyer that was referred to as 'ambulance chasers.' He was the guy who'd jumped first on the Class Action suit and had already received preliminary approval for registration of the action. So, she had to deal with him if she wanted to be a part of it.

She gazed around as she waited. The lobby furniture was all supple leather illuminated by the softest lighting she had ever seen in an office. The floors were marble, leading to a berber-type burgundy carpet down the hallways. Straining her neck a bit, she could see an entire line of offices stretching as far as her eyes would take her.

The tornado burst through a side conference room door. He rushed over and motioned for her to follow him. "Hello, Ms. Sutcliffe. I'm pressed for time today, so just follow me to my office and we'll make this quick."

They passed the reception desk on the way to the hallway—there was a large sign carved out of wood hanging on the wall behind the half-moon desk: 'Feinstein & Sons.'

She pulled the man's card out of her purse, to remind herself that his name was Dwayne Feinstein. He still hadn't been polite enough to formally introduce himself, not here and not at the hospital either.

She called out to him as they passed a line of small offices. "So, are you 'the' Feinstein, or are you one of the sons?"

He was rudely rushing ahead of her, demonstrating that he had absolutely no idea what the term 'gentleman' meant. Dwayne laughed in kind of a cackling way and turned his head to look back at her as he walked. "I hardly look like I could be the father, do I, Ms. Sutcliffe? Of course I'm one of the sons."

Shelby was completely turned off by the guy and their meeting hadn't even started yet. "Well, to be frank with you—and no offense intended—I have a tough time judging age with bald men." She couldn't resist.

He ignored her comment and led her into a large corner office, adorned even more lushly than the lobby. She didn't see one file or even a piece of paper on his desk. Just a computer and a phone.

Shelby couldn't resist again and gestured with her hand over his empty desktop. "You say you're busy. Doesn't look like it to me."

He ignored her again and plunked down in his executive leather chair. Shelby sat in one of the guest chairs and noticed that he was suddenly taller than her. He must have a pedestal floor installed underneath the desk. "Funny, now I'm looking up at you and a second ago I was looking down at you."

"Shelly, you seem to take some joy in making wisecracks."

"It's 'Shelby.'"

"What?"

"My name's 'Shelby,' not 'Shelly.'"

Dwayne opened a drawer, pulled out a file and flipped it open. He scrolled with his finger, then pulled a pen out of his pocket and made a notation. "So it is."

"You had to check your file to verify my name? My word wasn't good enough?"

The fat little man scratched his forehead and winced. "I think we've gotten off on the wrong foot here. Let's start again, okay?"

"Fine by me. What do you want with me?"

"Well, it's more like what I can do for you." He pulled a piece of paper out of the file and slid it over to her. "Just sign this document here, I'll witness it, and you're in."

"In on what?"

"Well, the Class Action lawsuit, of course."

Shelby crossed her legs and sighed. "Don't you intend to tell me how it works? What I have to do?"

Dwayne coughed into his fist. "It's simple. I represent you and all the families of the deceased victims. You'll be our main witness, being that you're the sole survivor."

"What if I prefer to have my own lawyer represent me?"

"You can certainly do that, but you still have to sign on to my Class Action. I'm the only lawyer who's been given the right of action. You can pay him yourself out of your own pocket—he won't have a contingent fee coming out of the proceeds of the lawsuit."

"Who gets the proceeds?"

"Well, you and the families, of course."

"And you."

"Of course 'me.' I have to be paid."

Shelby leaned forward in her chair. "What do you get?"

"The standard in Class Actions is forty percent."

Shelby laughed. "Are you serious?"

The lawyer rested his chin on his fists. "Yes, and it will be well earned."

"How much is the lawsuit for?"

He opened his file again. "I'm filing for 500 million. The suit will name both Flying Machines Inc. and Adventureland. That's fairly normal, to name the most obvious parties involved—the courts may decide to drop one of the names off and then the suit will be just against one. And I think that one will end up being Flying Machines Inc. I see no evidence indicating that Adventureland had any part to play in this accident."

Shelby whistled. "So you'll get a cool 200 million if the court awards 500?"

"Yes."

She couldn't believe what she was hearing. "So the balance of 300 million will be divided between me and the twenty-five families of the deceased?"

"Yes, but your share of course will be the smallest. You're alive and, unless you have any continuing crippling ailments, or mental deficiencies that you can prove were caused by the accident, you'll be low woman on the totem pole—you'll probably get a couple of million for your injuries and mental anguish."

"So, you get 200 million for my accident, and I get two million?"

"Yes—that's the way it would work."

Shelby shook her head.

"Look, Shelly, this is just the way it works."

"Shelby!"

The lawyer flinched. "What?"

"My name is Shelby!"

"Yes, yes…sorry."

Shelby stood. "Look, I just want to leave. Give me that sheet to take with me and I'll study it."

"No, you'll have to read it here."

Shelby grabbed it off the desk and started scanning it. Then she stopped reading and looked up. "This is a statement that you've already prepared. You haven't even asked me to describe what happened."

Dwayne sighed. "It's just a statement—you'll note it says 'preliminary.' There will be a deposition and you can tell your story then."

"No! I want to tell it now! And I want you to get it down right the first time!"

The lawyer held out his hand in a calming gesture. "Sit down…Shelby. Let me explain something to you."

Shelby sat and continued scanning the document in her hand.

"This lawsuit will be a slam-dunk. You could be a chimpanzee as a witness—it won't make a difference. What happened two weeks ago is a perfect example of why 'Strict Liability' is largely the law of the land. All I have to do is show that a rollercoaster caused death and injury. That there was no intervening cause—such as, say, an earthquake or tornado, or some other cause that made the tragedy happen other than just the fact that it was a faulty rollercoaster. I don't have to even prove negligence—I just have to show that this machine caused the horrible tragedy and that nothing else was involved. So…as I said…a slam dunk."

Shelby looked up from the document. "This will probably bankrupt Flying Machines Inc."

"Well, that depends on how much liability insurance they have. But…yes… even after the insurance pays, the company will probably drop into a graveyard. Their reputation will be shot."

"You haven't even asked me how I'm doing. How my injuries have healed, or how my mental state is."

Dwayne shrugged. "Doesn't really matter to me. I'm suing for 500 million collectively—how the plaintiffs' 300 million share gets divided is not really my concern. You can tell your story to the judge and jury—they might decide to apportion more to you based on that. But—none of that changes the total amount that I'm suing for."

Shelby frowned at him. "Why do you even need me?"

"As a witness, with your testimony, it will drive home the horror of it all—describing what you went through makes the horror real for the jury. The point is, with Strict Liability we're not going to be arguing 'fault.' The only thing that will be debated in court is 'quantum;' in other words, just the amount that will have to be paid. Strict Liability makes the lawsuit a sure thing—but not a sure thing as far as the amount is concerned. That's where I...the families...need you. Your story will sufficiently horrify everyone, which will jack up the amount that they decide to award. It'll sensationalize it; know what I mean? We're suing for both compensatory and punitive damages in this case. The compensatory damages are easy to ascertain: the loss of an income that would have been earned to the families; the future care needed for the families; college educations for their kids, etc. But it's the punitive damages part where the case needs you—those kinds of damages are intended to punish. They have nothing to do with anything specific such as lost earnings—they have everything to do with the horror value and how much the judge or jury feels that Flying Machines Inc. needs to be punished."

"But, isn't it just the insurance company that really gets punished?"

"Well, yes...as long as Flying Machines has enough liability insurance. If they don't, the company has to pay out of their own capital."

Shelby shook her head in disbelief and continued reading. Then she stopped. "Hey, this isn't right. Where did you get this information?"

"What?"

"This document says that once the coaster hit the split in the track the lap bars unlocked from the shock of the impact of the front car buckling."

"Yes."

"That's not right. I discovered that my lap bar was unlocked before we even reached the top of the second hill. I remember being afraid that once we careened over the top of the hill that my body would simply lift out of the train. The hill was so steep there was no way that lap bar would have kept me in. In fact, regardless of the split in the track we were all dead the minute those lap bars unlocked. The track didn't need to split in half to kill us. Luckily, I lifted myself up, out, and away from the doomed train as soon as it hit the split in the track. But no one else did. My seatmate Cheryl Sanders was gone the moment the train buckled—she got thrown, I guess, and I noticed her bar was in the 'up' position."

The lawyer scratched his chin. "You must be mistaken."

Shelby slapped the document onto the lawyer's desk. "I am NOT mistaken! I know what happened! Those bars were already useless before we even reached the top of the hill. I can't sign this document. And when we reach court, I will tell the correct version of this story."

"You're mistaken, Shelly."

Shelby smacked the palm of her hand down on his desk. "If I have to correct my name with you one more time I'm going to scream!"

Dwayne sheepishly started shuffling through his file again, until he found what he wanted. He waved the piece of paper at her. "This is the preliminary report from the NTSB—it states clearly that their investigation shows that the lap bars were crippled from the violent impact of the front car with the broken track—that it jackknifed, causing the lap bar ratchet locks to fail electronically."

Shelby laughed. "That's very funny. In their "investigation" they didn't even talk to the lone survivor—me. What kind of investigation is that?"

"Well, it's the NTSB—who do you think the courts will believe—you or them?"

Shelby rose from her chair. "Don't you want the truth? And I don't even see why this makes a difference to your suit. As you said, it's a 'slam dunk.'"

Dwayne stood up, too. "It complicates things a bit—it indicates that maybe there was another intervening cause of what happened, which, if that's the case, Strict Liability might not apply. Which means we'd have to prove negligence instead."

Shelby was dumbstruck. "You mean you'd actually have to do some work? To get at the truth? Is that what's bothering you? You're afraid that you may not be able to prove that Flying Machines Inc. was negligent? Hey, here's a brainstorm for you—if they weren't negligent, they don't deserve to be sued and they don't deserve to go bankrupt! Sounds like you'd rather have an untruth in your case, just so you can get your 'slam dunk!'"

"It's a complication we don't need. Why don't you just sign the form and let me take it from here? I promise I'll raise the issue with the NTSB."

Shelby chuckled. "Oh, you—who can't even get my name right—you'll promise me, will you? How's this for a suggestion—you talk to the NTSB first and get it straightened out. Then I'll sign a document that has a statement in my own words. How's that for a plan?"

The bald and fat little lawyer grimaced. Then he muttered, through clenched teeth, "Don't even give it another thought, Shelly. We can win this lawsuit without your testimony. No point in getting yourself all worked up. It looks like you're doing fine—you don't need to have this horrible memory dredged up for you again."

He then tore up the document that Shelby was supposed to sign and pointed to his door. "Have a lovely day."

CHAPTER 12

Nate awakened with a start. He could feel his heart pounding and sweat had soaked his pajamas right through. He shuffled into the bathroom, stripped off his wet clothes and towel dried his hair, which was plastered to his head from the perspiration.

It hadn't been a nightmare—more like a brainstorm.

Since he was sleeping alone now he didn't have to worry anymore about waking Stephanie when he had his sudden brainstorms. And he got brainstorms a lot—and, like now, most of them in the dead of night. At other times, they would creep up on him when he was daydreaming. Maybe because his mind was at rest? And maybe, as psychologists liked to say, dreams are just the brain's way of attempting to resolve the unresolved. Usually in bizarrely abstract ways.

Nate had awakened to the vision of a fist in front of his face. Just a fist, nothing else—and it was someone else's fist. A right-handed fist, and he knew it wasn't his because one of the fingers had a very large distinctive ring—kind of like a Graduation ring…or a Super Bowl ring.

He donned his dressing gown and wandered down to the kitchen. Poured himself a glass of milk and then stretched out on the couch in the living room. Sipping his milk while picturing the fist in his mind, he began pondering what the dream meant. It was so specific that it had to be meaningful. Meaningful to something that was going on in his life, and right now there was an awful lot going on.

He closed his eyes and concentrated. There had to be a message in this vision—it had to be a clue to something. And if history was any indication, Nate's brain would figure it out fairly quickly. He was confident of that. It was just the way his unusual brain worked. Over the years, he had come to understand its workings very well indeed.

His concentration was disturbed by soft footsteps. Then the voice of his wife. "You can't sleep either, I see."

He allowed his left eye to wander over in her direction. She was coming out of the kitchen with a glass of juice in her hand.

"No—too much on my mind, I guess."

Stephanie sat down in the chair opposite him. She let out a big sigh, and then spoke in a soft melodic voice. "What happened to us, Nate?"

Nate just shook his head.

She took a slow sip of her juice. "Did we just lose ourselves?"

Nate stretched his legs out on the ottoman. "I don't know, Steph. I think we just grew apart, and probably didn't really know each other as well as we thought we did. We wanted different things, that's all."

She leaned forward and put her elbows on her knees, resting her chin on her fists. "I still love you, Nate."

Nate shook his head. "No, you don't, Steph. C'mon, you have to face the facts. People who love each other don't fuck other people. I'm not angry about that anymore—it's just a statement of fact. I wasn't the right one for you—or I just wasn't enough for you. Either way, it doesn't matter anymore."

She started crying. "I just made a mistake. Why can't you forgive me?"

Nate frowned at her. "Steph, you made the same mistake at least twice. That should tell you something. It's best for both of us if we move on. And let's be honest here—we haven't been in love with each other for many years now, even before you fooled around. So, maybe your mistakes are partly my fault. My detachment might have chased you to other men. I dunno, maybe I got too busy with work and didn't put the effort into our marriage as much as I should have.

"And I let it drag on—I didn't pay attention to you, and I didn't try to fix it either. I kept promising myself that I had to do something about our marriage before I made a big mistake like you did—but I kept putting it off, kept finding other things to distract me. So, I just put up with you being in my life, when what I really wanted, I guess, was to have you out of my life. I didn't face it head-on like I should have."

"That's a pretty cruel thing to say, Nate."

"What? Crueler than fooling around on me?"

"I was drunk when those things happened."

"That's a weak excuse, Steph. All booze does is give people the courage and the recklessness to do what they really wanted to do in the first place. And then it becomes a convenient excuse for bad behavior. You know that, I'm not telling you anything revolutionary here."

"No, it wasn't that way."

"Sure it was—you know it was. Now you're just doing what I did for so long—not facing up to the truth. We're both at fault here, and there's no point beating ourselves up over it."

"I love you."

Nate pulled his legs back off the ottoman and leaned towards her. He spoke slowly and softly.

"Steph, you don't love me any more than I love you. You love our lifestyle, we both do. We got too comfortable and didn't pay attention to the things that should have been more important. We didn't pay attention to our souls.

"But don't worry—you'll be well taken care of. I won't give you a hard time about anything. I just want out—I need to start over and perhaps spend some time being by myself for a while."

Stephanie's face suddenly clouded over. "Well, what's going to be left over to take care of me after the lawsuit? There will be a lawsuit, won't there?"

Nate sighed. "Yes, there probably will be. And the company has liability insurance, so we should be well protected."

Her tone hardened. "But the business will probably fail, won't it? You'll have no problem starting over—you're an engineer. But I have no education or skills at all. What am I going to do?"

Nate chuckled. "I think I'm starting to understand why you started this conversation off by telling me that you still loved me."

Stephanie went silent, glared at him for the longest second, and then walked over to stand in front of the living room window. She stretched out her slender arm and shook her tiny fist towards the sky. "God, I hate you for what you've done to us!"

Nate looked on impassively at her pitiful little drama. But then, all of a sudden, he got the most extraordinary feeling in the pit of his stomach. A rush of excitement! At that same instant the answer he'd been waiting patiently for all night—actually in the form of an image—displayed itself in his brain.

He jumped to his feet. "That's it!"

Stephanie whirled around. "What?"

Nate rushed off in the direction of his bedroom. "No, it's not about you. But, thanks to you, something you just did brought it all back."

*****

Shelby parked her car in a parking lot just off L'Enfant Plaza in Washington, D.C. This was the office of the National Transportation Safety Board. She had a meeting in about five minutes' time with a senior official by the name of John Fletcher. The most senior investigator at the NTSB and the one who had personally conducted the rather quick investigation of the Black Mamba tragedy.

It had taken her a couple of days to actually get through to him. His calls seemed to be selectively screened—but once she finally identified herself as the lone survivor of the Black Mamba, she was able to connect. They talked briefly and he agreed to meet with her. He seemed nice, at least over the phone.

After only a few minutes wait in the reception area, a tall gray-haired man came out to greet her. He leaned towards her and held out his hand.

"Hello Ms. Sutcliffe. I'm John Fletcher and I'm very pleased to meet you... and I must say I'm also extremely pleased to see you looking so alive and healthy!"

Shelby smiled politely and shook his hand. She gulped when she realized what an important thing it was that he had just said. She was alive, and glad to be. And so far she hadn't been feeling any of the 'survivor guilt' that she had feared would creep up on her. Being a nurse, she had seen that reaction in many of her patients over the years.

"It's nice to meet you, too. Thanks so much for agreeing to meet with me."

He motioned with his hand in the direction of his office and they walked together down the hall. Shelby thought: *What a difference between this true gentleman and that slob of a lawyer I met with.* She decided that John Fletcher was one of those rare people whom you liked instantly. He had that special chemistry. Maybe it was his infectious smile or the gracious way that he had greeted her. He didn't do it in melodramatic fashion—didn't refer to the horrifying aspect of the accident—he just simply told her that he was glad to see her alive. He made her feel instantly comfortable.

"I'm sorry you couldn't get through to me the first few times you tried. We get so many enquiries from crackpots who are upset and vigilant about various accidents. We have to be so careful."

Shelby smiled at him—which was an easy thing to do with this John Fletcher gentleman. She thought he looked just like Cary Grant. He had that look about him that was captivating. John would be everyone's ideal of how the perfect grandfather should look and act. A classy man, for sure. She noticed the wedding ring on his left hand and guessed that his wife was a class act as well. How could she not be?

He led her into his office. She noticed that it was just a modest room, with furniture that looked like it had been bought at the local budget store. Quite a contrast to the egocentric opulence of Dwayne Feinstein's office.

John poured Shelby a cup of coffee and then sat down in the other guest chair beside her. Shelby was impressed—he didn't sit behind the desk, which always formed a natural barrier to good conversation. He made it more informal and personal by sitting beside her. She knew she was going to like this man.

"So, tell me, how is your recovery going?"

Shelby looked down at her hands, feeling a little self-conscious. "I'm doing fine. Remarkably, nothing was broken. I was just battered and bruised."

John smiled his Cary Grant smile. "That's great. What an ordeal for you—it's hard to imagine. How are you feeling about it all, though?"

Shelby smiled back. She didn't want to talk about how she felt—she'd been doing her best over the last couple of weeks to bury her feelings. Her dreams at nighttime exhausted her, constantly reliving it over and over again. She tried not to think about it while she was awake.

Keeping busy helped. Even meeting with that sleazy lawyer had helped. And being here, ready to confront John Fletcher about the NTSB report, was also helping.

"Mr. Fletcher..."

"Call me 'John.'"

"Okay...John. You can call me 'Shelby.' I'll get right to the point because I know you're a busy man. I visited with the lawyer who filed the Class Action lawsuit against Flying Machines and Adventureland. He wants me to join the action and testify."

"Yes, well, that would be the expected thing. Your testimony, I mean. And...I would expect also that you'll join the action?"

Shelby shook her head. "Not yet. I needed to get some things clarified first."

"Okay, I'm listening."

"It seems to me that the lawyer, Dwayne Feinstein, could care less about what really happened. He wants to hang Nathan Morrell and his company out to dry. He's relying on something that's Greek to me, something called 'Strict Liability,' which means he won't have to worry about who was at fault."

John rubbed his forehead. "That is how that legal principle works. He's correct."

"Well, to my understanding, it doesn't work that way if there was possibly something else that caused the accident."

"That's true—if there was a contributing cause, then the only alternative left for him is to prove negligence."

Shelby glared into Cary Grant's eyes, and she had no doubt in her mind that he could see into her soul—see her confusion and frustration. "You didn't bother to interview me. You prepared your report without even talking to me."

John stared back.

She persisted. "Why didn't you talk to me?"

He averted his eyes for just a second. Enough to make Shelby uneasy.

"It wasn't deemed necessary."

Shelby was starting to feel the same anger that she had felt in Feinstein's office. "Wouldn't it be *necessary* for you to know that the lap bars didn't deactivate upon impact with the broken track? That it wasn't the jackknife that caused them to pop open? The lap bars actually unlocked at least a second or two before the impact—I know that for a fact. I pulled up on it. And I'm the only one alive who can tell you that. If you had bothered to talk to me you would have known that."

John was rubbing his forehead with both hands now.

"John? Are you okay?"

"Yes...yes. I just have a bad headache."

"I have some aspirin in my purse. Do you want one?"

"No...no, it's okay. It'll fade in a bit."

Shelby paused for a second, then continued. "Your report stated that the lap bars came unlocked upon impact. And that's just not true. Something caused them to open before the train hit the split in the track. Isn't that a fact that's worth investigating? You have to admit it's weird. Why would that happen? Why would both of those things happen within mere seconds of each other?"

John glanced at his watch and stood up. "Shelby, I don't want to be rude, but I'm going to have to ask you to leave. I have another meeting starting in about five minutes."

Shelby stood as well. "Are you surprised at what I'm telling you? Does this alarm you at all?"

John walked over to his door and opened it.

"Thanks, Shelby, for coming here to tell me what you did. I'll take it under advisement."

She walked to the door. "What does that mean? I don't know what 'advisement' means with something as serious as this."

He smiled thinly—no longer looking like Cary Grant. "Goodbye, Shelby. Nice to have met you. Good luck to you."

CHAPTER 13

They were all there when Nate walked into the conference room. He was a bit late, but he knew they'd forgive him. He had a great relationship with his entire management team—a group of people who were the most talented he'd ever had the pleasure of working with.

He took his seat at the usual spot—head of the table. To his immediate left was his best friend and Vice President of Mechanical Engineering, Tom Foster— the one who'd experienced the hell at Adventureland right alongside him. And the one who he also now knew had a paralyzing fear of heights.

Next to Tom was Jim Watkins, Vice President of Finance. Anchoring the end of that side of the table was Robin Gilchrist. Robin was Vice President of Legal Affairs, and she was one of the best legal minds that Nate had ever met.

On Nate's right sat Ron Collens, Vice President of Electrical and Systems Engineering. Next to him was Ralph Woods, Vice President of Marketing. The last seat on the right side of the table was occupied by Helen Lacombe, the company's Vice President of Human Resources. She had a challenging job— the company's 600 employees were feeling very unsettled with what happened at Adventureland. They were naturally concerned about what the future of the company was going to look like after such a devastating setback.

Nate opened his file folder, took a quick glance at his notes, and then spoke to the group. They were all silent, no doubt wondering what he could say to make such a disaster look better. *Lipstick on a pig?*

Nate wasn't sure he could tell them anything to make them feel better—time would just have to take its own course. But, he was their leader and he knew that whatever it was he was about to say would either dash their spirits or lift them.

Luckily, Flying Machines Inc. was a private company. There were no external shareholders to be concerned about, nor financial regulators that they would have to account to. In addition, being a private company, their financial statements didn't have to be disclosed to anyone other than the folks around the table.

The executives were the shareholders—they were all Nate's partners, although he held controlling interest. Fifty-one percent gave him control, although he seldom had to swing his weight around with this group. They usually arrived at a consensus on everything that was decided. But in the event that there was a stalemate—which was rare—Nate would make the call, and his partners always respected his right to do that.

He looked up and scanned the faces of his team. Then he spoke.

"We've had an incredible setback. It was tragic and horrible, and no doubt the publicity alone is hurting us severely. Ralph can comment about that in a few minutes. I've assigned tasks to each of you, and I'll want you to report today to all of us your findings so far. So much is still up in the air, so I don't expect that you'll have all the answers yet. But we'll plod away until we get them.

"We're not going to lay down and die. We'll fight back. I don't think for a second that we did anything wrong. This is the most unusual accident in so many ways—there has been nothing like it in the history of rollercoasters, and we'll chat about that. There are answers—we just have to find them.

"I visited the lone survivor, Shelby Sutcliffe, in the hospital within a couple days of the accident. No severe injuries and I hear that she's been released now and is doing fine. A lovely young woman, no doubt. We won't be able to count on her being on our side though. She was very angry when she discovered who I was. So, her testimony probably won't help us at all—although, at this point, I have no idea what she will say or what she observed while on the ride."

Helen interrupted. "Nate, do you think the fact that you risked your life to save hers will have any mitigating impact on her testimony?"

Nate shook his head. "No, I'm not under any illusions about that."

He continued. "I have some things of my own that I want to share with all of you, but I'll leave that until a little bit later. Helen, since you asked the first question, why don't we start with your report? Go ahead."

"Well, from a Human Resources standpoint, everyone is in shock. Our people are worried, and for good reason. We've had no resignations yet, but I fear that will come. Some of our competitors will become predatory, sensing a death. They'll pounce and try to lure some of our best people away—particularly our engineers. They're in big demand. And, of course, our competitors aren't just in the thrill ride business—very few engineering firms specialize as narrowly as we do. Most do general engineering: bridges, dams, skyscrapers, aviation, automotive, etc. We specialize in just amusement devices, but our engineers are qualified to do virtually anything. So—we have a big field of competitors out there to contend with; they'll capitalize on the instability and try to steal our people. And, of course, they'll sweeten the pot by offering big salaries and signing bonuses."

Everyone around the table was nodding in agreement.

"Anything else at this point, Helen?"

"No, I just wanted to outline the lay of the land at this early stage."

"Fine. Thank you. Okay, Ralph, let's hear it from a Marketing standpoint."

Ralph Woods glanced around the table. All eyes were on him, because Marketing was the engine that drove any company. It was the finger on the pulse and its job was to create the right environment for healthy revenues to take place. He cleared his throat.

"Folks, things are happening fast. I've already received notices of cancellation on three of our lucrative merchandising contracts. And, as you all know, we don't just design and manufacture rollercoasters—that's just what we've become known for. But, what most of the general public isn't aware of is that we design and manufacture an entire range of amusement and resort devices. From waterslides, go-carts, Ferris wheels, and gondolas—right up to new prototypes of Formula 1 racecars and portable stages for rock concerts. We do virtually anything entertainment-related.

"Suddenly, no one's talking to us. All of the current projects we have on the go have had 'hold' orders put on them. But, even worse than that, our service contracts are being replaced mid-stream. As you know, a sizeable portion of our revenue comes from contracts with amusement parks for maintaining and servicing not only what we build, but for all rides and amusement devices, even those manufactured by others. We have the world-famous expertise that has driven amusement parks to outsource their maintenance with us. We've received several suspensions already and I expect more will follow."

Nate pointed his finger at Robin Gilchrist. "Robin, give us the legal view. Can they do that? We have signed contracts for all of these endeavors."

Robin nodded her head. "Yes, Nate. They have every right to do that. All of our contracts contain two-way exit clauses—or at the very least suspensions—in the event that either party is involved in any high profile public relations incident that might reflect badly on the other party—or cause a lack of confidence."

Nate protested. "But nothing's been proven yet!"

Robin cleared her throat. "No, and the contracts don't require that anything be proven. And you can understand why—the way the court and investigative process works, it might sometimes take years for proof to be clear. A party can't be expected to remain in a contract that might affect their business, suffering and waiting, while the courts drag their heels. And, think of it, even if something is proven, appeals can drag it out even further."

Nate picked up his pen and made some notes.

"Okay, Robin, I understand. Since you've taken the floor, why don't you fill us in on the legal landscape right now?"

Robin opened her file and glanced at the contents before speaking. "Okay, a Class Action has been filed by the legal firm, Feinstein and Sons. The court has accepted the registration—no preliminary court date has been assigned yet. All twenty-five families of the deceased riders have signed on. And...you'll find this interesting—so far Shelby Sutcliffe has not signed the petition. I don't know why."

"Hmm…that is interesting. Is that good news for us or bad news?"

"Hard to say—she's the only rider who's alive and of course her testimony will be important either way. But…and this is a big 'but'…perhaps there's something she knows that might not work in favor of the lawsuit. Maybe for that reason, they haven't pursued her. Or…she plans on launching her own lawsuit, which I seriously doubt. Any half-decent lawyer will tell her that her best chance at a settlement is to join the Class Action. By the time the courts get around to finally hearing her case, there might not be much money left to go around."

Nate nodded. "Which begs the question, how much money is there to go around?"

"We have liability insurance for 300 million."

And what's the Class Action filed at?"

"For 500 million."

There was a collective gasp around the table.

"So, we're 200 million short."

"Yes, but remember, they have to convince the jury or judge of that quantum. It might settle at far less than that—and these cases seldom get to court. They usually settle on the courthouse steps for much less than the amount filed."

Nate rubbed his forehead. "But, let's say worse case here. If it settles for 500 million, we'll be short."

"Yes. We'd have to sell assets."

Nate looked over at his Vice President of Finance, Jim Watkins, one of the best chartered accountants in Virginia. "Your assessment?"

Jim looked down at his notes. "Nate, we have 100 million in cash and securities. Another 50 million in hard assets. And 100 million in Directors and Officers Liability, but I doubt we could call on that—that's designed more for financial losses not related to death or tangible property damage. And then…we have all of our personal assets at stake. As directors and officers, we're personally liable under the law."

Nate raised his voice. "Hold on one second! The last market valuation of Flying Machines Inc. conducted with our auditors brought us to an approximation of 1 billion dollars in shareholders' equity." Nate gestured with his hand in a sweeping motion around the table. "Which is us collectively. That's what our investment in the company is worth. That's what the *company* is worth. So, we should be able to leverage that for bank loans to satisfy the lawsuit."

Jim's face bore a look of resignation. "No, Nate, that's not the way it would work. If the company can't satisfy the judgment out of insurance monies or liquid assets, Flying Machines Inc. will essentially be bankrupt. Our collective investment will be worthless."

Nate stared at Jim for a few seconds, then shook his head and looked back at Robin. "Okay, we'll just have to fight this. We'll prove that we weren't negligent."

Robin took a deep breath before speaking. "Nate, it doesn't matter. Virginia is a Strict Liability state. That's the law of the land. All we're going to be arguing in court is the quantum, not who was at fault. As long as the court does not see that there was another cause involved, or an intervening cause, it doesn't make any difference whether or not we were negligent. We're on the hook."

Nate leaned back in his chair and sighed. "You've explained that to me before, Robin. I'm sorry; it probably never really sunk in until this very moment. I guess it just didn't seem real to me before."

"I understand."

Nate leaned forward and started scribbling some notes in his binder. Then he looked up and proclaimed, "Well, there had to be an intervening cause—we all know that. We were not at fault. And I have a couple of things to share with you all in a few minutes. In the meantime, we need to do what we can to redeem ourselves. Our only hope is to prove what really happened. Tom, I asked you to get out to the site to see what you could find out—see when the NTSB would be ready to allow us and our insurers to have a look at the wreckage."

Tom took a long sip of his water. "I was looking for you around noon today, Nate, but apparently you had a business lunch. Wanted to bring you up to date before this meeting. Yes, I was able to visit the site this morning."

Nate was feeling encouraged all of a sudden. "Okay, great. What were you allowed to see?"

"Nothing."

"What?!"

"There was nothing to see. The Black Mamba has been entirely dismantled. And from what I was able to determine, the wreckage has been hauled away to an undisclosed location."

Nate stood up and slammed his fists onto the table. "They can't do that! That's ridiculous! How can we possibly defend ourselves?!"

Tom ignored the outburst and continued, "I was given the name of the NTSB guy, a man by the name of John Fletcher—the most senior investigator there. I called him and challenged him on this. His report is complete now. He emailed it to me and I'll share it with all of you. In any event, his response to my challenge was that the NTSB was claiming Eminent Domain on the wreckage."

Nate was dumbfounded. He looked over at Robin. "What the fuck is that?"

Robin swallowed hard. "It's a legal principle that allows governments to confiscate property if it is in the greater good to do so. I've never seen it used for something like this before, but this is the government—they can pretty much do what they want and trying to challenge them in court could take years, even if the courts allow such a challenge—which is unlikely."

Nate felt his left eye beginning to twitch. He couldn't believe what he was hearing. "I don't even understand why the NTSB investigated this to begin with. This is not normal at all."

Robin nodded. "I agree. But...again...this is the government and we're just a corporation. It's David versus Goliath."

Nate looked back at Tom. "Okay, give us the executive summary of Mr. Fletcher's report."

"It says that there was a faulty weld at the top of the second hill, and that it snapped right at that point."

Nate felt like he was going to explode. "That's absolute bullshit! I personally designed the superstructure and the track itself—the only welds used were on straight-aways and on the lower inclines of the hills. There were NO welds at the top of any hill. The tracks on those hills were solid steel!"

Tom nodded. "We know that, Nate. I'm just telling you what the report says."

"And what does the report say about the lap bars? They were in the 'up' position at the moment of the accident."

Tom looked at his notes. "Just says that the impact with the split track caused the bars to disengage."

Nate looked over at Ron Collens, his Vice President of Electrical and Systems Engineering. "What do you say to that? Is that possible?"

"No, not really. We could do some tests to make sure. But, those ratchet locking mechanisms were designed to open only three ways: upon entering the station at the end of the ride, manually if we had to, or...by remote control. They had their own dedicated radio frequency. I don't see how an impact with anything would cause those things to disengage."

Nate started pacing the boardroom, talking as he walked. "Okay, we have several things that make no sense at all. Let me summarize for us: the NTSB investigated an accident that is outside its jurisdiction; the wreckage has been dismantled and removed without us or our insurers having a chance to inspect it; the report says the accident was caused by a faulty weld in a section of the track where there were no welds; and last but not least, the report says the lap bars disengaged on impact when our knowledge tells us that would be unlikely to happen. Have I missed anything?"

Silence around the table.

"Okay, I'm going to share a couple of things with all of you. And what I'm going to share stays within this room."

Nate took a slow slip of water, then a deep breath. "You all know the... special...skills I possess. I notice things better than most, and can etch them into my brain for recall later. Sometimes, I don't take notice of specific details right away, but my photographic memory…or eidetic as they call it…can retrieve every detail, sometimes months later. Well, before the accident happened, I noticed a man…he was tall, well built, about forty years old or so…and snazzy dressed. Bald-headed and wearing expensive looking glasses. Designer frames. The guy raised his arm up in the direction of the second hill and his hand was in a fist. I thought he was waving at first, but then realized his hand was making a fist. I didn't think too much of it. A few seconds later, I saw a flash right under the track of the second hill. It was a sunny day, as you all know, and I wrote it off as just being a reflection of the sun. But…in hindsight, it was much more than that. It was almost like sparklers on the fourth of July—flashing, sparking. But, when I shifted my position I couldn't see it any more. So, I ignored that, too."

Nate paused and looked around the table. Some mouths were hanging open in shock as they took in his every word.

He continued. "When the train was falling, I noticed that some of the lap bars were in the 'up' position, and I couldn't understand how that could be. Sure, that was the wrong thing to be thinking at a time like that, but I couldn't help myself.

"The other night I had a dream. A fist in my face. Just a fist. I couldn't figure it out until my wife did something that triggered a memory. The memory of the man's fist being aimed toward the track. And the image in my dream brought the details in to me much clearer than my conscious memory recalled. It was a right-handed fist, and it had a ring on the third finger. Not just any ring—my first thought was that it was a graduation ring. But then I thought that the quick image I had of it told me that it could also be an even more distinctive ring than that.

"I went right back to bed after my wife did what she did to trigger it—and I concentrated hard before I fell off to sleep. The image came back clearer to me. I woke up and drew a quick picture. It was a large ring, with the image of five trophies in the center. On the upper rim around the center was the word, "Forty." On the lower rim was the word, "Niners." I estimated that this man I saw was in his early forties. So, I googled several years in the nineties and found images of this exact same ring from the year 1994. It was indeed the Super Bowl ring from 1994, when the San Francisco 49ers beat the San Diego Charges by a score of 49-26. And the image of the five trophies in the center of the ring signified that the 49ers were the first team to have ever won five Super Bowls.

"This man, whoever he was, played for the San Francisco 49ers Super Bowl champions of 1994."

There was a gasp around the table. Then Tom spoke…just one word…but it summarized how everyone felt. "Jesus!"

Nate pointed at Ron Collens. "You're the electrical and systems guy. What do you think about a guy standing on the Black Mamba's perimeter, pointing his fist at the second hill—the hill that supposedly split from a faulty weld?"

Ron was silent for a second, and then spoke slowly. "While you were talking about it, my first thought was that he was holding a remote unit. From your angle off to the right, it would look like just a fist, but that's the way you'd hold a remote."

"And what would that remote be doing?"

Ron paused again and looked around the table. "Most of you know that I was a Navy Seal. There's something we used to use all the time for quick burns through metal structures. It was a substance called Thermate—we used the military grade, Thermate-3, which could be simply painted onto a structure, fixed with a magnesium fuse, and set off by remote control. The stuff was so potent and generated its own oxygen that it could actually be used underwater. And it burns very fast, lightning fast."

Nate was scribbling notes. "Funny, that engineering convention I attended where I made that speech; a representative of AE911Truth spoke before me. He mentioned that residue of Thermate-3 was found at the base of the Twin Towers in New York."

Ron leaned his elbows on the table and rested his face in his hands. "We have to face the possibility here that this accident was sabotage. Which is a scary thing to think of."

Nate walked over to the side table and poured himself a cup of coffee. "Ron, could those lap bars also have been deactivated by the same remote control?"

"Yes, absolutely. If the man somehow managed to tap into the radio frequency we use, it would be a simple matter."

Tom jumped in. "Nate, we need to talk about who would benefit from sabotaging us. And there are several candidates, sad to say."

"Yes, there are. But…I'm not finished yet, Tom. I wasn't at a business lunch today when you were looking for me. I was meeting with a senior person I know down at Emergency Services. I demanded to know why the ambulance at Adventureland was unattended. And I also wanted to know why it took so long for additional ambulances to respond."

Tom cracked his knuckles. "I'm bracing myself."

"Well, apparently, the two ambulance attendants who parked the ambulance at the site, disappeared, never to be seen again. They were employed, with impeccable credentials, only two months before the accident. Parking the ambulance that day and abandoning it, turned out to be their last job. References were checked when they were hired. All came back fine. After the accident, those references were checked again, only to find out that the phone numbers were out of service."

Ron shook his head and cursed. "Fuck! This is way too weird!"

"Yeah, 'fuck' is right. And 'weird' is an understatement. But, brace yourself for this…the reason the other ambulances took so long to get to our accident site was because exactly two minutes before our accident an emergency call went out for assistance at a twelve car pile-up on the Woodrow Wilson Bridge caused by an overturned tractor trailer. All available units were dispatched.

"Only to find out that there was no such accident. It was a false alarm.

"Somebody went to great pains to make sure that there would be no emergency assistance at Adventureland that day. It's almost as if everyone on that rollercoaster was supposed to die."

CHAPTER 14

John Fletcher pulled into the driveway of his modest home in Georgetown, a beautiful historic section of Washington. He noticed right away that his wife, Linda, had been busy in the front garden. Splashes of color were everywhere— places where he had never seen color before.

Last week, she'd wielded her magic in the backyard, looking nicer now than in all the years they'd owned the old house.

Instead of getting out of the car, John turned the volume of the radio up a notch and reclined his seat. He wanted to take a moment or two to savor his favorite song—*their* favorite song: *The Way We Were*—and no one could sing that song quite like Barbra Streisand. The melodic range of her voice caused his eyelids to relax and close.

Yes, '*the way we were,*' he thought. Retirement was something he and Linda had been planning and looking forward to for years. They had been married for forty years—a lifetime—and he loved her as much today as he had on their wedding day. A beautiful church service—he could still picture his gorgeous bride in her flowing white dress, the very one that her mother had worn on her wedding day.

They were both so happy—planning their lives together. And working so hard over the years to reach this point—ironically, the point where he now had just one more year to live.

Two years ago, when his oncologist had given him the death sentence, he hadn't really believed it. He had very few symptoms, and death just seemed so unreal, so impossible. But, brain scans over the last two years confirmed that the tumor had continued to grow and the symptoms had become much more regular. The thing had a life of its own and it was stealing his in the process. He knew the end time for him was coming—and coming fast.

Linda had taken good care of him. At first, she'd fawned over him, treated him like an invalid. Until one day John got angry—told her that if she was going to constantly remind him that he was dying he couldn't bear to be with her. Couldn't bear to spend whatever time he had left watching her feeling sorry for him.

It broke his heart to tell her that. But he did it to get her attention—he never had any intention of leaving her. He just didn't want her looking at him that way and treating him that way. He wanted to retain some dignity and wanted their lives to be as normal as possible right up until the end.

She said she understood. And her actions since then showed that she did. In fact, she went in the opposite direction—started planning for what they would do years down the road, talking about what life would be like once John retired. Denial. And then she just poured her wonderful heart into every little hobby she could put her mind to. Gardening was the first thing she studied—took courses and bought all the tools. Her persistence was paying off. Their garden was starting to look like it was right out of a page from *Home and Garden* Magazine. *Bless her little heart.*

Around that same time, she became a voracious reader. Linda started reading anything she could get her hands on. Then joined a book club, attending meetings every week. Most book clubs met once a month, but this club was made up of readers just as voracious as Linda and one of the requirements of the club was that a new book would be reviewed every week. It was just what Linda wanted— to take her mind off what her and John were going through.

Several months before, though, she had finally started referring to the inevitable again—instead of trying to pretend it didn't exist. Not in a negative way though. One night she sat down beside John on the sofa, took his hand, and said, *"Let's do the bucket list."*

John was in shock. Didn't quite know how to answer her at first. Then he said, with a profound sadness in his voice, *"We can't afford it, sweetheart. I have to keep working."*

She rubbed his forehead, and then kissed it tenderly. *"We have to find a way."*

The subject was never raised again. But he knew that she knew he was right. If Linda had any expectation of having a comfortable lifestyle after he died, she needed him to work until the end—sad as that was.

The song ended, but Barbara's lovely voice still reverberated through his mind. John kept his eyes closed, totally relaxed now, a nice time to think.

He had no regrets about the past. He had married his dream girl and they had loved each other deeply for decades.

But then John caught himself—yes, he did have one regret. The fact that he and Linda were estranged from their son. He was living in Europe somewhere and they hadn't heard from him since he'd gotten out of prison a decade ago.

Their son, Vincent, had been in and out of the juvenile system for years. Raising him had been a nightmare for both he and Linda. He was a bad seed. Dealing drugs at a young age, breaking and entering convictions—then that night of the liquor store robbery it all came to an inevitable end. Someone finally got hurt—badly.

And John burst into Vincent's bedroom to discover him and his buddy counting the cash. Loaded handguns on the bed beside them. John had heard news reports just a few minutes earlier about a young cashier with a gunshot wound in the abdomen. Her partner, a young man, had been pistol-whipped into a concussion. John knew who had done the deed—knew in his heart and soul— and that sixth sense caused him to barge into Vincent's bedroom.

John didn't hesitate. He phoned the police and turned his son in.

Luckily, the two liquor store employees had lived, and they identified Vincent and his friend in a police line-up. Ten years in prison was the 'tough love' that John had helped deliver to his son. But he knew that it had been the right thing to do—it broke his heart, but his heart broke even more thinking that his son had caused such harm to innocent people. John was Doctor Frankenstein, and Vincent was his monster. He'd finally decided that he no other choice but to cage the monster.

His son never forgave him. Linda did, though. And as far as John was concerned, that was all that mattered.

With his eyes still closed, he shook his head in sadness. Life had dealt him some wonderful cards, but it had also delivered some unfathomable sadness. Was the tumor his punishment for throwing his own flesh and blood in prison?

And there he was—a year left in his life—still married to the only woman he'd ever truly cared about and all they could afford to do was wait. Wait until he died; wait until the NTSB sucked the last working hour out of him.

And there he was also—thinking about how he'd done the right thing twenty years ago, turning his only son over to the authorities. Yet, he'd just signed an accident report that he knew was a lie, signed a report that he knew would sink a decent company and ruin the reputations and lives of countless people who had done absolutely nothing wrong.

He, John Fletcher, a man who had always prided himself on doing the right thing. But, this time he couldn't, because he was being held ransom by a death sentence and the need to keep this stupid job so his wife could live on comfortably after he left. He needed Linda to be happy after he was gone. He wanted her to be looked after and not having to worry about anything.

This time he was doing the wrong thing—for the right reasons. But, it made him feel ashamed, made him feel like he had sold his soul. For the sake of 'national security.' How on earth could a rollercoaster accident affect national security? And who could have pulled off such a professional sabotage...and why?

The car was still running and the radio was still on. The soothing music had stopped and the news had taken over. The top headline was the wildfires in California, and the story went on to discuss how the years of drought in about half of the United States were nowhere near to coming to an end. That this was the 'new normal,' apparently.

Some towns were less than two years away from running out of water completely. And others had already resorted to attempting to purify sewage water to recycle as drinking water. There were no new sources of water anywhere on the horizon—and the rains weren't expected to ever come back to anywhere close to the extent that they were needed. The distribution of rain around the world had changed—countries that had suffered through hundreds of years of drought, were now seeing rain. And other countries that had always been able to count on plenty of moisture were now seeing drought. The scales had tipped—the world was being rebalanced, it seemed. First World countries were reverting to Third World status, slowly and inexorably. And the United States of America seemed to be one of the first victims of this rebalancing act.

Crops were dying in the fields, irrigation water was in limited supply, and there wasn't even enough water to properly fight the massive fires.

For a morbid second, John wondered how much longer the human race would have after he was gone. Did Earth itself have a massive tumor that was growing in an unstoppable fashion just like what was expanding in his brain?

He thought about his conversation with Tom Foster the other day—the engineer at Flying Machines Inc. How desperate and shocked the man sounded when John had explained what his report was going to say. How indignant he was when John told him that the determined cause was a faulty weld in the track. Foster insisted there were no welds on that section of the track—and of course John knew that he was right. But, he couldn't admit that. He had to remain silent.

John remembered hearing the hurt in the man's voice, the despair in his tone. John understood. And then the absolute desperation in his protests when John confirmed that the wreckage had already been hauled away to a location that he couldn't identify. Hauled away, as John painfully knew, so that no one else could look at the track and see that the steel had clearly been melted. Not snapped. Melted.

And the entire mess was due to be dumped into the sea in just a matter of days, somewhere off the coast of Florida—most likely closer to Cuba. No one would ever have the chance to see the atrocity. The evidence would be gone forever. The innocent people at Flying Machines Inc. wouldn't stand a chance. And John knew in his gut that something very sinister had happened—this wasn't mere sabotage. There was something else going on. That spook from the NSA was too smug, too arrogant, too unconcerned.

Once again, the memory of TWA Flight 800, from way back in 1996, tugged away at John's conscience. He had kept his mouth shut then. It was, even back then, the wrong thing to do for the right reasons.

And here he was doing the same thing again. History was repeating itself. The wrong thing for the right reasons. And with only one pathetic year left in his life.

At least when he'd sent his son to prison, it had been the right thing to do for the right reasons.

John reached down and pushed the power seat button—brought himself back into an upright position and then switched off the ignition.

He squeezed the temples of his forehead as he got out of the car. Pounding today, just pounding. He walked up to the front door, inserted his key and opened the door. Linda was in the front hallway adding some water to flowers she'd picked and lovingly assembled in a vase. She ran over to him and gave him a big kiss. A lingering one.

"I was worried about you. You're late."

"Had some things to do, hon. Everything's okay. Actually, can you go with me somewhere for just a few minutes?"

Linda looked at him suspiciously. "Is this a good thing?"

"Yes, indeed. It is most definitely a good thing, the right thing. I'm just going into the study for a second—need to write something down. Be right back and then we'll go."

John was back in a flash with a piece of paper in his hand. "Okay, let's go, hon."

John drove for only about five minutes—enough time to get them to a nearby mall where one of the few remaining phone booths still stood in ancient glory. A monument to a simpler time. A friendlier time.

He parked, and then turned his head to face Linda. "We're going into that phone booth and I want you to do the talking."

Linda squinted her face. "Darling, we have cellphones."

John shook his head. "Can't use a cellphone. And we can't use our landline. Has to be a phone booth." He handed her the sheet of paper. "When the man answers, I don't want you to identify yourself—just read these words."

Linda scanned the page and her mouth opened in shock. "John, what's going on? And why don't you talk to him yourself?"

"I can't. He might recognize my voice. And if the call's being listened in on, someone else might be able to identify me."

Linda's hand was shaking as she stared at the single sheet of paper. "I don't understand these words. They look ominous. Why will I be saying them? Why are you being so secretive?"

"Linda, do you trust me?"

"Yes, of course I do!"

"Then, just do this for me. Please?"

Linda paused for just a second, and then leaned in close to John and kissed his cheek. "I'll always do anything for you, you know that."

They both got out of the car and walked up to the phone booth. Before they went in, John glanced around to make sure no one was watching them.

The coast was clear.

He pulled the handset out of the cradle, dropped several quarters into the slot, and started dialing.

Linda grabbed his hand and stopped him. "What if it's a message machine that answers?"

"Just hang up if that happens." He continued dialing.

When it started ringing, John handed the phone to his wife.

Then he listened as she read out his written words in a halting, shaking voice. *"The wreckage has been hauled to Key West, Florida. It's at the main landfill Transfer Station. And it will be dumped at sea in a few days."*

John took the phone gently out of her hand and hung it back in the cradle.

CHAPTER 15

"I'm here to see Nathan Morrell. Would he perhaps have a few minutes for me?"

The pretty receptionist glanced up from her computer and smiled. "Do you have an appointment?"

"No, I just took a chance and dropped in, hoping he'd be free."

"I'm sorry—this is such a busy time right now. He only sees people by appointment."

"Maybe if you give him my name, he might make an exception?"

"I doubt it, ma'am—but I can try. What's your name?"

"Shelby Sutcliffe."

The receptionist's mouth hung open for a brief moment. "I thought I recognized you from the News." The girl stood up and held out her hand. "I'm Cynthia. I'm so pleased to meet you. You're so brave."

Shelby smiled politely. "Thank you—but not as brave as your boss."

Cynthia came around from behind the desk. "I'm going to check with Mr. Morrell. Be right back, okay?"

Shelby nodded and watched the girl hurry down the hall. She then took a seat in a plush leather chair in the reception area. Looking around, she could tell that the company was very successful—she wasn't surprised. And the artwork on the walls was very unique—all abstract paintings of amusement devices, including Ferris wheels, roller coasters, cable cars, carousels, racecars, and waterslides. No photos; just artwork, probably commissioned by Flying Machines specifically for their offices.

The floors looked like Italian marble, and the walls were adorned with a very subtle grass cloth wallpaper. Hanging from the ceiling above the reception desk, secured by heavy chains that penetrated through the ceiling—presumably anchored right into the concrete above—was an antique rollercoaster train, with five rows of seats. It was bright red with white stripes down the sides. The padded seats were black vinyl and Shelby could see that all these seats had for protection were lap belts—not bars—but actual *belts* like in a car. She felt a shiver run down her spine. The sight of this train suspended in the air was both frightening and ironic.

"We're having that removed. I'm sorry you had to see that, Shelby."

Shelby looked up at the tall, dark-haired man—the one with the voice of a news broadcaster. Her blue-eyed hero was looking down at her for the third time—the first had been from atop the Black Mamba's second hill, and the second time was while she was lying in a hospital bed.

Shelby stood up and smiled. "It's a shock to see an ornament like that in an office in the first place, but it does bring back some horrible images. I can see why you'd want to dismantle it now."

Nate looked up at the suspended train. "Yeah—too bad it has to go. That one has some real history to it—the first rollercoaster at Cony Island. It's about eighty years old."

"Wow. I hope you'll keep it anyway."

Nate nodded. "We're one of the financial sponsors of an amusement park museum in Vegas. It'll go there. That'll be its new home." He motioned with his hand. "Come, follow me. Would you like some coffee?"

"Yes, I'd love some."

"Great. I have one of those Keurig machines in my office—a fresh cup every time!"

He led her into his office—a nice bright corner one, with framed photos of rollercoasters on the walls. "Are those all yours?"

Nate nodded. "Some of them—and others are just some famous ones from different parts of the world."

She noticed some photos of snakes, too. "You like snakes?"

Nate chuckled. "I'm fascinated by them. Weird, eh? And all of my coasters are named after them."

Shelby sat down in one of the guest chairs while Nate brewed their coffees. "I guess you're surprised to see me."

"How do you take your coffee?"

"Just a bit of cream, thanks."

Nate handed her the coffee and she took a sip. "Um...good. Just what I needed."

He sat down in the chair beside her. Shelby thought that he was similar to John Fletcher that way. Both of them chose not to have the barrier of a desk in the way of a conversation. She was impressed.

"Yes, Shelby, I am surprised that you're here. Oh...you don't mind if I call you Shelby, do you?"

She smiled. "No, and what should I call you, Mr. Morrell?"

"Definitely not 'Mr. Morrell.' Call me 'Nate.'"

"Not Nathan?"

"I hate that name—too formal."

"Well, I think you suit 'Nate.' You look like a 'Nate.'"

He laughed. "These days, I'm not sure what I look like. I'm not sleeping too well—that's no doubt a problem you've had, too."

"It's getting better. But sometimes the nightmares come."

Nate scratched his forehead. "You know, you probably shouldn't be here talking to me—not with the lawsuit pending."

Shelby took a long sip of her coffee. "I'm not joining the Class Action. That's not to say that I won't sue you—I still might. But if I do, it will be with my own lawyer."

Nate nodded. "Is that wise? Your best chances are with a Class Action."

"I don't like the lawyer leading the action—and I don't feel comfortable with it all. There's something terribly wrong with this whole thing, Nate. Some things, like integrity, are more important than money. I'm kind of strange that way. Which is why I wanted to see you. I'm sorry for how I reacted at the hospital. I was just shocked to discover who you were and my emotions got the better of me."

Nate stood up and walked over to the window. "I understand, Shelby. It's been hard for me to accept that one of my inventions caused such horror. I don't understand it either. I know we did nothing wrong, and that's the frustrating part."

"Well, you'll get a chance to defend yourselves, I would presume."

"No—it's not turning out that way. We haven't even seen the wreckage and now it's gone. To some secret location. The NTSB report says that the track split at a faulty weld joint." Nate turned away from the window and looked at Shelby. "There were no welds on the hills, Shelby. It was all solid steel. It's impossible for the track to have split the way they said it did."

Shelby stared back, feeling sorry for this man who was obviously troubled—and for good reason. What he was saying reinforced the uncomfortable feelings she was having over this whole thing.

Shelby rose from her chair and moved closer to Nate. "I visited the NTSB myself. Met with a man named John Fletcher. He was the one who did the investigation. I asked him why he never interviewed me. He couldn't answer me. I asked him why his report stated that the lap bars disengaged upon impact with the broken track, when that wasn't true. Again, no explanation."

Nate frowned. "What happened with your lap bar?"

"It disengaged a few seconds before the train went off the track. I discovered that by pulling up on it. I was scared out of my mind—knew that I wouldn't survive the steep drop of the hill. But then it didn't matter anyway—the train went off the track and I pushed up all the way on the bar and shoved myself up and out of the car."

Nate started pacing his office. "Wow. This is interesting news. It supports something we discussed here the other day."

Shelby continued. "I told that to the sleazy lawyer and he didn't seem to care. In fact, he hinted that that information could actually hurt the action's chances of asserting something called 'Strict Liability.'"

Nate nodded. "Yes, it could." He continued pacing. "There are other things I could tell you as well, Shelby, but at this point I won't. Maybe over a coffee sometime. I don't want to sound like I'm defending myself by sharing stuff with you that's just preliminary or even just speculative at this stage."

"I understand what you're saying—but in my view, you should feel free to defend yourself and should be allowed to do so. It sounds like you're being denied that, which doesn't seem fair to me."

"By the way, I told that John Fletcher the same thing about the lap bar that I told the lawyer—funny, even though he gave no indication of being willing to change his report, there was a look on his face that I thought was odd. It wasn't the kind of look the money-grubbing lawyer had—it was more one of shame. Fletcher looked away, avoided my eyes. He looked ashamed. Then he just ended the conversation—not in an arrogant way. Very polite. But I got the feeling that he wanted to engage me, to say something supportive. He didn't but I sensed that he wanted to tell me something."

Suddenly, the door to Nate's office flew open, and in strode Tom Foster, followed closely behind by Ron Collens.

Tom was breathing hard. "Sorry to disturb you, Nate." He nodded at Shelby. "You too, ma'am." He directed his gaze back at Nate. "It's urgent that we talk."

"Can't it wait?"

"No, trust me."

Nate gently put his hand in the small of Shelby's back and ushered her towards the door. "I hope you don't mind. I'll walk you out."

As they were walking down the hall, Nate turned to her and said, "Those are two of my best friends and also partners in the business. I was going to introduce you to them, but decided that you've probably heard enough condolences to last you a lifetime."

"Yes, I have. And my stock answer is getting to be like a broken record. But…they probably recognized me anyway. In fact, your receptionist did."

They reached the lobby and Nate took her hand in his. "Well, if I hadn't seen you up close and personal, I would have remembered you from the News, too. The camera kinda likes you, I think."

She smiled slyly at him. "Aw…that's such a nice thing to say. But I think you're just trying to be extra nice and charming so that I won't consider suing you."

As Nate was turning to walk back to his office he flashed her a sly smile of his own. "You're right, Shelby. I'm damn good, aren't I?"

*****

"Key West?!"

Tom nodded. "Yup, that's what she said."

Nate was wringing his hands together while his two friends sat in front of him, literally on the edges of their seats.

"Did you recognize her voice?"

Tom shook his head. "No, and she seemed nervous—her voice kind of cracked a bit while she spoke."

"Jesus Christ—what were her exact words?"

"I'm not like you, Nate. I don't have instant recall. She just said that the wreckage had been taken to the landfill site—Transfer Station—at Key West, Florida. And that it was going to be dumped into the ocean soon—think she said in a few days."

Nate clasped his hands behind his head. "So, that's the secret location. And if they're going to dump it in the ocean, that says a lot. Normally, wreckage with that degree of high-grade steel would get melted down and recycled. It's astounding that they're going to just dump it at the bottom of the sea. They're trying to hide something. But what and why? And…who?"

Ron Collens jumped in. "Nate, there's a high crime underway here. This is just unbelievable. We can't let this happen. This wreckage is the only thing that could save us. The lawsuit will be bad enough—it'll probably bankrupt us. But, worse than that, all of us partners could be convicted of criminal negligence causing death. We could be facing years in prison. We're fighting for our very lives here."

Nate nodded. With one blue eye on Tom, and the other one on Ron, he grimaced and said, "I hear Key West is quite nice this time of the year."

CHAPTER 16

If any place could come close to convincing you that the world is flat and that you've reached the end of it, it would probably be Key West, Florida. It's the furthest point south a person can go in the United States while still being on land, and it's actually closer to Havana, Cuba than it is to the nearest American city, Miami.

In fact, it actually used to be part of Cuba—until way back in 1815, when Cuba was still part of Spain. Around the time that Florida was transferred by Spain to the United States, the little island of Key West was sold to an American businessman and then later annexed by the United States. So…it became a flaky little part of Florida and has retained that reputation to this day. Eclectic and nutty—but strangely alluring.

If you were a rooster you'd feel at home in Key West—they roam the streets at will and are more adept at dodging traffic than humans. Even just getting to Key West is an experience. If you fly, you miss the fun of driving over the narrow ribbon of road that connects all of the tiny little islands that stretch southwestward. So narrow a motorway that you feel like you're actually driving on the water. No less than forty-two bridges have to be crossed to get to Key West, including one called Seven Mile Bridge—made famous by the hair-raising chase scene in the movie, *True Lies*.

It's a town…or maybe a city…but that's a bit of a reach. It is indeed, though, an island unto itself and has an attitude all its own. There's probably no place on earth quite like it. People live and work there, but everyone always seems to be on vacation, even those who are working…or who say they're working. It's quiet and irreverent as hell—no one in Key West apologizes for doing nothing. Being lazy is a way of life. Life revolves around the beaches, sunsets, shopping, sightseeing… and Happy Hour, which starts very early and ends very late. It's the modern version of a Hippie enclave.

The buildings are painted in every color of the rainbow, and the arts community seems to dominate everything. But the word 'art' takes literary license with what your eyes see—most of it is probably created during Happy Hour. But the artists don't care—to them it's art and their way of looking at it is probably in an inebriated state anyway, so the creations probably look like masterpieces to them.

Ernest Hemingway must have found the little piece of paradise motivating. He wrote several of his books there and his famous home is on display for all to see, including the dozens of six-toed cats—and the odd seven-toed—that are all direct descendants of Hemingway's actual beloved pets. They inhabit the house and the grounds and are free to come and go as they please, while tourists snoop through the rooms and the gardens. The authorities don't even attempt to clear the cats out—they're a piece of history and feline reminders of the island's most famous resident. The cats are almost revered, sacred in their existence. Such is Key West.

Nate gazed out the window of the Embraer ERD—a small jet that only held about forty passengers. They were on the last leg of their trip—the first leg was a two and a half hour flight from Ronald Reagan National Airport in Arlington, Virginia, to Miami, Florida. That jet was thankfully a lot bigger than this one. Then several hours of layover in Miami until they could board this little puddle-jumper for the short forty-five minute flight to Key West.

He could see the airport off in the distance as they started descending—but they had never really gotten up that high anyway as the flight was so short. They had only flown at about 10,000 feet, so for the entire flight he had a great view of all the little islands that made up the Keys—a lot of them uninhabited, or barely inhabited.

He'd been to Key West before on vacation—he and Stephanie had come down here for a week many years ago. A week wasn't enough though. Not because he loved it so much that he wanted to stay. He didn't. But he knew the reason he didn't love it was because he hadn't stayed *long* enough.

It was one of the weirdest places in the world—but, strangely, also one of the nicest and most fascinating. Just the way of life—so foreign to what he was used to and what most people are used to. It was quiet, funky and fabulous—but a strange place with even stranger people. A single week didn't permit him to let go of his work ethic, didn't permit him to chase away the feelings of resentment he had felt for people that he'd labeled as 'flakes.' A week in Key West was only a blip—anyone who worked for a living back on the mainland wouldn't have enough time to get that relaxed laid-back feeling Key West hypnotized people with. He'd just simply never had enough days there to get hypnotized...or as the locals affectionately referred to it...'drunk.'

He bumped his elbow up against Tom's. His buddy had fallen asleep, even though the flight was a short one. Then he turned his head around to see if Ron was awake. Sure enough, Ron Collens, the former Navy Seal, had his nose buried in what Nate assumed was some vitally important document. Nate whispered,

"We're landing." Ron nodded and looked back down at his file folder.

Nate nudged Tom's elbow again. He stretched, yawned, and leaned his head forward so he could peek out Nate's window. Tom muttered, "Look at the color of the water. Beautiful."

"Yeah, this is a tropical paradise alright. There are so many islands in the Keys, but Key West is really the only one worth visiting. But it's so tiny—I think that's why everyone here is either stoned or drunk. The place is only eight square miles at the most. It would definitely give me 'island fever' if I lived here."

"So, I gather you didn't enjoy it when you and Steph came down."

"No, I wouldn't say that—I just couldn't get into the funky laid-back mood. Know what I mean? It's just a weird place—no one has any ambition here. No one seems to care about anything. That's not to say they don't have the right idea though—they'll probably outlive the rest of us poor slaves."

"Yeah, you may be right, but I can only laze around for so long and then it starts to drive me crazy."

The announcement came over the PA system to 'fasten seat belts.' The little jet descended faster and they could see the runway approaching.

Nate turned his head so both of his friends could hear him. "After we get off, we'll chat inside the Terminal and do a status check. The hotel's not far—well, nothing is far actually, but we have a potential problem that we need to be aware of. There's a big naval station on Key West."

*****

"I already chartered the helicopter when we were back in Virginia, so we'll fly over the site first—make sure the wreckage is there and take a few aerial photos."

Tom looked nervous. "Ron, I know you were a Seal and all that jazz, but you do know how to fly this thing, don't you?"

Ron smiled at his friend. "Well, now that we know you're afraid of heights, I might conduct some special dipsy doodles just for you!"

Tom grimaced. "No—don't even joke about that!"

Ron squeezed Tom's shoulder. "Don't worry—I'm an expert helicopter pilot. We all got a lot of training in the Seals, skills that came in handy for those of us who finally came to our senses and eased back into the real world."

Ron pulled two business cards out of his pocket and handed them to Nate and Tom. "I told you I would get these made up for us. Pretty official-looking, don't you think?"

Nate looked at his. His name would be 'Charles Duggett,' senior investigator with the NTSB. "I'm not crazy about my new name, but it sure looks like it'll pass muster."

Ron hoisted his carry-on bag over his shoulder. "Yeah, I think these will get us past the gate tomorrow so we can hopefully hike through the mess and get a close-up look."

Tom slipped his card into his wallet. "What hotel are we staying at?"

"The Almond Tree Inn on Truman Avenue—very close to here. Nice place, but we won't have much time to enjoy it."

Ron started walking in his take-charge military fashion. "C'mon boys. Let's get up in that chopper."

*****

The former Navy Seal fingered the controls expertly and they lifted upwards into the heavy tropical air. They each had their earphones on, with microphones attached. Nate was in the front seat next to Ron. Tom was right behind him.

Nate pointed northward. "That's where the naval station is, Ron. We have to stay well away from that."

"Yeah, I know, Nate. I was stationed there for a while. The landfill site is actually on the south side of Stock Island—the naval station is on the north side. It's tight. So, you're right—we have to be real careful not to stray near their airspace."

Ron turned the chopper on its side and swooped eastward. Within only a couple of minutes they were able to see the site, framed on the east by a deep waterway known as Safe Harbor, and on the other side by State Harbor. Nate could see that it wouldn't be much of a problem at all for the Transfer Station to load the mangled mess of the rollercoaster onto a ship, with two deep harbors to choose from.

Nate pulled his Canon camera out of his pocket. "Ron, take us down as low as you can over the site."

Ron nodded and fingered the controls. The helicopter began its vertical descent, and then slowly began swinging its way over the edge of the site. It was massive, and was piled high in several sections with what looked like construction materials and flattened automobiles. The place functioned as a scrapyard as well, by the looks of it.

Then Nate saw it. The gleaming white trestles, the shiny silver track, punctuated here and there by the black color of the train itself—or at least what was left of it. The wreckage had been placed near the far eastern edge of the site—which told Nate that the ship that was going to dump the mess into the ocean would be loading up on the Safe Harbor side.

"Take us down! Way down!"

Ron fiddled with the controls again and the helicopter descended once more.

They were very close now. "Turn us over on my side, Ron."

The chopper went into a smooth long turn over the mass of wreckage, and shifted effortlessly onto its side as it swooped across. Nate looked down at his creation. Now just a morbid pile of junk. It was sad to see it—his carefully crafted masterpiece had been unceremoniously dumped. Which seemed almost irreverent. Twenty-five people had died due to whatever it was that had caused the Black Mamba to go rogue. And the machine, that had been built with tender loving care, built for laughter and just pure unadulterated joy, was being deemed guilty without being allowed to defend itself. It had been judged and executed. As he looked down at his pile of junk, it felt to Nate as if it wanted to speak to him, to cry out in protest.

Nate was determined to listen. He positioned his camera up to the window and snapped away, taking countless photos that he and his team would have the chance to enlarge and examine later when they got back to Virginia. Ron made another complete circle, keeping the chopper angled onto its side as Nate clicked away.

He then pointed back in the direction of the airport. "We've got enough. Let's head back. Tomorrow we're gonna see it up close and personal."

CHAPTER 17

Ron gently eased the stick forward, and then slightly to the left. The nose of the Bell helicopter dipped and the aircraft veered off in the direction of the airport.

He loved this chopper—it was quite different from the attack helicopters he'd been trained to fly in the Navy. This one didn't have the same maneuverability or the speed—but it had a much smoother ride.

For some reason that he couldn't really define, he enjoyed flying helicopters much more than airplanes. He was qualified to fly both. The type of fighter jet that he had the most experience with was the F-18 Hornet, which was one of the Navy's favorite quick-strike aircraft. And in his career with the Navy, he'd had to make quite a few quick strikes.

He glanced around through the panoramic cockpit window. This chopper was one of the latest from Bell—a 206L4 model. He knew that one of the reasons why it gave such a smooth ride was the Rolls Royce Turbine engine—tried and tested through more than 150 million miles flown.

And for a commercial aircraft, it was quite responsive. It was equipped with a two-bladed rotor extended on a shaft above the roof of the cabin, and also a tail rotor that spun vertically, giving excellent directional control, especially at higher altitudes.

Ron loved flying—that's what he missed the most about being in the Navy. His rank upon retiring from the Seals was Lieutenant Commander. But he didn't get to fly very much during his last five years—those were his Seals days, and those missions usually involved him and his team being flown somewhere by someone else. And then just as quickly flown out again.

Instead of flying F-18 Hornets off aircraft carriers, his role as a Seal had been one of secrecy. Covert operations in the middle of the night in foreign countries that he never really got to see; at least not in the light of day. And killing more faceless nameless people than he cared to count. People who were just "targets." No more, no less.

After he did his five-year stint he'd had enough. He'd been in the Navy for a total of twenty years including his five years as a Seal. He'd earned his electrical and systems engineering degree at the pleasure of Uncle Sam, and at the expense of the American people. And also his pilot's credentials. He had to admit, the military was a great way to get an education that a person would be hard pressed to afford otherwise. So he had no regrets in that respect.

But, he had other regrets. His ability to kill without conscience during those Seal years still bothered him. He couldn't understand how he had been able to do that so easily. The Navy had given him the killing skills, sure, but what had they done to his mind?

Ron shook his head to bring himself back to the present. And the present meant soaring over the beautiful blue sea with his two best friends. He wished the three of them were there under different circumstances—wished they could just charter a boat and get out fishing for a few days. Fresh fish, barbecues and beers. With the two guys he loved and respected the most.

But, instead, they were in Key West trying to save themselves from a fate that might be worse than death. Bankruptcy and, quite possibly, the rest of their lives in prison. They didn't deserve this. The work they did at Flying Machines was not only state of the art, but it was also done with precision. They were the best in the world at what they did. And they didn't make mistakes that jeopardized safety. Ever.

Ron was forty-eight years old and had been out of the military for ten years. Civilian life had been good so far. It had been tough on the family when he was in the Navy; away far too much, especially during his time as a Seal. He'd missed so much with his wife, Monica, and their twin daughters.

But there was still a lot to live for—a lot of life that he wanted to be free to enjoy. He wanted to walk his girls down the aisle, hold his grandchildren and play with them until they exhausted him, take romantic vacations with Monica—and kiss her goodnight, every night, for the rest of her life.

But, instead of all that, his loved ones might be visiting him in prison and sneaking in chocolates at Christmastime as a special treat for him. Visiting with him for no more than an hour at a time once a week. Dropping off photos so he could see what he was missing and how they were all doing without him.

No. That was not the way it was going to be. He started feeling angry thinking about how badly they'd been set up. He wanted to know why. And he wanted to know who.

That indescribable 'killing feeling' was creeping back into his brain again—the feeling of absolute detachment, being able to picture a fictitious person and imagine how he'd do it. And he was trained to 'do it' in countless creative ways. He hadn't had this familiar overpowering feeling for many years. Until now, there had been no stimulus in his life to trigger it. But today he felt like a Seal again.

Ron blinked his eyes hard and then shook his head once more, symbolically trying to shake the thoughts out of his head. He could tell out of the corner of his eye that Nate was watching him.

"You okay, buddy?"

Ron smiled. "I'm doin' just fine. But how's our height-challenged friend doin' back there?" He turned his head around and grinned at Tom.

"Hey, I'm okay too—especially now that I know you're headin' back to the airport. Just get us down fast, please?"

"It's such a nice day and we paid for a minimum of two hours, I was thinking we should stay up a bit longer and tour around!"

Nate gazed around at the panoramic view. "It is beautiful up here. You're enjoying this, aren't you, Ron? The flying part, I mean."

Ron chuckled. "I feel like a little kid with a new bike. This helicopter is a treat to fly."

"Which do you enjoy more? Planes or choppers?"

"Oh, choppers by far. And they're actually more challenging to learn to fly than a plane, believe it or not. There's so much intricacy in a chopper."

Nate pointed. "I call that a 'stick,' but what's it really called?"

"Well, even we pilots just call it the 'stick.' But the official name for it is 'cyclic.' It controls the pitch, or angle, of the top rotor blades. Those blades are shaped like airplane wings so they provide the same kind of lift as in planes. When I shift the cyclic forward, the angle of the blades changes and the aircraft goes in a forward direction. The same applies in every direction I shift the stick. When the stick is in the direct center spot, the rotor blades are actually in a flat position, not tilted in any direction. And that's what allows a chopper to hover."

"Interesting. What's that tail rotor do?"

"It helps with maneuverability, especially at high altitudes. And counteracts the tendency of the aircraft to want to just turn round and round in one spot when it's hovering. It's a directional control aid."

Nate pointed back in the direction of the landfill site. "Since we still have this thing for a while, why don't we go back for one more run around the site? Won't hurt to get some more photos."

Ron smiled. "My pleasure, boss. More time in the air is just fine with me. Do you agree, Tom?"

He heard a groan from the rear seat. "Does it matter what I think? You guys never listen to me anyway. Have your fun—I'll just close my eyes."

Ron and Nate laughed as Ron eased forward and off to starboard on the stick. The sleek helicopter went nose down and over on its side—a smooth turn if there ever was one. They set a course back to the landfill site, which they could easily see off in the distance.

Ron sighed with pleasure as he felt the power of the chopper rev in his hand.

The stick gave the same sense of power that someone would get with his foot on the accelerator of a car.

Suddenly, he felt a chill. Not a cold chill, a different kind of chill. Something ominous. Something was wrong. It was almost imperceptible.

There was a slight shudder in the chopper—one that only a pilot could detect. And the stick in Ron's skilled hand felt different. Not as responsive. He pulled back slightly to test it. Nothing happened. *Shit!*

He was just about to try something else when the nose of the aircraft pointed violently upwards and the rotors roared. The helicopter started climbing at a breakneck pace. Ron pushed forward slightly on the stick, careful not to put it into a stall. No response again.

He shoved the stick into the center position, trying to force the craft to hover. Again, it was as if the cyclic was disconnected—what he was doing had no effect whatsoever.

Ron was vaguely aware of guttural sounds coming from Tom in the rear, and a cacophony of yelling from Nate through his earphones.

He yelled back. "Not now, guys! Just hold tight while I figure this out!"

His fist was clenched tightly on the stick—why, he didn't know, because it was doing nothing at all. Perhaps it made him feel like he was still in control.

The helicopter had a mind of its own now. He noticed on the altimeter that they had risen about 1,000 feet since the anomaly started.

Suddenly, the ascent slowed down—and then stopped. The aircraft started hovering. Ron pushed forward on the stick. Still nothing. Then, inexplicably, they started spinning around in a circle.

He could feel Nate's hand shaking his shoulder. He turned his head and looked into his frightened eyes. "I don't know what's going on, Nate! Let me work it!"

They were spinning around fast now—Ron could feel himself getting dizzy. Nate yelled. "Why are we spinning?!"

"The tail rotor's shut down. I'm going to try to restart it."

Ron stretched his sweaty hand out to the dashboard and punched the electronic ignition. Nothing. He glanced up at the instruments—everything seemed to be functioning normally except for the red warning light showing the tail rotor disengaged. His heart was pounding hard in cadence with the rotation of the rotors. Then, suddenly, that sound stopped too. An eerie silence descended upon the cabin. All three men were holding their breath.

Then they started to fall. Slowly at first, then faster and faster.

Tom yelled out, panic in his voice. "The engine's dead!"

Ron was trying desperately to figure it out—ignoring the outcries of his friends. First the aircraft had soared skyward all by itself with no command from him. Then it hovered. And then the tail rotor decided to shut down.

And the main rotors had stopped. He knew that there was an automatic protection built into the craft in case this happened. The rotors would begin what was called 'auto-rotation' where the blades would keep turning, but at a much-reduced rate of speed—the blades would create a small amount of lift that would keep the craft from falling to the ground like a rock.

They were still going to crash, though, and probably wouldn't survive it from this height. There was only so much lift the slowly spinning rotors could provide, and for a short fall it was survivable. But not at the height they were dropping from.

Their only hope was to re-start the engine, which could easily be accomplished on this model of helicopter even while in mid-air. He'd already tried to re-start the tail rotor with no success. Ron said a silent prayer that he'd have better luck with the main engine.

He hit the electric start button and waited. Waited for the comforting sound of the rotors whirling. There was nothing but ominous silence.

And, of course, the horrifying sight of the ground rushing up to meet them.

His two friends were dead quiet. He wasn't surprised—what could they possibly say? They were depending on him to get them out of this, but all of his options had been exhausted.

Ron had a sudden pointless thought: *If this was an F-18 Hornet I could eject; pull the handle, smash the canopy and pop up and out to safety.* But—for the obvious reasons—there was no ejection option available with a helicopter. You went 'down with the ship' in these things.

Suddenly, without warning or fanfare, that familiar comforting noise returned. Ron took a huge breath and exhaled hard as he heard, first, the main twin rotors, followed by the tail rotor. The helicopter was stabilizing itself at an elevation of 500 feet, and Ron had done nothing whatsoever to cause it to happen. His efforts at starting the engines had failed. The damn things had restarted on their own without his help.

Ron heard his two friends cheering.

He jiggled the stick toward him, trying to get the aircraft 'nose up' and back into a climb. He was uncomfortable with how close they were to the ground. No time or room for error if they started falling again.

But, the chopper clearly had a different plan in mind than Ron's. Instead of heading up in the direction that Ron jiggled, it went 'nose down' and dove. Swooping downward and then veering to the left—towards the water this time. Within seconds, they were over it, only 200 feet above the surface.

Ron frantically shoved the stick around in its radius, trying desperately to get some kind of reaction. But his efforts were fruitless. He cursed as the chopper leveled out over the water, 100 feet above the whitecaps. Then he swore again as the chopper dipped down even closer to the dangerous swells.

The thing decided to speed straight ahead and it seemed as if it was just skimming across the waves. Ron knew there was a real danger of the landing skids getting caught by the waves, and if that happened the helicopter would simply somersault at full speed into the sea.

He didn't want them to be trapped in a sinking death trap. As he was looking out the side window, gauging their distance from the water, he yelled out, "Unfasten your seat belts!"

Suddenly, Nate yelled out, too. "Jesus fuck! Look!"

Ron turned his head away from the side window and looked to where Nate was pointing. They were heading towards the shore now, towards a dock. And tethered to that dock was a massive cargo ship. The helicopter was on a direct line to crash into it broadside.

Ron pulled his hand off the stick and grabbed his chest. There was a pain that was crushing him, a pain he'd never felt before. Probably an anxiety pain, no doubt brought on by the horrifying sight in front of them.

Tom yelled, "Do something!"

Suddenly, the chopper, clearly still with a mind of its own, rose upwards at a steep pitch. As they swooped over the edge of the ship with only a few feet to spare, Ron was vaguely aware of the sight of panicked seamen diving prone to the deck.

The aircraft was climbing once again. Then—it stopped—and hovered.

The pain in Ron's chest was subsiding. He reached for the stick, to try one more time to gain control.

He throttled it forward.

It responded! He had control!

Ron didn't waste any time. The sooner they were safely on the ground, the better, before the thing decided to take them on another wild ride.

He aimed the craft in the direction of the airport and went full speed ahead. Strangely, everything seemed fine. It was totally responsive to his touch.

No one in the cabin said a word. He figured his friends were probably bracing themselves for another surprise, afraid to feel safe too soon only to have their elation dashed again.

Ron could hear their heavy breathing though, which didn't surprise him in the least. He was surprised that they weren't all dead of heart attacks.

He set the aircraft on a course for the tarmac near the hangar. Within a couple of minutes, they were above where they wanted to be. Ron hovered the chopper and lowered them slowly down to the circle. He shut the craft down, shoved the door open, and stumbled out onto the pavement. Followed quickly by his two stunned friends.

They staggered away a safe distance from the helicopter, and then all three promptly collapsed to the tarmac.

Nate was the first to speak, in between labored breaths. "What...the fuck... was that all about?"

Ron rose to a sitting position. "My guess? Someone else...was flying that helicopter. It certainly wasn't me. It was...like I wasn't even there. For those few minutes, chaps, I think we were in...in a drone."

CHAPTER 18

The helicopter charter facility was a dilapidated metal Quonset type structure, clearly in need of some TLC. But, as was typical of a lot of commercial buildings in Key West, the TLC thing would probably never happen. Most business owners on the island would prefer to just wait until the next hurricane and let the insurance company give them a new one.

And…there just never seemed to be a sense of urgency on this island anyway…about anything.

Ron Collens led the way into the building, pushing open an office door which was hanging precariously by one hinge. The poor shape of the building belied the high quality of the aircraft they chartered out.

Ron strode up to the counter, followed closely behind by Nate and Tom. The man he had rented the helicopter from was sitting on a stool behind the counter reading the comics section of the newspaper. Ron waited politely for the man to notice him, but he seemed to be seriously preoccupied with chuckling at the funnies.

Ron finally rapped his knuckles on the counter and the man looked up, clearly annoyed at being disturbed. He wore a baseball cap over shoulder-length blonde hair. Ron figured he was around fifty or so, but trying desperately to look like a Woodstock era twenty-year-old. A moustache, beard, tattered jeans, and a muscle shirt completed the bizarre image. A cigarette was smoldering in an ashtray within easy reach of the man's skinny arm. Ron figured, like with everything else in Key West, smoking bylaws weren't enforced.

But he wasn't here to talk about smoking. He wanted to know why he and his friends were terrorized in the skies over this hippie paradise.

The man took a long drag from his cigarette before deciding it was time to finally say something. "Yeah, can I help you, buddy? Wanna rent a whirlybird?"

Ron leaned over, resting his muscular forearms on the counter. "We just did—less than two hours ago. Don't you remember us?"

The man squinted. "Uh…yeah, sure. How was the ride?"

"The helicopter was out of control—and it seemed as if it was being flown remotely by someone else. Do you know anything about that?"

"Uh…no. Wanna smoke?" He held out a pack of Winstons.

"No, I want to know why the helicopter behaved the way it did."

Nate stepped forward and reached for the man's pack of cigarettes. "I'll take one of those. I could use a smoke right now."

The clerk laughed. "Hey, I got something stronger in the back if you want it. On me, my friend."

Nate flicked the lighter. "No, I don't do that stuff. Tobacco suits me fine."

"No problem, bud. Each to his own."

Ron persisted. "Did you folks let the Navy install telemetry in your helicopters?"

The man frowned. "Tele…what? What the fuck is that?"

"Are you the owner here?"

A belly laugh. "I don't own nothin', man. And that's the way I like it, know what I mean?"

"Can I see the owner?"

"He don't live here. Hangs out in Miami. Never see him."

Ron was losing his patience. "Do Navy personnel ever drop by here?"

"Well, of course. The Navy's our friend, man. We'd be nothin' on this little island without the Navy. We like them boys."

"Why would they come here to your place?"

"They do some work here for us. Hard to get qualified people on this island, so we put 'em under contract for all our maintenance stuff. I mean, they have whirlybirds over there, too, so it's easy for them to maintain ours. And we pay 'em pretty good, too. The Navy mechanics are good guys…and they even like a smoke or two once in a while. And our loose women." He grinned, displaying three empty spaces where teeth used to reside. "Know what I mean?"

Nate rubbed Ron's shoulder. "Time to leave. I think we just got our answer, and I doubt if we'll get anything else. This guy's harmless."

Ron nodded. They turned and headed for the door.

The clerk called after them, waving a sheet of paper in the air. "Could you fill out one of these customer satisfaction thingies? We like to know if our clients enjoyed their experience with us."

They kept walking, trying hard not to laugh. Tom muttered, "Brain-dead."

"Come fly with us again soon, y'all."

*****

Breakfast the next morning at the Almond Tree Inn consisted of every tropical fruit imaginable, along with the mandatory American breakfast of bacon and eggs. The three friends were sitting at a table beside the pool, enjoying the sunshine, the breakfast and the bikinis. Breakfast of champions.

But they didn't feel too much like champions. After breakfast, they'd be heading over to the landfill site, hoping to get a close up view of the wreckage. And they were still recovering from yesterday's horrifying ordeal in the air.

Ron put down his fork with finality. He was clearly finished eating and wanted to talk. "So, we know that Navy mechanics do maintenance work on those choppers. And, let's face it, after 911, it's reasonable to expect that a naval base would be concerned about any aircraft rental facility within a few hundred miles, let alone the five miles in this case."

Nate nodded. "Yeah, too close for comfort. And all that maintenance work would allow them to build in a few failsafe protection devices of their own. Just in case they needed to use them."

Ron nodded. "Our chopper was being flown remotely from an operator at that naval base; I'm convinced of that."

Tom jumped in. "So, why didn't they just crash us, for Christ's sake?!"

Ron shook his head. "No, that's the last thing they'd want to do. Think how that would look. The wreckage of our rollercoaster is in that yard and we were flying over that very yard. Too much of a coincidence to have three executives of Flying Machines Inc. die in a helicopter accident right where the wreckage of their rollercoaster is, a site they went to great lengths to keep secret. No—they just wanted to scare us away. Wanted us to realize how easy it would be for them to bring harm to us."

Nate frowned. "But who are 'they?'"

Ron took a long sip from his black coffee. "Don't know. The Navy could have been acting on instructions from someone much higher up the totem pole, not knowing why they were being asked to monitor us and scare us. Remember, military personnel are conditioned to simply obey, perform tasks, and not necessarily know why they're doing what they're doing. They could have just been performing a task they were ordered to perform. Someone probably flagged my name when I chartered that helicopter from Virginia—realized I was a partner with Flying Machines and that I was going to be right where the wreckage is. They're probably puzzled now though as to how we knew to come down here, because the location was supposed to have been classified."

Nate spoke again. "I'll repeat—who are 'they?'"

Tom reached for the coffee pot and poured. "Ron, what's this telemetry stuff you were asking the hippie about?"

"Hospitals use it, NASA uses it, and the military uses it. And a whole slew of other applications, like car manufacturers. Hell, it's used with virtually everything these days, including mobile phones. We just don't really think about it, we're so used to it.

"It's simply the installation of devices that can relay crucial data to a remote location. But that basic information gathering can be taken one extra step—remote use of that information.

"Remote controlled devices, such as missile-equipped drones, are used almost routinely now by the U.S. military in fighting terrorism in the Middle East—unmanned drones being "guided" by pilots remotely, sometimes thousands of miles away.

"So, the *use* of the telemetric data is the big difference. Everyone is accustomed to GPS, and, of course, stupid Facebook annoyingly tracking everywhere you go, everyone you're with. That's all telemetry. But when it's taken a step further to actually *control* the item in which the telemetry is installed, that's a different story. And drones are a perfect example of that. Our helicopter, in reality, became a goddamned drone the second they took it over remotely."

Nate reached up and tilted the umbrella towards the sun. "Didn't Boeing make use of remote control technology after 911?"

"Yes. Apparently, all of their jumbo jets now have telemetry installed, as well as the ability to remotely fly any of their aircraft from the ground if need be. If someone was considering hijacking a plane, it would be a waste of time for the hijackers to think they could actually take it over and steer it into high-rise towers. It can now simply be remotely flown from the ground by the authorities and landed anywhere in the world just by remote control. And there's nothing anyone in the plane can do to override what's being done remotely. Christ, we discovered that ourselves yesterday, didn't we? It's amazing technology and the applications are endless."

Tom folded his newspaper over to the second page, and held it out so his friends could see. "Coincidental that we're talking about this. Here's an article reporting about that Malaysia Airlines jumbo jet. It was a Boeing 777. The article says that it could have easily been remotely hijacked and flown to any destination in the world—that it didn't crash at all, despite the focus on searching the Indian Ocean ad nauseum. They're even saying that there are unconfirmed reports that the plane was landed remotely on the island of Diego Garcia down near the Maldives!"

Ron laughed. "I wouldn't be surprised in the least. In fact, Diego Garcia is a top-secret air force base—even us Seals had no idea what all went on down there. But one thing I do know—for that part of the world, Diego Garcia functions as 'drone central.' That's a fact."

Nate folded his napkin and stood. "I don't know about you guys, but yesterday's little episode was the most scared I've ever been in my entire life. And I design rollercoasters for a living, so scaring me is *not* an easy thing to do. Someone took over our chopper from a distance and bounced us around remotely, trying their fucking damnedest to terrify us into ignoring this whole thing. And the moves they were able to make with that chopper—how close we came to being killed—it's mindboggling. That was some pretty fancy flying for someone who wasn't even sitting in the cockpit!"

Ron stood up as well. "Yes. But what's really scary is this—what the hell have we gotten ourselves embroiled in? Why is this wreckage so sensitive that they would go to such trouble to scare us away from it? What is it that we and others aren't being allowed to see? And why?"

Tom slipped into his suit jacket. "Maybe we'll get some answers today, when we see our creation in person." He looked at his watch. "Our flight leaves mid-afternoon. We need to get out to that landfill site now if we want to have enough time to look around."

CHAPTER 19

Carl Masterson took off his glasses and began cleaning the lenses. These new glasses worked really well for him—his eyes had been getting worse these last few years, but at least now he could read without squinting or falling asleep. But the damn things got smudged so easily, it was frustrating. He slid them back onto his nose and then turned to his computer to check his emails.

Ah…the one he was waiting for. He picked up the phone, punched in a three-digit number and barked an order. "Got your note. Come on down to my office now."

He hung up the phone and walked over to his coffee stand. Poured himself a cup and sat down on his couch. He started thinking…about things. And there certainly were an abundance of things to think about.

First on his mind, how did those executives find out where the wreckage was? Someone told them and there were only a handful of people who knew. In his mind, he'd already narrowed it down, but he needed certain information to confirm. And he'd have that information in just a few minutes.

Carl felt restless these days—so much to do still, and everything had to be contained. He didn't need the complication of snoopy executives who just couldn't accept what was going to happen to their company. The fate of their company was a tiny issue in the big scheme of things. Of course, they had no way of knowing that.

But he had to be so careful—these guys were high profile. If anything happened to them, it might open a Pandora's Box. He couldn't afford that. Not with Operation Backwash in the final stages.

He walked over to his window. Carl's office was on the fourth floor of the National Security Agency headquarters in Fort Meade, Maryland. Just a leisurely thirty-minute drive from downtown Washington, D.C.

He looked out over the vast expanse of land that was Fort Meade; he loved the fact that he could look out, but no one could look in. All of the glass in the building was tinted one-way viewing. He had read in an op-ed column the other day that NSA headquarters looked just like a dark glass Rubik's cube. He chuckled—the guy was right; it did look like a Rubik's cube. And just like that toy, good luck to anyone trying to figure out what the NSA was all about.

Well, Edward Snowden had certainly done his best to let the world know what the NSA did, and the fallout wasn't good. That sniveling little nerd had aired their dirty laundry. But…like everything else that came out, the American people would accept it. And even though there was initial outrage, Carl figured there were more people on the NSA's side now than on Snowden's. If he ever put even one foot onto U.S. soil again, it would be the last thing he did.

The U.S. government had done such a good job of convincing their citizens that they had good reasons to be afraid—about everything—that they were probably at the point now where they really didn't mind losing some of their precious privacy and civil liberties if it meant being safe.

And that coward, Edward Snowden, was hiding out in Russia. Probably spilling more secrets to them than the NSA was aware of. He had accessed, and taken, a surprising amount of information and was no doubt keeping some of it in his hip pocket as a bargaining chip with the Russians, or as a trade for his life one day if the NSA finally succeeded in tracking him down. Indeed, 'knowledge was power,' and Snowden had found that out in spades.

Carl's eyes scanned the landscape. Fort Meade was a massive place—and an actual fort, too, although the fort part was completely separate from the NSA. The fort—or the modern term, 'military installation'—took up 5,000 beautiful Maryland acres. The NSA portion was relatively small, at only 350 acres.

The NSA building itself was impressive—three million square feet in total and it contained a post office, bank, restaurant, concierge office, and gymnasium. The NSA also had its own fire department and police force right on site.

The staff count at the NSA was kind of a secret, but the best estimate by most outsiders was 30,000. Carl knew it was closer to 80,000, scattered around the country and the world, with a lot of those employees being "off the books." And that same article that referred to their building as resembling a Rubik's cube, also described the NSA as the world's biggest employer of introverts and mathematicians. Carl thought that reference was pretty close to the truth. They did employ a lot of nerds—Snowden was a nerd. Maybe Snowden got brave after watching a rerun of that movie, *Revenge of the Nerds*.

Well, the NSA wouldn't be that careless again. Employees were monitored much more closely now and if there was even the hint of leaks, that threat would be eliminated.

It was only fitting that the NSA spy on their own people—Carl thought it was silly that they had been so cavalier about it in the past. Hell, the NSA spied on their own citizens and virtually the entire world, so why not their staff?

The NSA's mandate was to collect, decode, translate, and analyze information and data for foreign intelligence and counter-intelligence purposes. They were also tasked with surveillance on targeted individuals on U.S. soil. If those individuals moved to foreign soil, then the CIA took over.

The NSA was also authorized to accomplish its missions through clandestine means—bugging electronic systems and even sabotaging networks with invasive software. As a sideline, the agency also located targets through electronic means, and passed that information along to the CIA for assassination purposes.

The NSA tracked the locations of hundreds of millions of cellphones every day—to map their movements and relationships in detail. And most people would be horrified to know that the agency had access to all communications made on Google, Microsoft, Facebook, YouTube, AOL, Skype and Apple. All in the name of 'national security.'

And it didn't stop with that—personal email and instant messaging accounts were monitored, along with contact lists. And landline calls—they weren't exempt either.

Neither were the few remaining phone booths in the country. In fact, they were considered suspicious vessels of communication by the NSA, and for that reason alone phone booths still existed. The NSA wanted them to remain. Because people felt they were safe if they made a call from a phone booth.

So, phone booths made great bait. People who were planning nefarious activities against the United States would generally choose a phone booth over a landline or cellphone. Several terrorist attacks had already been prevented by the NSA just because the innocent fools thought they could safely talk from a phone booth.

All phone booth calls are not only tracked, but also recorded. And the software they used looked for certain key words or behaviors that would result in a 'flag' for a recorded call, triggering the need for an NSA agent or analyst to listen to it. That same type of software was used for all other activities too—on cellphones, email, etc.

The workload, as a result, was huge. Thousands of flagged communications were listened to or read every day, just to discern whether or not there was reason for concern. Carl thought: *No wonder the NSA is the world's largest employer of introverts. Who could do that all day and be happy about it?*

There were about a dozen separate divisions in the NSA—known as 'directorates'—but Carl knew there were a lot more that were not disclosed to the public, and some not even known to him. Each division was identified by a letter. Carl's division was 'Q'—Directorate of Security and Intelligence. That covered a big area for sure—in essence, everything eventually funneled up to him if it involved a risk to national security—and if something needed to be done about it.

Consequently, he was in the loop on most issues that threatened the United States of America. But not just terrorist threats—in reality, those threats were fairly well contained and not necessarily their biggest worry anymore. Although, that fact would never be disclosed to the American people, because the government needed them scared and pliable. The constant threat of terrorism was a great tool to accomplish that.

And also, if not most importantly, the hint of terrorism being rampant around the world gave the United States another great tool—that being the very powerful 'false flag.' Once in a while a government needed to accomplish something that required an excuse, or 'reason,' before it could be executed. The typical 'false flag' was usually a terrifying act that mimicked terrorism, but in fact was done by the government against its own people and its own soil. But always done with acceptable collateral damage—just enough damage and terror to give the government momentum.

And a 'false flag' operation was always done in a way to implicate someone else—another country, an organization, virtually anyone the government wanted to take action against. But wouldn't be able to otherwise, unless they succeeded in getting their people, and their allies, behind them.

One of the most ingenious 'false flags,' in Carl's opinion, was way back in 1962, termed as Operation Northwoods. The Department of Defense and the Joint Chiefs of Staff authorized an action that would have seen the CIA and other operatives committing acts of terrorism in Miami, Florida and Washington, D.C. But, those acts would be designed to implicate Cuba. Planes with Cuban insignia would be slammed into high-rise buildings, explosives would be detonated—in other words, all hell would break loose—all made to look like Cuba was doing it. But the wimp President, John Fitzgerald Kennedy, outright rejected the plan— even though the military had already approved it and was ready to launch.

Carl thought it was ironic that the documents pertaining to Operation Northwoods had been declassified for years now, but virtually no American was even aware of the proposed plan. It was out there for the looking, but no one was looking. People could even just google it; it was that easy and that available.

But, that's what made a 'false flag' easy. Even if people read it, they wouldn't believe it because the blind patriotism that the U.S. was so good at propagating somehow brainwashed its citizens. Which was a good thing for the NSA and the CIA. The naivety and stupidity of the people allowed total freedom for power to be abused any which way the government chose. And the mainstream Press wouldn't dare report on Operation Northwoods—even though it was a huge news story, a barbaric revelation. The Press just did what they were told, reported what they were ordered to report. Carl silently thanked God that there weren't any ethical journalists like that Walter Cronkite guy around anymore.

No wonder no one believed that 911 was a 'false flag,' although in fact it most definitely was. Carl thought it was amazing how similar the 911 operation was to

Operation Northwoods. It was just as if that old document had been dusted off and thrown back on the table in 2001, almost forty years after it was conceived. JFK thought he'd put a stop to something horrible back in 1962—but all he really did was cause a delay. And he paid for his cowardice with his life, the fool.

The NSA's mandate went much further than ensuring safety from terrorism and foreign powers—much further. Its role, in a nutshell, was just 'security'—period. If, for example, there was an economic or natural resource risk, the NSA would have to foresee that and recommend appropriate actions.

Which they always did. As a matter of fact, there was a serious risk that the NSA had reacted to many years ago already. The risk was identified and the solution was proposed. But this time, a President wouldn't be given the chance to say no. They weren't going to repeat the JFK mistake. It could happen without the President's authorization.

It was labelled 'Operation Backwash' and it was the most brilliant 'false flag' ever conceived. It had to happen—the very survival of the United States depended on it, and no wimpy President was going to stand in its way.

Carl's thoughts were disturbed by a knock on his door.

"Yeah, come on in, Roger."

A tall skinny man with glasses came through the door.

"Have a seat. Do you have what I need?"

Roger handed him a CD. "Yep, this is the recording of that woman's voice from the phone booth in Georgetown. It was flagged and we caught it."

"Good. Thanks." Carl waved his hand toward the door, dismissing him. Roger took the hint and left.

Carl popped the CD into his computer and listened to the nervous voice saying the words that told Carl everything: *The wreckage has been hauled to Key West, Florida. It's at the main landfill Transfer Station. And it will be dumped at sea in a few days.*

Those words told Carl everything simply because only a handful of people knew where that wreckage was being sent to. He opened up his map of Washington, D.C. and put his fingertip on a street.

Out of that handful of people who knew, only one of them lived within about five or six minutes from that phone booth: John Fletcher, Chief Investigator for the National Transportation Safety Board.

The man who had gotten angry with Carl when he insisted he sign a false report. And the same man who had actually yelled at Carl, asserting that the steel of the track had been melted, that it hadn't snapped.

Just another man with a small mind. Men like John Fletcher were perfect examples of one of the lingering problems with America, in Carl's view.

CHAPTER 20

"Wait a few minutes, guys. I'm going to change into something a little more official-looking."

Nate glanced at Tom and they both shrugged, as Ron walked through the lobby and down the hall towards his room.

It didn't take him long. About five minutes later, he was back, looking very official indeed. Ron was wearing his Navy officer's uniform—white high-collar tunic jacket with gold buttons, white pants, white shoes—the handsome image topped off by a white hat and black brim with the U.S. Navy emblem on the peak.

"I packed this in my luggage just in case I decided it might come in handy. And after seeing the Navy influence on this island, and the reverence that these locals seem to have for the Navy, I figured I'd wear it—might give us an edge. So, I won't use my NTSB identification. I'll just be the Navy consultant to the NTSB. Whaddaya think?"

Nate smiled and saluted. "Wow! I'm impressed—you look dashing! I wish I'd been in the military just so I could have worn one of those!"

Tom walked over and rubbed his hands along the black shoulder crest. "What's this mean, soldier?"

Ron laughed. "On the white uniforms, our rank insignias are displayed on the shoulder. On our black uniforms—which they actually call 'blue,' don't ask me why—the insignia is displayed on the sleeves."

Tom was still staring at the insignia. "So, two wide bars with a small one in the middle, and a star above—that's the insignia of a Lieutenant Commander?"

"Yes." He laughed again. "'Stand down,' Tom. You're embarrassing me."

"Well, I can't help it if I'm blown away by your appearance. Never seen you like this before. I feel like I have to obey you or something now. Are you gonna start giving us orders?"

"You bet I am! Starting right now—why don't you pull the keys out of your pocket and get the car out of the parking lot. An officer can't be seen walking to a car, now, can he? You have to pull up out front for me!"

Nate jerked his head toward the door. "C'mon, Tom. We'll both get the car—and I'll hold the door open while our esteemed friend here crawls into the back of our rented Ford Taurus."

The three friends laughed. Ron adjusted his hat, pulling it down a bit over his eyes. "Oh, I forgot about the Taurus. Suddenly, I'm humbled!"

*****

As they were driving down Front Street approaching the Transfer Station parking lot, Nate looked out over Safe Harbor on his left. He was able to make out the jagged edges of the Black Mamba's skeleton poking up from the pile near the harbor's edge.

He'd had a different view of this just yesterday—but it seemed like it was longer ago than that. Nate guessed that his brain was trying its damnedest to make yesterday's nightmare flight a distant memory.

As he gazed out through the mouth of the harbor, he noticed a large cargo ship heading straight for the inlet. It looked like Safe Harbor was its intended destination and, if so, there was no doubt in Nate's mind that his rollercoaster was about to go on its one-way cruise to the depths, never to be seen again.

The parking lot was right in front of the office. There was an entry point on the left with weigh scales that vehicles would drive onto if they were loading or unloading refuse or trash. Other than that, the facility was wide open for entry and there didn't seem to be any security personnel, none that were visible at least.

"Okay, fellas. Before we get out of this car, let's just muse about what we're going to say. How we're going to dupe our way in there."

Tom reached into his suit pocket and pulled out a folded newspaper article. "You guys know how much I like to read the news. Well, I found this little article. Refers to a school bus accident in the Keys a couple of weeks ago. It was a bunch of choir kids—the thing rolled, killing three of them. And it says here that one of them was the son of a Navy officer from the naval station. Anyway, this article is an update to the original story—states that the investigation has been completed and it was determined that it was driver error, that there was no fault with the bus. I'm figuring that that bus has already been hauled here, awaiting the wrecking ball. Where else would they take it?"

Nate scratched his head. "I agree—it's probably here. So, your idea is that we pretend we're here to look at the bus?"

"Right—we can't exactly come right out and say we want to look at the coaster, especially after what happened yesterday. I'm guessing that any request like that would be 'red flagged.'"

Nate licked his dry lips. "Okay, so we'll say that we're the NTSB and that we're here to do our own quick inspection before the bus gets flattened. And school buses are in the NTSB's jurisdiction if they choose to get involved, so that wouldn't raise any eyebrows."

Ron jumped in. "Well, my uniform might come in handy then, too. We can say the Navy's involved indirectly because the child of one their own was killed on the bus."

"Yep, that fits nicely."

Ron took a sip from his water bottle. "God, it's so hot already—especially in this darn uniform!"

Tom turned his head around to face the back seat. "Well, buddy, that's what you get for showing off!"

Ron laughed. "Speaking of putting on a show—what if our little skit goes wrong? What if the bus isn't in this yard? We'd have to have another reason for being here."

Nate nodded. "You're right. Then we'd have no choice but to state that we want to see the coaster wreckage, too. That would be our backup plan—nothing to lose. We just come right out and say that since we're here anyway, and we're the NTSB, we don't want to miss the opportunity to have one final look at the wreckage. Make sense?"

Tom opened his car door. "Sounds good to me. Let's get to it, guys. Our flight leaves in a few short hours."

Nate led the way into the little office. There was a female attendant behind the counter. She looked up, surprised. A place like this probably didn't get too many visitors. Most people that came here would be coming to dump something—so they would drive right onto the scales and then have to answer questions to the other attendant in the booth outside. The woman in the office probably didn't have contact with anyone for most of her workday. Now, all of a sudden, three men were standing in front of her, one of them resplendent in uniform.

"Y...yes? Can I help you, gentlemen?"

Nate smiled and handed her his fake business card. "I'm Charles Duggett with the National Transportation Safety Board. My associate and I want to take one final look at the school bus that was involved in that fatal accident. And the Lieutenant Commander here is representing the Navy's interests—one of the children who died was the son of a naval officer."

She smiled at Ron. Maybe she had a thing for men in uniform. Nate thought that perhaps it was indeed a good idea after all that Ron had dressed up.

"That was a very sad accident." She pointed through the window to the northeast corner of the scrapyard area. "Yes, we still have the bus. It's scheduled to be crushed tomorrow, so your timing is perfect. Feel free to have a look around."

"Thanks so much. We won't be too long."

She smiled, more at Ron than Nate. "Take all the time you want."

They walked out of the office and headed in the direction of where she had pointed. When they rounded the first corner they could see the yellow school bus—badly crunched in on one side.

Nate shielded his eyes from the sun. Then he pointed. "That driveway leads directly to our wreckage. And, look, that cargo ship is just a few minutes away from docking. It's going to get busy over there real soon."

Nate noticed a stationery crane mounted on the rear deck of the ship. It wouldn't take them long to load the wreckage with that thing.

"We have to move fast. Ron, I think you should stay here with the bus, and pretend you're inspecting it, get underneath it and dirty up those pretty dress whites. Go inside, too—just be visible, look like you're doing something.

"And in that white outfit you'll be more visible than Tom or I. If she walks out to take a peek, she'll see you and be reassured. While you're doing that, Tom and I will take a look at the wreckage and, if we're lucky, get some photos of the damaged section."

Ron shooed with his hand. "Okay, good plan. Get going."

Nate and Tom jogged off in the direction of the Black Mamba, or, what was left of her. Within two minutes, they were there. For a few seconds they just stood and stared. At their masterpiece. It was the first time they'd seen it since the accident. They hadn't been allowed back to the site again after it had happened, and it was eerie looking at it now, in this place—a twisted pile of junk, in a junkyard. But, it was still their junk.

Nate motioned with his hand. "You start over there at that end, and I'll start here. Move fast. That end doesn't seem to have anything piled. So, you won't have to worry about being up high. I'll take the higher spots at this end. We don't have much time. If you find the section of track we're looking for, give me a whistle."

Tom nodded and ran down to the far end of the wreckage. Nate stared up at the ominous sight in front of him. Then he climbed. It was just a mass of twisted metal. He made his way to the top and then got down on his hands and knees and peered through the trestle pieces. He could easily make out the track of the first straightaway—the one that would have led out of the station and up the first hill. There was also a sequential identification number that was engraved in the steel— Nate made sure that, in all his structures, numbers in sequence were engraved in each track section before any welding of pieces took place.

Nate picked his way along the top of the wreckage and followed the silver track, which was several feet below him. He scanned it with his eyes; saw where it would take him. He crouched and worked his way monkey-style along the top of the twisted wreckage—saw that the track now had a curve to it. He knew he was looking at the first hill. In this case though, the track of the first hill was lying on its side, curving off to his left.

He noticed that the way it was lying, just dumped in the spot it was in, it was leading back down to the ground in a gradual slope, leaning up against piles of trestles on the way down. It was leading back down to where Tom was. And Nate knew that after the first hill would come the fateful second hill—the hill they wanted.

He saw Tom picking his way through the wreckage below. Nate put his thumb and forefinger to his mouth and whistled. Tom looked up and Nate pointed down at the track—then raised his forefinger to signify the number '1.' Tom nodded his understanding and crawled underneath some twisted pieces of metal. Nate watched him edging along the ground following the silver strip of track. Most of the track had been bent and twisted mechanically for shipping purposes, but it was still largely intact—parts of it looked like spaghetti, but it was easy enough to follow along like a puzzle, especially with the numbering sequence.

Tom whistled back to Nate. Nate couldn't see him now, but he knew approximately where he was. He slid feet first between two sections of trestle, and then swung with his hands. He had an open section ahead of him, heading down. He moved, hand over hand, down to where he knew Tom was. When he was ten feet from the ground, he let go and landed deftly on his feet. Then he advanced at a crawl—the area Tom had crawled through was almost like a 'mechano-set' tunnel. Nate actually had one of those neat mechano kits when he was a boy—that was when he first discovered his love of building things.

He heard another whistle. Nate allowed one eye to roam to the right, and the other to the left. Then, through the mess, he saw the soles of Tom's feet; about 60 feet ahead of him down a trestle tunnel on his left. He took off at a fast crawl.

Nate examined the curve of the track as he crawled and ran his fingers along the edges. He could tell by the numbers that this was the second hill and where Tom was, up ahead, was probably where the peak would have been. He followed the curve of the hill—for an instant he thought how weird it was to see the hill track bent in a tight loop and on its side, instead of standing majestically erect like he'd designed it to be.

Tom was digging with his hands. Nate raised his head to get a better look and banged his forehead hard against one of the trestles. *Damn!*

He rubbed his head and shook off the pain. "Tom, what are you doing?" He crawled faster and stopped right behind him.

His best friend turned his head around and stopped digging. "Nate, this would be the exact spot where the split in the track would be. See the way the curve cuts back in? But the bastards buried it!"

He resumed his digging. Nate could see that his hands were cut from scraping against the jagged metal track supports. He glanced around and saw what he needed. A single piece of metal rod support. "Back up, Tom. I'm going to use this—it'll be faster."

Nate rammed the metal rod into the ground where Tom had been digging and began levering underneath. He could feel resistance about three feet down. Stood up and began pushing down on the free end.

At the same time, he heard the horn of the ship—it was getting ready to dock. And there were sounds of activity about 100 yards to his right—dockside. The dock crew was getting ready, too.

He grunted and strained his biceps to their limits, pushing down harder and harder on the rod until he felt the piece underneath it give way. The hidden section emerged slowly from the dirt to the sound of scraping metal. Nate gave the rod one final push and up popped one jagged end of the track.

Tom reached down and grabbed it—yanked up as hard as he could and then pulled it over on an angle away from the ditch it had been concealed in.

Kneeling over the broken section of track, they gasped in unison. "Christ, look at it! It's been melted—those edges are hardened molten steel!"

Nate pulled his camera out of his pocket and began snapping away. "No point in pulling up the other end, Tom. It'll obviously look the same as this. Ron was right when he guessed what might have happened. When I described that flash I saw, and the man holding his fist towards the second hill, Ron said it sounded like remote-detonated thermate. Thermate melted our track. It didn't snap. It was melted. Who the fuck would do this? And why? It was mass murder, for Christ's sake!"

Tom rubbed his muddy fingers across his face, wiping away the sweat and leaving streaks of dirt in their wake. "Let's get out of here, Nate. We got what we needed."

They began to crawl back the way they had come in, moving fast now, banging their heads into dangling pieces of trestle along the way. Finally, they emerged from the twisted metal tunnel and struggled to their feet.

Two men stood in front of them, pistols in hand.

"Hand over the camera."

Nate was out of breath from the frantic crawl through the twisted mess. And he felt an anger building in his belly. They had come this far and discovered exactly what they needed; what would clear their names if anyone would listen. And now this.

"I can't do that."

The two men were gorillas. Dressed in military fatigues, both were at least six and a half feet tall—or at least it seemed that way to Nate. Bald heads, square jaws—military to the core.

"You're not authorized to be here. This wreckage is off limits."

Tom waved his hand in an arc. "I don't see a warning sign. We were just souvenir hunting—this is a famous rollercoaster and an infamous accident. We just wanted something to sell on eBay."

One of the gorillas laughed. "You think we're stupid? We know who you are. And right now, we're gonna go for a walk over to that ship there, and you can go for a little ride with your rollercoaster. Move!" He waved his pistol in the direction of the driveway leading to the dock.

Nate and Tom turned in the direction of the dock and started walking, hearing the footsteps of the goons behind them. Nate thought: *This is how it's going to end. No one will let this evidence see the light of day.*

They turned a corner in the driveway and Nate glanced up one last time at the twisted wreckage of the Black Mamba. His creation, his masterpiece—the end of him.

Suddenly, there was another voice, a comfortingly familiar one.

"What's going on here? Why are your weapons drawn?"

Nate and Tom turned around just in time to see the two gorillas doing the same—and they were saluting while shoving the pistols back in their holsters.

The gorilla in charge said, "Sir! Weapons secured, sir!"

"Good. Again, what's going on here? Who are these people?"

Nate thought: *Ron is one darn good actor!*

"These men were snooping around the rollercoaster wreckage, sir. Taking photos. We asked for their camera and they refused. We were just in the process of taking them to the ship."

"And who are they?"

"We were instructed to keep a watch out for them. These look like the executives from the company who designed the rollercoaster."

"Did you check their identification?"

"Not yet, sir. Just face recognition from photos. We were ordered to be vigilant about visitors here."

"Ah…I have the same orders as you do."

"With all due respect, sir, who are you? We weren't advised that a Navy liaison would be here for the loading of the wreckage."

"I'm Lieutenant Commander James Fielding. Does that name not mean anything to you? I'm attached to the naval station."

The gorillas paused. Then the second man pulled a cellphone out of a holster on his hip. "You'll understand that we have to check this out, sir. I'll just make the call."

Ron nodded. "Sure, no problem."

The man's index finger punched the number into his phone right at the very instant that Ron's very different kind of punch landed in the middle of his throat. He started choking and the phone fell from his hand. While it was still in mid-air, Ron's left foot shot out, sending the phone flying into the pile of twisted metal.

The other gorilla gasped and yanked his pistol out of its holster. Ron's right foot moved so fast that it was a mere blur. The soldier's gun was gone in an instant. He struck out with his fist, but Ron spun out of the way. Then he turned his back into him, grabbed the man's arm and threw him effortlessly over his shoulder. He hit the ground with a thud, but like the trained soldier he was, he was back on his feet in a flash. He advanced on Ron, who stood his ground with both fists extended in front of him.

The first soldier was on his feet now too and both were moving slowly towards Ron, side by side. He was down in a crouch, white suit smudged with dirt from crawling around in the bus. When the men were within four feet, Ron faked a punch with one hand and then executed a perfect 360-degree spin at lightning speed, his right foot carving an arc in the air, connecting with the chins of both men consecutively. He made it look like child's play. And his speed made it impossible for them to react in time.

They grunted and went down. Ron didn't waste any time waiting for them to regain their alertness. He dropped to the ground between them and put a hand underneath each of their heads, squeezing hard at the bases of their skulls. His fingers knew exactly where to press. The soldiers' eyeballs rolled up into their foreheads and their bodies went still.

Ron leaped to his feet and looked back at his two friends. "Don't worry, they're just unconscious. But we'd better get out of here fast!"

CHAPTER 21

It was her favorite spot for lunch.

The 'Sunshine Café.' A happy name, she thought. And it did indeed embrace the sunshine, with some funky tables set up on an outdoor patio. It catered to clientele who wanted charm, great service and darn good food. Just a few blocks down the street from the hospital, it was a calm refuge for her. Especially after a morning of surgeries. Lunch here was always perfect for her. It was far enough away from the medical center that most of the doctors and nurses avoided it—in fact, most just ate in the hospital cafeteria.

Shelby hated the cafeteria. Not that the food was bad—it wasn't. It was just that it wasn't an escape for her. She needed her escapes, needed her solitude. While most people would describe her as a social creature, she really wasn't. She could turn it on and off when she needed to, but she really did enjoy being alone. Loved her own company, her own thoughts.

Sometimes, she wished she wasn't that way.

And most times she wouldn't really give her lifestyle much thought. The fact that she was alone, had no one special in her life. For a while, when she was younger, she actually had spells when she was angry with herself. Why was she so choosy? Why was no one right for her?

She'd dated a lot of men in her life—maybe she was expecting too much, but she just never got that special feeling with any of them. That wonderful feeling that made her want to get to know them better, or want to spend more time with them. That feeling had always eluded her and she wondered if maybe her expectations were just too high. Perhaps she watched too many movies, wanted that romance that films portrayed so well.

Most of the men she'd dated had seemed nice at first, and most were very good-looking—Shelby had never had any troubles attracting handsome men. But, after a few dates, the lure of their looks faded into oblivion, because their personalities and intellects seemed flat. It was something they all seemed to have in common—just not much going on, empty suits. And self-obsessed. She couldn't stand being around self-obsessed people. And it seemed as if more and more people she met these days had that despicable quality.

So, she decided that she'd rather be alone by herself, than alone with someone.

Shelby was thirty-two years old and the biological clock was ticking away. She wanted children in her life, but it had to be with the right father. She wasn't one of those women who was content to be a single mother; she believed strongly that a child needed both mother and father figures. Shelby was just old-fashioned that way.

She sighed and looked at her menu. There were so many items to choose from—she'd been coming here for two years now and still hadn't tried all the entrees. The coffees were to die for, but the milkshakes were so good that they were worth killing for. And the creativity that went into every meal. It wasn't just a meal at Sunshine; it was darn pretty, too, and she loved that.

She knew the owner—a pretty blonde woman named Sarah. Shelby knew that every night back at home after a long day at the cafe, poor Sarah would be cooking chickens, and then bringing them in the next day to be prepared for that day's meals. Chicken was a popular item—Sarah had no choice but to cook tons of them because that was what the customers wanted. And she also did all the baking—all of the creative cakes that brought Sunshine such notoriety were her creations. She was one busy woman.

Shelby felt a tap on her shoulder. Another woman she knew in the café, and in fact her favorite. Ali was her name, and she not only greeted and served her favorite customers, but she also did a lot of the cooking in the kitchen. The special stuff, the gourmet stuff, the pretty stuff.

"You're looking radiant today, Shelby!" Ali leaned down and gave her a hug, and a kiss on both cheeks. A British tradition, and Ali was as British as they came. Shelby always looked forward to seeing Ali—she made her day. Always happy, always willing to take the time to ask about her life…and actually listened, too, which was a rarity these days.

"Thanks, Ali. I'm not feeling too radiant though. A couple of tough surgeries this morning—and we lost someone on the table."

"Oh, gosh—I'm so sorry. What happened?"

Shelby wiped a tear away from the corner of her eye. "It was a little boy, defective heart valve. We replaced it with a pig's valve, but it didn't take. Cardiac arrest right there on the table."

"I'm sure you all did everything you could."

Shelby looked into her friend's beautiful eyes and kind smile—one of those smiles that just lit up a room and touched everyone who was fortunate enough to be kissed by it.

"I know in my gut that we did—and my surgeon took it really hard, too. It's one of those things that you never really get used to, even though it happens more often than people realize."

Ali leaned over the table and whispered, "I'm sure that little boy is watching you right now and thanking you for trying. Don't tell Sarah, but your lunch is on the house today. I can hear that little boy talking to me in my head—saying that you deserve a free lunch!"

Shelby smiled. "Thanks, Ali. You'll have to let me buy you a coffee sometime."

Ali laughed. "Rubbish to that! We'll go have a glass of wine!"

"Okay, it's a deal!" Shelby pointed at two items on the menu. "I'll have these, Ali. No hurry—I have a couple of hours before my next surgery."

With that, her friend was off like a flash into the kitchen. Shelby knew that Ali would prepare the meal herself—she wouldn't trust it to anyone else. That always made Shelby feel special. After what had happened at the hospital that morning she needed to feel something different than the desperation she'd felt in the operating theatre when they'd been trying in vain to revive that little boy. His cute pixie face was one she'd never forget.

Shelby pulled her phone out of her purse and started checking her messages. Ali came back and served her coffee, to help tide her over until the meal arrived.

She smiled when she saw her messages. There was one from Nate Morrell. Just five simple words: *How about that coffee sometime?* She lifted her eyes from the screen and gazed off into space. And thought to herself. *Should I?* She smiled again when she silently answered in the affirmative.

Suddenly, she wasn't alone with her thoughts anymore.

He was just there. She'd been off in such a daydream about Nate that she hadn't even noticed him taking the empty seat across from her.

He didn't smile, didn't introduce himself, didn't even say 'hello.' He was just… there. Shelby shivered.

She managed to find the words. "Who are you?"

He spoke. "That doesn't matter."

"Why are you sitting here? There are plenty of empty tables."

He rubbed his left hand over his right, which is when she noticed the ring. A big ring, unique, adorning the third finger of his right hand. And his hands were big—wide and strong, with wrists to match. With his broad shoulders and barrel chest, he looked like he'd been an athlete in his younger years. He was dressed all in black, which added to the sinister look. The man's head was bald and he wore the strangest glasses. Tinted lenses connected to frames that were wide near the front and then split into two prongs which joined together again as they reached his tiny ears. But, even with the tinted lenses, she could tell that his eyes were as black as midnight.

"We need to talk, Ms. Sutcliffe."

Frowning, she asked, "How do you know my name?"

He didn't blink. He just stared right through her. Shelby shivered again. This man was giving her the most horrible feeling.

"You need to join the Class Action lawsuit."

"Are you a lawyer?"

He ignored her question. "The action may not succeed without your testimony."

"I don't know why this is any business of yours."

Ali arrived with her lunch—eggs benedict and a side salad. She turned her attention to Shelby's lunch guest—a puzzled look on her face. "Excuse me, but would you like to order something, sir? I could make a recommendation if you're in a hurry."

The stranger answered with his eyes still boring into Shelby's. "No, nothing for me."

Ali hesitated, then turned her attention to Shelby. "Is...everything okay?"

Shelby hesitated for a second, and said, "I don't know this man, Ali."

Ali took a step closer to the table. "Sir, perhaps you might be happier at another café?"

He turned his head and looked directly into Ali's eyes. With a voice laced with menace, he said, "Leave us for five minutes. I have something important to propose to Ms. Sutcliffe. In five, I promise I'll be gone."

Ali looked at Shelby, a question in her eyes. Shelby felt that shiver again, but something made her nod to Ali in reassurance. She didn't want her involved in this, whatever 'this' was. Ali grimaced, looked at her watch and then back at the stranger. "Okay, five minutes. I'm timing you." Shelby watched as Ali strode confidently back to the kitchen. Despite the unsettling experience she was going through with this dark stranger, she felt comforted by Ali's confidence. She knew that Ali would look out for her, as she probably did for all of her friends.

She turned her attention back to the stranger. "I don't understand why this is any business of yours, but I've chosen not to join the action."

"That would be a big mistake. The action has to succeed—there are many families depending on it."

"My testimony wouldn't help. I already discussed this with the lawyer, Dwayne Feinstein. He wanted me to testify that the lap bars became disengaged at the time of impact. That's not what happened—those bars became unlocked before the train hit the split in the track."

His eyes became even darker. "No, that's not what happened. They became disengaged when the train hit the broken track. That's what you'll testify to."

Shelby held her head high, indignant. "I'll do no such thing. That would be a lie. And I think I would know—I'm the only one alive who knows what happened."

The man pulled a checkbook out of his suit pocket. "What will it take to change your mind? I'll write you a check right now to make it worth your while. Name it."

Shelby couldn't believe what she was hearing. This man, whoever he was, was offering to bribe her to testify to an untruth. And why did this make all that much of a difference? She didn't understand why this was such an issue. They could still try to make their case just based on the broken track itself. If she stayed silent on the issue, no one would know that there was something strange about the accident.

"I don't want your money. I won't be bought off to lie. You've chosen the wrong woman, whoever you are."

A big hand reached across the table and grabbed hers. She tried to pull it away but his grip intensified. A thumb slid underneath her wrist and started pressing hard on the area where her pulse was. To anyone watching, it would look like they were just holding hands, but for Shelby, the man's thumb was beginning to exert excruciating pain in an area where she never imagined she would experience such pain.

"I don't think I've chosen the wrong woman. I think you have a price like every woman does. And I think you'll make the right choice."

He released the pressure and withdrew his hand. Pushed his chair back and stood up, glaring down at her.

"If Feinstein doesn't hear from you by this Friday, I'll find you, and we'll have another little chat. Well…maybe our next chat will be a wee bit longer."

Then he was gone.

CHAPTER 22

During the two days Nate was away in Key West, Stephanie had been a busy little bee. Half the furniture was gone, her three closets that had been bursting at the seams were now empty, and some of Nate's favorite gourmet cookery had escaped.

But she'd left him a cute little note. *'I've moved in with a friend. We'll talk as we get closer to the divorce proceedings.'*

Nate chuckled. He was able to guess what kind of "friend" it was. Well, hopefully he had lots of money to keep her in the lifestyle she'd become accustomed to.

This was better anyway. He was glad she was the one who'd decided to move—less hassle for him, and he got to stay where he was most comfortable. And he wouldn't have to force himself to be nice to her, tiptoe around on eggshells.

He sat down on the edge of the bed and checked his phone messages. He smiled—a nice text reply from Shelby: *'Yes, I'd love to meet for coffee. Day? Time?'*

He walked over to the closet, pulled out his favorite golf shirt, and thought, 'Well, how about right now?'

*****

It ended up being wine, not coffee. A nice little bar in Old Town, not far from Nate's office on King Street. It was around 7:00 in the evening and she met him at the 'Rendezvous Point' lounge.

Nate was sitting in a corner booth when she strolled into the bar. Wearing white jeans with heels and a purple t-shirt, she looked pretty hot. Nate noticed all the eyes turning to watch her as she walked over to his table. He understood why—it was hard not to notice. She was indeed striking. And her looks were made all the more special to Nate knowing they had a special bond between them. She wasn't just an attractive woman—she was the woman whose life he'd saved. That was special.

He stood up and greeted her. She gave him a hug and a kiss on the cheek, and then slid into the booth. Nate slipped in next to her.

When the Merlot came, Nate held up his glass in a toast, and they clinked. "To second chances in life."

Shelby laughed. "Well, considering everything, I'd say that's the most appropriate toast I've ever heard!"

Nate shuffled in his seat. He was a little bit nervous—they had gotten off to a rocky start when he'd visited her in the hospital, although they'd had a nice visit when she came to his office. But he still didn't know the status of the lawsuit, and he wanted to know whether or not she intended to sue his company. He wouldn't feel totally comfortable talking with her until he knew.

"How are you feeling now? Everything healed up okay?"

"Yes, I'm doing fine now—as far as recovery from the accident's concerned. There are other things, though…"

Nate topped up both their wine glasses. "Do you have anyone you can talk to about how you feel—what the next steps for you are?" He was fishing.

"No—other than my mom and sister, there's no one I can turn to that I'm all that close to. I kind of keep to myself most of the time—unless of course I'm going on junkets with the Coaster Crazies, or skydiving. At times like that, I'm with groups of people who I know fairly well. Well, with the Coaster Crazies, I did know them…that little group that I hung with is gone now, of course."

Nate lowered his head. He knew that it all must be bothering her more than she would even admit to herself. He tried to change the subject. "I didn't know you were a skydiver—tell me about that."

Shelby laughed. "It kind of goes along with this daredevil thing that I've had most of my life. I don't understand it—I'm just a nut that way, I guess. I learned to do it when I was a teenager. My mom wouldn't sign the permissions and waivers when I was younger. She told me that she wouldn't be party to me killing myself! So, I had to wait until I was eighteen when I was legally allowed to sign the forms myself. My mom still wasn't happy, but she respected that it was a decision I was able to make without her.

"Anyway, I took the course and had my first jump. Came off the wing of the plane spinning and when the chute opened up from the tug from the static line the lines got all wrapped around my legs. So I was kinda upside down for half the flight down—had to unwind myself before I could enjoy the ride. I was then way off course and ended up landing in the top of a tree!"

Nate shook his head in shock. "God that must have been scary. I don't think I could do that."

She reached across and rubbed the back of his hand. "I think we both found out the hard way that there are things people are capable of doing in a split second that they probably couldn't imagine doing if they had time to think."

He nodded. "Yeah, you're right on that."

They switched over to coffee and dessert. Both had eaten dinner earlier in the evening, so decadent desserts were in order. And they both had to drive, so the wine had to come to an end.

The next hour was spent talking about their lives. Nate confessed to her about where his marriage stood and that Stephanie had now left. And Shelby opened up to him about how her love life, for some reason, had been a total failure so far.

He found that hard to believe. She was such a charming, intelligent lady, and darn easy on the eyes. But she admitted to being a loner, and had standards that no one had ever seemed to be able to measure up to. Nate thought that was a good thing—and wished he'd set his sights higher when he'd married. He'd rushed into something that was so important. He should have gotten to know his bride a lot better than he had. It was just something he'd fallen into…seemed like a good idea at the time.

Three hours went by in a flash. She was really easy to talk to—and fun. She was outspoken and had a good sense of humor. He was enjoying Shelby's company immensely, made a little bit easier in knowing that his wife was out of his life for good.

"Shelby, I need to ask you this. Are you going to pursue a lawsuit against my company?"

She paused, which made Nate nervous. "I've been saving this to tell you. I'm a little bit scared about something that happened yesterday."

Nate leaned in closer to her. "What happened? Does it have something to do with the accident?"

She nodded. "I was having lunch by myself in a little café near the hospital. This man just sat down at my table and told me that I have to join the Class Action. I asked him who he was and he wouldn't tell me. Then I told him that I wasn't going to join the lawsuit because the lawyer wanted me to lie about the lap bars.

"He said that I had to testify that the lap bars became disengaged on impact. I said no, that I wouldn't say that. He offered to write me a check to convince me to testify to that. I said no again. Then, he grabbed my wrist and squeezed hard with his thumb. Told me I had until Friday or he'd pay me a visit again. He really hurt my wrist. And Friday is two days away—I don't know if he was serious or not, but I'm nervous that I might see this man again."

Nate knew that Shelby was a confident woman, he could easily tell that. But her voice had been shaking when she was telling the story of her encounter with the stranger.

"Maybe you should go to the police. Tell them this story and describe him. They might be able to do a police sketch and locate him."

"I don't think they'd do anything. It would be my word against his. How can I prove that he threatened me? How could I prove that he hurt my wrist? Any witnesses in the café would say that we were just holding hands. That's what it would have looked like."

She was right. There was really nothing for the police to act on. "Describe him to me, Shelby."

"Tall, broad shouldered kind of guy, could have been an athlete at one time. Bald, with these expensive-looking tinted glasses. Oh, and he had this big ring on his right hand—never seen one like it before."

Nate's mouth went dry. He sat up straight in his seat and took a deep breath. "I've seen that man before."

"What? Where?"

Nate pulled out his wallet to pay the bill. "Are you going to sue us? I know you won't join the Class Action, but are you going to sue us separately?"

Shelby touched his hand lightly. "No, I'm not. This whole thing seems so dishonest and it seems as if someone's trying to stack the deck against you. You can take my word on that. I won't be suing."

"Okay, I will take your word. I sense that with you, your word is good. Come to my office tomorrow afternoon—say around 2:00? Can you get off work?"

Shelby nodded. "No problem. I don't have any surgeries tomorrow, so I'm just on call. I'll switch my 'call' shift with another nurse."

"Okay, good. I'll answer your question…and many more…tomorrow. I want my partners to meet you and hear what you have to say. And we'll let you in on everything. This is a mystery beyond comprehension."

*****

Nate introduced Shelby to Tom and Ron, closed the door to the conference room and then took his seat at the head of the table.

"There's coffee over on the credenza, Shelby. Help yourself."

"Thanks, but nothing for me right now."

"Okay. So, to start things off, I wanted you guys to hear what Shelby has to say about the accident, and what's happened to her since then. And I intend for us to share what we know with her. It looks like we're all in this together, and there are some puzzling and troubling things going on that we need to share." He looked at Shelby. "Okay, tell my partners what's been happening."

Shelby detailed, first, the accident itself and how she noticed her lap bar was unlocked before the train collided against the broken track section. Next, she outlined her meeting with Dwayne Feinstein, and how he told her that she was mistaken about the lap bars. He showed her the NTSB report, which stated that the bars unlocked upon impact with the broken track, and not before.

She then told them about her visit with John Fletcher at the NTSB.

"He seemed like a really good guy…but kind of sheepish, almost ashamed. Hard to put my finger on it, but he seemed to be avoiding my eyes when I confronted him about his report. I asked him why he didn't bother to interview me, and that if he had, he would have discovered from me that the lap bars opened before the impact. And…it seemed to me that he wanted to tell me something…but couldn't."

Tom jumped in. "I talked to him, too. He's the one who told me that his report would say that the track split due to a faulty weld. I objected to that—he didn't argue with me, but wouldn't change his report either, despite me telling him that there were no welds on that part of the track. Also, this Fletcher guy is the one who told me that the wreckage was being hauled away to an undisclosed location. That we—the ones who were being hung out to dry for this accident—weren't allowed to look at the wreckage or know where they were hauling it to."

Nate directed the conversation back to Shelby. "Tell us about the guy who visited you the other day."

She did. There was silence in the room after she described how he'd hurt her wrist and about the veiled threat he threw at her if she didn't sign on to the Class Action by Friday.

Nate addressed the group. "This man Shelby described to me—this sounds like the same man I saw that day at Adventureland, raising his fist toward the second hill. Ron, you thought that sounded like he was aiming a remote control device."

Ron leaned back in his swivel chair. "Yes, and after what we discovered down in Key West, I'm convinced that he was using that remote to detonate a fuse—a fuse that had been attached to material called Thermate-3, a military grade substance that can be painted onto steel and burn through it in seconds. It was probably painted on the underside of the track where it couldn't be noticed. And…Nate, you said you also saw a flash at that exact spot seconds before the accident."

Nate nodded. "And now we know, firsthand from Shelby, that the lap bars came unlocked before the impact. So, they might have been disengaged by that same remote control unit."

Shelby jumped in. "Hold on a second. What's that you said, Ron, about Key West? What did you find out?"

"We found the wreckage down there, ready to be hauled out to sea. The broken part of the track had clearly been melted—it was easy to see that it was molten metal that had hardened since the accident."

"Jesus! It was sabotage then!"

Tom mumbled, "More like mass murder."

Ron twirled his pen. "Actually, I don't think so, Tom."

"What?"

"I'll tell you what I think in a second. Anyway, Shelby, the way we found out about Key West was an anonymous phone call that Tom got—from a woman. She just told us where to find it and hung up. Someone had a pang of conscience."

Nate got up and poured himself some coffee. "That guy who visited Shelby, it sounds like he was wearing that same Super Bowl ring that I saw the guy at Adventureland wearing. He fit the description in every other way as well. And another thing that Shelby doesn't know—all the ambulances were redirected that day to a phony accident on the bridge. And the two guys who had parked the ambulance that Tom and I jumped into—they just disappeared."

Tom reached over for the water jug and poured himself a tall one. "God, this talk is giving me a dry mouth. Here's something we need to consider also—for someone to have painted or sprayed Thermate on the underside of the track and attached fuses, they would have had to have been part of the maintenance crew at the amusement park—or one of our guys. And for that bastard with the remote to be able to find out the radio frequency we programmed for the lap bar locks, there had to have been an inside man for that, too. Maybe the same guy?"

They were all nodding at this ominous statement.

Ron Collens jumped up from his chair and walked over to the white board. "Let's jot down what we know."

Ron picked up a marker pen and wrote out a list of the key points:

Nate saw a man raising his fist towards the second hill.

He thought he saw a flash on the track.

He saw some of the lap bars in the 'up' position as the train fell.

The ambulance was unattended and all other emergency vehicles had been diverted to a phony accident.

Shelby's lap bar became disengaged before the train hit the split in the track.

She was pressured by the lawyer to testify that the lap bar was disengaged only upon impact, and then pressured again by this mysterious stranger. And pressured by implied threat to join the Class Action.

This mysterious stranger who Shelby met, and similar to the guy Nate saw, would seem to be the same person. And from Nate's description of the ring on his finger, he may have played for the San Francisco 49ers in the 1994 Super Bowl.

John Fletcher, the chief investigator for the NTSB, seemed to be hiding something when he talked to Shelby.

This accident was assigned to the NTSB despite it having no jurisdiction in amusement park accidents.

Someone had a conscience attack and phoned Tom anonymously telling him where we could find the wreckage, and that it was going to be dumped into the ocean.

On our visit to Key West, our helicopter went out of control, and seemed to have been taken over by a remote operator. It was flying itself and it appeared to be a deliberate attempt to scare us away.

When we searched the wreckage, we discovered that the track had indeed been melted at the point of separation.

We were accosted by military personnel at the site in Key West. We had to get a bit rough in order to escape. They seemed intent on taking Nate and Tom onto the ship that was going to be hauling away the wreckage.

And there must have been an inside man, or men, working at Adventureland or for Flying Machines, in order to paint the Thermate onto the track and to disclose the radio frequency to disengage the lap bars.

There was total silence in the room when Ron finished the list. You could hear a pin drop. The list was overwhelming. Everyone was just staring at the white board, obviously trying to make some sense out of it all.

Tom spoke first. "Ron, a few minutes ago you said that you didn't think this was mass murder. What did you mean by that?"

Ron moved away from the white board and sat back down again.

"This was a professional job. Mass murderers don't do things as sophisticated as this. And it has been designed in a way to make it look like an accident. The threats against Shelby and the attempts to get rid of the wreckage before anyone else could inspect it, just underline the fact that someone wants this file closed and for it to be labeled an accident."

Tom jumped in. "But twenty-five people died!"

"Yes, they did. I think this was a 'diversionary murder.'"

Nate frowned. "What are you talking about, Ron? In English, please?"

Ron laughed. "Sorry, bad habit of mine. Let's narrow this down to some basics. This was designed to look like an accident. And the lap bar disengagement, to me, was a back-up plan. It was to ensure that everyone on the coaster died. Just in case the Thermate fuses didn't light from the remote activation, Plan 'B' was to disengage the lap bars. Both of those things were done with the mere press of a remote. If the track didn't melt, then at least the bars wouldn't have held anyone in as they went over the hill because that was the Plan 'B'. Therefore, both of these things together guaranteed that everyone would die."

Shelby piped in with a smile, "Not *everyone!*"

Ron smiled back. "Yes, Shelby, you were the wild card that they didn't foresee, thank God." He continued, "Then, to make it even more inevitable, a fake multi-vehicle accident on the bridge was called in to Emergency dispatch, and the two ambulance attendants—obviously 'plants' and not really ambulance attendants—who parked the ambulance at the park, just simply disappeared. So, there were no paramedics available to save lives if there were any to save. The ambulance fiasco was just another back-up plan. We'll call that Plan 'C.'"

Tom spoke up again. "Okay, this all makes sense, Ron. Overall, a pretty brilliant plan if this is the way it indeed happened. But—cut to the chase. What's a 'diversionary murder?'"

"That's a type of murder that's designed to look like something else. First, to make it look like an accident. Secondly, to make it look like just a horrific mass casualty. To draw attention away. Everyone would be focused on the 'accident' part, and the high body count—and nothing else. So, two things diverting attention away from what was really intended. Just like a 'head fake' in football."

Nate said, "I think I know where you're coming from. Spit it out."

"I think that only one person was intended to be killed on that rollercoaster. The other twenty-four victims were, sadly, just collateral damage."

CHAPTER 23

Carl Masterson parked his car in a lot just off L'Enfant Plaza and walked into the lobby of the NTSB headquarters. It had been a beautiful day so far—he'd actually enjoyed the drive down from the NSA compound in Fort Meade, Maryland. He usually didn't—for some reason he could never relax in the car. Maybe it was the music he usually played—seventies heavy metal.

Today, with so much on his mind, he decided to suck it up and listen to some soft jazz. And it seemed to have worked. He was breathing easy, his heartbeat wasn't racing like it usually was, and he could almost feel the possibility of a smile crossing his face. He just had to find something funny and test that out.

In fact, today he felt like he was in his twenties again—playing football for the 49ers.

Those were the days. His glory days—well, college ball was probably more glorious, if he was being honest with himself. He'd been a star fullback at the University of Southern California, got drafted in the first round by San Francisco, and then made his debut in the NFL. His childhood dream had come true.

And he'd had a couple of good seasons as the starting fullback. Things were going well until that damn scandal. The old stripper claimed rape—well, it wasn't rape at all. She'd wanted it and willingly came back to his hotel room. She was just a tramp.

And the courts agreed with him. He was acquitted of all charges. She was a gold-digger, looking to tell her story to the tabloids. And hoping she could succeed in a civil suit against a well-heeled NFL sophomore. Even after he was acquitted of the criminal charges, she didn't give up, the fat bitch. But she failed again.

But, goddamnit, the scandal took two years off his career. He was suspended until the criminal case was heard, then back on the roster. But after that he needed time off constantly to fight the civil case—suspended again, this time on a morals clause. When he was finally cleared, he then had to deal with the non-stop protests and bad publicity about discrimination, and favoritism towards athletes. Yes, he was an athlete, and yes, she was black.

He'd kept in shape throughout, knowing he'd win eventually. He wanted his spot in the starting line-up back. But, success in sports is a fleeting thing. If you're unfortunate enough to fall onto the injury list, someone else slips in and gets noticed. When you finally come back from the injury, there's a new hero in town.

And if you're falsely accused of a crime or something scandalous, the sting remains even when you're cleared. People still remembered that you'd been accused, and they certainly all remembered the salacious little details of his case—a black stripper, an NFL football player, kinky things that she said he did—nothing was kept private. Everyone he knew was embarrassed as hell, and ashamed to be seen with him.

And Carl was embarrassed, too, because his world had been laid bare for all to see. And the jokes thrown towards him by fellow players, about the stripper being fat and old—that he was a desperately horny man who wasn't equipped to hit on someone with youthful beauty, that he had to scrape the bottom of the barrel.

Carl admitted to himself that he'd made the mistake of stumbling into the wrong joint that night. It turned out to be not one of the higher-end strip joints; the ones that featured young nubile strippers, the classier girls. No, the one he stumbled into was a kinky underground place that featured transvestites, fat girls, black girls and over-the-hill girls. And the girl he picked up had three strikes against her: fat, black and over-the-hill. The locker room jokes that he had to endure throughout that whole affair were painful, and the Press had had a field day with him, too.

So, when he finally came back onto the roster in 1993, he was a forgotten man. Someone else was the starting fullback—and he'd missed almost two years of active play. He was good enough to get through training camp, but only good enough to make the 'taxi squad.' Which meant he was on the team, but not really. Kind of in the background in case they needed him. He never even dressed for games. Was never on the team jet.

But then, in 1994, he'd earned his way back—not to the first string, but at least on the bench. He was a bencher, a filler—in case a first stringer got injured. And sometimes playing on special teams—kickoff returns, boring things like that.

But—he was still a part of the team, and got to enjoy the glory of winning the Super Bowl in 1994. Didn't contribute much—made a few blocks, things like that—just enough to get his sweater dirty, which was something every bencher wanted at the very least. A little dirt smudged on the face always helped, too—great to have when the Press took photos after the victory. You got to look like you contributed something, anything.

But he felt that he had earned his Super Bowl ring, nonetheless. Carl looked down at his right hand and admired it. Then he rubbed the ring for good luck. He did that before every important meeting or confrontation—a memory of his days of glory.

Well, he was a winner again—just not in the sports field anymore. Before the NFL, he'd managed to complete his law degree at 'So Cal.' And, when he left the NFL, he went right back to college and earned a Master's degree in Criminology. Then two years with the FBI after that.

One day, out of the blue, he was recruited to join the largest spy agency in the world, the National Security Agency. He'd moved up fast, now in the position of Director of the rather clandestine Security and Intelligence division. He had a small staff—only about thirty in total. Very specialized people, all talented in specific areas.

His staff was small by design—the most sensitive material and actionable events came under his area. Most of the other departments collected and analyzed information and that was it. But his department was charged with doing something about the information—be that strategic planning, communications… or other things.

What they did was so sensitive he couldn't run the risk of having too many eyes and ears seeing and hearing what they did. He needed to maintain control and keep a lid on things. So, even he himself did fieldwork—usually the most sensitive stuff. He kept those things close to his chest.

His staff was an odd collection of specialists. There were marketing experts for the communications area, systems experts, strategic planners, a few engineers and scientists…and a couple of assassins. And of course there was Carl himself—skilled at martial arts, a trained lawyer and a criminal psychology expert. Being a former athlete did nothing for him, however. In fact, no one even remembered him, because he hadn't even had the chance to make his mark way back then.

But he had his ring. No one could take that from him. And most people didn't even recognize it for what it was. He was always surprised about that. Unless they got a close-up look at it, the only comments he got were: "Nice ring," or "Boy, that's a big ring."

Carl took the elevator up to the fourth floor of the National Transportation Safety Board, and walked up to the receptionist.

"I'd like to see John Fletcher."

"Do you have an appointment?"

Carl pulled an NSA shield out of his pocket and held it out in front of her face. "No, I don't."

"Oh, I see. The NSA. Okay, what's your name, please?"

"We don't give out our names—national security reasons."

"Well, who do I say is visiting?"

Carl sighed. God, this girl was thick. "You just say 'the NSA;' that's all you have to say."

Looking flustered, she picked up the phone and punched in a number. Then she hung up without saying anything and hurried off down the hall. Carl took a seat and waited.

In a few minutes, John Fletcher made his appearance. Carl noticed a slight scowl appear on John's face the moment he saw who it was. Carl smiled inside.

"You again? What do you want now?"

Carl stood. "I want us to have a little chat in your office."

John jerked his head and led the way down to his office. Once inside, he closed the door behind them and sat down at his desk.

"I signed your report. There's nothing else to say."

Carl allowed his lips to curl up in the corners. The kind of look he used to give to opposing linebackers on the football field. "You signed something else, too. A confidentiality agreement. Have you been faithful to that agreement, John?"

"Yes, I have been."

"Has your wife been faithful to that agreement, John?"

"I don't know what you're talking about and my wife never signed an agreement with you anyway. It's a moot point."

Carl rubbed his ring. "It's not a moot point—not if you asked her to do the talking for you."

John just stared back. Carl could tell he'd hit a chord.

"Funny thing, the executives at Flying Machines knew exactly where to go, where to find the wreckage. They flew right to Key West, flew over the junkyard and then made a personal visit there. Funny, huh?"

John shifted in his chair. "I never told them anything."

"Another funny thing happened. A woman phoned one of the executives, Tom Foster, from a phone booth in Georgetown only five minutes from your very house. She told him where the wreckage was. Now, isn't that a funny coincidence?"

"That could have been anyone."

"Really, John? Do you believe in strange coincidences like that? An educated man like you—one who has investigated virtually every serious accident in this country over at least the last thirty years? Someone like you who is trained to look beyond mere coincidence?"

"Again, it could have been anyone."

Carl pulled a mini-cassette out of his pocket. "I have the tape of her voice on this cassette. Would you like to listen to it with me?"

John shook his head. "There would be no point in that. It's not my wife's voice. I suggest you leave."

"Would you be interested in knowing that we did a voice match? It is indeed your wife's voice."

John sat up straight in his chair. "How on earth could you get my wife's voice to do a match with?"

Carl laughed. "Are you forgetting that I'm with the NSA, John? You yourself, in our last meeting, were angry enough to remind me of the Edward Snowden affair, and how the NSA is so adept at listening in on private conversations. I appreciated that reminder, John."

John opened his mouth to say something, and then changed his mind.

Carl rubbed his ring again. Things were going well. Now he needed to do a good job of bluffing so that John would open up a bit. He needed to make John feel safe, calm him down—he might come clean with him if Carl did this effectively.

He allowed his voice to slide into a conciliatory tone. "So, don't kid a kidder, John. I know what you did—you got your wife to make that call. It was your conscience talking and I understand that. You have integrity and it was a tough thing for you to deal with, signing a report that you knew was false. Even though I told you it was for national security reasons, the good guy in you who believes in truth and justice came through.

"Sometimes I hate my job, John. I have moments of conscience all the time and I have to fight those back for the good of the country. But...you don't have the training I've had, and you haven't had to endure some of the terrible things I've seen—nor the scary things that I know the country needs protection from. I expected too much from you. I realize that now."

He noticed that John's jaw seemed to be relaxing a bit. "So, what happened just happened, period. Can't put the genie back in the bottle. All I want from you—need from you—is just for you to be honest with me and tell me if you've told anyone else about this. About the report being false, about how the accident really happened, things like that. All I'll do is contact those people and have them sign confidentiality agreements. Then we'll be done."

Carl was feeling confident. John's face had really relaxed now. He waited. John licked his lips and wiped the sleeve of his right arm across his forehead, soaking up the sweat that was glistening on his brow. Then he stood.

"Get the hell out of here, you dishonest prick! Do you really think I'm that stupid? Not only do you want a false report filed, I'm convinced that you and your spooks committed mass murder. I told you what I found—I found melted steel. That's evidence of Thermate. And those lap bars did not disengage upon impact—I know that for a fact. Seeing you sitting there in front of me, spouting your crap, makes me sick."

John walked to his office door and yanked it open. "Get out! I don't want to see you again, whoever the fuck you are!"

*****

Carl felt unsettled the entire drive back to Maryland. Even the soft jazz wasn't helping.

He hadn't handled that as well as he could have. He had no idea if Fletcher had confided in anyone else. There might very well be loose ends out there, but Carl couldn't tie them up if he didn't know what they were.

Well, he would just have to deal with what he knew. This Fletcher guy was a loose cannon. But Carl had to assume that at this stage all the man had done was to get his wife to make that call. Carl knew nothing that would indicate anyone else had been told anything, and certainly nothing else had come to his attention. So, maybe this could be contained. With a little fear.

He could kill him—but that would just draw more attention. The NTSB investigator who had signed the report for a high-profile rollercoaster accident dying suddenly? That would just be too coincidental. He had to shut him up— make him realize he was serious. That this was serious. Operation Backwash could not be jeopardized by a moralistic accident investigator. And if Fletcher knew what Operation Backwash was all about, he might even agree with Carl.

But, of course, he couldn't be told. That operation was classified and it would remain that way. No, he would just have to put the fear of God in John Fletcher.

Gas leaks had been quite common the last few years in the United States. In some cases, entire neighborhoods had been leveled. Houses flattened, its sleeping occupants left even flatter. These things just seemed to happen in this day and age of high efficiency appliances and central heating. Gas was volatile and unpredictable.

Sometimes, they were indeed accidents...and sometimes they weren't. The average American citizen couldn't tell the difference.

CHAPTER 24

Dinner had been lovely. Candlelight, pasta, some red wine, and a wee bit of dancing afterwards. John Fletcher had never really learned how to dance, but Linda was really good and she'd patiently showed him a few steps over the years. At least now he wasn't embarrassed when she persuaded—or, more like coerced—him up on the dance floor. He'd managed to move around without stepping all over her toes.

She'd worn his favorite dress tonight—beautiful purple, a slight dip in the front showing just a hint of cleavage, bare on the shoulders, low cut in the back. And she'd donned her favorite black dancing shoes, too—that was John's first hint that she'd be dragging him up onto the floor.

They'd talked and laughed for hours, trying hard to forget the grim death sentence John's tumor had given him. And they did forget—for a while. They reminisced about their forty plus years together, and both knew that they'd do it all over again if they could.

John just loved her dearly. There had never been anyone else. While he knew that a lot of his friends had fooled around on their wives over the years—and loved to brag about it—it wasn't something that ever occurred to John to do. He felt sorry for his friends, sad that they hadn't found that special person like he had. He never lectured them, never judged them—usually just shrugged his shoulders and said something like, *'Whatever turns you on.'*

And John, with the good looks he'd been blessed with, would have had an easier time picking up women than any of his friends. One of his best friends, Gary, said to him one time when they were having a beer together: *'John, if I had your looks I'd be in bed with a different girl every night!'*

And John had been hit on numerous times during his forty years of marriage—he had no problem letting them down gently. And he never regretted doing that. It just wouldn't have felt right—and he would have been thinking of Linda the whole time anyway, thinking about how much she loved and trusted him and how much he loved and trusted her.

No, he couldn't betray that—and never would. It was too good to ruin.

He glanced over at her as he made the last turn to reach their home in

Georgetown. Her cheeks were flushed from the wine and the dancing, and her auburn hair was a little out of place from the breeze flowing in through the open sunroof. She sensed that he was looking at her and smiled at him. A warm smile, one that didn't need any words. But, she said them anyway. "I had a lovely time, John. We should do that more often."

John pulled up in front of the house. Linda's car was in the driveway, so he always left his on the street. Their garage was full of junk, so neither of their cars had ever seen the inside.

But...this was Washington. Garages were meant for storage down here—there were hardly ever any weather issues to be concerned with.

As he shifted the Lexus into park, she reached over and squeezed his hand. "I love you, John." Then tears started to stream down her cheeks. "And...I'm...going to...miss you." She started sobbing and covered her eyes with her delicate hands. "You...don't know...how much. I can't imagine...life without...you in it."

John wrapped his arm around her slender shoulders and squeezed her tight. "Don't think about it, hon. Please. Let's not be sad during the time I have left. Hey, a few months ago you suggested the 'bucket list.' I have some vacation coming—why don't we take off for a while and go someplace nice? Whaddaya think, girl?"

With her hands still covering her eyes, she nodded her head. John could still hear her sobbing. "Let's go inside and plan it. Okay?"

John got out and walked around to her side, opening the door for her. She kissed him as she got out of the car. "You and your planning—this time I'm not going to make fun of you. Yes, let's go plan. How about Bora Bora?"

Once inside the house, John said, with a sly smile on his face, "I think our best planning is done in bed, don't you think? We'll do our own little Bora Bora under the sheets!"

Linda winked. "I'll meet you upstairs, you devil."

He watched her as she negotiated the stairs, still a little bit tipsy from the wine. "Hold on tight to that railing, Lindy."

She turned her head, and called down to him in a singsong voice, "I love it when you call me 'Lindy.'"

John laughed. "I usually only do that when I'm horny!"

"I know! That's why I love it!"

John walked back into the hallway and picked up the envelopes sitting on the phone desk. Flipped through them—nothing important, just a few bills. He heard Linda getting ready upstairs—toilet flushing, tap water running.

He knew that in just a few minutes she'd be in bed. He liked to wait until she was nice and relaxed like that, kinda dozy—then he'd crawl in next to her and enjoy her gentle sighs and moans as his fingers began to roam over her body.

Yes, a little vacation, just the two of them with none of their 'couples friends' along, would be really nice. They hadn't done that in a long time and John regretted that. Especially now as the clock was ticking away on him with every precious day.

And especially after that unsettling visit the NSA spook had paid him the other day. That guy knew—they'd recorded Linda talking from the phone booth, for God's sake. John never even thought that was possible. So, now, unwittingly, he'd dragged Linda in on this strange affair. Hopefully, the way John had sent the guy slinking out of his office, he would leave John alone now.

Despite his regret at them discovering what he, through Linda, did, he was glad that the Flying Machines executives managed to see the wreckage before it was dumped at sea. John knew he'd done the right thing; it helped a little bit with his guilty conscience over signing that phony report.

Ah…the sound of the closet door in the bedroom creaking open. Linda was no doubt slipping into one of his favorite negligees right this very moment. John felt a familiar stiffness in his crotch as his imagination began to take over.

*****

The jet black Ford Explorer was parked across the street and five doors down from Fletcher's house. The driver kept his eyes peeled—the main floor lights were still on, but the upstairs bedroom lights had just gone out. He saw the shadow of a lone figure moving around in the living room area.

He reached his arm out of the window and aimed a tiny little remote control at Fletcher's house. It was powerful—had a range of 300 meters. And it was configured for a sequence of two presses of the button. His superior had made it clear how this would work tonight, and he had to follow the instructions to the letter.

The man turned to his partner sitting beside him. "Okay, now!"

His partner jumped out of the car and raced towards the gold Lexus, a tire iron brandished in his right hand. He raised it and smashed it on top of the sunroof and then took a baseball swing at the front windshield. Then he raced back to the Explorer.

The car alarm on the Lexus started blaring and the driver of the Explorer knew that Fletcher would be out the front door within about ten seconds.

Once he saw the front door open, he would press once on the remote. That would cause a slight popping noise in the kitchen that no one in the house would notice. The gas valve on one of the stove burners would open by remote, allowing the gas to seep into the kitchen at a rapid flow.

When he would press the remote a second time, a tiny little gadget hiding on the top of the Fletchers' kitchen cabinets would come to life. A cute little thing—

at a quick glance one would just think it was a bee or a hornet. But, in actual fact, it was a robot. The thing would gain liftoff from the top of the cabinets, and swoop down and around the kitchen in tight little circles.

A nanorobot—slick, high tech, innocent looking, and very very tiny. In this case, it was also very very deadly.

Nanorobots could be used in a variety of ways, for a myriad of missions— they could carry things, drop things, attack things, and be programmed and directed to do almost anything. They were the tiniest drones yet invented.

For this mission, the thing was designed to do two things. The driver would wait a sufficient number of seconds before pressing the remote again; because he wanted there to be sufficient gas buildup before the drone did its work. If it was sent flying too early, it could get damaged in those close quarters and not have time to do its work at the exact right moment.

And its work was to simply emit sparks as it flew. This little nanorobot was specifically designed as a "sparker." Its nickname was, of course, 'Sparky.'

*****

John finished looking through the mail and threw the envelopes back onto the desk. With an expectant smile on his face, he began his climb up the stairs, a randy bounce in each step.

Suddenly, the screeching sound of a car alarm broke the night stillness. John headed back down the stairs, pulled back the curtains and peeked out the front window. Yep, it was his car. The head and tail lights of the Lexus were flashing.

John cursed, opened the front door and ran down to the street. Right away, he saw that the sunroof and windshield had been smashed in. *Vandals!* Cursing again, he whirled his head around, looking in all directions. All he saw was a black SUV halfway down the block that was just finishing a U-turn and heading quickly in the opposite direction.

John ran after it, waving his hands in the air and yelling. It kept going. It was dark, but the streetlights illuminated the license plate and the occupants for just a split second. John needed glasses for reading, but for distance he was pretty good. He locked the plate number in his brain. There were two people in that vehicle, who either saw who did this to his car—or, more likely, *were* the ones who did it.

John walked back toward the house, looking sadly at his beloved Lexus as he passed. For the moment, he had to get his keys so he could shut off the alarm. Nothing else he could do—he'd phone the police in the morning, and give them the license plate number. Right now he had better things to do—although he had to admit, he was not as horny now as he had been just a few minutes ago.

He heard the upstairs window slide open. Linda poked her head out. With panic in her voice, she called out, "John, I smell gas! Something's…"

Suddenly, there was a concussion—a blast that knocked him off his feet and several feet backwards in the air. John struggled to catch his breath, rolled from his back onto his knees and gasped. It was like the air had been knocked out of his lungs. As he struggled to his feet to a loud ringing in his ears, he called out, "Linda!" He couldn't hear himself yell the word, but he knew he yelled it.

Standing upright for just a few seconds, he could tell that most of the house was on fire, while parts of it had completely disappeared. He could see down the side of his house clear to the rear yard, through what used to be the garage and the kitchen. Flames were flickering through the front living room windows, or at least where the windows used to be.

He took a couple of steps, calling out Linda's name again, then staggered from the dizziness and fell straight forward onto his face. John struggled to his feet again, blood streaming, his nose hard to breathe through—probably broken.

Forcing himself through sheer will to stay on his feet; he looked up at the window where he had last seen Linda's pretty face pleading with him about… something.

He called out her name again, and was vaguely aware of lights in the other houses coming on, neighbors filing out into the street.

There were no flames coming out of the second floor window, but there was certainly lots of smoke. The main floor was hopeless—the fire was raging. John worked his way over to the tall elm tree that adorned their front lawn. He found the strength to grab onto the first low-hanging branch, and then swung himself up, straddling it. Then the same for the next few branches until he was up adjacent to the bedroom window.

He was close enough that he could just make it. He stood on top of the branch he'd been straddling, holding onto the branch above for support. Then he hurled himself toward the windowsill, grabbing the edge with both hands and yanking himself up and in through the window.

He crashed to the floor. The smoke was so dense in the room that he couldn't see a thing. John's eyes were tearing up from the acrid smoke and he was finding it impossible to breathe. So he just held whatever breath he still had and started feeling around on the floor with his hands.

He found her right away, just back from the window that she'd been calling to him from. He didn't check for a pulse—no time for that. They had to get out now or they'd both be dead in seconds. Out of the corner of his eye, he saw flames licking away under the bottom of the closed bedroom door. The fire was just a few feet away from them now.

John swooped her up in his arms and staggered back to the window ledge. Now that he was standing, it was even harder to breathe—the smoke was much heavier, starting just a few inches off the floor. This gave him hope—she had been lying down on the floor, where the smoke wasn't as thick.

Cradled in his arms, he gently edged her out the window and stuck his own head out with her for a breath of fresher air. Drinking it in, he wondered, *what the hell am I going to do now?*

Then he heard their voices. Three men standing on the lawn beneath the window, arms outstretched. His neighbors. "Drop her to us, John! We'll catch her! Hurry!"

He hesitated for just a second, but realized he had no choice. He couldn't possibly carry her down the tree. If he just dropped her straight down, her body would miss the branches of the tree. She'd be okay—they'd catch her.

Just before he let go of the love of his life, an unexpected thought crept into his brain: *Linda will be pissed at me when she wakes up. Dressed in this sexy little negligee, she'll be horrified when she finds out that our neighbors saw her this way.*

Amidst tears that he wasn't sure were from the smoke or from sheer anguish, he allowed his arms to go slack and watched her body fall in slow motion to the waiting arms below.

They caught her and all four went crashing to the ground—Linda safely on top, head cradled by one of the men.

John crawled out onto the window ledge and threw himself toward the outreaching branch. Then he swung from limb to limb until finally tumbling to the ground from about ten feet up.

He crawled over to his Linda, who was surrounded by their neighbors. He could hear sirens approaching. John pushed several people out of the way until he finally reached her side.

John snuggled his face up against hers and then felt a gentle hand on his shoulder. He thought—hoped—for a second that it was her hand, but it was just one of the catchers.

He looked up from Linda and stared into the eyes of his friend.

The man's head shaking, eyes saying it all, John didn't need to hear his words. But he was forced to hear them anyway; those words that he'd never imagined he would hear in the short life he had left.

"She's gone, John."

CHAPTER 25

Carl handed a sheet of paper to his assistant, Alex. "I want you to access the Inova Alexandria Hospital records and check on the condition of this man."

Alex studied it for a second and then asked, "Is he one of ours?"

"No, he's not."

"Is he currently an in-patient?"

"As far as I know, yes. Why?"

Alex wrote a couple of notes on the paper and then looked up. "It's just a lot quicker if we know which database of records to hack into. I'll get on it—should only take a few minutes."

Carl nodded. "Shut the door behind you."

He swiveled his chair around and gazed out the window at the Fort Meade landscape. Yes, all had gone well last night. All according to plan. He'd watched the news this morning and the explosion was featured as just a secondary story on the local news channel. Just another gas explosion. They happened so regularly now throughout American neighborhoods that most people just yawned and took another sip of their coffee.

The initial investigation by the Washington fire marshal declared it a gas leak—all gas lines to the street were shut off as a precaution, and the site was still being surveyed. But there wasn't much left to survey—Carl had seen the news footage. The destruction was so complete that it was hard to believe a house once stood there. After the initial explosion which took out the kitchen and the garage, the fire had moved rapidly throughout the rest of the main floor and up to the second floor. Within half an hour, the house had basically disappeared.

Too bad about the Fletcher woman, but a message had to be sent. Carl had actually wished John Fletcher had been successful in saving his wife—she didn't have to die to get John's attention. The explosion, fire, and fear of losing her would have been enough to scare him—but in hindsight maybe this was better anyway. Her death would hit him much harder and should serve to convince him to keep his mouth shut.

Carl knew that Fletcher was just a few years away from collecting a pension, so his job would be important to him—especially now with him being all alone.

That job would be his entire life from now on. And by now Fletcher must be well aware of the influence that the NSA had on his employer, the NTSB—enough influence that Carl had been able to insert himself into the rollercoaster investigation and force Fletcher's boss to agree to the phony accident report that Fletcher had been ordered to sign.

Surely Fletcher would be thinking of those things as he mourned his wife—and wondering to himself also if the gas leak was truly an accident. That's exactly what Carl wanted him to wonder. He wanted there to be some shadow of a doubt in his mind, enough to make him one very careful man.

Carl spun around in his chair at the sound of knuckles rapping on his door. "Come in."

Alex came bounding in with several sheets of paper. "I have what you want."

"Boy, you guys are fast! Okay, tell me what I need to know."

Alex looked at his notes. "This John…Fletcher, yes, he was admitted last night for smoke inhalation and a few cuts and bruises. He also needed to be sedated due to shock. Sounds like he's coming around now, lungs are still being monitored closely. One was in danger of collapsing, but on the mend. Some bad headaches reported on his chart, too, but those are from the brain tumor…"

"What? Hold on—go back! Brain tumor?"

Alex shuffled his pages and held one up for Carl to see. "Yes, this is his medical summary from radiation treatments he's been having at the hospital. Prognosis terminal—looks like he has about twelve months left."

Carl rubbed his temples with both hands. "Leave those records with me. That'll be all, Alex. Thanks."

Once again, Carl swiveled his chair towards the window. This was how he relaxed, looking out over the vast terrain that surrounded Fort Meade. He felt protected here; powerful, immune from the world. He decided to try to take his mind off the news he'd just heard. Got up, walked over to his wall safe and took out a file. He sat back down in front of the window and opened the folder. It was quite thick, containing about six inches of documents.

He pulled one item out of a sleeve pocket. It was a map of Canada. Carl scanned the little black dots marked for various locations on the map.

Then he sighed, laid the folder on his lap and gazed out the window again. Not even this file could distract him from what he'd just learned.

John Fletcher was dying. He was a man with nothing to lose and nothing to gain.

*****

Impatiently, she asked, "Where do I sign?"

Dwayne Feinstein opened up the document.

"All the signature pages are marked with paper clips. And I used pretty pink ones just for you."

Shelby looked up at him and scowled. "Just give me a pen so I can get the hell out of here. There's a stink in this office."

Dwayne handed her his gold Cartier pen. "Now, no need to get snarly, Ms. Sutcliffe…actually, do you mind if I call you 'Shelly?'"

She tapped the pen hard on the desk. Dwayne winced.

"I minded it the last time and I mind it just as much now! My name is 'Shelby!' Do you think you'll be able to get that right in court? I don't think the jury will find you too credible when you can't even get the name straight for your only witness!"

She began flipping the pages to each of the pretty pink paperclips and signed one page after another until she was done. She didn't even bother reading what she was signing.

Then she unceremoniously tossed the expensive pen onto the desk. "Are we done?"

"Yes, for now. There will be a deposition of course. I'll let you know about that and prepare you for it, coach you a bit on what to say, things like that."

"We already agreed upon what I would say."

Dwayne smiled. "Yes, we did. I'm glad your memory became clearer. It's not unusual for memories to be confused right after a traumatic experience—it usually takes a few days for the accurate memories to show up. So, to be clear, you will testify that your lap bar became disengaged at the moment the train impacted with the edge of the broken track. Correct?"

Shelby lowered her eyes. "Yes. That's what I'll say."

Dwayne stood up and walked to the door. He opened it and ushered Shelby out into the hall. "We're all good, then. My coaching of you will just concentrate on how you will testify, what words you choose to use. It'll all go smoothly and you'll be a rich woman after this is all over."

Shelby nodded, turned on her heel and headed for the elevator.

The lawyer called after her. "Goodbye, Shelly."

*****

Nate picked up his phone and punched in her number.

"Hi, Nate. It's done."

"Good. Did he buy your sincerity?"

"Well, I can't be nice to that man no matter how hard I try. He can't even get my name right. So I didn't play it too eagerly—that would have been phony and he might have seen through me, suspected that something was up. I just said that I could live with testifying the way they want me to—that my memory was probably wrong. But I needed him to see that I still disdain him. I think he would expect that."

"Yeah, makes sense, especially considering how unpleasant your first meeting was. Shelby, at least this buys you time. Today was the deadline from that guy who visited you in the café. So, now you won't have to worry about bumping into him in some dark alley."

"Yes, I feel relieved. And it does just buy time. This case won't go to court for quite a while yet, so I can still drop off the Action in plenty of time. Maybe we can figure out some of this puzzle before then."

"That's the plan. Oh and, as we discussed, I've arranged for my graphic designer to pay you a visit tonight after you get home from work. His name is Paul Fortier. A brilliant artist, especially with sketching images of people. He used to be a police sketch artist until we lured him away to the fun side. He does all our advertising images."

"Okay, I'll wrack my brain to get the best recollection of that guy. I hope I do a good job for Paul."

"You'll be fine. I'm getting him to do a sketch for me this afternoon, based on the guy I remember seeing at Adventureland. I haven't told him your guy and my guy may be the same person—I don't want him influenced. Then, after those sketches are done, we'll compare them."

There was silence at the other end.

"Shelby? Are you still there?"

"Yes, yes, I'm here. Sorry, I was just thinking about something. Listen, Nate, could I interest you in dinner Sunday night? My place? I'm a great cook!"

It was Nate's turn to be silent. But just for a second or two. He blurted out, "You bet! I'll bring the wine. Email me your address."

"I sure will. See you around seven o'clock Sunday night, then. And bring a Chianti, because we're having pasta!"

Nate clicked off and smiled. Dinner with Shelby would be nice—he was glad she'd asked. He caught himself the last couple of nights wondering what it would be like to spend some alone time with her. Well, now he'd find out.

He picked up his phone again and punched in an extension. "Hi Ron, grab Tom and come down to my office."

Nate put the phone back in the cradle, walked over to his side stand and poured a cup of black coffee. Taking a sip, he pondered how much they had to do and whether or not their efforts would result in anything tangible.

His door opened and in walked his two friends. "Pour yourself some coffee, guys, and take a seat." They both passed on the coffee.

Nate sat down on the couch and put his feet up on the coffee table. "We have a lot to do, guys, and we're running out of time."

Tom crossed his legs and raised his hand in the air. "I, for one, think we should march into the NTSB office and demand that the investigation be reopened. Tell them what we found down in Key West and how someone gave us a tip-off."

Nate shook his head. "Not yet, Tom. We have a few things to do first—but I don't disagree with your idea. We just need more before we do that.

"In fact, I'll start with you. I want you to get the passenger list for everyone who died on that rollercoaster. Photos, bios, the full Monty. Use whatever resources we have, but if you have to go out and hire some specialists, you have my green light to do that. Do whatever it takes—we want to know all there is to know about those poor souls, what they did, what they didn't do, what messes they were involved in, scandals. Everything."

"Okay, hopefully there will be some answers in what we can dig up. As Ron said the other day, this whole thing does smell of what he calls a 'diversion murder.' If one particular person was meant to die on that coaster, something is going to stand out."

"Yes. We might get lucky." Nate then pointed at Ron. "Ron, with your systems engineering expertise, I'm hoping you'll be able to hack into NFL records and get the complete team roster, including backup players and 'taxi squad' sitters. Hell, even trainers, coaches—everyone associated with the San Francisco 49ers in their Super Bowl win back in 1994. Anyone who was an active member of the team in any capacity was probably entitled to a ring. So—we're talking possibly dozens of men here."

"That should be easy. I'll get right on it."

"Photos, too—but also do a database search on all those names to track down where they are today, along with current photos of them if there are any out there on the Internet. The guy I saw at Adventureland wore that Super Bowl ring, and it sounds like the man who accosted Shelby at the café was wearing one, too. I'm ninety-nine percent certain it's the same man."

Nate stood up. The meeting was over and his friends took the hint.

As they were leaving, Nate said, "Tom, tell Paul Fortier that I'm ready for him. He can sketch me a killer now."

*****

Shelby walked into the hospital cafeteria. She planned to have a quick lunch before her shift started. She looked at her watch—plenty of time actually; two hours to kill before her first surgery.

She thought about going to the Sunshine Café for lunch, but after the encounter she'd had with that strange man she was still a bit reluctant to go back there. Even though everything should be okay now. She'd signed on to the Class

Action, so his threat had achieved what he'd wanted it to achieve. She was looking forward to seeing what Nate's sketch artist would come up with for each of them. And…she was definitely looking forward to dinner with Nate on Sunday night. She hadn't cooked dinner for a man in at least a decade, so she figured her heart must be telling her that Nate was pretty special.

Shelby grabbed a tray, helped herself to a ham sandwich and a tomato juice, and then walked over to an empty table. She was just about to sit down when she noticed one of her nursing friends, Carol, sitting all by herself. She moved over to her table. "Carol, penny for your thoughts?"

Carol looked up. "Oh, Shelby, sorry, I'm a bit distracted and I've worked a double shift, too. Time for a nap, I think!"

Shelby sat down. "How are things down there in Emergency?"

"Oh, hectic as usual. Sometimes I wonder how long I can keep up the pace. The hours are far too long and these double-shifts every two weeks are killers. How about you up there in Surgery?"

"Lots going on—quite a few heart operations. And we lost a little boy a few days ago. It was horrible. I haven't been sleeping well at all since that happened."

Carol winced. "That's tough when it's a child. They have their whole lives ahead of them. I had a real tough one to deal with last night, too. Not a child, but a sweet man who lost his wife in a house fire. Did you hear on the news about that gas explosion?"

"No, I didn't hear about that. What happened?"

"It was across the river in Washington—Georgetown, to be exact. They say that it was a gas leak. The poor man—he's in his sixties—tried to save his wife. They'd been together forty years. He climbed a tree, jumped through the window, and then dropped his wife out the window down to some neighbors. But…it was too late. We treated him for smoke inhalation—it was pretty bad, but thank God he's coming along better today."

Shelby shook her head. "That's so sad—together forty years."

"Yeah, breaks your heart, doesn't it? And he's such a sweet guy—he was talking to me about his wife. He absolutely adored her, I could tell. And…you know, he's a dead ringer for Cary Grant. Can't believe how close the resemblance is. Even sounds like him!"

Shelby perked up at that. "Cary Grant? Carol, what's his name?"

"Uh…Fletcher. John Fletcher."

Shelby jumped up from her seat. "What room is he in?!"

CHAPTER 26

John turned his head to the side and watched the nurse change the bandage on his left shoulder. It had taken twenty stitches to get it sewn up tight. John remembered now how he did it. That very last branch he'd smashed into on his way down the tree. It had a sharp knot that tore into him as he dropped to the ground.

It didn't hurt. Except when they stitched him up. The intern in Emergency had offered to freeze the shoulder, but John refused. He just gritted his teeth and sucked it up. He wanted to feel the pain and actually wished it had hurt more than it did. He wanted it to hurt; right now he wanted everything to hurt.

There had been a stream of visitors to his room all day. Some reporters, too; after the fifth one, he asked the nurses to chase them away if any more came up to his floor. There was nothing he could tell them anyway. He didn't know anything. The nurses were great, especially Carol, the primary nurse who had supervised his care ever since he'd been checked in.

John closed his eyes. He pictured Linda with her head poking out of the upper window, calling out to him—panicked about the smell of gas. Then the explosion. And when he got to his feet, one side of the house and the garage were gone, and the portion of the main floor that was left was in flames.

He opened his eyes and eased himself up into a sitting position. The nursing assistant saw him struggling and rushed over to help him. She propped up two pillows behind his neck and upper back. "Better now?"

John forced a smile. "Yes, thanks."

"Be careful, Mr. Fletcher. Your lungs have improved, but we need to still be careful."

"When will I be out of here?"

"Looks like tomorrow—but I'll check with Carol when she gets back from lunch. We'll let you know for sure later on. You're probably anxious to get home."

John looked down at his lap. "I don't have a home anymore."

The nursing assistant put her hand up to her mouth and gasped. "Oh, I'm so sorry. It was just an expression. I didn't intend to sound so insensitive."

John forced another smile. "It's okay, dear. Don't worry about it. I know you didn't mean to say it like that."

He pulled another pillow off the side chair and stuffed it behind his head.

What happened?

A fire department official told him this morning that they suspected there had been some kind of gas leak in the kitchen, from the gas stove. But the destruction was so complete that there would be no way of determining that for sure, or how the leak was caused. There was nothing left to look at.

They'd given him some calming drugs last night and again this morning. He was apparently quite agitated when they brought him in, not speaking or thinking clearly. He knew Linda was dead, but that's pretty much all he'd been aware of last night.

It was only this morning that he remembered what she was calling out to him from the upper window. He knew she'd been concerned about something, but for the life of him he couldn't remember what it was until this morning. She had smelled gas. That's what she yelled out to him.

John closed his eyes again. Thoughts were coming into his head faster now—the medication had worn off and things weren't such a blur.

What was I doing outside?

Then he lurched up as the memory came to him. The car alarm! Someone had vandalized his Lexus! He had been on his way upstairs to join Linda in bed, when the alarm sounded. That's why he was outside.

He shook his head and concentrated harder. He retraced his steps in his mind—seeing the damaged car, looking around in all directions...there was another car!

A black one...a Ford...Explorer. It was making a U-turn down the street and drove away in the opposite direction. John concentrated on the image of the car...a license plate. It was: W23865.

John reached over and pressed the call button for the nurses' station. In less than a minute, she was standing beside him, concern in her eyes.

"Don't worry. I'm okay. I just wanted to know if that police officer who was here before is still out there in the hall. I'm more alert now—I'd like to talk to him again."

"Yes, he's down in the coffee lounge. I'll go and get him for you." She rushed out of the room.

Within minutes, the detective was sitting in the chair beside the bed, with his iPad on his lap, waiting patiently for John to tell him what he recalled.

John took a deep breath, and then exhaled slowly. "My car was vandalized. That's why I was outside. With the destruction of the house, no one has probably noticed yet that my sunroof and front windshield were smashed. The car alarm went off and I went outside. Discovered the damage and saw a car driving off. It was a black Ford Explorer. And I remember the license plate number."

The officer worked his fingers over the iPad. "Give me a second while I pull up the vehicle registration site." He fiddled with it a bit, sighed, and fiddled again. "God, this site is always so slow." He waited for a second, then said, "Okay, I have it. Give me the plate number."

"W23865."

The officer looked up at him, a curious expression on his face. "Are you sure there's a 'W' as a prefix?"

"Yes. Absolutely sure."

The officer turned off his iPad and stood up. "I'm sorry, Mr. Fletcher. There's nothing I can do to help with that. I'm sure the vehicle was just in the neighborhood anyway. You didn't actually see anyone hitting your car."

John's mouth hung open in shock. As the officer began walking to the door, John found his tongue.

"What? I just gave you a license number from the plate of the car that was there seconds before the explosion! Why wouldn't that be relevant? And why didn't you complete the check on it? It was at your fingertips!"

The detective turned and faced him. "Mr. Fletcher, that wouldn't have helped. We can't access those types of license plate numbers. We're blocked. The 'W' indicates that it's a military car—army, to be precise, probably out of the closest army base at Fort Meade. That's out of our jurisdiction."

With that, the officer left. John was simply astonished. Army! And Fort Meade rang a bell in his head. It was in Maryland and only about a half hour drive north of Washington.

Things were swirling around in his head. He'd just lost his wife and now he was alone. He had a possible witness to what happened, or maybe even a possible perpetrator, and the police's hands were tied.

And John knew firsthand about 'jurisdiction.' The officer said the police had no jurisdiction with the military. John didn't have jurisdiction either in that rollercoaster accident; but that didn't matter—he was forced to investigate by the NSA for whatever goddamn reason.

John suddenly felt the blood rush to his head. In a flash, it hit him.

The NSA! They're based in Fort Meade, too, side by side with the Army installation!

CHAPTER 27

Shelby rushed down the hall to the room number Carol had given to her. She knocked on the door and then peeked her head around the corner.

She recognized him right away—even with his head in his hands. He was sobbing, his shoulders shaking. For a second, she thought of turning around and leaving, but instead she walked slowly over to the bed and sat on the edge. Even though she worked in a different department, she was still a nurse and may be able to be of some comfort to this poor man.

Softly, she said, "John?" He pulled his hands away from his face and for an instant looked embarrassed to be caught crying. "It's okay, John. Do you remember me? Shelby Sutcliffe?"

He nodded and rubbed a sleeve of his hospital gown across his eyes.

"Hello, Shelby." He looked her up and down. "You're a nurse here. I didn't know that."

"Yes, I work in surgery. Can I get you anything while I'm here?"

"No, I'm fine—just a bit sentimental right now."

Shelby reached over to him and squeezed his shoulder. "I'm so sorry to hear about your loss. Your nurse, Carol, told me you were here. I wanted to just pop by and tell you how sorry I was to hear. You and your wife were together a long time—it must be so hard for you."

She saw a fresh tear run down his right cheek. "It is—to lose her that way is the hardest part, though. Knowing she was scared and basically suffocating to death. I...didn't get there...in time. I tried...but I wasn't fast enough."

Shelby squeezed his shoulder again. "She knows that, John."

"I was the one who was supposed to go first."

"There are no rules for these things, John. Sometimes fate intervenes."

He grimaced. "No, there *was* a rule for this one, Shelby. I have a brain tumor—about a year left to live. Maybe a wee bit more, but that's about it. I was worried about leaving her behind, and now I'm the one left behind. Why wasn't it me? Linda still had a long life ahead of her."

Shelby was at a loss for words. What could she possibly say? It was just so incredibly sad. He lost his wife in a horrible explosion and fire, when all the while they had both been preparing for *his* death.

She spoke in almost a whisper. "Are you sure I can't get you anything before I go?"

He looked up at her and Shelby was surprised by what she saw in his Cary Grant eyes. They were still glistening a bit from the tears, but they now had a fixation to them—a steely determination.

John returned the whisper. "Tell me, honestly. Have you signed on to that Class Action lawsuit yet?"

She felt he was someone she could trust—sensed that when she'd first met him, when he seemed almost ashamed that his report said the opposite of what Shelby knew happened on that rollercoaster. She knew she could tell him the truth and, at that moment, after what he'd gone through, she felt he deserved that more than anything.

"I did, John. It's a long story, but I did it to buy time. Some strange things have been going on and someone threatened me. A scary guy just came up to me one day, sat down, and told me that I had to testify that the lap bars disengaged at the point of impact. I intend to eventually drop off the lawsuit—I'm working with the executives at Flying Machines to try to get to the bottom of this. They've had some scares themselves."

John reached out and grabbed onto her hand, squeezing gently. "I want to help. I'm sorry I stonewalled you when you came to see me. I knew that what you were telling me was correct. Those lap bars opened and they shouldn't have—and that wasn't caused by the impact. I also know that the track was melted, that it didn't snap. But, at that time, I was being a realist. I was forced to sign a phony report. I wanted to keep my job, benefits and life insurance intact until I died. I needed Linda to be looked after."

Shelby squeezed his hand too. "I understand."

"I don't know if you do. You see, now I'm not motivated anymore. I have nothing now. Nothing to live for; nothing and no one to care about. But I feel that I have to do the right thing—I've looked the other way before, but I can't this time."

He reached out with his other hand and squeezed both of hers. "Introduce me to your friends at Flying Machines. I want to join you folks."

Shelby felt her heart soar. "John, that's wonderful. I'll let them know."

John Fletcher nodded. "It's not so wonderful, Shelby. You see, now I want revenge too."

CHAPTER 28

Carl Masterson was staring at his computer. Not quite believing the latest assessments that had just been sent to him.

Opinions and predictions about the most dangerous national security crisis that the United States of America had ever faced.

No, it wasn't terrorism. And no, it wasn't Russia or China.

It was water. The lack of it.

A couple of years ago it was estimated that a full half of the world's population would be facing severe water shortages by the year 2050. That assessment had now been accelerated to the year 2025. The latest assessments were coming from not just scientists and engineers within the United States, but also from the World Health Organization. It wasn't science fiction, it was real.

And it didn't take a rocket scientist to understand why. The damn world's population tripled in the twentieth century and it was expected to increase by another fifty percent in the next fifty years. And the use and abuse of renewable water had grown six-fold. And there wasn't any more fresh water in the world today than there was a million years ago. Some would be surprised to know that water just couldn't be replaced.

India, one of the most populous countries in the world, was predicting now that their groundwater supplies in major sections of the country would be completely gone in about five years.

Several "think tanks" around the globe had already predicted that there would be 'water wars' in the not too distant future. In essence, water was 'blue gold,' very precious, and nothing could survive or thrive without it. Just like oil had been the motivation for numerous wars, now the world's attention would turn to water. It would be the source of conflict at a scale that the world had never seen before. Global in nature—the infamous two World Wars would pale in comparison.

Well, the United States of America was still the world's superpower, Carl thought. If anything, this crisis added credence to the investment in the military that the country had made over the last century. *We can basically take what we want if push comes to shove.*

The demands for water had not only increased due to world population growth, but also due to alternative forms of energy such as nuclear power. Fresh water was needed to cool the reactors and nuclear power was now a prominent energy source around the world. The ripple effect from not being able to cool reactors would be monumental. Not just loss of power for the cities of the world, but the catastrophic effect of meltdowns. The world had already seen three of these meltdowns—and a lack of water would guarantee a meltdown epidemic.

Aside from the effects of climate change, there was an incredible wastage of water from irrigation practices. Approximately sixty percent of water withdrawals were for irrigation—but in arid regions this rose to ninety percent. On top of that, industry drew down twenty percent for their purposes, households used ten percent, and four percent just evaporated away and got dropped somewhere else. And not always where it was most needed.

America's two most populous states, California and Texas, had suffered through crippling droughts in the last several years, and there was no end in sight. Snowpacks in California's Sierra Nevada, the source for the state's greatest mountain reservoir, stood at only thirty percent of normal. Disastrous. And both of these states were usually abundant agricultural producers; now that was in jeopardy too. The water requirements were huge for agriculture—growing just one kilogram of potatoes required one hundred liters of water, but that paled in comparison to the thirteen thousand liters needed for just one kilogram of beef.

The water shortage could cause Americans to literally starve to death, if they didn't parch to death first. And the wildfires in the southern states—it was so dry there that these monsters popped up with just the tiniest spark. Fresh water was needed to fight these—such a waste considering that the United States was desperate for water just to sustain life itself.

Carl scanned a list of cities and towns at imminent risk in America; there were about five hundred in total. Ones that were designated as being in danger of running out of fresh water within two years or less. He knew that this list would increase in size—he got these updates every week, and twenty more had been added since last week's update.

Despite the inconveniences associated with water conservation, the average American still didn't realize how serious the situation was. They still watered their lawns, expected golf courses to be emerald green, and fully anticipated that their utility bills would come down. And complained when they didn't. They were living in a dream world.

The ones who really knew how serious it was were the farmers. They were fully aware that the end of the world was fast approaching—it was only logical. If countries couldn't feed themselves, then…

Climate change was the wild card. Despite the world population explosion and the increases in demand for water to nurture all the new energy and industrial sources that the world had ushered in, there was this 'thing' going on with the climate. Glaciers in massive retreat, rainfall that wasn't falling in the areas that were usually dependable. Heatwaves that were breaking records, causing more need for water and energy, while worsening the drought situation at the same time. Let alone the massive forest and grass fires caused by the heatwaves.

The world was in crisis. But the United States didn't have to join the world in this crisis. The country was strong and perfectly capable of taking what it needed. It just had to make it look like it was being done for other reasons; or that something horrible drove them to do it for honorable reasons. A 'false flag.'

Carl turned off his computer. He remembered back to when Operation Backwash was first conceived. It was way ahead of its time back then, and progressive in its thinking. And now things were so serious that it had to be put into action. Carl had no doubts about that and neither did the people who signed his paycheck.

He turned his thoughts back to John Fletcher; a 'loose end' that he hadn't anticipated. Fletcher was a dead man walking. Such a man would not experience fear. And this was what was worrying Carl. A man without fear was a dangerous man indeed.

CHAPTER 29

Tom Foster was looking over the list in his hand as he walked into Nate's office. "Okay, buddy, we have it. The list of riders on the rollercoaster along with their brief bios. Wanna go over it together?"

"Great news, Tom! But no, I'll study it on my own—I'm in a bit of a hurry. Have to finish up here and then get home to change—I have a date tonight."

Tom grinned at him. "I'm glad to hear that you're getting out again. Anyone I know?"

Nate laughed. "A gentleman never tells, Tom. And if I told you, you'd be hounding me for details—and as I said, a gentleman never tells!"

"Okay, okay Mr. Privacy. I'll respect that. But…if you do hitch up with this mystery woman one day, I expect to the 'best man.'"

"Did you ever have any doubts? But—you were the best man at my first marriage and look how that turned out. Maybe you're a bad omen!"

Tom laughed. "Not fair! No, I think you can blame yourself for that one. I think Stephanie's low-cut blouses blinded your judgment!"

"Could be. Hey, sit down for a second—a couple questions for you."

Tom walked over to the living room area of Nate's office and took his usual seat. "What's wrong with this picture? It's a beautiful Sunday and you and I are here in the office working."

Nate stretched out on the couch. "I know, I know—we must be mad."

"So, what are these burning questions you have for me, Nate old buddy?"

"Well, I was looking through the maintenance logs for the Black Mamba and I noticed that two days before the accident your team did the final mechanical inspections on the train and the track. Did you notice anything unusual at all?"

"No—well, not that was reported to me anyway. I never personally do those inspections—I just oversee, as you know. All my hands-on work is done in the factory prior to the erection. But my team was all over the track and the train that day, and no one reported anything unusual."

"So, you weren't out at the site that day?"

"Sure, I was there—but my team were the ones up high. As you know, heights aren't my thing anyway."

"Yeah, I know that now."

Tom laughed. "Yeah, my secret's out. But, at my level, I think you pay me too much to be crawling around scaffolding and hanging from trestles anyway. We have 'people' for that. But, speaking of 'people,' there is something I found out that I need to tell you about. It may be nothing but it's just one more strange thing in this whole affair."

Nate stiffened. "Uh-oh, I'm afraid to hear this."

"As I said—may be nothing. But one of our maintenance crew, in fact one of the guys who was up in a sling for that final inspection, took vacation right after the accident. But—he never came back. There's no sign of him. We've tried to reach him with no success. I reported him missing to the police this morning—it's just been too long now to assume that he went on a simple little bender."

Nate wrung his hands together. "What's his name? Have I met him?"

"Bill Shanahan. No, I don't think you've met him. He's an engineer we hired out of Cal Tech. A good guy, too—this seems out of character for him. Which worries me—you'll recall that we presumed that there had to be an 'inside man' for this. If indeed Thermate was painted onto the underside of the track and the remote radio frequency for the lap bars was given out to someone, there had to be someone either at our end or at Adventureland who did those things."

Nate nodded, pausing for a few seconds before answering. "Okay, this may be good news and bad news. If he is the one and we can find him, we can get some answers—or at least the police can. If Bill is a witness to or a participant in sabotage, then that will clear us and maybe lead to who planned this and why. But if we can't find him, it's another dead end that we can't prove."

"Yes. I'll keep on top of it. The police will be searching his home today—promised they'd get back to me."

"Okay, let me know as soon as you hear anything." Nate stood. "Now, it's time for me to go get ready for my date! Don't ask..."

*****

Tom Foster got the usual ecstatic greeting from his two kids when he came in the front door of his expensive home in the ritzy Del Mar area of Alexandria. Joey was five and Katy was four. Darling kids—he loved them dearly. Sophie called out to him from the kitchen. "Hi, sweetie! Dinner will be ready in about an hour."

Tom bounded into the kitchen and gave her a big wet kiss on the back of her neck. "What are we having tonight?"

"Well, it is Sunday, you know. The day you're not supposed to be working! But...despite my anger about that, I'm making our traditional roast beef and

Yorkshire. Okay? Happy?"

Tom smiled and kissed her on the lips this time. "You bet! I've just got a few things to do—an hour will be plenty of time for me to get them done. Then I'm all yours for the rest of the night."

Sophie kissed him back. "I'll hold you to that!"

Tom turned and headed back down the hall. "I'll just be in my study, hon."

He headed into his office and closed the door. Took off his suit jacket and threw it over the stool. Then he poured himself a tall scotch and stretched out on the sofa. Tom took a long sip of the burning liquid, winced at the sting, and then sighed.

And he started thinking.

Things were such a mess—his life was a mess, and with each day it seemed to be spinning more out of control.

He knew that the police would never find Bill Shanahan. Bill was the convenient 'patsy,' and the powers at work had made sure that Bill would never be found again. He would simply be labeled as a 'missing person.' No proof that he had done anything wrong, and no proof that he hadn't. He was just like the wreckage of the Black Mamba that was dumped in the Caribbean. If you can't find it you can't prove anything, either way.

When Tom had chosen Bill Shanahan to be the patsy, it was merely a case of "eeny, meeny, miney, moe." There was nothing bad about Bill, nothing particularly special about him. He was chosen simply to draw attention away from Tom. On that day of the final inspection, two days before the accident, Bill hadn't even been there. In fact, Tom was the only one up there hanging from a sling, at that spot, on that day. He'd doctored the records to make it look as if Bill and a team of two other engineers had done the inspection.

Those two other engineers had indeed been there, but they were doing work in the mechanical room—they hadn't been up underneath the track. And no one yet had dug any deeper. Now, with Bill gone, they probably wouldn't. The records showed that he was there and now he was gone. The Flying Machines executives would assume that Bill was the 'inside man,' but of course wouldn't be able to prove a damn thing—because he was probably at the bottom of the Potomac.

Tom wasn't afraid of heights—he loved heights. But he needed everyone to think that he was terrified of being up high. That was all an act—to take him off the list. And now with Bill as the patsy, he was reasonably confident that no one would suspect him.

And the list of riders on the doomed rollercoaster that he'd just given to Nate today did indeed contain all of the names—but there was one name that was deliberately misspelled. And, as a result, had a different bio. That other person was indeed dead, too, but from a heart attack a couple of months ago, not from a rollercoaster accident. So the bio would be for the dead man, but the list would indicate he died on the coaster, not from a heart attack. Tom couldn't invent a totally different name—it had to be similar in case anyone did any checking. If the spelling mistake was discovered, it would simply be written off as just a spelling mistake. It was a difficult name, after all, and an easy mistake to make.

Shelby was still the wild card. No one was supposed to survive that day— the main reason why Tom had faked the vertigo attack. He was hoping that Nate would not climb up the superstructure by himself. And that Shelby would eventually tire and tumble to her death.

But, true to his friend's hero nature, he went anyway. Shelby's assertions about the lap bars disengaging before the impact had opened up a can of worms. If she hadn't survived, that wreckage could have been dumped in the ocean without anyone being able to testify that something went wrong with the lap bars. Now, if she managed to get people to listen to her, that would certainly cast suspicion on the entire accident.

And the way she went stomping into John Fletcher's office had caused poor John to have a moment of conscience—resulting in the man's late wife making an anonymous phone call to Tom himself.

Tom had no choice but to disclose that anonymous tip to his partners—all phone calls at Flying Machines Inc., as with a lot of companies, are recorded for customer service reasons. A warning comes over the phone to the caller just before they speak, advising about the recording. Fairly common practice now.

So, Tom was put in a tough position, and had been forced to share the phone tip with his partners. If he hadn't, they would have found out anyway when the recordings were listened to in the tech department, and Tom would have had some serious questions to answer.

And while his partners had no idea it was Fletcher's wife who gave the tip, Tom knew. His contact at the NSA had told him who it was.

His 'contact'—a man whose name he still didn't know. Tom had met him, but still had no idea who he was, except that he was from the shadowy NSA. And while it sounded like the man who Nate had seen and whom Shelby had met were one and the same person—what those two didn't know was that their descriptions of him sounded bang-on with the guy who Tom had met, too.

The man had simply slid into the booth that Tom was sitting in at a restaurant three months ago. It was shortly after the announcement had been made about the inaugural ride of the Black Mamba, and the list made public of the lucky Coaster Crazies members who were chosen for the honor of the first ride.

The NSA man said very little at first. He just opened his laptop, made a few keystrokes, and then turned it around so Tom could see it. He recognized what he saw right away.

All Tom said was, "What do you want?"

And he was told.

The next step for Tom was to visit an abandoned warehouse in the middle of the night to meet with a shadowy figure—someone else without a name—who demonstrated to him the fine art of applying military grade Thermate-3 to steel structures. It was pretty simple—just had to be applied with a brush to a specified thickness, and the stuff's color was even disguised to blend in with the color of the steel track. They'd thought of everything. Then he learned how to apply the tiny magnesium fuses, and was given the substance that would have to be used to adhere them.

So, after that late night meeting, he had his supplies. A container of Thermate, a brush, four magnesium fuses, and adhesive.

He was also given a remote control unit, which he had to program with the radio receivers contained in the fuses, as well as configure the radio frequency to be exactly in line with the frequency used for the unlocking of the lap bars. Then he had to meet the spook again and give him back the programmed remote.

Yes, his friend and former Navy Seal, Ron Collens, had figured the whole scenario out perfectly. The clever bastard. He'd guessed it right.

And even though Tom was the 'inside man,' that still didn't stop his contact at the NSA from arranging to scare the shit out of all three of them down in Key West. The prick didn't care that Tom was on that helicopter, too.

Yes, Tom was the 'inside man.' The reluctant 'inside man.' He still had no idea what this was all about—had been given no reason at all as to why one particular rider on that rollercoaster had to die that day, and everyone else with him. Tom didn't know anything beyond what his singular job was.

Ron had been right on that point, too. This had been a 'diversion murder.' A grizzly mass murder to cover up the murder of one.

Tom was now an accessory to a mass murder.

But he had decided three months ago that that was better than having his secret double life exposed. And he still felt that way. What his wife, children, extended family and friends thought of him was paramount. In fact, if they found out what he was, he knew he would simply kill himself. There could be no other choice.

He had been a cursed male his entire life. He hated the way he was, had tried to fight it, but always to no avail. He was simply...cursed. A piece of human garbage who would repulse everyone if they knew what he really was.

The NSA spook had calmly and softly explained to him that they were capable of tapping into every single Internet entry, transaction, communication, and download. Nothing was sacred...or secret. And neither were Tom's clandestine activities.

The international child porn ring that Tom was an active member of had been discovered a decade ago, and watched ever since. The NSA had no inclination to bust the ring—instead they chose to use it for national security purposes. Most of the two thousand members were well-placed, well-heeled, and, well...useful as hell. Instead of busting the network, the NSA was better served in blackmailing the members where it served their purpose.

And Tom apparently served their purpose right now.

He wasn't paid a cent for what he did—all he was promised was secrecy. His double life would remain his to enjoy.

But, the problem was, Tom didn't enjoy it anymore. His affliction had become more of a curse than he ever imagined it would. Now it was responsible for the deaths of twenty-five innocent people. No, make that twenty-six including Bill Shanahan.

It was bad enough that Tom was sick in the head.

Now he was a killer, too.

CHAPTER 30

He tried not to think of it as a 'date'—focusing on that just made him nervous. It had been more than a decade since he'd been on one, and there he was starting over again. There with a brand new woman and one that he happened to be very attracted to. Which made him even more nervous.

And they'd met in a rather unconventional way, to say the least—not many couples could boast that they'd met hanging off the side of a rollercoaster. That intense experience did make their connection unique. Even if nothing happened between them, they would always remember that and would always be special in each other's hearts.

Nate had saved her life and she had put her life in his hands.

He was sitting at the dining room table. A scented candle was burning and flickering in a gold leafed wine glass that Shelby told him she'd brought back from the island of Murano. It was the most beautiful wine glass he'd ever seen. She said she'd never even had one sip out of it yet—she liked it better as a candle holder because the flames were enhanced so much by the deep red of the glass interspersed with pure gold swirls. He had to agree—it made a great candleholder.

Dinner had been wonderful. She made a perfect veal parmigiana with a side plate of spaghetti and chicken meatballs. The sauces on each dish were just perfect, enhanced by the Chianti Brolio that Nate had brought.

Nate leaned his head to the side and watched her working in the kitchen. She was putting the final touches on their tiramisu dessert—he loved tiramisu. How had she known? Woman's intuition? Or did he just look like a tiramisu kind of guy?

She looked so adorable—humming away in the kitchen, her cute little butt moving in time with the jazz music that was playing softly on the stereo. She was wearing bright white shorts and a yellow halter-top. It was indeed a hot night, so Nate assumed she just wanted to be comfortable. But as a man, he kinda figured she was also dressed in that cute casual way just for him. And he loved it.

Shelby was nicely tanned, which stood out in stunning fashion against the bright clothes she was wearing. She was easy on the eyes, especially with that beautiful blonde hair that flowed down over her shoulders. The sparkling blue eyes finished off the image.

They'd spent dinner laughing about some of the events in their lives. She told him some more stories about her skydiving adventures and giggled about the rollercoaster experiences she'd had with the Coaster Crazies.

Nate asked her if she intended to remain with that group and she told him she just couldn't. Even though she was a daredevil and still intended to skydive, she didn't think she could ever get on a rollercoaster again. The thought of it gave her the chills and made her feel faint. She told Nate all about the weird fainting problems that she'd had since she was a kid—the doctors had no idea what caused it, but they suspected sudden spikes or drops in blood pressure. Something she just had no choice but to live with.

Nate told her about his marriage to Stephanie—all the gory details. And he lamented how they'd never had kids, but also said he was sort of glad they hadn't, now that they were divorcing. Kids from broken families always came out a bit damaged—in one way or another, and sometimes the effects didn't show themselves until several years down the road.

He discovered that they both loved horror movies and disaster flicks. Anything exciting or with some buzz to it. They also seemed to like the same foods, loved wine, and neither were keen on the club scene, preferring instead gatherings at home. He hadn't told her yet about his childhood football accident and resultant eidetic memory. He'd leave that for a later date. Didn't want to spook her!

Travel was something Shelby enjoyed as well—and that was one of Nate's passions. He thought to himself how nice it would be if this relationship developed to the point where they could take a vacation together. He was looking ahead already and fantasizing in his mind about them doing "couples" things together. Nate knew he was getting ahead of himself—this was after all only their first date. But, he couldn't help it. She was having that kind of effect on him.

Although, it felt as if he'd known her for a lot longer than he had. It helped that they were comfortable with each other, could be themselves. Nate felt totally at ease in her company and enjoyed her immensely.

His thoughts were interrupted by a humming Shelby dancing into the dining room carrying their desserts.

They both dug in—delicious. She was indeed as good a cook as she'd boasted. He loved that about her. The confidence and spunkiness she exhibited. Gave a dimension to her personality that most people lacked. She wasn't afraid to speak her mind and stand up for herself—he'd observed that about her.

She looked up, dabbing at some errant dessert at the corners of her pretty mouth. Then she smiled mischievously at him. "Well, what do you think?"

"It's delicious! And your mouth looks wonderfully clean!"

"No, not that, silly! Of course it's delicious—I made it! No, I'm talking about that skydiving idea I mentioned to you."

Nate winced. "Gee, Shelby, I don't know. I can't picture myself doing that."

She made a pouty face, and then said to him in a teasing voice, "Oh, you big baby."

Nate protested, "I'm not a baby—I'm just scared shitless!"

"Honestly, you'd love it, Nate. We'll do a tandem. I'll be with you the whole way. In fact, there's a family rally coming up in a couple of weeks. All the regulars will come out for the day, and the families come along to watch. There's a picnic as well, and music. It's a fun day—an annual event. Whaddaya think, big baby?"

Nate sighed and surrendered. "Alright. Email me the details and I'll join you."

Shelby shrieked with joy and clapped her hands together. "You've made me so happy! And I get to show you off to some of my friends there—they're gonna love you!"

Nate grumbled, "I just hope I survive to love another day."

She pouted again. "Okay, I can see you're nervous about this—and I understand. The thought of jumping out of a plane is a bit scary, scarier than a rollercoaster by far. So, no pressure. If you don't want to do it, I'll understand. I'll only register myself for the rally—I won't even list your name as a guest. That way, you don't have to feel committed, okay? If you want to come, you just come, and I'll register you at the last minute. Deal?"

Nate grinned. "Okay, deal."

"It'll be held at a private airfield just on the outskirts of Alexandria. This is the club I belong to—the Virginia Sky Pilots. We have a little hangar there where we keep all our own equipment, but we also have plenty of outfits for guests." She pretended to study Nate for a second. "Yeah, I think I can get you outfitted with a nice pink jump suit and matching helmet."

"Gee, now I'm really excited!"

She laughed. "Honestly, you have nothing to worry about. You'll love it! It's such a wonderful experience. I'm actually a certified Jumpmaster now, so you'll be in good hands."

"Well, that's the first part about this that I like."

"What?"

Nate grinned. "Being in your hands."

Shelby smiled at him warmly, and Nate could see that her cheeks were suddenly flushed.

He broke the uncomfortable silence, rose from his chair and walked to the front foyer where he'd left his briefcase. He opened it up and took out a sheet of paper, holding it against his chest.

Nate sat back down in the dining room. "Okay, you little daredevil. Time for us to compare sketches. Did Paul leave his sketch with you?"

Shelby went into the kitchen and opened up a cupboard; returned to the dining room with a sheet of paper held up against her chest, too. With a sly grin on her face she said, "You show me yours and I'll show you mine."

They both put their sketches face up on the table. And gasped in unison. The sketches were so identical, it was uncanny. The bald head, strong jawline, cold black eyes behind designer glasses.

They looked up from the sketches and Nate whispered. "It's the same guy, for sure. Whoever the hell he is, he does get around. And who he works for is anyone's guess."

Nate then told Shelby all about their little adventure down in Key West—about the helicopter that took them on a wild ride, seemingly flying itself. And about what they discovered in the scrapyard—the molten metal at the spot where the track split. Then how he and Tom were accosted by the military and, if it hadn't been for Ron saving the day, might have been forced to board the ship that was primed to head out to sea to dump their wreckage. And maybe dump him and Tom, too.

"God, it's obvious that someone doesn't want you guys nosing around. They tried to scare you off. And what you discovered with the molten metal jibes with what I learned the other day."

Nate perked up. "What?"

"You know about that NTSB investigator, John Fletcher? He's the one Tom talked with originally when the inspection was done?"

"Yes, right. He told Tom that the track split at the non-existent weld." Nate shook his head in frustration. "The prick. He's the one who also confirmed to Tom that the wreckage was being hauled away to a location he couldn't tell us about, and that we weren't allowed to inspect it ourselves. I'd love to get my hands on that guy."

Shelby smiled. "Well, you're going to get your chance."

"What do you mean?"

"You'll recall that I met him, too, after the accident. I went to his office and confronted him about the report that the lawyer told me about. Where it said the lap bars disengaged at impact. I was angry with him that he didn't bother to interview me."

"Yeah, I remember that."

"Well, I told you that he seemed out of sorts when I met him—seemed ashamed, like he wanted to tell me something."

"Okay, where are you going with this?"

"I met him again the other day. At the hospital—he was checked in as a patient. There was a gas explosion at his house. John tried to save his wife, but it was too late. He told me that he has a brain tumor—that he has about a year

171

left to live. But now he has nothing to live for. He said he was forced to sign that false investigation report—didn't say who forced him. But he admitted to me that he knows the track was melted and the lap bars didn't disengage on impact. He wants to meet with us. He's at the point now where it no longer matters to him if he keeps his job, benefits and life insurance. He only went along with the falsification because of his wife. Didn't want to leave her destitute when he died."

Nate just stared at her, mouth open wide. Then he found the words. "This story just gets weirder by the day. I can't believe this. So now we have the chief NTSB investigator on our side. That should be a big help. Sad to hear about his situation though, and the death of his wife. He must be very despondent right now."

Shelby crossed her arms across her chest. "It gives me the chills when I think about what happened to him and his wife that night. Must have been so terrifying for both of them. But, I also get the chills when I think of one other thing he said to me."

"What was that?"

"He said he wants revenge now. I don't know what he meant by that—it wasn't *his* rollercoaster that killed twenty-five people, it's not *his* company that's going to get sued and maybe go bankrupt. So, I don't know what he meant by that."

Nate nodded. "Maybe when we meet with him we'll find out more. But…that is an odd thing to say. The only thing that occurs to me is…does he suspect that the gas explosion wasn't an accident?"

"I…don't know. I never thought of that."

"Okay, well, let me know when he's out of the hospital and wants to meet with us. Oh, I have one other thing I want to leave with you." He got up and walked back to the foyer to retrieve his briefcase. "I should have just brought this damn case back to the table with me, but I was trying to be polite!"

Nate opened the briefcase and pulled out a folder. "Here. This contains a complete list of the riders who were killed on the rollercoaster. Along with photos and any bios we could dig up on them. Tom just finished the report today. I've gone through it, but nothing jumps out to me at first glance. But you've ridden a lot of coasters with these people, so some of them you probably know, at least casually."

Shelby took the folder, opened it and started scanning the list. She made the odd little comment and nodded several times, as she ran her finger down the pages. Suddenly, her finger stopped at one name. Then she shook her head and continued running her finger down the page.

Nate noticed her hesitation. "I noticed you stopped at one name. What was that all about?"

Shelby shook her head. "No, nothing at all. I just didn't remember that name, but then when I saw the photo it came back to me."

"Okay. Well, study it a few times and see if it jogs anything at all in your mind—even the most insignificant detail might be important. Read the bios— see if they jog anything, too. I'm sure you chatted with some of those people occasionally, about jobs, families, troubles, etcetera."

Shelby nodded. "I will, Nate. I'll give it a good look."

Nate got up. "Well, I'd better get going. Early morning tomorrow and a long day ahead."

Shelby got up, too, and walked him to the door. Then she spun him around gently and wrapped her arms around his neck. Gave him a squeeze and a kiss on the cheek. Nate pulled his head back and studied her.

"You know, Shelby Sutcliffe, the last time our faces were this close was when I threw you up against the trestle after you almost fell. I pinned you with my body while studying your face carefully. But you'd fainted and your eyes were closed. I must admit, I like it much better this way—I can gaze into those blue eyes of yours."

She flashed him a tender smile, almost a thankful smile. Nate then leaned in and kissed her gently on the lips.

CHAPTER 31

It was another typical Monday morning. For some reason Mondays were one of the busiest days for surgery. She'd just finished assisting with an appendectomy, which went fine, but the gall bladder operation first thing that morning had some complications. First, the surgeon who was scheduled to perform the surgery was called away on a family emergency, so another specialist was substituted at the last minute. The patient was just being prepped when he heard the news and almost had a panic attack. They managed to calm him down and the surgery went ahead as planned.

But maybe the substitute surgeon had indeed been a bad omen for him. Once inside, they discovered cancerous tumors in the region surrounding the gall bladder. So, they simply closed him up again. He was still in recovery and Shelby didn't envy the surgeon who had to give him that news when he awakened.

She did love surgery—it was always different. No operation was exactly the same and the patients all had their unique characteristics. She enjoyed the "lifesaving" nature of surgery the most. Sure, there were disappointments, too, but there were far more victories than defeats, and she was the kind of person who always focused on the positives. She felt she had one of the best jobs in the world, because most of the time what she did was give people hope and make them happy again. A second lease on life, and who couldn't be happy about a job that allowed you to do that for people, even if they were people you didn't really know?

Shelby removed her scrubs and headed on down to the cafeteria. Time for lunch and after such a busy morning she was darn hungry. Hadn't had time for breakfast—she'd slept in. Wanted to stay in dreamland after such a lovely date with Nate the night before. The alarm had gone off, she set the snooze button, and then five minutes later hit it angrily with the palm of her hand when it buzzed its rude reminder. She didn't set it again, preferring instead to relive their dinner date in her mind and take her chances that she'd wake up on her own.

Half an hour before her shift started, she awakened for the third time, in a panic. No time for a shower, she just threw some clothes on and ran to the car. Normally, Shelby walked to the hospital, but her lazy extended wake-up wouldn't allow that this morning.

Despite the frantic morning, she smiled at how nice it had been just to lie there in bed and remember the nice time she'd spent with Nate. She was very attracted to him, she had to admit, and he was so different than anyone else she'd ever dated.

Even though he was good looking and very successful, he wasn't the least bit into himself—modest to a fault, and interested in virtually everything that Shelby had to say. Nate was a very attentive man and seemed to possess an incredible memory. She would mention something very insignificant, something that normally wouldn't stick in someone's mind, but he would remember it and raise it later on in the conversation.

That kind of amazed her—it demonstrated to Shelby that he was paying close attention to her and, if he remembered something minor like that, he would surely remember the big stuff. Most of the men she'd dated couldn't even remember the big stuff—probably because they were too busy thinking about what they wanted to tell her about themselves.

Shelby really hoped that Nate would join her for the skydiving rally. She knew he'd enjoy it, especially someone like him who earned his living designing thrills.

Remembering back to his gentle kiss when he left, she felt a smile come over her face. It was so nice to have a date end that way. She compared that short moment to other dates—when she'd been groped in cars, or had her ass squeezed on the dance floor.

And trying to explain to some lout why she really wasn't interested in wrapping her mouth around the penis of someone she barely knew. *Sorry, dude, not that kind of girl. You can find those girls anywhere, but I'm not one of them.*

She remembered feeling insulted—and kind of dirty—after being out with guys like that. Guys who started out nice, but then turned out to be pigs.

She often wondered after those dates what it was about her that made men think she had such little self-worth. What messages was she sending out? But after deliberating about it, she cut herself some slack. It wasn't her problem—it was theirs. She was a classy lady, but some men just weren't capable of recognizing that. Or, they just didn't care about that—it wasn't what they wanted. Maybe they were somehow convinced that every woman was cheap, or just some piece of meat.

For guys like that, there were never second dates.

But for Nate, she hoped there would be a second…and a third…

She entered the cafeteria, chose a corned beef sandwich and cream of asparagus soup, and took a seat at the corner table near the window. It was almost empty today—most people must have chosen to go out for lunch. Shelby regretted that she still hadn't had the courage to return to the Sunshine Café since the day that strange man made his appearance and threatened her.

That reminded her of the papers in her purse. Manipulating her sandwich with one hand, Shelby struggled to open her purse and pull the sheets out with the other.

First, she laid the sketch face up and gave the man another look. She shivered, folded it up and shoved it back in her purse.

Then she started scanning the list of the twenty-five coaster victims that Nate had provided her with. She finished her sandwich and started in on the soup—delicious. She was savoring every morsel of this food today.

Just like last night, she used her finger to guide her eyes down the list of victims. Which reminded her for a second of Nate. She'd noticed last night, just for a moment, that his eyes seemed to wander slightly—when he'd asked her about what she'd noticed on the list, one eye was looking at her while the other one was still trained on the list. She made a mental note to ask him about that. It was a bit weird. Or, on second thought, maybe she should wait until they knew each other better—he might be self-conscious about it.

As she sipped her soup, she ran down the list quickly. Then flipped to the other pages—the ones that contained the photos and bios. She saw her friend and seatmate, Cheryl Sanders, and couldn't stop the tear that suddenly blurred her vision.

Shelby hadn't known those people all that well, but Cheryl had been the exception. They always sat together on rollercoasters and, once every month or so, got together for lunch or dinner. And the others—well, they would meet at some Coaster Crazies club meetings that sometimes had guest speakers, and almost always at those meetings there were film showings of rollercoasters from around the world.

She actually remembered one film that featured another one of Flying Machines' coasters—the Boomslang in Tokyo. It was known for its sharp jolting curves and breakneck speeds, and had been on the list of rollercoasters for the Coaster Crazies to visit sometime in the future.

Since they always got to chat together at these meetings she got to know the others a little bit. And she remembered some things about each of them. Of course, the Coaster Crazies were a worldwide group and there were 5,000 members, and even locally there were about a hundred in just the Alexandria chapter of the club. The twenty-six chosen to make the inaugural ride of the Black Mamba were drawn by lottery. She thought sardonically, *yes, weren't we the lucky ones.* So, since there were so many members in just her chapter alone, it was impossible to really get to know people.

But Shelby had always used little memory tricks to help her remember people's names, things like word association or images. Like, with Cheryl Sanders, when she first met her she used Cheryl's hair color to help remember her last name—it was sandy blonde.

She looked at another name on the list: Rod Hockney. For him, she always thought he looked like a hunky hockey player, so that locked his name in her memory. She chuckled as she continued on down the list. One lady's name was Virginia Semen, and it hadn't been hard for her to come up with images to remember that one.

Her finger stopped again—at the same name that had made her hesitate last night. She didn't know what it was, but something just didn't seem right. She flipped to the bio pages and saw his photo. Yep, it was the same guy she knew casually. She'd only chatted briefly with him a couple of times.

She read his bio—a dentist in Washington.

That didn't sound right. Shelby wracked her brain.

Out of all the names on the list, this was the only one that was giving her a funny feeling. And if he'd been a dentist she would have remembered that.

She looked hard at the name: Alexei Draminov.

The photo was right, but the bio didn't seem right—and the name, just like last night, left her cold. There was something wrong.

Shelby sat back in her chair and folded her arms across her chest. *What image or word did I use to remember this man's name? I know I used something.*

Yes, he was indeed Russian. She remembered that. But, an American, born and raised in the United States. He still had family back in Russia, she recalled, and was pretty sure they were in Moscow.

He had the stereotypical Russian features: stocky, wide in the chest, square-shaped head, and strong jawline. Very distinct eyebrows and cold hard eyes. But he was a pleasant man, very friendly, but a little bit shy. Laughed easily, those cold Russian eyes twinkling behind thick-lensed glasses.

Shelby retrieved an image—standing beside the coffee machine during an intermission at one of their meetings. There were several of them, talking about what they did for a living. She replayed the scene in her mind—could hear the others talking. And then Alexei spoke.

He worked for the government! He wasn't a dentist!

She also recalled him talking about the forty-minute drive it took him to get down to Alexandria from the Fort Meade area of Maryland.

So, he wasn't a dentist, nor did he live in Washington! The bio was way off base.

Then she fixed his face in her mind and remembered back to when she'd first heard him introduce himself. Tried to remember what words or images she'd used to remember his name.

A dragon!

Shelby whipped her cellphone out of her purse and turned it on. Waited for it to warm up, then went to her 'favorites.' Clicked on the website for the Coaster Crazies. Then she entered her private membership number and password. Up came the 'Members Only' page, with buttons for upcoming activities, news, and videos of various rollercoasters.

There was also a complete listing of members worldwide. Shelby clicked on that and the list came up. There were 5,000 members, but the list could be refined by country and alphabetically. She clicked on the United States, and then went to the 'D' section of the list.

She scrolled. And there he was.

His name wasn't Alexei Draminov. It was Alexei Dragunov.

'Dragon.'

CHAPTER 32

John Fletcher donned just a casual suit today—he'd worn his best suit yesterday at Linda's funeral. These were only two of several new suits that the insurance money had bought for him. Of course everything now would be brand spanking new, and until his house could be rebuilt the insurance money would at least pay for accommodations and all those basic needs he would have—such as clothes.

Today didn't deserve a really good suit. It was just a meeting, not the burial of his lifelong lover.

It was such a sad day for John yesterday. But everyone was great. They all came over to him and gave their condolences, but they didn't really know what to say afterwards. Conversations were short—quick messages and hasty retreats. They held his hands and whispered how they'd felt about Linda. Offering their help with anything he might need. All of them trying not to look too sad—but also trying not to look too happy either.

Funerals were always a delicate balance. He didn't blame people for feeling uncomfortable; he'd always felt that way, too, at funerals for friends over the years. What could you really say to make someone feel better?

John was living in a rented house just a few blocks from where the charred remains of his home were. At least he was still in the neighborhood, with all the memories that he and Linda had. He knew those familiar surroundings would make him sad, but he wanted those reminders. He wanted to feel sad. And angry. Anger was the new love of his life.

John Fletcher had nothing to live for now. He was looking forward to the imminent end of his life, when he'd be able to join Linda again. But he had things to do first.

He wanted justice. And justice wouldn't come from the justice system. He'd pretty much given up on that. Any system that forced him to sign a falsified report that incriminated an innocent company and its executives wasn't much of a system. There was no hope that he would get anywhere working through proper channels.

He'd worked through channels his whole life, looked the other way when the

TWA 800 lies were spouted to the world; called the police on his own son twenty years ago and sent him to prison with his testimony; and signed the phony report for the Black Mamba accident. And then the minute he tried to do one little thing to rectify his mistake—by asking Linda to make an anonymous phone call to tip off the Flying Machines executives—he'd gotten her killed.

Working through the system over the years had brought him nothing but grief. And now he was without the person he cared about the most in the entire world.

And he was still without Vincent. John had hired a lawyer in London to take whatever steps were necessary to track down his son. Vincent had a right to know that his mother had died. John knew he was in Europe somewhere, so maybe a few posts in the newspapers of the major cities would get some results. The London lawyer would take care of that. He also authorized him to hire a private investigator to see if any trails could be uncovered. There had to be some trails— credit card transactions and Internet communications alone; unless he'd changed his name, which would make things more difficult.

It hurt John to know that Vincent was unaware that his mother was gone. And Vincent didn't even know that his dear old dad had a year left to live. Not that he'd care about that, but John was sure he'd care that his mom was gone.

John was meeting with the Flying Machines people down at their office in Alexandria. Shelby Sutcliffe would be there, too. That sweet feisty woman—he liked her.

He wanted to help them. John wanted to do one important thing before he died. And he wanted to be able to tell Linda when he saw her again that he got the people who had killed her. And he was going to get them—if it took until his dying breath, he would get them.

After the NSA spook visited his office and told John that they had taped Linda's anonymous phone call from the telephone booth, John was a bit worried that they might have to look over their shoulders. But he'd been naïve—didn't really believe in his heart that anything bad would happen to them. Then the guy had tried to trick him into telling him who else he'd told about the wreckage in Key West.

John knew that the track had been melted. And he was ordered to sign a fake report, to deny his own professional investigation. He'd seen the melted track for God's sake. He knew that something horrible had happened there—it wasn't an accident at all. He just didn't know why such a horrific act was committed.

Then that fateful night when he was out on the street with his vandalized Lexus, he saw that other vehicle do a U-turn and speed away. In the hospital, the police officer confirmed that the license plate had been for a military vehicle. And he knew that Fort Meade was the closest major military installation, the same place where the NSA was based.

It was all starting to fit. Those twenty-five people on the Black Mamba were murdered. His wife had been murdered. Someone was very desperate to try to keep things covered up. Something was going on, but John didn't care as much anymore what that actually was, and he didn't really care about getting justice for the rollercoaster victims either.

That wasn't what was driving him. He wanted to just do the right thing one last time, and if that led to uncovering what was going on, so much the better.

No, more than anything, he just wanted to squeeze the life out of the person or persons responsible for Linda's death.

For the first time in his life, John Fletcher felt absolutely no fear.

He was already dead. And his bucket list was a blank page.

*****

Nate was waiting for everyone to make their appearance in the boardroom. Shelby had just arrived a few minutes before and Tom was in his usual seat. Still to show up were Ron Collens and the newest member of their informal little team: John Fletcher, from the NTSB.

Nate had some papers on the table in front of him and he waved one of them in the air. "Tom, looks like a big mistake was made in checking the bios for the victims. You had the name spelt wrong. A guy named Alexei Draminov should actually have been 'Dragunov.' The guy you'd listed was a dentist—Shelby caught this mistake, and she says the real guy worked for the government."

Tom fidgeted with his hands. "I don't know how that could have happened. Let me see that?"

Nate slid the sheet of paper over to him. Tom looked at it, and then glanced at Shelby. "Are you sure about this?"

She nodded. "Yes, absolutely."

Ron Collens came into the room and took a seat across from Nate. "Sorry I'm late, guys. Was just finishing up that little thing you asked me to check on, Nate."

"That's okay. We're still waiting for our special guest to arrive, anyway."

Tom folded the sheet of paper with the two names on it, and shoved it inside his suit pocket. "Let me run a check on that new name, Nate. Sorry about the mistake."

Nate waved his hand. "No, don't bother. I asked Ron to take a look at it for us."

Tom pulled a handkerchief out of his pocket and wiped his brow.

Are you okay, Tom?"

"Yeah, I'm fine. It just seems extra hot in here today." Tom got up and walked over to the wall thermostat, giving the dial a spin. "No wonder—it's eighty degrees in here!"

Just then, the door opened and in walked Cary Grant. Nate was shocked at this first glance of the man—Shelby had warned him about the matinee idol looks that John Fletcher possessed, but he still wasn't prepared for it.

He got up and shook John's hand, then introduced him to Tom and Ron. John sat down beside Shelby and took her hand in his, squeezing it gently. "So nice to see you again, dear, and thanks again for visiting me in the hospital. It helped me more than you know."

Shelby smiled warmly at him. "My pleasure, John."

Nate started things off. "John, we're all so sorry about your loss. You must be still in shock. Our condolences. But we are glad you've agreed to help us despite the loss you've suffered. This is such a weird mystery that just keeps getting weirder and anything you can share with us would be appreciated. Would you like to tell us your side of things?"

John nodded. "I'll be brief—mainly because I'm not feeling too communicative these days, as you can probably appreciate. In a nutshell, I was forced to sign that investigation report—forced by my boss and some shadowy man from the National Security Agency. I know from my own inspection that the steel on the track was melted—I'm a metallurgical engineer, and my experience told me that it was probably done with Thermate."

Ron jumped in. "I agree, John. That was my initial guess, too. And the photos my colleagues took of the wreckage down in Key West show the molten metal."

John nodded and continued. "You all probably know that I'm dying of a brain tumor. About a year left to live. That was the reason I chose to go along and just shut up. The wrong thing to do, I know, and I'm ashamed of that, but I was worried about benefits and life insurance remaining intact.

"At that time, my wife, Linda, was still alive." John paused to wipe a tear away from his eye. "My conscience started getting the better of me, so I asked Linda to make an anonymous call to you, Tom. You and I had chatted over the phone about my inspection report, so I figured you were as good a person as any to give the tip to. I wanted you guys to see the wreckage before it was sunk in the Caribbean."

Tom wrung his hands together. "Yes, thanks for that, John."

John let his eyes roam to everyone at the table. "I'm convinced that my wife was murdered because of that phone call."

He paused to let that comment sink in, and then continued. "That night, we were out to dinner. When we got back, Linda went upstairs and I was just about to join her when my car alarm went off. Went outside and discovered the glass had been smashed on my car. Then I noticed another car a few houses up the street doing a U-turn and speeding off in the other direction. I got the license number.

"I walked back toward the house and suddenly all hell broke loose. A gas explosion tore the house apart. It was too late to save Linda." Some more tears, which John wiped away with the back of his hand.

"I believe that the car alarm was intended to draw me outside. I think they knew that the husband would normally check something like that in the dead of night rather than the wife. My best guess, is that the scum in that vehicle I saw, used a remote control release on the gas valve; a receiver and device they must have installed while we were out to dinner. Then they must have used the remote control again to trigger something that would cause a spark. There's no way of knowing any of this for sure—the destruction of the house was total. So, I'm just speculating, but I think I'm pretty close to the truth."

Nate was jotting down notes as John talked. "Sorry to interrupt, John. But why would they want to kill your wife? You'd already signed the report—you did what they wanted."

John grimaced. "That same NSA guy who forced me to sign the report paid me a visit after Linda made the anonymous call, and after you guys had trekked down to Key West. He told me that he knew the phone booth was close to my home, and that they'd taped Linda's voice. And he had a voice match—God knows these clowns can do anything—so he knew it was Linda's voice. He wanted to know who else I'd told about the wreckage. I got angry—threw him out of my office, told him I thought he and his cronies had committed mass murder. Told him again that I knew that Thermate had been used."

Ron interrupted. "John, originally when he asked you to sign that false report, did he tell you why?"

"Just that it was for national security reasons."

Nate leaned his elbows on the table and stared at John. "So, you're convinced that they intended to kill your wife. But not you?"

"Not me—just Linda. I don't think they wanted the coincidence of me turning up dead. I was the one who investigated that horrific coaster accident, and they already knew that you guys saw the wreckage so you knew it wasn't an accident. If you raised alarm bells, it would look really bad if I suddenly became dead.

"No, they wanted to scare the shit out of me by blowing up my house and if my wife died, all the better. They wanted me out of the house—that's why the car was vandalized. And I think they knew that I would know it wasn't an accident. They *wanted* me to know. But I'm certain they *didn't* know that I'm dying, so being frightened about my future is now a moot point."

Ron turned his laptop on. While he was staring at the screen, he asked, "Did you check on that license plate number?"

"I tried to—gave it to a policeman. He told me that since it had the prefix 'W,' he wasn't able to access it. The 'W' told him it was a military vehicle."

Ron nodded. "Yeah, that's 'Army' to be exact—probably a pool car out of Fort Meade."

"Yes, and guess where the NSA operates out of? Fort Meade!"

"You're right, John."

Nate pulled the sketch out of his briefcase and slid it over to John. Shelby followed his lead with her sketch. "Is this the guy from the NSA?"

"It sure is. Bang on, both sketches."

"Was he wearing a large ring on his right hand?"

"Come to think of it, yes. He kept rubbing it."

Nate lowered his voice. "John, I saw that guy at Adventureland a minute or two before the accident, with his fist raised at the track—we're guessing that in his fist was the remote control that caused the Thermate to ignite, and the lap bars to disengage."

John whistled. "Geez!" He directed his attention to Shelby. "And where did you see this guy?"

"Out of the blue, he dropped down in the seat in front of me at a restaurant. He threatened me into joining the Class Action lawsuit, and told me I had to testify that the bars opened on impact."

"Did he give you his name?"

"No."

"I didn't get his name either. Refused to give it to me for national security reasons."

Ron was clicking away on his laptop. He looked up at John. "We've concluded, John, that the mass murder was done to cover up the murder of just one person. We don't know the reason yet...but I think we've just discovered who the person was that they wanted to kill."

Tom perked up. "Who do you think it was, Ron?"

Ron turned away from his keyboard and stared at Tom. "I've received some information from my contact at 'Anonymous'—that rogue group of pesky hackers and troublemakers. I checked that name out that you seemed to have misspelled."

Ron looked back at his computer screen. "Looks like Alexei Dragunov worked for the NSA. Out of Fort Meade. He's an American, but from Russian heritage—still has family back in Russia. Looks like Mr. Dragunov was assigned to the Russian Unit of the NSA, as an analyst. They have separate units there that are dedicated to tapping into communications for virtually every country in the world. It allows the NSA to specialize and focus on world hot spots, and also of course make use of the multiple language skills of some of their operatives."

Nate looked over at Tom and frowned. "That was a pretty serious oversight, Tom. Every rider on that rollercoaster has been checked out and no one else's occupation jumped out at us. But *the* one—the *only* one—who worked at the NSA, is the one whose name happened to be misspelled. And now after what John has told us, we know that our mystery man, who's been literally pushing all the buttons, is from the NSA as well."

Tom nodded. "I agree. Let me check with the people I assigned to this and find out how it happened."

Nate tapped his fingers on the table. "I asked you to do that checking yourself."

"I know, but I have good people—and I was busy with other things. Leave it with me, Nate. I'll find out and heads will roll."

"Who did you assign to this?"

"I'd rather not say right now. Let me get back to you."

Nate cracked his knuckles. "Are you trying to protect someone, Tom?"

"Maybe—until I find out more. As I said, leave it with me. Heads will roll, I promise you."

Nate shook his head. "I don't care about heads rolling, Tom. I'm only interested in how this mistake happened and if it was accidental or deliberate. It's a glaring error, and it seems far too coincidental to me."

"I agree. I'll get on it."

Nate looked back at Ron. "Anything else to report on this guy?"

"Yeah, and there will be more to come, too. But, in the meantime, you all may be interested in knowing that Anonymous have checked Dragunov's known contacts. The one and only Edward Snowden is listed here as a close ally and friend when they both worked at the NSA together. And...as the entire world knows, Snowden is now hiding out somewhere in Russia, having been granted asylum by Putin. It's been rumored that he's living in the Moscow area. And, as we've just discovered, Alexei Dragunov just happens to have had family living in the Moscow area."

There was absolute silence around the table. Several stunned mouths were hanging open until Nate broke the stillness.

"Another coincidence."

CHAPTER 33

The meeting was at a bar in Old Town Alexandria, just a short walk from the Flying Machines' offices. Ron Collens was going jacketless today, with the temperature in most of Virginia expected to soar close to 100 F. All he had with him was his laptop case. He wouldn't need anything else—and knowing the skills of the man he was meeting with, he may not even need that.

He and Chet Mathers had served together in the Seals; comrades in arms. Friends for life. They had each saved the other's life at one time or another, and would owe each other for that until the end of time.

Chet, like Ron, was a Systems Engineer—but with talents and skills way up in the stratosphere. He owned his own software company and had become immensely successful, specializing in the entertainment field. That industry required creative solutions to their challenges, and Chet's company had gained a reputation that surpassed all others.

Chet also had a secret occupation—a volunteer one. He was an 'Anon,' an active member and one of the founders of the shadowy quasi-activist group, 'Anonymous.'

Anonymous was an international group of hackers, but more appropriately labeled as "hacktivists." Their symbol was a stylized version of a Guy Fawkes mask, made famous in the movie, 'V for Vendetta.' Anonymous members wore these masks whenever they protested in public.

The group, which originated in 2003, now numbered in the thousands around the globe. They were originally just written off as pranksters, hungry for publicity. One of their first targets was the Church of Scientology, with online pranks, embarrassing revelations, and 'denial of service' attacks on the church's website.

Those establishment figures who didn't take Anonymous seriously were caught by surprise when they suddenly became emboldened with their newfound notoriety. Because next on their impressive list were several sensitive government agencies of the United States, Israel, Australia, Spain, Turkey and the United Kingdom.

They didn't stop with governments—new victims were added to their list, including PayPal, MasterCard, VISA, and Sony.

Anons then publicly supported WikiLeaks, Occupy movements, and more recently Edward Snowden.

An unstated vow that Anonymous seemed to have was to use their impressive skills to fight oppression, corruption, and dishonesty in governments and corporations. Supporters of the group have referred to them as "freedom fighters" and "digital Robin Hoods."

Critics abound, too, and of course from the predictable circles: governments and large corporations. Called "anti-religious and racist," "cyber lynch mob," and "cyber terrorists," the group had made their presence felt in painful fashion and in all the places they wanted it to be felt.

In 2012, TIME Magazine even elevated the group to the position of being a "person," calling Anonymous "one of the most influential people in the world."

From what Ron could gauge from Chet, the group had very few rules for its members. The three most important guiding principles were: to not disclose identities; to not talk about the group with anyone; and to not attack the media. They were motivated by primarily one thing: 'an unrelenting moral stance on issues and rights, regardless of direct provocation.'

The anthem of Anonymous that a lot of the members seemed to use in communications or warnings was: *We are Anonymous. We are Legion. We do not forgive. We do not forget. Expect us.*

Ron knew far more about Anonymous than he was supposed to know. But his close relationship with Chet gave him special privileges, and Chet knew that Ron would never betray him to anyone. Ron had actually been invited by Chet to join the group years ago, but he'd declined. It just wasn't his thing.

And he'd never had a reason before to tap into his relationship with Chet. But this time, he had a reason and Chet agreed to help without question, providing he remained 'anonymous.' Ron and his partners needed help and he wasn't shy about asking his old military buddy for a favor. And he knew that Chet certainly wouldn't hesitate to ask him either—the bond between military comrades was a strong one indeed and it lasted a lifetime.

Ron walked through the door of a politically cheeky-named bar called 'The Confederacy.' He strolled to the very back and saw his friend sitting alone at a booth. Ron slid into the seat across from him and they saluted each other. Then, with big smiles, they shook hands.

"So, are we on for golf next Thursday—same time, same place?"

Ron gave a thumbs-up sign. "You're on, bud. A hundred bucks a hole?"

"I hate to take your money, but I will. After I beat you, I'll buy the drinks though."

"Yeah, yeah. I'll book the tee-times for us. So…hate to rush you, but I have a meeting in an hour. Can we get to it? We can talk pleasantries next week."

The waiter came by with a couple of draught beers. Chet paid him and included a generous tip. "I took the liberty of ordering for us while I waited patiently for you."

They clinked glasses in a toast. Then Chet leaned his head forward over the table and lowered his voice.

"I'm glad you came to me. From what you've told me, I think that what you guys are going through is just a travesty. Sounds like something is up, something big."

"Well, I filled them all in on your initial findings—about Alexei Dragunov being with the NSA and possibly associated with Edward Snowden. And the fact that he might still have family living in Moscow—which made all of us wonder if Snowden is hiding out with one of those families."

"Yeah, and you can bet the American government is wondering about that, too."

"But, Chet, none of that explains why they would have wanted to kill Dragunov."

Chet nodded. "We'll get to that in a few minutes. I don't really know for sure about that yet either, but I do have a bit of a trail. Let me talk to you first about that NFL roster of players from the 49ers Super Bowl team of 1994.

"We went through the entire list, then did extensive database tracking of the history of each of the players, coaches, trainers—the whole bunch. The list totaled about seventy people.

"Approximately thirty percent are dead, several are in hospitals or in chronic care, quite a few live out of the country and rarely return here even to visit, some are Little League coaches, and some are still involved with the NFL or in the sports broadcasting industry.

"There were really only three who stood out as being in the category of the person you outlined: one was a Secret Service agent, now retired; one is with the CIA based in Egypt; and the third one couldn't at first be traced to our current time, so he looked suspicious to us."

Ron whispered. "Who is he?"

"A man by the name of Carl Masterson. He was a star fullback, but a scandal kinda sullied his career. He worked his way back to the second string of the 49ers just in time for the '94 Super Bowl. He has both law and criminology degrees, and worked for the FBI for a while. Then he disappeared off the radar."

Ron swore under his breath. "Just our luck. That does sound suspicious, but a dead end."

Chet smiled. "My friend—you weren't listening to me. I said *'couldn't at first be traced;'* the operative words being *'at first.'*"

"Okay, my friend—cut to the chase."

"Well, considering what we found out about Dragunov, we decided to hack into the databases of both the CIA and the NSA. Nothing at the CIA. But bingo! We found him at the NSA! He's quite high up in the ranks; that's why he was blocked from tracking. Dragunov wasn't blocked because he was just a lowly analyst, but this Masterson guy is a Director of the Security and Intelligence division, whatever the fuck that means. He works out of Fort Meade in Maryland and we have his home address in Maryland as well. In addition, he spends a lot of time in Washington—credit card transactions trace him nicely."

"Do you have a current photo of him?"

Chet turned on his laptop, made a few keystrokes, and then spun it around for Ron to see. "Here's the photo from his driver's license."

Ron whistled. "That's the guy! I've seen the sketches and it's him for sure!"

Chet laughed. "We're good, huh? We can pretty much do anything, Ron. Hacking is really easy if you know what you're doing. Damn illegal, too—so I trust you to keep this on the 'down low' as regards Mr. Carl Masterson of the NSA. You didn't get this from me, or Anonymous."

Ron paused to let it all sink in. "Don't worry, Chet. But I can hardly wait to tell the others. We're making real progress now."

Chet slid his laptop back around and entered a few more keystrokes. "I'm not finished yet. You're going to find this very interesting. When Alexei Dragunov died on that rollercoaster, he was actually unemployed. He was fired—described as a layoff for government cutback reasons—just over three months ago. Around the time that you guys announced your inaugural ride of the Black Mamba. And at that same time you announced the names of the riders from the Coaster Crazies who had been chosen to ride. I thought it was coincidental that he was fired just a short time after that. And even more coincidental was an email that Dragunov sent just a few days before he was fired."

Chet entered a few more strokes. Ron was chomping at the bit. "Chet, tell me, for God's sake."

Chet sat back in his chair and stared at the screen. "We found this email. We have no idea who it was sent to, and there was no reply to it. He encrypted it, but we decoded it. And this email might have been why he was let go—and then murdered. I don't know, maybe I'm reaching here. But the email is definitely in code; we have no doubt about that. Our coding expert has given me an opinion. But, let me first just read out what the email said:

"Hi there. Hope you're well. I have to have an operation next week. Damn teeth. Hurting so much, infected, and I have to drink tons of water just to flush the puss out. Hey, did you know that eighty percent of the bottled water we get here in America is imported from Canada? Interesting, huh? I love Canada, don't you? Such a beautiful country. I want to head up there this summer and hang out at the Great Lakes. I hear they have masseuses on the beaches that

will also wash and scrub your back for you. Have you ever had a backwash from a beautiful woman before?"

Ron drained the rest of his beer. Suddenly, he was extra thirsty so he signaled to the waiter to bring them two more.

"That's kind of a strange message. It seems pointless. But why can't you discover who he sent it to?"

"He followed a certain path. It was routed through several different countries; different IP addresses, and then…ended up in Moscow. To an IP address registered to an Internet café. Whoever accessed this email did so by simply signing in with an account password."

"Jesus! Do you think…Snowden?"

"That's exactly what I'm thinking."

The waiter served the second round and Chet paid him again. Ron took a long slug. "I'd have to stare at that message for a long while to see what kind of decoded sense it might make. So, why don't you speed the process up for me, Chet, old buddy?"

Chet folded his hands together. "As you know, we have thousands of people in Anonymous around the world—but we're still a tight-knit group despite the large numbers. I can tap into the skills of anyone I choose to, and we're all kind of a…brotherhood, know what I mean? I think you do—it's similar to the military. Anyway, we all know who's good at what so I went to a contact in South Africa, a former CIA operative who went rogue, living now under an assumed name. He was one of their foremost decoding experts. Brilliant mind.

"Anyway, I sent this email to him and asked for his opinion. He says it's definitely in code, and not that difficult. Done by an amateur, which of course someone of Dragunov's rank at the NSA probably would be. The word 'operation' would be the first clue and his reference to teeth. My contact hacked into his dental records and there's no record of any operation on his teeth pending—in fact, Dragunov hadn't visited a dentist for over a year. The second clue that stands out is the unnecessary mentions of having to flush his mouth out with water and that Canada supplied the U.S. with most of its bottled water. Silly information that was out of context in an email that, as you said, seemed to be pointless to begin with. But…it wasn't pointless.

"Then he talks about visiting Canada and going to the Great Lakes. Well, the Great Lakes are nice, but the water's cold and the beaches aren't that nice. These are big lakes, kinda like small oceans. If you wanted to visit the lakes in Canada, you'd go to the smaller resort lakes in Ontario or British Columbia. So, that's a clue in itself.

"Next he talks silly nonsense about getting his back scrubbed and washed on a beach in the Great Lakes. My contact checked on that—there's no such service on the beaches of the Great Lakes in Canada. And Dragunov ends the email with asking if the recipient has ever had a 'backwash' before by a beautiful woman. So—the words 'wash and scrub your back' get switched around to 'backwash.'"

Ron looked at his watch. "I gotta run in a few minutes, Chet. Speed it up for me."

"Okay. I think Dragunov had been in touch with Snowden all along. I think this email was sent to Snowden in Moscow, and I do believe that he set Snowden up with his relatives there for a place to stay once Putin granted him asylum. And…I think that Dragunov stumbled across something else, either at Snowden's request or all by his lonesome. This email was trying to find out if Snowden knew about this other matter. Dragunov was waiting for a reply…which he never got."

"What is that something else?"

"We don't know exactly. But our decoding expert in South Africa is 100% certain that it at least pertains to water, pertains to Canada, pertains to the Great Lakes, and is known in official NSA channels as 'Operation Backwash.'"

CHAPTER 34

Carl hated the look of these two guys. Sure, they were good at their jobs, but they looked weird. Tattoos up their arms, with a few other creative etchings circling their necks, in their ears, on the top of their bald scalps. They looked identical in that respect—maybe they got a two-for-one special at the tattoo parlor?

Carl was a bit of a conservative—he couldn't help but look down on people who marred their bodies that way. A few of his teammates in the NFL had those damn markings too, and he had tended to gravitate away from them. Anyone with tattoos always made him think "trailer trash."

No matter—these two were always reliable and creative in every challenge Carl threw their way. They'd never failed him yet. And he would need them to be that way once again. They were known within the intelligence community as two of the most efficient assassins on the market.

He passed each of them two photos with names and addresses written at the top. "Memorize these faces and their details, and then burn the photos."

One of the guys frowned. "Isn't this the guy whose house we blew up? You told us then that we had to draw him out of the house—which we did."

"Yes, that's correct. But the situation has changed and he has to be dealt with now. You have two choices for this man—an accident, or a suicide. But it can't be seen as a murder. Clear?"

They both nodded their colored bald heads.

The other killer was looking hard at the second photo. "She's pretty. Such a shame."

Carl couldn't resist. "That kind of lady is out of your league anyway, so don't be too broken-hearted."

The guy looked up at Carl and sneered. "No one is out of my league."

"Sure. Okay, with this girl, it has to be an accident. Suicide wouldn't be believable for her, not like it would be for the man. So, you only have that one option."

"No problem." They both rose to leave.

"Oh, one more thing." He handed them each a piece of paper. "This

192

information was lifted from their online calendars. It will give you a concise idea where they're going to be and what they'll be doing over the next two weeks."

"Time frame?"

"I just told you—within the next two weeks. And don't forget to burn those documents after you've memorized everything."

As they left his office, Carl glanced at his watch. He had a meeting with two logistics officers from the Pentagon in about ten minutes. They needed an update to take back to their bosses, and Carl was glad that everything about Operation Backwash itself was on track. It was these damn loose ends that he hadn't anticipated, but he had no choice but to just deal with them. Which was exactly what he was doing.

He opened the folder that he'd be referring to during the meeting. An 'executive summary' of Canada was at the top of the pile of reports.

Canada—a lovely place. He'd been there many times. And, my God, they seemed to have water coming out of their ying-yang. Canada actually owned access to about thirty percent of the entire world's fresh water. And their citizens were spoiled by how much they had—rationing was seldom an issue in Canada. In fact, Canadians were one of the largest per capita consumers of water on the globe—a whopping 326 liters per person per day.

And the Great Lakes System was the mother lode of fresh water. With the exception of the Polar ice caps, the Great Lakes were the largest source of fresh water on the planet; a mind-boggling 95,000 square miles. Those lakes alone held twenty-two percent of the world's fresh water.

And luckily for the United States, the five Great Lakes straddled its border with Canada. Four of them were shared equally with Canada and managed jointly between the two countries by the International Joint Commission, which was set up under the Boundary Waters Treaty of 1909.

The U.S./Canadian border, the 49th Parallel, ran directly down the middle of the most northern body of water, Lake Superior, then through the middle of lakes Huron, Erie and Ontario. Lake Michigan, the fifth Great Lake, was the only one totally within the border of the United States.

Lakes Erie and Michigan were the key aspects of Operation Backwash.

Lake Erie was the one that America would steal the water from, and Lake Michigan would be the site of a 'false flag' terrorist attack.

The Boundary Waters Treaty dictated how much water each of the two countries was entitled to, and it had never been renegotiated and it was unlikely that it ever would be. Canada was resource-rich, and it felt that it was entitled to keep its resources and its fair share of the water that the border defined.

Operation Backwash would basically redefine that border for them, and tell the Boundary Waters Treaty to go fuck itself.

America was running out of water—fast. And its relatively tiny neighbor, at least from a population standpoint, had resources that every nation in the world coveted. The lucky thing for America was that it shared a border with the most resource-rich nation on the planet. And the temptation was just far too great. The solution to America's water woes lay north of the 49th Parallel. America had actually tried to take over Canada back in the war of 1812, but the damn British and French had held them off. Well, colonialism was dead now and Canada was on its own. Too bad for them.

Carl jerked out of his daydream at the sound of his office door opening. These guys from the Pentagon never bothered to knock.

He rose from his chair to greet them. They waved him back down.

The tall guy was General Tetford. The short guy was General Halperson. These dudes didn't have tattoos.

Tetford started things off. "Okay, we're getting close, Carl. We understand you've had some loose ends and we don't want to hear about those. We trust you'll just take care of them."

"Consider it done."

"Good, so, we need to report back to the top brass as to where we are right now on all of the preparations. Why don't you start with the tunnel update first?"

Carl shuffled the papers in his folder until he came to the report that he wanted.

"The tunnel is almost finished. It's been a five-year project—stretching from the Illinois River to the southwest tip of Lake Erie. When it reaches Lake Erie, it will be fifty feet underground, so when it punches through into the lake it won't be noticed. That's the eastern end of the tunnel. At the western end, it will have two branches—one diverts off through the banks of the Illinois River, which as you know feeds the Mississippi. The water levels will be dramatically boosted in the Mississippi, a situation that has been dire for us up until now. Not just water levels for drinking and irrigation, but also shipping up the Mississippi from the Gulf of Mexico has been dramatically altered due to the low water levels. Ships can't be loaded to the same level as they were five years ago because the river's so shallow now, which is causing shortages of goods to our northern cities.

"The second western branch of the tunnel dives down deep into the Cambrian-Ordovician Aquifer, which will flow from there into the nation's most precious and crucial one, the High Plains Aquifer. This is one of the world's largest aquifers, lies under eight states and underlies 17,500 square miles. And right now it's only at thirty percent capacity—it's the most important aquifer we have and it's the most depleted. So, this tunnel branch from Lake Erie will dramatically boost the High Plains Aquifer—a major triumph for us. Agriculture and ranching will be helped tremendously, and we might even be able to start watering our golf courses again."

Halperson finally spoke. "Any problems with the tunnel construction?"

"Not really any to speak of. The good thing is, and the reason we chose Lake Erie, is that the tunnel goes entirely under U.S. soil, so we don't have to worry about Canadian officials asking questions about noise reports. Sure, we've had our own citizens complaining about mechanical noises underground and sounds of muffled banging—especially at night when it's normally expected to be quiet. But, people all over the world have been complaining about noises like that—probably because other countries are building tunnels and bunkers, too. Usually, when these things get reported, municipalities pretend to investigate, and the nutbars start blaming the noises on aliens. So, thank God for the nutbars—they help us more than they realize."

"What equipment have you been using for this tunnel? It's going to be a long one—240 miles if I recall?"

"We decided to go with a Pipe Jacking system—less chance of collapse. It's very simple, but slow as hell. Pipes are rammed through the bedrock by a pneumatic hammer at the rear. At the front is a Tunnel Boring Machine—the pneumatic hammer and TBM work in harmony with each other. The TBM in front cuts through the rock, while the hammer continuously rams the pipe forward. We built vertical shafts along the route from the top, so we could access the TBM for repairs along the way. And more pipe just gets added as the project moves along. Once the final stretch is completed and we burst through the banks of Lake Erie, the TBM will be shoved forward and down into the depths of the lake. At that time, the water will begin to flow in massive volumes, toward our Illinois River and High Plains Aquifer. Our problems with water will be largely resolved. And, you're right, General, the tunnel is about 240 miles in length, traveling underneath parts of three states: Illinois, Indiana, and Ohio."

Halperson nodded and jotted down a few notes on his pad. "Whereabouts will it punch through into Erie?"

"About halfway between Toledo and Cleveland."

Tetford walked over to the coffee stand and poured himself a cup. "Okay, that all sounds good. How long until completion?"

"Should be completely done and ready to punch through into Lake Erie no later than a month from today."

"Good, now tell us where we are on the other aspect of Operation Backwash—the 'false flag.'"

"Okay—well, that part of the operation will be coordinated with the tunnel completion date. We'll be using Lake Michigan and the areas surrounding it, which as you know is totally within our borders, so an attack on Lake Michigan will be viewed as an attack on the United States. We'll be starting to leak information to the media that we've picked up "chatter" about a possible chemical weapons attack on the United States. We won't say exactly where, but we'll drop little hints. The objective of this is, once the attack happens, that we'll be justified in lining all of the Great Lakes with U.S. troops—on our side of the lakes. We won't be invading Canada, but we'll have heavy troop presence on all five lakes, which will just be seen as logical defense. The citizens of our country will be appalled and be totally behind us, and our allies will sympathize with us after the attack happens. Our reason for being there will be declared 'national security,' which of course we're entitled to do under International Law.

"Troop presence along the Great Lakes will then be permanent, and will delay any possible discovery by the Canadians of our tunnel—which by then will have already punched through into Lake Erie."

"Won't the Canadians notice the water level drop?"

"Not really—at least not for some time. And then we'll just deal with it when that happens. What can they do anyway? Attack us? I don't think so—they're not equipped for that. The deed will be done and it will be the 'new normal.' The water levels in the Great Lakes have been dropping anyway for the last few years due to the hotter summers, less snow, and dryer weather. And the Canadians have almost finished their plans for damming off James Bay from Hudson's Bay. Since hundreds of rivers flow into James Bay, the dam project will turn James Bay from salt water to mainly fresh water. Then, the next step of their plans after that is to divert water from James Bay down to Lake Superior—which eventually flows into Erie. Voila! Water levels return to normal, and we'll be then getting much more than the share we've been historically—and legally—allowed."

"Sounds brilliant. Describe the attack to us."

"The attack will come from the Canadian side of the border—so we'll blame the whole mess on a terrorist cell operating out of Canada, and of course lament the weak security in Canada as being the root cause of a horrific attack on the United States. We've planted information relating to a plant that we leased near Sudbury, the largest Canadian city close to Lake Michigan. That plant has been leased in the names of some prominent Muslim activists in Canada—they aren't aware of that, of course, but they're going to become the most hunted people on the planet after the attack happens.

"That plant has actually been used by us to manufacture about a million little nanobots—the major components are nano in size, but the actual machines will be about the size of grasshoppers and, when they fly, it will even *look* like a swarm of grasshoppers. They'll be loaded onto a truck and driven to a point on the Canadian side close to our border—then launched from there into the air, programmed for the western shores of Lake Michigan."

"Which U.S. cities will be impacted?"

"We expect casualties in both Green Bay and Milwaukee. Nothing beyond that. In total, we expect maybe five thousand deaths."

Tetford nodded. "Continue."

"Each of these little bots will be loaded with Hydrogen Cyanide. Once the bots are released, they'll be programmed to fly to the western shore of Lake Michigan and then simply self-destruct. On destruction, the cyanide will be vaporized and begin to spread. The good thing is, Hydrogen Cyanide doesn't survive well in water—so we'll be able to say that the terrorists intended to poison our water system, but didn't understand the science as well as they thought. So, we'll have some deaths in cottages along the lake and in those two cities I mentioned, but our water supply won't suffer from our 'false flag.' And the attack will justify U.S. troops controlling the shores of the Great Lakes, on the "lookout" for more attacks—and we'll be perceived and thanked for actually "helping" Canada with their security. Our tunnel will go undiscovered and our troop presence will provide us with even more options if we wish to use them down the road."

Generals Tetford and Halperson abruptly stood and headed for the door. No goodbyes, or even any thanks for a job well done.

Tetford looked back at Carl before leaving. "Make sure you tie up those loose ends."

CHAPTER 35

"He's identified the guy. He's no longer the 'mystery man.' Ron's friend at Anonymous tracked him down from the NFL roster—the prick's name is Carl Masterson. He's fairly high up at the NSA. Lives and works in Maryland."

Tom stood up and walked over to the window in Nate's office. It was early in the morning and there was still heavy commuter traffic outside. He solemnly watched the congestion, and then said, "That's great news. Now we just have to decide what to do about him."

"Ron's discovered a few other things as well. This Dragunov guy was fired three months ago from the NSA—apparently he sent an email to Moscow that might have been his downfall. Something to do with a plot called Operation Backwash, which apparently involves the water up in Canada—the Great Lakes region. Ron thinks the email was sent to Edward Snowden, and it was tipping him off to something that Dragunov stumbled onto."

Tom started pacing the office. "This sounds like one tangled web."

"It has been from the beginning, that's for sure. I've asked Ron to join us—he should be here in a few minutes. His friend had some more information that he wanted to pass along. He's on the phone with him right now. Maybe he can fill in the blanks a bit for us when he gets here."

*****

"Okay, there's something strange going on, Ron."

"Well, we already knew that—tell me something I don't know!"

Ron could hear Chet tapping on his keyboard at the other end of the phone. "Brace yourself. I've hacked into Carl Masterson's phone records. Traced the recipients for all the phone calls he's made, and there's one that pops out at me. One of your partners, Tom Foster. I've tracked twenty phone calls made to his cell phone in the last three months. And I did a reverse check—almost as many calls from Foster back to Masterson."

"What?!"

"Sorry to tell you this news, but I figured you'd want to know right away. The records don't lie. I don't know what's going on, but I would hazard a guess that Tom Foster was the 'inside man.'"

"Jesus! He's not only a partner, but he's also one of our best friends! I can't believe this! What would he have to gain from this?"

Ron could hear Chet rapping his fingernails against the mouthpiece. "Nothing financial, that's for sure. I checked his bank accounts—no unusual deposits. Unless he has an offshore account somewhere that might be out of reach for us to find."

Ron could feel the blood boiling in his veins. His right hand was squeezing the phone so tightly that his fingers had turned white from the lack of circulation. "Chet, I can't thank you enough for this. Leave it with me. Anything else you find out, let me know right away."

"Okay—be careful, my friend."

*****

Ron Collens marched down the hall towards Nate's office—he felt like he was back in the Seals, stalking a known terrorist. Readied for the kill, hands swinging confidently by his side, face flushed from the adrenaline.

He felt betrayed—they'd been going through hell, and this "friend" of theirs had probably been setting them up every step of the way, allowing their nameless, invisible enemy to always stay one step ahead of them.

Lives had been lost, their company was in peril, Shelby had been threatened, John Fletcher had lost his wife—and who knew what other dangers awaited them all, just because they wanted to clear their names in a tragic rollercoaster accident. And their partner, Tom Foster, had been doing his damnedest to make sure they never did. But why? What was his connection to all this?

He swung open the door to Nate's office and stormed in. His eyes went to Tom right away, sitting in the guest chair in front of Nate's desk, jotting down notes while Nate talked.

Ron closed the door behind him and, in a raised voice, said, "Don't give that guy any more information, Nate!"

Through blurry eyes, he saw the stunned look on Tom's face. That look turned to fear when Ron walked over to him and grabbed him by the necktie with one hand. He used the necktie for leverage as he exerted his considerable strength to yank Tom out of the chair and up into the air. The man started choking as the terrifying sensation of being hanged began to send warning signals into his brain. Ron brought his other hand up, too, giving him more leverage as he hoisted Tom well above his head.

Tom was choking and gasping—he brought one feeble hand up to his necktie, trying desperately to relieve the pressure. With the other hand he started banging on Ron's head. Ron ignored him and started swinging the man back and forth, increasing the tension on his neck. Tom's legs were kicking out in every direction.

Ron was vaguely aware of Nate yelling something and could sense that he was on his way over to the scene. Then he dropped him—actually just flung him outward. Tom crashed up against the coffee table and lay prone on the floor gasping for breath.

Nate grabbed Ron by the shoulders and spun him around. "What the fuck are you doing? Have you gone stark raving mad?"

Ron backed away from Nate and turned his attention to Tom on the floor.

Out of breath, Ron said, "You might...be better off asking our friend...that question, Nate."

Tom was starting to come around—he'd raised himself into a sitting position on the floor and loosened the necktie that just a few seconds ago had been functioning as a noose, strangling the life out of him.

Looking puzzled, Nate looked down at Tom. "What's Ron talking about, Tom?"

"I...haven't...got...a clue." Tom was rubbing his neck and stretching it from side to side.

"Explain yourself, Ron. You've just come close to killing our friend here, right in front of me."

"He's no friend of ours, Nate. That's just an illusion. I've just been told about phone records that show the NSA spook, Carl Masterson, and our Tom Foster here in regular communications together, long before the Black Mamba crashed."

Tom struggled to his feet. "There...has to be...some mistake."

"No, there's no mistake with those records, Tom. You're the mistake. You're the inside man."

Tom raised his arms out towards Nate in protest. "Nate, I told you about that engineer of ours who went missing after the accident—Bill Shanahan. He was the one up in the sling that day of the final inspection. Don't you remember me telling you that? He might have used my cell phone to make those calls to the NSA guy—to cover his tracks."

Ron took a step towards Tom, causing him to flinch and slink backwards. "You pathetic prick—I never said anything about a cell phone. I only said I had phone records. What made you say it was a cell phone?"

"Well, I just assumed..."

"You assumed nothing! And as far as Bill Shanahan is concerned, before I came to this meeting I went down to your department and checked with the two other engineers who were at Adventureland on that final inspection day. They'd been doing last minute checks in the mechanical room that day. I asked them if they recalled Bill being there—both said no, that the only other person there was you. And that you were doing all the outside work."

"They're just not remembering correctly."

"Both are pretty smart guys—but more to the point, they said Bill was down in Dallas doing an inspection there. I checked—he indeed was. His expense accounts back that up. Then I checked the maintenance records for that day of the final inspection, which you signed off on—and they show him being there, inspecting the track and the train. So, how could he have been all the way down in Dallas and way up north here in Virginia at exactly the same time? Someone doctored the records. Explain that, Tom?"

"I...can't."

"Was Bill your patsy, Tom? And did you have him killed? The same way you callously went along with killing twenty-five innocent people on the coaster?"

"I..."

Nate stepped forward and grabbed Tom by the lapels of his jacket. He pulled him to his feet and threw him back against the wall. "What the fuck did you do, Tom? And why?"

Tom started dribbling. Nate reared his fist back and smashed it into his nose. The blood started pouring instantly. Nate hit him again—this time in the solar plexus. Tom doubled over and began spitting blood.

"You murderous son-of-a-bitch! I can't believe what I'm hearing! I've known you forever!"

Tom suddenly stood proudly erect and pushed himself forward off the wall. "You guys...are making...a mistake. We have to...look into this. I'm being set up. You have to admit...we've been up against...incredible forces since this began. I would never have done the things you're alleging. Give me three hours—that's all I ask. I think I can follow a trail from what you've told me."

Ron looked over at Nate, hoping that he wouldn't give in to his friend's request. But he did.

Nate growled, "You have three hours and no more. Only because we've known each other for so long. After that, I'm calling the police. Don't make me regret this."

Tom's face showed instant relief. It made Ron sick to see it. He wouldn't have been so generous.

Tom held out his hand to Nate. "Thank you, buddy. I'll prove myself to you."

Nate shoved his hand away. "Get the fuck out of here. I'll shake your hand after you prove Ron wrong."

*****

Tom Foster moved fast. Packed a small suitcase, grabbed his passport and headed for the door. Sophie was still at work—a part-time job with a real estate office. And Joey and Katy were in school.

201

On his race home from the office, he'd arranged for a bank transfer of several hundred thousand dollars to a bank in Bangkok, Thailand. Sure, it could be traced, but they'd never find him there. A soul could get completely lost in Bangkok. He'd move the money around to different banks once he was settled in, but it didn't matter—they couldn't touch him there.

And while his sick affliction had brought all of this down upon himself, he figured if he was still going to live out his years he might as well live like he was meant to live.

Tom had thought of suicide, but realized at the last minute that he just didn't have the courage.

So, he'd live in Thailand, where every perversion he'd ever imagined would now be available to him on a daily basis.

Yes, it was a curse—but it was the only life Tom had left now.

CHAPTER 36

The hangar was sitting just a short taxi ramp in from the private airstrip. And it wasn't much of an airstrip. Just long enough to handle the typical jump-planes. It was dark and deserted, after the bustling activity all day with legions of people getting things ready for the next day's big rally.

The two interlopers had no problem gaining access to the building. A cheap lock that was easily compromised, with no visible signs of entry left behind. They were pros—and also expert skydivers themselves, having served with the Airborne Rangers.

The two men, outfitted in black from head to toe, headed straight for locker number 213. They knew this was her locker because a rental fee was being charged monthly against her credit card, and the online reservation form she'd completed identified the number assigned to her.

There was a combination lock, but that wasn't a challenge either. One man donned earphones and held what looked like a stethoscope up against the lock as he slowly turned the dial. Within minutes, the lock was open and the contents of the locker laid bare.

They dragged out a thick package—a sack containing precious cargo that had been carefully folded by its owner, with not only extreme care, but also special expertise—life-saving expertise.

One of the men shone a flashlight inside the locker. "Ah, ha—she has a tandem chute as well." He pulled that sack out and laid it on the floor several yards away from the other one. "Okay, you go to work on the single chute and I'll deal with the tandem."

They quietly went about their tasks—pulling the chutes out of the sacks and completely unfolding them. Then just re-folded them again, but slightly different than the way they came out. An errant fold here, another one there—they knew exactly which folds would cause the chutes to be impaired. Like most expert skydivers, they knew that the cause of most skydiving fatalities was incorrectly packed parachutes.

After finishing with the main chutes, they followed the same procedure with the reserve chutes—taking them out of their sacks, unfolding them and re-packing them in a slightly different fashion. Just enough to cause catastrophic failure.

Everything went back into locker number 213 in exactly the same spots. Nothing looked out of place. And the two men knew, with cold confidence, that whichever parachute she chose to use tomorrow would fail.

*****

Nate was on his way. It was about a half hour drive out to the private airstrip, and he didn't know whether he was looking forward to it or not. He was anxious to spend the day with Shelby, but he wasn't sure he wanted to do it floating down from a height of 15,000 feet.

Why did Shelby have to belong to a group called the Virginia Sky Pilots? Why couldn't it be something like the Virginia Movie Buffs?

Well, he knew that was just the way she was—she was a daredevil and even the terrifying Black Mamba accident hadn't kicked that tendency out of her. Sure, she was afraid to go on a rollercoaster again, but that hadn't depleted her thrill of adrenaline rushes in general.

Nate chuckled to himself. There he was, a rollercoaster designer, who was afraid to jump out of a plane! And as for Shelby, he still wouldn't change a thing about her—her daredevil attitude was one of the things he found attractive about her, probably because he had long outgrown that stage and sometimes wished he had it back again.

And...it was just simply one more aspect of Shelby Sutcliffe that he loved. So, he didn't mind joining her for one of her passions. Although he hoped that their next date might be just a simple movie!

They'd actually seen each other quite a few times since that first dinner date two weeks ago—mainly on lunch breaks and after work for drinks. Both of them had been pretty busy, so no time to devote an entire evening to each other. Nate hoped that would change soon.

Today was actually a good escape from the other things on his mind—well, one thing in particular: Tom Foster.

He'd been missing now for five days, ever since that meeting when Ron and Nate had roughed him up. The evidence against Tom for being the 'inside man' had been overwhelming, but, despite that, Nate had agreed to give him three hours to straighten it out.

He'd leaned in favor of loyalty towards his long-time friend and partner. And—he just hadn't wanted to believe it. He was in denial. Nate should have listened to Ron and called the police right away.

When he finally did call the police, it was too late. Tom had left the country and he'd been traced to Thailand—along with 600 thousand dollars of his family's money. The trail grew cold in Thailand. The police surmised that he'd just disappeared into the quagmire that was Bangkok, and he certainly had the funds at his disposal to change his identity and obtain a new passport.

Tom's wife, Sophie, was distraught, as were the kids. Nate had paid Sophie a visit to try to find out whatever he could. She knew nothing, but took the opportunity to grill Nate about what happened to cause Tom to leave. Nate didn't tell her anything, but left the hint with her that the reason he couldn't tell her was that it was now a police matter.

Nate still found it almost impossible to believe—that someone he'd been so close to for most of his adult life could have betrayed him and committed such a horrific act.

What was the connection between Tom and that NSA guy, Carl Masterson? Why had they been communicating with each other? And was Tom really the one who had applied the Thermate to the underside of the track and attached the fuses? So much for his apparent fear of heights.

Nate knew that his inability to be objective about Tom had caused them to miss their best opportunity yet to find out what this was all about. He only had himself to blame—Ron had done the proper due diligence which had incriminated Tom, but Nate had given the prick the benefit of the doubt. And then he had just fled the country.

He should have tied him to a chair and beat the shit out of him—and then the truth out of him. That's what he should have done.

He shook his head—shook the thought out of his brain. Today was an escape into the wild blue yonder, and he had to concentrate on just enjoying himself and letting the distraction work.

And what a distraction this was going to be! Flying through the air with the greatest of ease with a beautiful blonde strapped to his back!

He'd only been driving for fifteen minutes when he saw the sign for the turn-off to the Virginia Sky Pilots airfield. As soon as he saw it, his stomach started doing somersaults. And his mouth suddenly became dry. Hell, now he wouldn't even be able to give Shelby a proper 'hello' kiss!

Nate pulled his BMW up into the parking lot beside the small hangar building. He noticed several tents set up attended by a bunch of people—he guessed for registration. And inflatable jumpy houses for the kids—and there were lots of kids there already. Running around, jostling, laughing. And...much to his joy, there were several food tents. Hot dogs, hamburgers, pizza—a few of his favorite foods. They must have known he was coming!

He was wearing a pair of shorts and a t-shirt. Shelby had told him to dress light—he'd be donned in a 'onesey' jumpsuit, with a soft helmet called a "frap hat." It had to be soft on tandem jumps because his head could snap backwards and injure Shelby who'd be strapped on behind him. And he wore sneakers— they used to make jumpers wear heavy boots, but not anymore. It was thought that the boots protected the jumpers' feet upon landing, but history had proven that wrong. More injuries to ankles were caused by bad traction when hitting the ground, so sneakers worked best.

Nate walked inside the hangar and saw Shelby right away. She was standing in front of her locker already decked out in a yellow jumpsuit. She shrieked when she saw him, and ran over—throwing herself in the air, wrapping her arms around his neck and her legs around his thighs.

"I was afraid you weren't going to show! I'm so happy you're here. You're gonna just love this!"

Nate kissed her lips with his dry mouth. "Can I have a hamburger when this is over?"

She winked. "You can have more than that!" Nate's mouth suddenly went even dryer.

She lowered herself to the floor and pulled him by the hand. "Come over here to my locker. I have a nice brown jumpsuit for you—I tried for pink, but they were all out!"

Nate laughed and snapped his fingers. "Oh, darn!"

While Nate slipped into his suit, Shelby deftly strapped the parachute sack to her back. Then she spun him around and fastened a harness to him, clipping it around his thighs, his chest and shoulders.

"What's this for?"

"Silly boy—since I'm the only one with the parachute, you need to get attached to me. You'll be attached to my chest—I'll snap you on to me just before we exit the plane."

"Oh, God!"

"Sounds ominous, I know—but it's perfectly safe. You'll love it. We'll be jumping today from 15,000 feet. And you don't have to worry about a thing—I'm a certified jumpmaster and instructor, with over 1,000 jumps under my belt. And you can easily see that I'm still alive!"

"Yes, I'll give you that. You're very much alive!"

"Just to give you some scope of what we'll be doing, Nate—we'll freefall for about sixty seconds at about 120 miles per hour. A tiny little chute will pop out as we exit the plane, called a 'Drogue' parachute.

"All that will do is just slow us down in freefall—otherwise we'd be falling at 150 miles per hour, which sometimes is too risky a speed to pull the main chute. So the Drogue will just give us a bit of drag, nothing more than that.

"We won't be able to talk during freefall—too noisy with the wind rushing.

But once the main chute opens we'll be able to chat the rest of the way down, which will be about a six minute ride. When we approach the ground, I'll tell you when to lift your legs up—then I'll control the landing. Just keep your feet out of the way and let me take the landing."

Nate was trying hard to find saliva to swallow with, but there seemed to be none available. "What if the main chute doesn't open?"

"I'll pull the main chute at around 5,500 feet from the ground." Shelby held her wrist up. "See this on my wrist? This is an altimeter—tells me when to pull.

"But, as a safety precaution, in case something happens on the way down and I can't pull the chute, the main chute is equipped with an AAD—Automatic Activation Device. It's programmed to engage the main chute at an altitude of 2,000 feet just in case it hasn't been pulled by then. And…if the main chute doesn't open, I also have a reserve chute. It's not as big or as safe, but it will provide some level of lift for us. So, you see? Nothing to worry about!"

Nate gulped. "Yeah, right. Can the parachute handle the weight of both of us?"

Shelby laughed. "Oh, easily. I have two different chutes that I use—one for when I jump solo, and another one for tandems. The tandem chutes are bigger and able to handle more weight. They're rectangular and quite big—about 500 square feet when fully inflated.

"However, if we did have to use the reserve chute, we won't slow down as much—so we'd hit the ground harder. I can tell you though, in all the jumps I've made, I've never yet had to pull my reserve chute."

Shelby reached into her locker and pulled out a knife in a sheath, and two pairs of goggles. "Here, put your goggles on and adjust them so they're comfy."

Nate slipped the goggles over his eyes and adjusted the band. "What's that knife for?"

"Just to shut you up in case you scream too much and annoy me!"

"Ha, ha…very funny. Seriously, what's the vicious looking knife for?"

Shelby clipped it to the waist of her jumpsuit. "In case something unforeseen happens and I have to cut away the main chute."

She suddenly yelled out to someone coming through the door. "Brenda, you made it!" She ran over and grabbed her by the hand, pulling her towards Nate. "This is the guy I've told you about—Nate Morrell. My hero—the one who saved my life! Nate, this is my skydiving buddy, Brenda Walgren."

Nate held out his hand. "Pleased to meet you, Brenda. You going up today, too?"

Brenda smiled at him. "So nice to meet you, too—and thanks for saving my dear friend here. Yes, I'm going up in the same plane with you guys, as a matter of fact." She looked down at a piece of paper in her hand. "I see that one other jumper is with us and we go in fifteen minutes."

Nate gulped. "Oh, God…"

Brenda spun the dial of the combination lock and opened her locker. "Nate, I felt just like you on my first jump—but honestly, it's just a wonderful safe feeling. Once you get that jumping out of the plane part out of the way, there's nothing to it. You'll be fine—and you're jumping with one of our club's finest."

Nate put his arm around Shelby's shoulders. "That makes me feel better. And…I'm not surprised that she's one of the best."

Shelby smiled and leaned up on her tiptoes, kissing Nate tenderly on the cheek.

"We'd better get out there. Brenda, see you in the plane!"

"Okay, I'll just be a couple of minutes. Don't leave without me! And…maybe a beer at the booze tent afterwards?"

Nate muttered. "I think scotch would work best."

Both women laughed. And for one last time, as he walked outside and towards the ominous-looking plane, Nate cursed, "Oh, God,"

*****

Shelby knew they were almost at the point. It normally only took six minutes for these sleek little jump planes to reach 15,000 feet. She looked out through the little window beside them—a beautiful day for Nate's first jump. Sunny, not too much wind. She leaned her head forward from where they were sitting on the floor near the back. The first jumper, a guy named Jake, was positioned right beside the doorless opening. He edged his ass forward and sat on the edge. Then the jumpmaster yelled, "Now!"

Jake leaned forward and did a somersault out of the plane. He was gone.

Brenda was next. Amidst the swirling noise of the wind rushing through the door opening, she managed to yell back, "See you on the ground! Good luck, Nate!"

She slithered forward on her bum and hung her feet over the edge. Then the command came and she was gone, too.

Shelby leaned forward and whispered into Nate's ear. "Okay, darling. Our turn. Slither forward to the edge, lift your feet up in the air and lean back against me."

Nate didn't say a thing, but he did obey her. Once he was positioned with his legs hanging out of the plane, Shelby strapped his harness to hers in three spots down his body. "Okay, legs up in the air and let me do the rest. Just go with it."

His legs lifted; Shelby eased them both gently over the edge and pushed Nate downwards, guiding them into a gentle somersault down and away from the plane.

They were airborne. She checked her altimeter—already at 14,000 feet. They would just enjoy the ride now for another forty-five seconds, then she would pull the main chute.

She stretched her arms out wide and motioned for Nate to do the same. Then, for aerodynamics, she used her feet to pull Nate's legs up between hers. Then she just spread her legs wide and relished the experience.

She was hoping Nate was enjoying the ride of his life. And later, back at her house, she intended to give Nate the second ride of his life. Two in one day—what man could ask for more?

Shelby scanned the horizon and could see Brenda soaring in freefall slightly below them and behind. She checked her altimeter. Just a few seconds to go.

Then she saw something else. Something that made her heart stop.

CHAPTER 37

She was struggling. Brenda never *ever* allowed herself a full freefall for the full sixty seconds. She always pulled her main chute at around 10,000 feet; had never been confident enough to allow herself to fall to the 5,000 foot level. Shelby and Brenda had chatted about this many times—Shelby had encouraged her to give it a try so she could experience the full joy of freefall. But Brenda's logic was that she wanted plenty of time to react if the main chute didn't open. Wanted to be able to stay as calm as possible to get the reserve chute out and inflated.

Shelby gazed down in horror as Brenda twisted in the air. She was pulling frantically at the handle for her main chute—then doing the same thing with the reserve handle. Back and forth, alternating between each handle. Nothing was happening.

Shelby glanced at her altimeter—they were already at 7,500 feet. And Brenda was about a 1,000 feet lower. Brenda's main chute should have opened up 3,500 feet ago.

Thoughts were racing frantically through Shelby's brain—a rapid processing in mere milliseconds, her training and instincts coming through on auto-pilot. And she not only had Brenda and herself to worry about; she had Nate strapped to her chest, too.

The dreaded light-headedness started settling in again—she could feel it beginning to overcome her and her eyesight began to blur. *No! Not now! Don't do this to me!*

She screamed as hard as she could—no one could hear her, of course, not even Nate at the speed they were falling accompanied by the deafening rush of wind.

She screamed once again and her head started to clear. Not wasting time, fearing that it would come back again, she reached down to her waist and ripped the knife out of its sheath. Then she reached up and cut the line to the little Drogue chute, the one that had deployed as they left the plane. The little contraption that was containing their freefall to 120 miles per hour.

Shelby needed to go faster than that, and she needed the maneuverability to be able to control her movements to precision, and the Drogue would interfere with that.

As soon as the Drogue was cut, their speed increased dramatically. She could tell Nate noticed, as he turned his head around and looked up at her. Shelby merely made a calming motion with one hand, then pointed down to where Brenda was. Then she made a swooping motion with her hand. He nodded. Shelby figured he understood, but it didn't matter—she wasn't asking permission.

She went to work. Instinct was in charge now, partnered by sheer terror for her friend. Shelby roughly pushed down on Nate's head and shoulders, causing them to begin to assume a downward attitude. Then she lowered her own head straight down just above Nate's and pushed his legs inward, squeezing them together with her own legs. Now their legs formed a sleek posture of no resistance. Next she grabbed his arms and extended them outward in front of him and joined them with her own.

Instantly, their speed went from relatively sublime to pulse-pounding. Shelby knew that the position they'd just assumed, particularly the 'head down' position, had the potential of increasing their air speed to almost 250 miles per hour. She looked ahead and slightly downward. They were approaching Brenda very quickly, and she had to make sure to apply the brakes before they slammed into her.

Shelby's goggles were starting to fog up, and some light-headedness was coming back. As they continued to dive like eagles, she screamed with all her might. Her head cleared—she'd fought the fainting episode off once again. Even her goggles had de-fogged.

Shelby could see Brenda's face clearly now—and she could tell that Brenda saw her, too. The look on her face was one of abject desperation and horror. She was still yanking away on the handles, hoping for some kind of miracle.

Shelby knew that she was Brenda's only hope for a miracle. They were very close now—Shelby pulled back on Nate's head just as she raised her own, spread their arms out wide and did the same with their legs. Nate seemed to instinctively know what she was doing and moved easily to her cues.

She then pulled back on his shoulders and arched her back to the farthest extent she could. They were perfectly parallel to the ground and their sideways movement had stopped. They were falling at the same pace as Brenda and only about twenty feet separated them.

Shelby made subtle movements with their conjoined bodies in order to close that distance quickly, being careful to avoid spinning into an accidental "head down" position again. If they raced downward, past Brenda, there's no way they could come back up. There was absolutely no room for error.

They were close now, very close.

Shelby stretched outward with her right hand, and Brenda did the same with her left. Their fingers touched, then they both bent their fingers to get a clasping effect.

It worked! She yanked hard and Brenda slammed into their two heads. Shelby grabbed onto Brenda's harness with her right hand, and then checked the altimeter on her left wrist. They were now at a heart-stopping 4,000 feet above the unforgiving ground. She would have normally pulled her chute at no lower than 5,000 feet, particularly when she was on a tandem jump. And now it had turned into a trio jump. Too much weight falling for one chute to handle safely, and not much altitude left for the canopy to slow them down sufficiently.

Shelby had one more precaution to take before pulling the ripcord of her parachute. She was worried that the faulty chutes that were strapped to Brenda's back might still decide to open, and if both of those chutes opened at the same time as Shelby's opened, or even afterward, they could have a serious problem of conflict between chutes. The tangled mess would be unable to inflate properly and all three of them would just continue their freefall at over 150 miles per hour, straight into the ground. And she was deathly afraid that the AAD on Brenda's chute might also somehow trigger that troubled chute into opening at the programmed 2,000 foot level, which would just cause it to collide underneath Shelby's canopy, rendering it useless.

She didn't have time to tell her what she was going to do, and neither would Brenda even hear her with the overwhelming rush of wind noise. She had to simply act on instinct, and the 2,000 foot level was approaching fast—her chute would automatically open at that point and she had to dump Brenda's before it possibly opened, too.

With her one hand holding onto Brenda's harness, she reached down with the other one and dragged Nate's left hand up and around Brenda's waist—then pulled it in tight. Nate understood. He shot his right hand up and did the same thing. She was now wrapped up tight and on an angle that was below Nate. Shelby couldn't reach the buckles of Brenda's harness now because of Nate's body being in the way, so she yanked her knife out of its sheath once again and with several quick swipes managed to cut the harness free. The wind grabbed the crippled contraption and swept it away.

Shelby looked down at Brenda and gave her the 'thumbs up' sign. Brenda just stared back at her, expressionless, while Nate held onto her for dear life.

She stole a glance at her altimeter—2,200 feet.

Then she felt the pull as her Automatic Actuation Device did its assigned work. It felt as if they were yanked upward, but that was just an illusion, as their rapid downward motion was slowed so dramatically it gave the impression of 'lift.'

She glanced around—they were a long way from the 'drop zone.' She couldn't even see the huge white triangle that would have been painted on the ground. In their attempts to just stay alive, they had drifted well out of range.

The ground was coming up fast—not as fast as it had been during freefall, but much faster than a normal parachute drift. This canopy wasn't designed for three people, and neither was it designed to be pulled only 2,000 feet above the ground. Shelby knew they would have a hard and fast landing, which might prove to be just as fatal as a freefall into the ground.

She looked down at the landscape. They had drifted so far that they were on the outskirts of Alexandria now, and the ground that they were going to hit was solid concrete—not the soft gentle fields that the airstrip was surrounded by.

Shelby reached both hands up, grabbed onto the toggles, and began to steer them at different angles. She couldn't allow them to hit a concrete road or building—there had to be something better. She spun them around with quick pulls on the toggles and gazed outward. She was hoping for a clump of tall trees that were growing close together—something that would soften their landing and catch them before hitting the ground. And she was worried about power lines—a skydiver's worst enemy. As they were now close to Alexandria, they might be headed for some exposed lines which wouldn't be easily visible at the height they were at.

Then she saw the best of the worst options.

Water!

It was a small lake or reservoir a short distance to the northeast. They would just make it.

Now that the parachute was open, all three of them were upright. They could talk, now that the rush of the wind had stopped.

But Shelby didn't talk, she yelled. "Nate, that lake is our safest option. I'm going to steer us over there. We're still going to hit the water fairly fast and hard. When we get about fifty feet above the water I'm going to steer us back into the wind. That will slow us by about 15 miles per hour."

Shelby looked at Brenda. "Do you hear me, Brenda?"

No expression on her face; no reaction to Shelby's voice.

"I think she's in shock, Shelby. I'll look out for her when we land. What do you want me to do?"

"At thirty feet above the water, I want you to drop Brenda. I'll yell out the order. You and I'll keep drifting, so we'll be a few feet past her when we hit. No chance then of collision. At twenty feet above the water, I'm going to disconnect you from me. You'll then drop to the water. Do a cannonball; much safer at the speed we'll be hitting. We'll just have to hope for the best with Brenda—she's not responding."

Nate turned his head back toward her again. "Roger on that. What about you?"

"I'll hit the water after you. But I need you to drop first well away from the parachute so that you can come after me. I'll disconnect myself from the chute right after I disconnect you, but the chute will probably still drape on top of me—it's so big. I might need you to free me."

Nate just nodded and squeezed Brenda closer to his chest.

They were over the lake and drifting down fast. It was always so deceiving over water, trying to ascertain how close to the surface you were. If they dropped while they were still too high, it would be certain death. Shelby glanced at her altimeter—sixty feet, fifty feet, forty feet…

She spun them around with the toggles, tugging harder on the back toggle to open the canopy towards the wind. She was relieved that the slowdown effect was almost instantaneous.

"Drop her, Nate!"

He shook his head and held on!

"Nate—drop her!"

He shook his head again.

Shelby couldn't wait any longer. She reached down with both hands and disconnected Nate's harness at the three spots. He and Brenda dropped toward the water. Shelby was aware of Nate flipping his legs upward with Brenda on top.

As Shelby disconnected herself from the parachute, she could see them hitting the water with Nate in a curled sitting position, arms locked at the elbows and stretching toward the sky, holding Brenda safely above the surface of the water. He took the full force of the hit.

Shelby was free of the chute. She pulled her legs up to her chest and folded her arms over her knees, keeping her head upright. She hit the water hard, felt the searing sting in her bum. She went down deep, and then opened her eyes. Sure enough, the parachute was settling into the water right above her.

Shelby swam sideways for a bit, but then panic caused her to start reaching toward the surface. She felt disoriented—it looked as if she was past the canopy, but once she reached what she thought was the surface, it was nothing but the nylon of the parachute.

The panic was taking over—and the lightheaded feeling was starting to return. She moved along the surface, feeling the pressure on her lungs as the oxygen was quickly depleting. She kicked hard with her legs and pressed up at the surface with her hands.

But the parachute's death shroud seemed endless. And the feeling that she was about to faint was causing fear to take over. She couldn't think clearly. And she couldn't scream now to chase the faintness away. If it happened now, she would surely drown.

And a thought kept nagging at her brain. She had a tool to get her out of this mess. What was that tool? She was starting to feel drowsy—had the urge to open her mouth to breathe, but something in her brain told her not to do that.

Suddenly, she felt a strong arm wrapping around her waist, and a slight pressure at the side of her hip. Pulling at something. What was it?

Then the flash of a knife, frantically tearing into the smothering fabric of death above her.

CHAPTER 38

Carl Masterson was sitting in his office at Fort Meade, Maryland, enjoying his morning cup of black java. He savored the aroma first, then took a long, labored sip. *Ahh...the rush!*

He pondered in his mind how his two assassins would pull off the jobs he'd assigned to them. Knew that they'd follow his instructions to the letter, but in a macabre way he was curious to know how they would do it.

He made the decision that Shelby Sutcliffe had to die once he'd learned from Tom Foster—before the coward disappeared—that she was only pretending to join the Class Action lawsuit, and instead had joined the Flying Machines crew to help prove their innocence. He knew that the feisty lady was going to blow the whistle at some point—perhaps even in court, allowing that slob of a lawyer, Feinstein, to think that she was going to testify that the bars disengaged on impact. When in reality she would shock the court by telling what really happened—and that she'd been threatened to testify falsely. Then everything would start unravelling. All due to words from the pretty little mouth of the star witness; someone who not only looked good, but was also a nurse, and a sympathetic character who had survived a horrific accident. She would be entirely believable.

So, it was her loss in not just going along and collecting a cool two million dollars. Now she would...simply...die. And be shut up forever. The Class Action would succeed without her testimony, and the Black Mamba episode would remain classified in official records as simply an accident.

And that John Fletcher guy—well, he was a ticking time bomb. He'd done the investigation, he'd seen the molten metal and deduced correctly that Thermate had been used to bring the rollercoaster down. The self-righteous prick had already used his wife to tip off the Flying Machines executives as to where the wreckage was—and gotten her killed in the process. And now Carl knew that Fletcher had a terminal brain tumor. So, he was not only a ticking time bomb, but also potentially a very loose cannon. Someone who had nothing, and no one, to live out his final year for. Carl was convinced that such a person could not be frightened into silence—he would be completely incapable of feeling fear.

Both of these people were dangers to the operation and they were loose ends that had to be tied.

Carl knew that he probably wouldn't hear from his two men until both jobs were done—true to their prior modus operandi if they received an assignment to kill two or more parties related to the same case subject, the killings would usually be done around the same time. Or at least within a few short hours of each other. The reason for that was the worry that once word got out about the first death, the other one would go underground, or speak out in public about what they knew just to protect themselves.

So, Carl would wait patiently. He wouldn't be able to totally relax until he heard that both Shelby Sutcliffe and John Fletcher had gone to the 'great beyond.' And, of course, it would be entertaining to hear how his two creative killers had accomplished the task. Carl always liked to enjoy the silver lining of any situation and the entertainment value provided by contract kills was always amusing to him. Sometimes, he laughed out loud at the outrageous methods these guys occasionally used. Well, he didn't care how they did it as long as neither death looked like murder. She had to die in an accident, and he had to die in either an accident or through the appearance of suicide.

Carl stood up from behind his desk and walked over to a large map of the world that he had just purchased the other day, now hanging on his far wall. He studied the Great Lakes region, in particular Lake Erie, imagining in his mind where the tunnel's forward movement was at that very moment. In his estimation, there would only be about five miles left to go. They were close, so close.

His eyes roamed down to the great state of California, then over to Nevada, Arizona, Texas and New Mexico. These five states were in dire straits from the punishing drought, and food was going to start costing the United States a ton of money. Food they'd never had to import before would now have to be shipped in and paid for at usury prices. Countries that America had never had to buy food from before would be licking their lips at the opportunity to stick it to them.

Their fruit would have to come from Mexico, Egypt and third world countries in the Caribbean. And their wheat and other grains would have to be bought from Canada. America's standard of living would fall, towns and cities would fail, farmers would be thrown out of work—and the tourist trade would dry up. Who would want to fly to the United States on holiday if the lakes and rivers were dry, if green foliage had turned brown, and if they couldn't even get a glass of water—or had to be told that the water they were sipping was simply recycled sewage?

Oil had been the propellant for America's economy over the last century— and now water, or the lack of, threatened to kill it and also decimate the country's superpower status. America would become a pathetically needy nation and, while no one liked needy people, a needy country was even more pitiful.

217

Carl's eyes moved across the map to northern Africa, and Libya in particular. He remembered back to when they had first strategized the plan that became known as Operation Backwash. A bunch of them sitting around a large table, marvelling at what Muammar Gaddafi had pulled off in Libya. And it occurred to them that they could do exactly what he did, but it wouldn't have to be even a fraction of the size that he designed. And they would do it in reverse.

Gaddafi had brought water *from* an aquifer to his cities and the driest areas of his country. The U.S. would take water *from* a large body of water and divert it *into* a depleted aquifer and the dying Mississippi.

Yes, the iconic leader of Libya, the man who preferred to sleep in a Bedouin tent at night rather than in one of his palaces, had created the world's most ambitious civil engineering project. The man who the United States and other NATO countries had propagandized into a madman in the eyes of the world, was actually a genius. Who would have thunk it?

The Great Man-Made River Project, so named, was a vast network of pipes that drew water from the world's largest aquifer—the Nubian Sandstone Aquifer System. This aquifer was discovered by Libya in 1953 by accident while they were searching for oil reserves. Turned out that this marvel of nature had accumulated from the last Ice Age and was just sitting there waiting to be taken. So, Gaddafi, the little Bedouin genius, decided in 1983 to get the ball rolling. He stated his vision to the world: *My people will have fresh water for the next 1,000 years and I will undertake a project of "greening" the desert.*

The arrogant little bugger actually said that he intended his country to be "self-sufficient" and not dependent on anyone. He wanted certain parts of the Sahara to be transformed into fertile agricultural lands, providing good jobs for farmers and reducing the country's need to import meats, fruits and vegetables.

The Western media—prodded by governments of course—declared the project as the "pipe dream of a madman." But, by the turn of the new century, the marvel of what the man had done couldn't be ignored any longer. Engineers around the world began referring to the GMRP as a "masterful work of engineering," which it truly was. And the aquifer was so huge, it would indeed last for 1,000 years. Libya would indeed rise to a position of prominence, not just in the Middle East, but in the entire world.

Gaddafi installed 1,750 miles of underground pipes, making it the largest network of pipes and aqueducts on the planet. It was designed to deliver over 5 million cubic meters of water a day to cities all across Libya. Not just for drinking, but for irrigation as well, in order for Gaddafi's dream of "greening" the desert to be realized. Palm trees started growing in places where they'd never been seen before. A full seventy percent of Libya's citizens could turn on their taps and receive fresh water, a luxury many had never enjoyed before.

218

This damn Nubian aquifer was vast—the little desert-dwelling Arab had really lucked out. He'd discovered by accident that he was sitting on top of an Ice Age miracle that contained a mindboggling 100,000 cubic miles of groundwater, the world's largest fossil aquifer system. Gaddafi had clearly been born with a horseshoe up his ass.

That all changed of course when NATO forces attacked Libya in 2011 and, instead of a horseshoe, someone shoved a knife up his ass just before he was executed. Clearly a war crime, he'd been taken prisoner and deserved to be protected under the Geneva Convention, but America and its allies had never given a shit about stuff like that in the Middle East—Arabs were just a bunch of primitive beings intent on destroying the Western way of life.

That moment and the eight months of bombing that preceded it, ended Gaddafi's ambitious dreams for his country. He just went the way of Hussein, Noriega, and so many other dictators who'd gotten too big for their britches and had actually started believing their own headlines. *We couldn't have that happening.*

Carl shook his head as he marvelled about what the little Arab had accomplished. He still couldn't quite believe that such genius and vision came from a man who slept in a fucking tent. Who could believe that a man like that could rally the engineering talent to build almost 2,000 miles of pipe through tunnels, and drill 1,300 wells—some of them 1,500 feet deep to access the aquifer.

Carl also remembered a quote that Gaddafi had spouted to the Press back in 1991. It went something like: *"After we finish this project, America's threats against Libya will double. They will create reasons to harm us, but their real reason will be to stop this achievement and keep the people of Libya oppressed."*

Carl chuckled. *How right he was!* But what Gaddafi didn't fully appreciate was his brilliance in pulling off this engineering marvel, the envy of the world, without borrowing one fucking cent from international banks! The arrogance! A measly little Arab country of only four million people was able to build this monstrosity without a single dollar of debt. *Hell, in America, with a population of 300 million, we can't even build a fucking bridge without borrowing money!*

Gaddafi never really saw it coming though. First, there were the 'Arab Springs' popping up across the Middle East—first Tunisia, then Egypt, then Libya—and eventually Syria. Each of those uprisings were stirred up and manufactured by the CIA and other intelligence agencies of the West.

No, Gaddafi just never saw it coming. That alone showed how stupid and naïve he really was. Maybe he wasn't such a genius after all? Did he really think the world would allow a primitive Arab in a tent to rise to such prominence, waving the resource stick in our face? He already had oil, now he had water. How much more would he want? Well, he had already started musing about an Arab currency for oil sales—ignoring the American dollar as the reserve currency. *Sorry—not an option, Muammar.*

The bombs and missiles started falling in 2011, and eight months later it was over. NATO decided it had a moral obligation to intervene in the civil war that had been fired up and stoked by the CIA. By the time the intervention was over, parts of the engineering marvel that Gaddafi had created were destroyed, slamming the Libyan people back fifty years. Now, instead of seventy percent of the people having access to fresh water, it was only forty percent.

And the little dictator had been executed. Carl didn't know the whole story, but from what he did know, the NATO attacks had been most aggressively supported by France. For the first time in their modern military history, France had led the way for NATO. Which Carl always thought was kind of strange— and added credence to reports that surfaced in 2012 that a certain prominent French politician had conspired with Libya to have his 2007 re-election campaign financed by Libyan money—to the tune of fifty million Euros. And added credence also to reports that a French assassin had infiltrated the "mob" that had dragged Gaddafi kicking and screaming out of a sewer pipe. And that after that knife was brutally rammed up Gaddafi's ass, this same assassin put a gun to his head and pulled the trigger.

Because a dead Gaddafi wouldn't be able to talk about his special relationship with France.

And to this day, the Libyan people, who were now suffering once again from water shortages, probably weren't aware that tanker ships were leaving Libya's harbors every week laden with water destined for the United States of America.

CHAPTER 39

Volunteers with the Virginia Sky Pilots hunted around the countryside for two hours until they found it. Six of them in four-wheel-drive Jeeps scoured the land until they saw an anomaly. A gray sack lying in a field of dandelions.

When they returned to the hangar with the prize, Nate was sitting in a corner with Shelby. He had his arm around her shoulders, which were wrapped in a warm blanket. She'd changed into a dry set of clothes from her locker when they returned. Nate's clothes were still wet, but he didn't care. They'd be fine until he got home, and it was still so hot outside that he welcomed the feel of moist clothes against his skin.

But Shelby was a different story. She was shivering despite the ninety degree heat, and Nate knew it was probably more from the shock of what she'd gone through. She'd managed to hold it together during their desperate freefall flight and expertly took care of all of the details to get them safely down into the lake. And had managed to fight off the fainting spells the entire time they were in peril. But landing in the water and getting stuck under the chute had taken its toll on her.

After Nate had succeeded in tearing through the nylon parachute with Shelby's knife, they broke through the surface, desperate to just breathe again. They gulped it in, both panting heavily, but once the joy of breathing fresh air again was over, they realized they would have to just tread water—there was nowhere to go. They were stuck with their heads popped through a four foot opening in the nylon. Nate used the knife again to make the opening a bit larger but they couldn't swim until they cut the thing right through to the edge.

Both of them were having a tough time at that point, but especially Shelby. She was exhausted, and told him that she felt a fainting spell coming on again. Nate urged her to just scream away and she did. It helped, but she still seemed disoriented.

He knew he could easily swim by himself underwater again, underneath the nylon canopy to the outer edge, but there was no way Shelby had the energy for that. And he didn't want to leave her alone to tread water while he swam for help.

So, they were stuck in this tiny opening, treading water, and Shelby was getting more and more tired by the second. Nate continued hacking away at the nylon—hard work because he had to use one hand to hold the material and the other one to wield the knife. All the while treading water with just his feet.

Suddenly, she was there—diving in from the shoreline.

He knew that Brenda had survived their fall. Shortly after they hit the water, she came out of her daze. The force and temperature of the water had snapped her out of it. Nate ordered her to swim to shore, which was only a forty yard jaunt, while he dove under the parachute to search for Shelby.

But now Brenda was coming for them. She reached the outer edge of the floating parachute and grabbed onto it tightly. She yelled, "Hold onto the edge you've cut! I'm going to pull you in!"

And she did—inch by painstaking inch, she dragged the cumbersome nylon sheet, swimming backwards with just her feet, both hands on the edge of the chute. The more progress she made, the faster they were traveling. Once she got past the 'dead in the water' inertia, the canopy moved faster and Brenda's task became easier. Nate and Shelby just held on tight.

Once on shore, they had all just collapsed to the ground. And then they enjoyed a group hug. A jeep arrived along the shore and drove them back to the airfield; no one said a word about what had happened. No one even wanted to think about it. What almost happened to the three of them, but particularly Brenda, was too horrifying to consider. All Nate knew at this point was that he was never going to jump out of a fucking plane again—he didn't care how much Shelby still enjoyed it or how much she begged him. He wasn't going to do that again. It was a suicide mission.

But more than two hours had gone by, and now they had to think and talk about what happened. They had hung around for that very reason. Brenda and Shelby wanted to take a look at Brenda's parachute sack once it was found. They had to know.

Nate saw the Jeep pull up out front and Brenda ran out to greet it. She came back in with the sack in her hand and dropped it on the floor in front of them.

"Are you up to this, Shelby?"

Shelby nodded and pushed the blanket off her shoulders. Then she knelt down on the floor beside Brenda. "Let's go real slow, Brenda—unfold it very carefully, and let's look at each fold."

Nate got down on the floor beside them and watched as their expert hands went to work. They knew exactly how a parachute should be folded and packed, and from what Shelby had told him, even one fold out of place could cause catastrophic failure.

It didn't take them long. Just three folds in, they saw it. One fold was going in the opposite direction, and the pilot chute was stuffed underneath this particular fold with two of the suspension lines wrapped around it. With the pilot chute disabled, there was no way the main chute would have opened—the little pilot chute's job was to be first out of the sack, grabbing onto the wind and pulling the main chute out behind it. The pilot chute was trapped in a way that it would never have seen the light of day.

Brenda gasped. "I pack my own chutes—there's no way I would have ever packed it like that! I would have had to have been stoned at the time to fold it that way!"

Shelby opened up the compartment for the reserve safety chute. These reserve canopies were much smaller and they didn't have to have pilot chutes in order to open. But—this one had been clearly sabotaged, too. Folded in the opposite way from standard accepted practice, there was no wonder it didn't open either.

Shelby's face had gone completely white. She whispered, "Brenda, go get the tandem chute out of your locker. We'll look at that one, too."

Nate rubbed Shelby's back. "You okay, hon?"

"No, I'm not. I feel a chill again."

Nate reached behind him and dragged the blanket off the chair. He wrapped it around her shoulders as Brenda returned with the tandem sack.

The girls went through the same procedure for both the main canopy and the reserve chute. Once finished, they just sat back and stared at each other.

Brenda spoke first. "One parachute packed that way is tough enough to explain, but both parachutes? That's almost impossible to fathom. Someone wanted me to die today."

Shelby lowered her head into her hands and started crying. Nate pulled the blanket around her tighter and kissed the back of her head. "Shelby, thanks to you, no one died today. You were in control the entire time. We owe our lives to you."

Brenda crawled over to Shelby and hugged her hard. "It's okay. Let it out. Today was a shock for all of us. But Nate's right—we both owe our lives to you. I couldn't believe it when I looked up and saw the two of you diving toward me. I've never seen such a precision freefall before in my life—thank God you did the most perfect manoeuvre *today* instead of some other day. And even though you're an expert skydiver, I doubt if you could ever pull that off again—it was amazing. I hope you never *will* have to do a stunt like that again!"

Shelby lifted her head and wiped her eyes with the back of her hand.

"No one wanted you to die today, Brenda. It was me they wanted."

Brenda and Nate just stared—mouths hanging open in shock. Nate broke the silence. "What do you mean? It was her chutes that were tampered with."

"They thought they were tampering with my equipment. The locker Brenda uses is actually my locker. Locker number 213 is *my* locker. Remember, Brenda, you asked me to trade with you about three years ago. You've always been so superstitious about numbers, and the numbers in 213 add up to 6, which you said was your lucky number. So, I traded with you."

Brenda's hands flew to her mouth. "God, I'd forgotten! But, that was so long ago!"

Shelby nodded. "Yes, it was. But the official record still shows me as the renter of locker 213. And I pay that rental fee every month. And you're paying the rent for the other locker: the one I use—the one that's in your name."

She wrapped the blanket around her chest and pulled it up just under her chin.

"I was supposed to die today. Not you."

CHAPTER 40

It was another late night for John Fletcher. Why he was putting in such long hours at work, he didn't quite know. There was really no point anymore. Maybe it was because he didn't have Linda to come home to. Or that their beloved house had burned to the ground and all he had to return to now was a depressing rental. No sense of ownership or belonging anymore.

He almost always came home on time when Linda was alive. They rarely missed having dinner together. It was like a daily tradition for them—talking about their day, all the little things they did: the silly things, the important things, and all the things in between. There was always something to talk about. But, sometimes they didn't even talk at all. They didn't need to—just being together had always been enough for both of them, and once in a while silence was a special treasure, a comforting sense of tranquility.

Sometimes after dinner, accompanied by coffee and maybe a liqueur or two, they enjoyed a game of chess together. John was a really good chess player and it had always been hard to find someone to play with who could challenge him. So, ten years ago he'd reluctantly taught Linda to play—she begged him, he groaned, she begged him some more. He figured it was just a passing phase—that he'd spend hours and hours teaching her this difficult game, she'd enjoy it for a while, then give up. And he knew that after he beat her a few times she'd definitely throw in the towel. And, for John, playing chess with a rookie who would probably take five years to reach his level of play, it would be a boring experience every time she asked to play.

Well, was he ever surprised! After the teaching was over and the real games began, it only took Linda about twenty matches before she started making him sweat. He knew his wife was clever, but he really didn't think chess would be something she'd rise to. She wasn't known for her patience and chess was one of those slow-moving games that required gobs of patience and endless waiting.

John smiled as he remembered the first time she put him in checkmate. He'd just stared at the board, not believing what had just happened. And there she was, dancing around the living room, happier than a child on Christmas morning.

She was thrilled that she beat him and, at the very moment of that victory,

John developed new respect for the love of his life. And while he didn't relish being beaten, he was delighted that he now had a chess partner who could give him a run for his money. It was no fun playing someone whom you could easily beat. There was no challenge or sense of satisfaction in that.

John turned onto his street and rubbed the cuff of his shirt across his eyes. Tears came easily these days—it didn't take much. A scene in his mind, an image of her smiling face, the sound of her voice haunting his memory. Anything at all would bring the tears. He knew time would be a big healer, but he didn't have much time so he figured that this was probably the way it would be for him the rest of his days. And that was okay. He had no reasons to be happy, so he might as well experience at least one emotion.

Well, there were actually two emotions that now dominated his being: sadness and anger.

The anger wouldn't go away either. And now that he knew so much more—including the name of the NSA spook, a plan would soon formulate in his mind. He couldn't wait too long because he just didn't have that long.

John pulled into the driveway of his two-storey rented house, a far cry from the beautiful home that he and Linda had nurtured for most of their adult lives. She'd had the garden looking so lovely before she died—she was so proud of it, and John was proud of her *for* it. He was glad there was no garden to speak of at this house—he would only regret that Linda wasn't wielding her magic.

He forlornly got out of his car, trudged up to the front door and inserted his key. Turned the handle and stepped inside. He sighed as he tossed his briefcase onto the bench in the hall and wandered down to the kitchen. A beer might be nice—it was still so hot outside, and inside it wasn't much better. The rental house didn't have air conditioning, so sleeping at night wasn't pleasant.

They were waiting for him in the kitchen.

Sitting at his kitchen table with pistols in their hands aimed directly at his head.

They were big guys, both bald, with tattoos that marred their necks and even the tops of their heads.

John just stood in stunned silence. He stared at them. Funny, he didn't feel afraid at all—in fact, it didn't even really surprise him all that much. But he didn't know what to say, so he just waited. And he couldn't move—not with those guns aimed at his head.

One of the tattoo twins decided to speak. "Mr. Fletcher, we're going to go down into the basement. We have things all set up for you. Please move."

John turned around slowly and walked to the basement door. He flicked the light switch and began the steep walk down. This basement was just a storage room—nothing was finished down there and there was lots of junk left over from the last tenant.

He could hear their heavy footfalls behind him. When he reached the bottom he saw right away what had been 'set up' for him. A noose was hanging from a steel beam which ran across the underside of the ceiling. And a stool was positioned underneath.

So, he was supposed to commit suicide tonight. It occurred to him in that instant that Carl Masterson had finally discovered that John was dying. And that there was no motivation for John to remain silent anymore. So he was a danger that Masterson hadn't foreseen. And he was right. John was a danger.

He also realized in that instant that these two men couldn't leave any marks on him. They wouldn't shoot him, they wouldn't beat the shit out of him—those things would ruin the suicide angle. Just like the murder of Alexei Dragunov: twenty-four other people had to die that day on the rollercoaster to ensure the illusion of an accident instead of a murder. And the murder of John's wife— disguised to look like an accidental gas explosion. They, whoever 'they' were, were going to great lengths to make murders look like accidents.

In his case, they'd decided to make his murder look like a suicide. Smart choice—his wife was dead, his house was gone, his son was estranged from him, and he was dying of a brain tumor. Suicide would be believable.

He walked into the middle of the basement room, followed by the two killers. He just stared up at the noose and, for one insane instant, he smiled. He looked back at the two of them, and said, "Isn't that cute?"

One of the men said, "Let's just do this the easy way, Mr. Fletcher. It won't take long and if you don't struggle, you won't feel any pain."

"Really? Have you ever had a noose around your neck? Do you know what it feels like?"

The other guy was getting impatient. "We're wasting time. Just stand up on that stool and we can get this over with."

John knew what he had to do. He was in his sixties, but was in excellent shape. And he had a hard head. He'd discovered that when he was a boxer in college. Had taken countless hits on the head that would have knocked lesser people unconscious. But not John—he'd become known as the boxer who no one could knock out. His notoriety as a boxer had gained national attention—qualified for the U.S. Olympic team, but had to drop out due to a knee injury. John still worked out at the local gym and even sparred once in a while. He wasn't what he used to be, but he was still pretty darn good.

But that head of his was still very hard.

John shook his head. "No, I'm not getting up on that stool. You'll have to drag me up."

The impatient one stepped forward. But the other one put a hand on his shoulder. "Be careful. No marks. Be selective."

John felt a burning rage in his gut. An anger was building inside of him such as he'd never experienced before. He could feel the adrenaline pumping through his veins as it occurred to him that these might be the same guys who had driven off in the car the night that his lovely Linda died. The guys who blew up his house while Linda was calling down to him from the upstairs window. John felt his fists clenching, fingernails digging into his palms.

Then he just turned around and ran full tilt into the wall. Full force. His forehead connected with the wood joist and he bounced backwards and fell to the ground. He was slightly dazed, but not too much. That famous hard head had served him once again. He reached up and could feel the wetness of blood oozing out of his forehead.

"Jesus! Are you crazy, man?"

John got to his feet and stared at them. "Yes, I'm crazy. Come and get me. I challenge you to drag me up onto that stool. But, gee, how are you going to explain this lump on my forehead and all this blood? Kind of hard to get those if you're hanging yourself, don't you think?"

The impatient one moved toward him again, gun in hand. John met him halfway and grabbed the barrel of the gun. He rammed it up against his own forehead. Then he seethed, "Come on, you piece of shit! Pull the trigger! I dare you! Do it!"

The calm one lurched forward and grabbed his partner from behind. But not before John yanked the gun out of the stunned man's hand. He figured that this was a new one for these guys—dealing with someone who wasn't afraid of one single fucking thing, not even the barrel of a gun.

John had the gun by the barrel—he quickly flipped it around and pointed the barrel at the impatient guy. Then he pulled the trigger. Nothing happened—he wasn't surprised.

He spun the cylinder out of its lock. Sure enough, each of the six chambers were empty.

John smiled at them. They looked back at him, stunned. "I can see that no one was taking any chances tonight. These guns of yours were just props—just to scare me. Couldn't take the chance of one of them going off and actually causing this to look like a murder, could you?"

The calm one stepped forward. "This is going to happen a different way, Mr. Fletcher. Now that you've abused yourself, we'll have to make your death look like a different kind of suicide. Like off a bridge onto the expressway. That would leave severe bruises. So, don't be too smug—we can leave all the marks we want now."

"Go ahead. I don't give a fuck."

The impatient one rushed John. He sidestepped him and brought his elbows down on the back of his neck, crushing him to the ground. John could feel the rage surging inside him. He wanted blood, and these fuckers weren't going to throw him off a bridge, that was for sure. In fact, they weren't getting out of there alive.

The calm one threw a punch at his face which was easily deflected. John countered with a punch to the man's gut. He doubled over. They'd clearly underestimated him. Clearly underestimated a man with nothing to lose. That wasn't the kind of person they were used to killing.

John dashed over to a corner and hoisted up a large spade. He held it in front of him like a javelin and ran full speed at the impatient one who was just getting to his feet. The man screamed at the very instant that the spade pierced his abdomen. John kept his forward motion going and propelled the man back against the wall. He knew he was dead when he could hear the metal of the spade clanging against the wall behind. The spade had gone clear through him.

He whirled around. The calm one had assumed a karate stance. John laughed. "You don't know who the fuck you're dealing with, do you? They didn't tell you that I'm not capable of fear, did they?"

The man started circling, with his hands curling slowly in the air, feet poised for just the right opening. John wasn't going to give him one. In fact, he was just going to surprise him.

Instead of backing away from the threatening feet that were slightly raised at their heels, ready to spring like a cobra, John just growled and ran at the man. Once he was inside three feet, the man's feet were ineffective. He tried, but it was a useless gesture.

John brought his knee up hard into the man's balls, causing him to scream out in agony. Then he grabbed him around the throat and pressed hard against his Adam's apple. The man choked and gasped for air.

John released his hands from his throat and then pounded them inward against his ears. The bald-headed tattooed killer screamed in agony as his eardrums burst. John then brought his face to within inches of the killer's. "You blew up my house, didn't you? You killed my wife, didn't you?"

Not waiting for an answer, John reared back and then rammed forward, head-butting the man. Then he brought his face up close again—he was staring now into the killer's dazed eyes. "You're the one who's going to die tonight. Let's not let that noose go to waste, huh?"

John dragged the dazed man up onto the stool and held him erect. He wasn't reacting to anything. John didn't care. He slipped the noose over his head and positioned the knot to the back and slightly to the side of his neck. Then he slid the knot tight.

John Fletcher, chief investigator with the NTSB, was a man who had always gone along—had always done everyone else's bidding just to stay on the safe side.

Had always done his best to do all the right things, had ignored the lies of TWA 800, and had ignored the lies of the Black Mamba accident.

And John Fletcher had caused the murder of the sweetest person he had ever known.

Yes, all those things were true. John knew it and there was nothing he could do to change the past.

But this he could do.

He stood back and admired the sight of his hostage slumped and barely standing on the stool, noose fastened tightly around his neck.

He gave the stool a football kick, sending it flying across the room. Then he just watched impassively as the killer twisted, choked, lurched and gasped in the damp air of the dingy basement. In less than a minute, there was silence. A deathly silence.

John turned his head and stole a quick glance at the other guy, still half standing against the wall with a spade through his stomach.

And the only semi-rational thought that popped into his head was that the spade would come in handy later on in the backyard under the cover of darkness.

CHAPTER 41

Nate was keeping a close watch over Shelby. The trauma from what had happened up in the sky was still with her, but she'd gotten progressively better the last couple of days. After their near-death experience, she had been afraid to go back to her own house alone so Nate went with her—then he suggested she just pack a bag and stay at his house. She jumped at the offer. They both felt better—it was far safer.

So now they were roommates—Nate made up a room for her in the older wing and he continued to sleep in his familiar room in the newer section. Tonight he had done steaks on the barbecue along with a nice selection of vegetables. He was a good cook—Shelby was surprised. Well, at least on the barbecue he was good—a guy thing, for sure. He never spent much time in the actual kitchen of the house and, with the beautiful year-round weather in Virginia, there weren't many days when he couldn't barbecue.

They were stretched out on the double chaise lounge in his backyard, relaxing with a bottle of wine after the generous meal. His yard was very private—a wall of trees and bushes all around the property, so thick that not even one brick of the houses on either side of him could be seen. It was a private little oasis and he loved it. Loved the seclusion and found that it was a great way to relax, especially lately with all that had been going on. And he loved looking at the water shimmering in his small kidney-shaped swimming pool. The subtle blue lights along the edge added a magical quality to his little piece of paradise.

It was already dark and the solar lights had come on, painting a soft romantic hue around the yard. He turned his head and glanced at her—she was gazing up at the stars with a pensive look in her eyes. Her beautiful blue orbs twinkled, even more seductively than the stars.

As he looked at her, drinking in her beauty, he marvelled at how strong she was. And how skilled. The stunt she'd pulled when they were thousands of feet in the air was nothing short of amazing. What bravery! She'd referred to him as being brave after he'd saved her from the rollercoaster superstructure, but that was nothing compared to what she had done. Her precision dive, which Nate figured was tough enough solo let alone tandem, was breathtaking. He could still feel the incredible speed—the way his cheeks were shoved back and felt like they were fluttering, the tingling in his legs and hands as he saw the ground rushing up at them, his heart pressing into his chest. It was exhilarating while at the same time scary as hell.

And then, the way she adjusted their heads and bodies to slow their descent at just the right time—knowing she wouldn't have a second chance. There was only one shot at halting their rapid drop, and she pulled it off—positioned them right beside Brenda, who by that time had probably given up all hope.

Shelby had been like an angel from heaven.

And now she knew that someone had tried to kill her—that it was her parachutes they thought they'd sabotaged. What a terrible thought to be occupying her brain. Two near death experiences—one on a rollercoaster and another one in the sky—anybody would be in shock after such back-to-back horrors. And then to find out that someone had tried to kill her; in fact, both times someone had tried to kill her. The first time she was just collateral damage, but this second time she was the actual target.

Nate reached over, held onto her hand and squeezed it gently.

She turned her head towards him and smiled lazily. "That was a lovely meal, Nate."

"A lovely meal for a lovely lady."

"Aww…that's a sweet thing to say. You are a sweet man, you know that?"

"It's easy to be sweet with you. And what a hellcat you are! I still can't believe your daring and poise up there in the wild blue yonder. You have my extreme admiration, dear lady. I've never seen anything like that in my life—hell, I actually experienced it right along with you, except that I didn't have a clue what to do. I just followed your lead."

"And you followed it very well indeed, dear sir."

Nate winced. "But my neck still hurts a bit with how you pushed it down so roughly when you started your daredevil dive." He reached up and rubbed the back of his neck with his hand, just to help illustrate his whining.

"Oh, you are a big baby, aren't you? Let me fix that for you." She gently eased him over until he was lying on his stomach. Then she pulled his t-shirt up and over his head, dropping it on the ground beside the chaise.

Shelby straddled his back and her fingers went to work. Nate was amazed at how strong they were. For such a wisp of a woman, she had strengths that a person wouldn't notice at first glance—both mentally and physically.

He hadn't actually been faking it with the neck—it had been a bit sore ever since the skydive, but he knew that could also be stress. Regardless, he was feeling the tension release with every squeeze of her fingers.

Suddenly, he felt a wetness on the back of his neck where her fingers had been. A tongue had replaced the fingers and it was swirling around in circles—he could actually see the circles in his mind that she was drawing on his neck. He concentrated on that as she made the circles larger and larger. The effect was so relaxing that he could feel himself slipping away.

Then she moved back, slowly—actually more like a slide. He could feel her hands pulling down gently on his shorts, then heard the sound of the material making contact with the paving stones.

Her tongue was curling up his ass now, just slightly between the cheeks. He moaned softly as the wetness of it and the swirling movement stirred his senses. Her hand slipped underneath and Nate arched his back to give her easy access. Her fingers found his penis and began stroking it.

Nate couldn't take it any more—once she touched his penis that was his cue. He rolled over underneath her and arched his back again, raising his penis up towards her mouth. He saw that she was already naked—how had she done that? He figured he must have actually dozed off for a minute or two and didn't realize it.

She shook her head, rejecting his penis, and just crawled forward on his chest. Then she leaned down and kissed his mouth hard, pressing her tongue through his lips. They parted eagerly and their two tongues met—swirling, seeking, searching for something.

He raised his crotch up and found her, entering her easily. Her wetness was intoxicating to him and he surged upward with gentle thrusts. She moved easily with his rhythm and they were one. Her tongue continued to swirl—he was amazed at the magical moves it could make. The passion he felt for her was racing through every inch of his body and the heat they were generating in the eighty degree nighttime temperature was extreme.

He felt the sweat on her body and he knew that she could feel his. Nate had his hands on her bum and was pulling her in motion as his thrusts sped up. She moaned, and whispered, "Not yet."

Nate didn't want it to be 'yet' either, but he was finding it hard to hold back. And the heat between the two of them was becoming unbearable. He had to cool it down.

He eased up into a sitting position without missing a beat. Shifted sideways and rested his feet on the ground, their tongues still swirling furiously together. Then he rose to a standing position, taking her with him. He staggered over to the side of the pool, his hands holding firmly onto her bum, her arms wrapped tightly around his neck. Joined together as one, Nate stepped over the edge into the cool soothing water.

The relief was instantaneous, and their movements became even more furious. Being immersed in water, the ease of their thrusts was even more pronounced. Nate spun her around and leaned her back against the pool liner. He put one hand behind her head to protect it and the other one on her bum. He pulled up hard and then moved himself in and out with quick, sharp movements. She gasped, grabbed onto his hair and pulled his head back. He looked into her eyes and could see that she'd just experienced what she'd begged him to wait for. Only then did he allow himself the same. An exhilarating moment that came as a huge relief.

*****

Both of them were spent, back on the chaise lounge dozing peacefully together under a fleece blanket.

Then the phone rang.

Nate jerked awake and reached down to the patio, feeling around blindly for his phone. He found it underneath the chaise, picked it up and clicked 'talk.'

"Yes?"

"Hi Nate. It's John Fletcher."

"Oh, John, how are you?"

"Not good. I need to see you."

"Tonight?"

"Yes, I don't want to say anything over the phone. Can I come over?"

"Well…sure, John. If it's that important you better get over here. You have my address here in Old Town. We'll wait up for you."

Nate clicked off. Still partly in dreamland, Shelby looked up at him with a question in her eyes.

"We'd better get dressed. John's gonna pay us a visit."

Shelby sat up and pulled the fleece blanket around her. "Why? What's wrong?"

"He didn't want to say, but the tone of his voice was strange, distant. Something's happened."

CHAPTER 42

Carl picked up the phone on the first ring. He was hoping—praying—that it was his two men reporting back to him on those special assignments he'd sanctioned. The two weeks were up and he was worried. Carl should have heard something by now. He'd made it clear that he wanted them dead within the two weeks. Every day he'd been scouring the online death notices and logs from morgues. Nothing yet.

But, no, it wasn't the call he'd been hoping for. It was General Tetford from the Pentagon.

"Masterson, are those loose ends tied up yet?"

"I'm still waiting to hear, sir."

"Let me know as soon as you know."

"I will."

"The reason I'm calling is that I've just received some new estimates from the Army Corps. of Engineers. They tell me that the water level drop in Lake Erie is going to be far more severe and noticeable than your team predicted. It won't be easily explained as just being a result of hot dry weather. No one will buy that."

"What are their estimates, General?"

"About twelve inches over the first seven days."

Carl tapped on his keyboard and pulled up the draft of an encrypted email. "General, I sent you a message yesterday with some updates on Operation Backwash, including a contingency item we added. Did you get it?"

"I haven't had time to read emails, Masterson. Just tell me."

"Well, to give us some flexibility of controlling the water flow from Lake Erie through our tunnel, we're adding a hatch that will be installed at the opening. We're building a steel superstructure around the mouth of the tunnel, secured in the bedrock. The hatch will have the capability of being radio-frequency controlled. We'll be able to open and close it at our discretion."

Tetford let out a deep breath. "Okay, I like that. We can let it surge and allow the water level to drop. And if there are eyebrows raised by the Canadians and they start monitoring it closely, we can close the hatch and let the scrutiny cool off a bit. Then let it surge again—it'll probably drive them crazy, but at least we'll be in control."

"Exactly. But, General, we can't fool them forever. We'll just have to deal with it when they do figure it out."

"Yes, I agree. But, they might discover the tunnel early if they use submersibles."

"The Canadians already have unmanned submersibles operating in the Great Lakes. But so do we. We'll put extra patrols around the tunnel opening and make sure that no Canadian submersibles get close. But we're also going to be using 'cloaking' technology. I put that in the email to you as well. Holographic signals will be emitted down the tunnel, conducting along the metal of the pipe, recreating the image of a solid bank. As long as the technology doesn't fail us, the tunnel won't be visible. If their submersibles take photos of the bank below the surface of the water, it will appear as a normal solid bank of the lake. But what they'll be photographing will be a hologram."

"Okay, well, you've built in some good contingencies. I like this stuff. Good—I feel better. And when the Canadians eventually do catch on, we've got some economic weapons at our disposal. We can threaten to tear up the NAFTA treaty, causing crushing trade deficits for them. We're their biggest trading partner—they'll suffer more than we will. And we can level all sorts of accusations at them about how lax their border security is, allowing terrorists to launch an attack against us from Canadian soil. And, of course, we'll have our troops surrounding our side of the Great Lakes. If they want to make a serious issue of us stealing their water, we can get tough."

"On that point, can our theft of water be termed as a trigger for their allied agreements with countries like Great Britain? Would the Brits be obligated to help defend Canada against such an act? In other words, is it an 'act of war'?"

"No. Allied agreements require a country to be actually attacked. We're not attacking, we're merely stealing—and the theft is occurring from our side of the lake, through our bank of the lake. So, they wouldn't have a leg to stand on if they went whining to the Queen."

"Okay, we're on solid ground."

"Now, Masterson, are we on track for the terrorist attack?"

"Yes, we've planted all the information about the Muslim cell operating out of Toronto. We've created and planted 'chatter' about a planned attack. We know the RCMP has already picked up on this and have launched a quiet investigation. The grasshopper nanobots are finished and ready to be launched from the Canadian side of the border. They're all laced with hydrogen cyanide. We just have to give the word and they'll be in the air."

"They'll be seen."

"Yes, but we've planted stories over the last few weeks about grasshopper swarms throughout the U.S. The insect populations are high this year—even the Weather Network forecast a large storm system coming in, but it turned out to be just a grasshopper swarm. So, people are inclined to believe that these things are common now. There won't be any adverse reaction to our swarm. It'll just be seen as normal with the times."

"Alright. I'll wait for your next update. And after I read that email you sent me, I'll probably share it with a few others here as well."

*****

Nate ushered John into the living room. Shelby was enjoying a cup of hot chocolate and she jumped up and gave John a big hug. John hugged her back and flashed her a big smile. But that smile disappeared fast.

"John, can I get you something to drink?"

He took a seat in a wing chair opposite the couch. "No, Nate, I'm fine." Nate sat on the couch beside Shelby. If John was surprised to see Shelby at Nate's house, he didn't show it. But what was showing was a big welt on his forehead.

They both waited patiently for him to say what was on his mind. He definitely sounded troubled about something.

Then he sighed and let it out. "Two men were waiting for me when I got home last night. They had a noose hooked up to my basement ceiling—intended to make my death look like a suicide."

Shelby put her hands to her mouth and gasped.

"As you can see, they didn't succeed. I killed them. First time I've ever killed anyone. And it doesn't even bother me all that much. It was kill or be killed."

Nate swallowed hard. "Did you...phone the police?"

John shook his head slowly. "I buried them in my backyard. The...way I killed them...would be hard to explain. It was too extreme to claim self-defence."

Shelby still had her hands over her mouth when she asked John a muffled question. "How did you...kill them?"

"I don't want to tell you. Let's just leave that alone, okay?"

"Okay."

"There was no identification on their bodies. No cellphones. Nothing. No car keys either—so they must have been extra careful and just had a car drop them off. I'm convinced these were the two guys who blew up my house. I asked one of them—he didn't answer me."

John reached into his pocket and pulled out a piece of paper. He threw it onto the coffee table. "I found this in one of their pockets. You'll see that it has my address written on it. But of more concern right now is that it has the address of Virginia Sky Pilots written down as well as your home address, Shelby. In one of our conversations you told me you were a skydiver. So, putting two and two together, I think they were planning to visit you next."

237

Shelby laid her head back against Nate's shoulder. "They already did, John."

Nate told John the story about the skydiving incident. When he was finished, John just shook his head in dismay. "We have to go public on this as soon as possible, just to save our lives. If they came for us once, they'll come for us again. There are more where these scum came from."

Nate nodded in agreement. "John, are you now prepared to tell what you know—publicly?"

"Yes, I sure am. I'm done with this. That's one of the reasons I wanted to see you tonight. I have a personal mission, which I'll tell you about another day. All I want to do is live long enough to carry it out. But for you two, you have long lives ahead of you. There's something really insidious going on; the lengths they've been going to to silence us have been extreme. They're not fooling around. Whatever they're trying to keep secret is very serious. And it might indeed be that Operation Backwash thing that Dragunov had alluded to in his email to Snowden. Whatever the hell that is, that may be their precious secret. It seems obvious that Alexei Dragunov was the one they wanted to kill on the rollercoaster."

"You'll lose your job if you speak out, John. You'll be going against the official report."

John stood and walked over to the window. He looked out at the starry sky, then spoke very softly; so softly they could barely hear him. "I don't care anymore. First, I want to help you good people stay alive. Then, I have one more thing to do. After that…I want to…see her again."

Nate walked over to the window to join him. "I was just thinking—I'm scheduled to speak at another convention next week. They've assigned a topic to me, but if you're willing to do this with me, we could shock them all with this story instead. All the Press will be there, so we'd catch them all by surprise. If I called a separate Press Conference just to deal with this, the NSA and other government forces might do their damnedest to make sure that no one showed up. Or…make sure we didn't show up. But, this way, they'll all be there—it'll go viral probably while we're still speaking. It'll pop up on all the social media."

John turned to him and held out his hand. "Count me in. Let's set the fucking record straight."

Nate shook his hand and was surprised by the sheer power in John's handshake. He hadn't noticed that on the other occasions they'd shaken hands.

It was difficult to imagine that this strong, healthy, good-looking man was actually dying.

CHAPTER 43

Nate, being one of the guest speakers, had been favored with three extra admission tickets to the convention. So, tagging along for the experience—an experience none of the other attendees at the convention knew they were going to get—were John Fletcher, Ron Collens, and Shelby Sutcliffe.

All of the speakers were allowed to sit in the front row with their guests, so that's where they'd be until Nate's name was called. Their plan was that once that happened, two of them, John and Shelby, would head up to the podium with him.

This was the same venue where Nate had delivered his speech, 'The History of Rollercoasters,' shortly after the accident. The Walter E. Washington Convention Center was one of the few facilities that could handle such a huge crowd. Once again, it was being hosted by the National Society of Professional Engineers.

And, once again, the theme of the convention was a controversial one. And the society wanted its guest speakers to address the subject from their own personal viewpoints. The topic of Nate's speech was supposed to be: 'God Particle or Devil's Dust.'

Of course, he wouldn't be saying one single word about the God Particle. He would leave that to others, and there were plenty of physicists and engineers at the convention who would talk that topic to death. Nate would be talking about something entirely different.

The purpose of the convention was to have the audience hear different viewpoints on the controversial Large Hadron Collider, a monstrosity that defied a layman's description, located in an oval-shaped seventeen mile tunnel beneath the Swiss/French border. This abomination used powerful magnets to, in simple terms, smash beams of protons together at close to the speed of light. There were several installations like this around the world, but this was clearly the largest and most ambitious.

The LHC had actually been shut down since 2012, when it was reported that its experiments did indeed result in discovering the 'Higgs Boson' particle in 2012, which was nicknamed the 'God Particle.' Nate, despite being a highly skilled engineer, didn't quite get it. Apparently, this subatomic particle helped explain why much of the mass in the universe existed. That part he understood—the part he didn't get was why anyone should care, and why we would want to tamper with something that, according to some prominent physicists, was potentially a dangerous thing to unlock.

The LHC had needed a long rest, because it was gearing up now for its biggest, most ambitious run yet. Not satisfied with just finding the God Particle, the governments who were sponsoring this experiment wanted more. This time, the objective was to find other heavier particles, particularly the particle that produced 'dark matter,' that invisible substance that made up ninety-five percent of the universe.

This was where the controversy lay—with the LHC due to be fired up again in January of 2015, scientists around the world were challenging the project, calling it reckless, and warning of how it could unleash something so dangerous that it might not be able to be contained. Earth itself could be in peril if the experiment opened up the wrong Pandora's Box.

Nate read last week that preparations for the restart had already begun, with one-eighth of the giant collider being cooled to its operating temperature—a chilly -271 degrees Celsius, a temperature colder than outer space. And the remaining sections would be cooled to the same extent in the months ahead, getting ready for the big 'dark matter' hunt.

But, this time—which is what was scaring a lot of scientists—the monster would be smashing protons together at an energy level almost double of what had been needed to discover the 'God Particle' back in 2012. People were starting to get scared; well, at least people in the know were getting scared. The average person on the street had no idea what the LHC was and probably thought the 'God Particle' was just some new designer drug.

Most people would probably be shocked if they knew what this obscene use of taxpayers' money was actually doing way down there under the ground, and what chances it was actually taking with the future survival of the planet. Nate personally believed that some things were best left alone. And the National Society of Professional Engineers knew his views—which was why they had asked him to speak from an opposition standpoint.

Nate would have loved to have done just that—the stupid LHC project was insanity as far as he was concerned. But today he had more important things to discuss. He and his friends were going to ambush the podium and make a scene. The mood of the convention would turn on a dime and be distracted in a direction that no one could have anticipated. He intended to talk about his own 'dark matter.'

The four of them had met several times in the last few days leading up to the convention. Ron had been the voice of reason. Nate wanted to just tell everything they knew, but Ron rightly pointed out that there were some things they just couldn't say. They couldn't disclose that they knew the identity of Carl Masterson of the NSA. Nor could they mention their theories about Alexei Dragunov and the meaning of the email he'd sent to someone in Moscow. They couldn't say that they suspected he'd sent it to Edward Snowden. And neither could they say that Dragunov was the one who was the intended murder victim on the rollercoaster.

No, they couldn't say any of those things. Because to do so would open up a can of worms, making their situation even worse. Hacking into federal databases was a federal crime, and to admit they knew all of those things would bring an investigation down on their heads. And Ron could not fathom exposing his friend from Anonymous—that man had dug deep for them on the condition of total anonymity.

So, they had to stick to the facts as they knew them to be, and deal only with those facts that were known through means other than hacking. They had to realize that they really couldn't prove anything. And if they even mentioned that there was possibly some sinister scheme underway called Operation Backwash, they would be branded as nutcases. Because, again, they couldn't prove it, had no idea what it even was, and that very information had been obtained by illegally hacking into the NSA database.

To a certain extent, their hands were tied. But they could say enough to possibly clear Flying Machines Inc. in the pending lawsuit. Just enough to cast doubt—and once they'd had their say up at the podium, the courts and the public would know that there was enough evidence to indicate that an intervening cause had brought the rollercoaster down.

And putting themselves in the spotlight would most likely dissuade any more attempts on their lives. After today, they would be too high profile. Their deaths would be high profile. And Nate suspected that the NSA didn't want any of this to be in the spotlight—for whatever their reasons were, and for whatever Operation Backwash was.

The NSA, and whoever else was involved, had gone to great lengths to make the rollercoaster incident look like an accident. And since then, there had been the explosion at John's house, the skydiving horror, and the attempt to kill John by making it look like suicide. Every event had been designed to look like anything but murder.

Nate leaned forward and looked down the row at his friends in the four seats beside him. "Are we ready?"

They all nodded nervously. Nate smiled. "We're gonna be fine. Just follow my lead. And the place is packed with Press. This LHC topic is so controversial, it's attracted a lot of attention. I noticed CNN, NBC, ABC and all the major newsprint organizations. Let alone the social media that everyone in this room has access to. We're gonna give 'em all more than they bargained for tonight."

Shelby licked her lips and whispered, "When will we be up?"

"I didn't want to tell you this before, but I'm the first speaker. So, don't be nervous—just look at it this way—we'll get it over with fast and leave."

Nate turned his attention to the stage. The Master of Ceremonies was walking to the podium. It was about to begin.

The MC delivered his opening remarks, setting the tone for the speeches that would follow. He gave some brief history about the LHC project and briefly outlined what the benefits were, and what the possible risks were with such a project. Then he bowed out and told the audience that he would leave it to the speakers to go into greater detail.

The moment had arrived. He announced Nate's name. Nate stood, along with John and Shelby, and together they walked up onto the stage. The MC looked at Nate with a question in his eyes. Nate waved him off and continued up to the podium.

John and Shelby flanked him while Nate adjusted the microphone to his height. He could hear murmurs in the crowd; probably, like the MC, they were puzzled as to why there were three of them up there.

Nate stood tall and erect, cleared his throat, and began.

"Ladies and gentlemen. It's a pleasure to be here speaking to you once again. Most of you know who I am—or should I say, how infamous I am. Yes, I'm the CEO of the company that designed the Black Mamba, the subject of one of the most horrific rollercoaster accidents in history. And, of course, with the way my company and I have been portrayed in the Press, and will be portrayed in the upcoming Class Action lawsuit, you would think that I'm also a killer.

"I have two associates up on stage with me tonight. To my right is John Fletcher, Chief Investigator with the National Transportation Safety Board. John is the man who conducted the investigation into the accident. And to my left is Shelby Sutcliffe. Most of you might remember her from the news stories that came out after the accident. Shelby is the lone survivor of the Black Mamba mass murder."

There were loud gasps and murmurs in the audience. Several members of the Press were standing now—cameras were clicking away and video rolling. He had their attention.

The MC walked up to Nate and whispered in his ear. "What the hell are you doing?"

Nate turned his head towards him and whispered back. "Something I should have done weeks ago. Go back to your spot. I have the microphone."

Things had quieted down a bit. But Nate knew he had to speak fast now just in case someone decided to call Security and have them hauled off the stage.

"My topic tonight is supposed to be: 'God Particle or Devil's Dust.' Well,

I'm not going to talk about that—there are plenty of other experts here who know more about that subject than I do. What I'm going to talk about is how my rollercoaster was sabotaged. And how twenty-five people died, perhaps in order to kill one person. The accident wasn't an accident—it was mass murder.

"After the accident, the investigation was mysteriously assigned to the NTSB. Strange, because amusement park accidents do not fall under their jurisdiction. Then my team and our insurance company were denied access—we weren't allowed to see the wreckage. Before we knew it, it had been hauled off to Key West, Florida, of all places, and dumped into the Caribbean Sea somewhere off the coast of Cuba.

"I went down there with two of my engineers and we had the opportunity to see the track before it was disposed of. We could clearly see that the metal of the track had not snapped—it had been melted.

"Right now, I'm going to ask John Fletcher from the NTSB to step forward and give you his assessment. John is fully aware that he will probably lose his job after tonight, but he's decided to take that chance to tell you what he knows." Nate turned to John. "The podium is yours, Mr. Fletcher."

John adjusted the microphone higher, then cleared his throat.

"Ladies and gentlemen, I did indeed conduct the investigation into the accident. And I signed a false report. I was forced to do so by both my superior and a senior official from the National Security Agency."

There was noise in the crowd again at the mention of the NSA. Members of the Press were moving closer to the front of the stage. There was some heckling coming from the back row, but Nate couldn't make out what they were saying, and whether they were on their side or not. It didn't matter—he didn't give a shit who was on their side.

John continued.

"I don't know who the NSA man was, or why they wanted the false report issued. But I went along—and that was my mistake. I can't in all conscience allow this good company, Flying Machines Inc., to be incriminated or sued based on false information. I saw the track. As Mr. Morrell said, it had been melted and my original report stated that.

"It was sabotage, and my expertise led me to believe that a substance called Thermate-3 was used, equipped with radio frequency fuses having the capability of being set off by remote control. And I believe that same remote control device was used to unlock the lap bars.

"This accident was staged as a mass death trap—no one was supposed to survive. It is my opinion that disengaging the lap bars was the saboteurs' back-up plan. If the fuses in the Thermate-3 failed to ignite, then the failure of the lap bars would guarantee the same result—mass murder. But they didn't bargain on one thing—that there would be a survivor. So, on that note, I introduce you to the lone survivor of the Black Mamba murder scene, Shelby Sutcliffe."

Shelby smiled at John and shuffled nervously up to the microphone. Nate stepped forward and adjusted the height of it downward for her.

She looked out at the audience. And promptly froze.

Nate put an arm around her shoulder, and whispered, "It's okay, go ahead. I'll stay right here beside you."

She wobbled on her feet and whispered back. "I feel it coming on—feel like I'm going to faint."

Nate looked directly into her eyes—could see them rolling a bit, saw that the color had left her face. He whispered again, "Just do your thing. Scream into the microphone."

For a split second, Shelby looked at him like he was daft, then nodded and took his cue. She leaned toward the microphone and just screamed with all her might. And again. Then one more time for good measure.

Nate looked out over the audience and saw the shocked looks on most of the faces. The cameras were clicking away even more furiously.

But Shelby was okay. Like the trooper she had always proven to be, she cleared her throat and began to speak.

"Sorry to have shocked you all. I felt like I was going to faint up here, and if there's one thing I learned from hanging onto the side of the Black Mamba's trestle structure, it's that screaming at the top of my head chases away fainting spells. So that's what I did then, and that's what I just did now.

"I was asked to join the Class Action lawsuit, but I was told by the lawyer that I had to testify that the lap bars disengaged upon impact with the broken track. And after I refused, I was paid a visit by that very same NSA man who forced John Fletcher to sign a false report. He threatened me into joining the lawsuit and told me in no uncertain terms that I had to testify that the lap bars disengaged on impact.

"I'm here to tell you tonight that that was not the case. And I would know—I was there, and I'm the only one alive who can tell you what really happened. Before the train jackknifed with the broken track, I had accidentally pulled up on my lap bar. The thing came up in my hands, with ease. It was already disengaged before the impact and, when I looked over at my seating partner, she was gone from her seat the instant the train left the track. Her lap bar was in the up position. Everything you have heard and read is an absolute lie."

Shelby stepped back from the microphone and Nate took over again.

"Ladies and gentlemen, that's all we have to say tonight. We have digital copies of John Fletcher's report and his photos of the track—as well, we have photos of the track as we saw it down in Key West before it was dumped at sea.

Interested Press members are welcome to contact my office tomorrow and we will provide those items to you.

"As for what happened, we are at a loss to explain why someone would have pulled off such a heinous act. And we are at a loss to understand why a government agency would try to cover this up, and force two people to lie. You can form your own conclusions. In my view, this should now be an FBI matter and I welcome the opportunity to talk to them about this if they're interested in pursuing it. At the very least, I want the Class Action lawsuit dropped and the good name of myself and my company restored. Thank you."

CHAPTER 44

The last two days had gone by in a blur—the uproar raised by the speeches at the convention was all the news; the only news. Immediately after they'd finished saying what they needed to say, Nate, Shelby, and John left the convention hall. Ron stayed behind just to gauge the reaction from the audience and from the convention organizers. According to him, the remainder of the speeches went over like lead balloons. No one seemed interested in the Large Hadron Collider— the buzz was all about Flying Machines Inc. and the shocking revelations that had been made up at the podium.

Some of the Press stuck around, but most of them fled from the convention center, trying desperately to be the first to file their stories. And boy, were there a lot of stories. Twitter was going nuts, every online news page covered the event, including photos and videos, and of course the twenty-four hour news stations were covering it ad nauseum. All of them trying to put some kind of terrorism spin on it, which is pretty much what they tried to do with everything these days.

The three of them had clearly made headlines and now there were more questions than answers. And everyone wanted answers. Nate and his friends had some of the answers, but, following Ron's advice, they knew they couldn't share them with anyone. They would be open to prosecution themselves, and that's the only focus there would be.

Since at least one branch of the government seemed to be involved in the rollercoaster mass murder up to their necks, they would all close ranks and go on the offensive. All would be lost. The Flying Machines executives, Shelby and John, would lose credibility; their chances of coming out clean would be slim to none if they were charged with the federal crime of hacking into government databases.

John Fletcher had spent most of the last two days at the Flying Machines' offices with Nate and his team. As had Shelby. She took a short-term leave of absence from work and the hospital understood. In fact, they preferred it—with all the publicity, the Press were hanging out at the hospital hoping to interview her. It was disrupting hospital operations.

So, to keep it less chaotic, Nate put out a press release advising that they would all be available for scheduled interviews and photo shoots, for a period no longer than two days. At those sessions, the Press would also be given flash drives with photos of the melted track as well as John's original inspection report, the one he'd been ordered to bury.

The Press ate it up. They hounded them for as much information as they could get—yet all they got was the same information that had been spoken of at the convention. Nothing more, nothing less. They didn't disclose the sabotage of the parachutes, and neither did John mention the attempt on his life—for obvious reasons.

At the end of the two days, Nate got the call he'd asked for during his speech—Special Agent Andrew Hopkins of the FBI phoned. He wanted to meet and interview all four of them. Nate eagerly agreed. It was the meeting he wanted.

Finally, something was going to happen.

*****

"We're going to ask a series of questions, and whichever one of you wishes to answer feel free to just speak right up." Agent Hopkins started the meeting off with no fanfare. Some pleasant introductions of himself and his partner, Special Agent Angela Norbury, but aside from that, smiles and small talk were non-existent.

They were meeting in the boardroom and, in addition to Nate, there were Ron, John and Shelby. Nate also asked Robin Gilchrist, his Vice President of Legal Affairs, to sit in. Just in case.

Hopkins pulled a small recorder out of his briefcase, turned it on and set it in the middle of the board table. "We'll just tape this meeting, if you don't mind."

Robin reached across the table and turned the machine off. "Put that away, sir. You're not recording anything."

"And what's your job here?"

"I'm the Chief Legal Officer—so, as an officer of the court, you'll abide by my wishes. As of now, you can consider all four of these people my clients."

Angela Norbury retorted, "There's no need for such legal formality. We're just trying to get to the bottom of this."

"In that case, if you don't want formality, you'll abide by my wish that this meeting not be recorded."

Hopkins pulled a notepad and pen out of his briefcase and asked in a tone dripping with sarcasm, "Are we allowed to take notes?"

Robin answered him in the same sarcastic tone, "I don't think that question deserves an answer."

Hopkins nodded. "Okay, then, I'll start this off. Mr. Morrell, why did you mention the NSA in your speech the other night?"

"Because it was relevant."

"Why was it relevant?"

Nate frowned. "You obviously have transcripts of what each of us said. Ms. Sutcliffe was approached and threatened by the same man who visited Mr. Fletcher. That man identified himself as being with the NSA. He forced Mr. Fletcher to sign a false investigation report. And he threatened Ms. Sutcliffe to join the Class Action and testify to something that was a lie. Does that all sound relevant to you?"

"Do you know the name of this man?"

"No," Nate lied.

"Do you have proof that he was with the NSA?"

"No, but Mr. Fletcher's superior was in on the meeting when the NSA forced the issue of the false report. Check with him. He must have seen some credentials."

Norbury jumped in. She was sitting directly across from Nate and had a file open in front of her. "Yes, we've talked to him already. Gary Tuttle, Director of Operations at the NTSB. He said he doesn't recall any other report—that the one on public record is the only one that was issued, and that Mr. Fletcher provided that to him after his inspection. And he doesn't recall anyone from the NSA being involved in any meetings regarding the rollercoaster investigation. Mr. Tuttle also said that Mr. Fletcher is delusional, and that his employment has been terminated as of today for incompetence and unprofessional behavior."

John jumped to his feet. "What?! I'm just learning this from you? No one has said anything of the sort to me!"

Robin stood up and put a hand on John's shoulder. "Sit down, John. As of now, I'm representing you in a wrongful termination lawsuit against the NTSB."

Norbury continued, "The NTSB will countersue for libel and slander. That so-called 'original' report and those photos Mr. Fletcher has now distributed widely to the Press, have already been debunked as being forgeries—that they were completed 'after the fact,' as well as digitally altered to show earlier dates."

John jumped up again, only to be gently pulled down by Robin. She responded, "I guess we'll see the NTSB in court, then."

Nate was staring across the table at the upside-down notes that Norbury had in front of her. The arrogant little ball-breaker had no idea Nate could read them. Not only read them, but also take a photo in his mind and flip them right side up. He smiled pleasantly and rapped his knuckles on the table. Norbury looked up at him.

"Are you trying to get my attention, Mr. Morrell?"

"Yes, I am." Nate was looking at her with his right eye, and watching Hopkins with his left. He saw the man's hand subtly flick a button on the recorder. Without turning his attention away from Norbury, he said, "Agent Hopkins, I saw that. Pass that machine over here to me—you can have it back when you leave. This is my office and, unless we're under arrest, you will abide by our rules while you're here."

Hopkins scowled, then slid the recorder across the table. Nate turned it off and passed it over to Robin.

Nate stared at Norbury and kept his silence for a few seconds. Then, "Agent Norbury, you say that the NTSB denies meeting with anyone from the NSA, correct?"

"Yes, that is correct."

"Then why do I see in your notes the name 'Carl Masterson,' and a title next to his name of 'Director of Security and Intelligence, NSA'?"

Norbury looked at him in astonishment, then quickly closed the file. "You must be mistaken.

"Oh, really? Do you think I just pulled that out of the air?"

"I don't know what you're trying to stir up here, Mr. Morrell. You may already be in a lot of trouble with the comments you made at the convention. I would tread carefully if I were you."

Nate pressed on. "Your notes also contain the words 'Thermate' and 'magnesium fuses.'"

Nate noticed the blood had now drained from her face. But, as an FBI agent, she had been trained to recover fast, which she did. "Well, Mr. Fletcher himself mentioned in his speech the other night that in his opinion Thermate-3 had been used, along with magnesium fuses."

"Oh, he did, did he?" Nate opened his file folder and held up a sheet of paper. "This is the official transcript of our speeches. Mr. Fletcher did indeed mention Thermate, but at no time did he say the word 'magnesium.' In fact, he said—and let me quote exactly: 'radio frequency fuses.' So, why do your notes use the word 'magnesium?' That sounds pretty specific to me. Do you know more than you're admitting, Agent Norbury?"

Norbury lowered her eyes. Then she suddenly pushed back her chair and stood, grabbing her file folder. "I don't know what game you're playing, Mr. Morrell, but you're in a lot of trouble and you don't seem to realize it."

Agent Hopkins stood as well and together the two of them headed for the door. He looked back and said, "Those photos prove nothing. They could be of any track anywhere—you could have melted some track yourselves and used it for your photos. I think you're a desperate man, Mr. Morrell. Your company is going down because of your gross negligence and you just don't seem to realize that yet."

Nate laughed. "Really? You underestimate us. Silly for us to let you come here today, thinking that you might want to get to the bottom of this. It seems to me that the FBI is already at the bottom of this, twisting around in the same pig shit that the NSA is. Oh, before you leave, Agent Norbury, please answer me one more question. Why were the words 'Virginia Sky Pilots' also jotted down in your notes?"

*****

"Masterson, you said you were going to tie up loose ends. This fucking mess has gone viral now! What the fuck are you doing over there?"

Carl held the phone away from his ear. The yelling from General Tetford was especially painful this morning after his night of drinking with some old NFL buddies.

"General, something went wrong. My men never got back to me—something's happened to them."

"I don't give a shit if they went to Mars! *You're* accountable for this! You were supposed to take care of it. Too late—these people can't turn up dead now. Call off your dogs."

Carl winced. "I realize that. But we're already in damage control. I've read all the news reports of their speeches the other night. I'm in tune with you, don't worry. The FBI is working to discredit them, and we've done amendments to all the online records. By the time we're finished, these people will look like neurotic nutcases."

Carl could hear Tetford cursing under his breath. "Make sure we're on track for Operation Backwash. None of this needs to change any of our timetables. Agree?"

"Nothing has changed. These assholes are just an annoying distraction."

*****

John Fletcher walked into the backyard of his shitty little rental house. What a joke the yard was compared to what Linda had created back at their dream home. He stomped on top of the two graves that he'd dug. The grass seed was already starting to take—little sprouts were popping up here and there. Soon, it would look normal again. He made a mental note to get out tomorrow and water them again. These seeds needed lots of moisture in the early days after planting. He'd learned that from Linda.

Back in the house, he took the stairs down to the basement. He just stood there, staring up at the noose that was still hanging from the ceiling. For some reason, he hadn't discarded it yet. Didn't know why—maybe it was just an important reminder to him that he'd almost lost the opportunity to carry out his

250

mission.

John went back upstairs and sat down in the kitchen. He hadn't eaten dinner yet, but he wasn't hungry anyway. He could tell that he was losing weight—his appetite wasn't what it was. Perhaps that was a sign that the end was coming? His doctors had warned him that might be one of the first signs that motor signals weren't getting through. That, as well as the gradual loss of other functions. But he didn't think so. He figured it was just the stress of what was going on, and the single most important thing on his mind: the 'thing' named Carl Masterson.

John picked up the phone and dialed Ron Collens' home number.

Ron answered on the first ring. "I was expecting your call, John. Don't know why, maybe because of how agitated you were at the meeting today. I was agitated, too—but somehow I managed to restrain myself."

"Yeah, I am agitated—but also more focused than ever, Ron."

"It sure was hopeless with the FBI today, wasn't it? So much for justice and the search for truth. Those clowns are out to bury us. I thought Nate was brilliant, though. Making sure they knew that we knew what side they were on was a clever tactic. They're on their guard now."

John smiled as he thought about the way Nate had thrown those curve balls. "He is a brilliant guy, for sure. And how the hell was he able to read all that upside down?"

Ron laughed. "Oh, that's a long story. Nate has a few gifts that were given to him on the football field when he was a teenager. They come in handy sometimes. He'll probably be willing to tell you the story over a beer one night. Or maybe four!"

"I'd love that—except that I'm running out of nights. I'll have to pin him down on those beers soon."

"Yeah—I understand." Ron coughed. "So, John, what's on your mind?"

"Carl Masterson is on my mind. And it's clear from the meeting with the FBI today that we need to find out what Operation Backwash is all about. And I think you and I can do this without Nate or Shelby being involved. We should keep them out of it, I'm sure you agree."

Ron was silent for a few seconds. John held his breath and waited for the former Navy Seal to take the bait—bait he knew he wouldn't be able to resist.

"Tell me what you need from me."

John sighed with relief. "First of all, I'll need your help. Secondly, I'll need you to obtain three items."

Ron whispered when he asked his next question—almost as if he knew what the answer was going to be. "What items do you need?"

"Three items that I know with your background and connections you'll be able to get for us: Thermate-3; radio frequency magnesium fuses; and a remote control programmed to the fuses."

*****

John was lying in his new replacement bed looking up at the ceiling. He missed the bed that he and Linda had shared for so many years. That one had fit his body perfectly, and had a lovely imprint that Linda's body had created on her side of the bed.

On nights when she was up late reading, he would go to bed and run his fingers down the subtle curve in the mattress. It had always given him comfort. When she wasn't there, it was a reminder of her. Almost sacred, like the Shroud of Turin.

Now there was nothing. There was just him. All alone, without the one he'd been selling his soul for to make sure she'd be taken care of. He could still see her lovely face calling down to him from the second storey window that fateful night. Could see the worry lines on her face at smelling the gas. Calling down to him, fear in her voice. Then the explosion. And when he'd struggled back to his feet, her gorgeous face was no longer in the window. At that moment, even before he'd climbed the tree, he knew in his gut she didn't have a chance.

A sweet innocent person like Linda didn't deserve to die that way. Not *any* way. He was the one who was supposed to go first, not her. The hate in his heart was overwhelming. Someone was going to pay.

He started drifting off. He knew that he was drifting because bizarre images started appearing in his mind. The beginnings of dreams—he marveled at how amazing that was. He always knew that he was seconds from falling asleep as soon as irrational images and ideas popped into his head.

Suddenly she was there.

Her pretty face right in front of his eyes. John thought his eyes were open, but in this state of early REM he wasn't quite sure. She smiled at him, and then tenderly kissed his lips. Her hair was flowing down on either side of her face, and she was wearing his favorite dress. He glanced down at her left hand and saw the wedding and engagement rings that he'd picked out for her all by himself decades ago.

Then he saw her hands rise from his shoulders. She was floating now, face still close to his, but her hands and feet were no longer supporting her. Instead, her hands were on his head. Rubbing, massaging. He sighed—those hands were so familiar to him. No one else's hands would ever do—these were the hands he loved.

And then she spoke—in a whisper. "I love you, John. I always have and I always will. My hands will make you feel better, you know they always do. Just relax and let me do what I know I need to do. Just go to sleep—I'll be with you all night. I have work to do."

Her fingers were pressing and probing now, exploring his entire scalp—back and front, right and left. Then they stopped at one point on his head and began pressing hard, very hard. It didn't hurt—in fact it was the most exhilarating feeling he'd experienced in his entire life.

John closed his eyes and puckered his lips. He felt her again. She kissed him and gently slid her tongue between his lips.

The stickiness in the crotch of his pyjamas added reality to his dream. It had happened quickly and only from a kiss. So much time had passed already—he had no resistance to her.

Was it a dream? John kept his eyes closed, in fear that if he opened them she'd be gone.

She seemed oblivious to his orgasm and just continued to work her fingers into his scalp.

And he didn't want that to stop. Ever.

CHAPTER 45

Carl Masterson pulled out of the driveway of his luxurious country home in Crofton, Maryland. His eyes always roamed when he drove through his property. Carl's driveway was at least a quarter of a mile long, framed by mature oak trees that formed almost a tunnel-like effect. His spread was ten acres—not that he used more than just the space his house occupied. He never had the time. Someday, he hoped to grow some vegetables, maybe get some horses. And most definitely a dog.

He didn't have any kids—hell he didn't even have a steady girlfriend. Had never been married and had never really wanted to be.

To him, women were just objects. To treat them like real people meant having to put up with the emotion and their unreasonable demands. He preferred to just have the occasional lady drive out to visit him, and then kick her out before the sun came up. He didn't like to wake up in the morning to see what he'd been messing around with. And he didn't care if it cost him money—he had plenty of money, and having the real thing was certainly better than browsing porn sites.

No, he preferred to be alone. There wasn't one warm spot in his heart for anyone. He didn't know why he was like that. He'd had a good childhood, his parents were wonderful—but he just didn't care about people. Carl just tolerated them. He hadn't had any brothers or sisters. Maybe that was it? That he'd never really been properly socialized?

He turned left at the end of the road and headed toward the main highway. It was only a twenty minute drive to his Fort Meade office and he always enjoyed it. It was so isolated out there in the Crofton area. Served as a real escape for him from the pressures and unpleasantness of his job. And lately there had been a lot of them.

When this was over, Carl intended to spend a couple of weeks at a Club Med down in the Caribbean. Lots of loose women at those resorts and he wouldn't even have to pay for them. And all the women who went to Club Med never wanted nor cared about a relationship, which suited him fine. They just wanted to get drunk and fucked in the tropical heat, and that was all he wanted, too.

He thought back to the meeting he'd had with the FBI the other day—all prompted by those stupid speeches Nate Morrell and his two friends gave at the convention. He knew the FBI would have no choice but to look into their allegations. They found out quickly who he was—Gary Tuttle at the NTSB had caved and given them his name. That opened up a firestorm of phone calls back and forth between the FBI, the NSA and the Pentagon.

General Tetford had given the agents their marching orders—hadn't told them anything at all except that the lid was on this entire thing, and that national security was at stake. Carl loved using that term 'national security.' It was the ultimate crutch. Got you out of anything.

When they met with him, they tried their best to probe—just curiosity, he guessed. But he stuck to the party line that Tetford had set. *Sorry, national security.*

So, the FBI had no choice but to just shut up and bury the whole thing. They'd not only had orders from Tetford, but also the FBI Director herself.

But, they met with Carl anyway. Probably just wanted to put a face to the name. Funny though, they mentioned that they'd done some digging on Shelby Sutcliffe. Turned out she was involved in a near-fatal accident a week before, with some organization called Virginia Sky Pilots. Some parachutes had been sabotaged. The FBI agents asked him if he knew anything about that. He answered honestly when he said that he didn't, but he couldn't help but think to himself that Shelby's near-death experience had been the work of his two men.

And where the hell were they? They had just disappeared into thin air! And John Fletcher was obviously still alive, too, so they had failed on both counts. It was a real mystery.

Well, Carl wasn't going to think about Shelby Sutcliffe or John Fletcher any longer—nor the executives at Flying Machines Inc. It was 'hands off' now—they had gone public and there was no margin anymore in having them killed.

He could just concentrate on Operation Backwash. Watching the master plan swing into action. Just days away now.

Step One was punching the tunnel through the banks of Lake Erie and beginning the massive theft of precious water from Canada.

Step Two, the very next day, was the launch of the million-plus hydrogen cyanide laden grasshopper-bots from the Canadian side of the border. Thousands of Americans would die, but the action would convince Americans and the world that the Canadians were weak on terrorism—hell, the wimps hadn't even supported the U.S. in the war in Iraq. They'd refused to be part of the action, stating publicly that the war was unjustified and illegitimate.

Well, they should have known that their public humiliation of the United States would come back to haunt them one day. The Canadians showed no fear whatsoever of their giant neighbor and clearly forgot the U.S. mantra: *'If you're not with us, you're against us.'*

So the horrific terrorist attack on U.S. soil would show the world that the U.S. was justified in protecting the vast Great Lakes system militarily; that Canada just wasn't capable of keeping that precious resource safe.

When Step Three kicked in and U.S. troops lined the border areas around the lakes and set up permanent camp, it would just be one more step to actually crossing the border and taking control of the entire lake system.

More tunnels would follow. The tunnel into Lake Erie was just a 'shot across the bow.' And who would blame the U.S.? When Canada couldn't even stop terrorists sitting right under their noses in their attempts to poison the water system? A water system that was shared up until now equally with America? How could America sit idly by and watch it happen again? They couldn't and that's the way the world would see it.

The Islamic cell based in Toronto that the attack would be blamed on, was already set up to take the fall. Sure, these people were probably already there as sleeper agents for Middle East terrorist groups, but so far they'd done nothing. They were supposedly a religious group. *They are fucking Arabs for God's sake—they are all terrorists deep down inside.*

Well, pretty soon they wouldn't be sleeping any more. The NSA had planted solid indisputable information linking this Toronto group to the Islamic State of Iraq and Syria, otherwise infamously known as ISIS—the militant terrorist group that was currently tearing their way through Iraq and Syria, causing both countries to be on the brink of total collapse. And, perfect timing, these wingnuts had already issued threats of terrorist attacks against the United Kingdom and the United States. So, blaming the hydrogen cyanide attack on ISIS would be entirely believable.

Current events had primed the world to accept this 'false flag' as being exactly what it would appear to be. As for the deaths that would occur, the NSA and the Pentagon just viewed those as being necessary for the larger cause. That cause being the assurance of fresh water security for America, and the maintenance of its high standard of living.

And, of course, maintaining its position of dominance around the world as the only true superpower left. As far as Carl was concerned that alone was worth lying, stealing...and killing...for.

CHAPTER 46

Nate was sitting in his office munching on a corned beef sandwich, when Robin Gilchrist burst through the door.

She was excited. "Have you talked to Shelby this afternoon?"

"No, do you want to talk with her? She's at home cleaning my house right now." Nate smiled. "God, I sure love having her staying with me, Robin!"

"I'll bet you do. No, I don't need to talk to her—you can pass along the news yourself."

"What news?"

"You knew she was meeting with a judge this morning, didn't you?"

Nate nodded while swallowing a big chunk of corned beef. "Yeah, she told me she'd been summoned. Didn't know what it was about, but figured it must have had something to do with all the news coverage about what she said at the convention."

"Well, it sure did. The judge she met with was the one who had originally certified the Class Action lawsuit. I just got off the phone with the court clerk. That judge has decided to de-certify the Class Action. And...get this...he's launching an investigation that may possibly lead to Dwayne Feinstein being disbarred."

Nate jumped to his feet, grabbed Robin in a bear hug and whirled her around in the air. He couldn't wipe the smile off his face. "God, that's incredible news, Robin! I can't believe this!"

Robin put her hands on Nate's shoulders and pushed him back. "You're stronger than you realize, Nate. You've squeezed the breath out of me!"

"I'm sorry—couldn't control myself!"

Robin straightened out her blouse. "It's all due to your gutsy move to go public at the convention. You guys sure stirred things up. When the judge heard Shelby's version of events this morning, and how Feinstein had told her how she had to testify, he was furious. His decision was swift."

"Geez—so what does this mean exactly, Robin?"

"It means there won't be a Class Action. But we're not out of the woods. The families of the victims can still sue us, but they'll have to do it individually. Which some might do. But here's the kicker—because of Shelby's story, and the photos of the melted track that have appeared in the news along with John Fletcher's original report, there's very little chance of Strict Liability being applied. There's reasonable doubt now that there wasn't an intervening cause. Which means that anyone who sues us will have to prove negligence, which of course will be virtually impossible to do."

Nate was wringing his hands together. "Robin, in your expert legal opinion, what do you think the chances are that we'll be successfully sued now?"

Robin held her right hand up and made a zero with her thumb and forefinger.

Nate yelled, "Yes!" He reached out for her again.

Robin held her hands up in the air. "No, Nate—no more hugs!"

Nate smiled sheepishly. "Sorry, I'm just excited. Our great company's going to survive, Robin. I can hardly wait to give the news to everybody."

"Again, I have to caution you that we're not totally out of the woods. So, be careful about giving too much assurance to everyone."

"I know, I know—but that's just the lawyer in you talking."

Robin smiled warmly at him. "Yes, boss, that is just the lawyer in me. Friend to friend, I agree with you—I think we're going to be okay. But, the lawyer in me has to ask a question—where is John Fletcher? He's not answering his phone or returning messages. The court clerk tried to reach him, too, because the judge wants to talk to him about the coercion he was put through."

"I don't know. He was fired, as you know, so maybe he's taken a little trip to get his mind on other things?"

"Maybe. That's why I tried to reach him—to start the proceedings for his wrongful termination suit."

"Give him a couple of days. John's been through a lot. He'll turn up. He's probably just lying low for a while."

*****

John Fletcher was lying in the middle of a road in the community of Crofton, Maryland. There were only a couple of houses on this stretch of dead-end road, so he was pretty safe. Until one particular car came along, heading home to one particular house.

About fifteen minutes ago, he'd passed Carl Masterson on the highway coming back from Fort Meade. Then John sped ahead to the spot where he was right now. Lying on the highway with his car parked along the side at an odd angle, with its driver's door wide open. He clearly looked like a driver in distress—perhaps a heart attack, or a mugging. Someone who needed to be saved. John figured even a heartless animal like Masterson couldn't help but stop.

At least that was the plan. And it was Ron's plan. His contact at Anonymous had given him the address to Carl's home along with the make of his car and license plate number. It was then just a simple matter of both of them staking out the exit from Fort Meade and waiting for the right car to come along.

The plan was that John would speed ahead and position himself on the highway near Carl Masterson's home. With Ron following at a safe distance behind.

When Masterson pulled over to help, Ron would pull up behind him.

What would happen after that was also mapped out—to a point. There was an old abandoned shack that Ron knew about only a short distance away. Located in the Globecom Wildlife Management area south of Crofton. It was a desolate area—virtually ignored by tourists, populated instead by some fairly serious animals. The old cabin had been a hiker's outpost, but hadn't been used by anyone in years. Some of Ron's contacts had used it before, but Ron refused to tell John how they'd used it. John didn't care—it sounded perfect.

But there was something else about the old cabin, too. For the last two days it had been inhabited. Ron had already taken someone there, soon to be joined by Carl Masterson. This other person was a bonus that neither of them had counted on. And the timing of it caused them to move up the timetable on grabbing Carl.

It was only fitting that the two of them be together in the shack.

Because the other person was Tom Foster.

Ron's friend at Anonymous had managed to track Foster down in Bangkok. It wasn't hard, at least not for Anonymous—only two Americans had registered new passports in Thailand within the last few weeks and a quick examination of passport photos online enabled Ron to identify Foster. He'd disguised himself— had a fashionable beard and had grown his hair out. Wore fake glasses as well. But he was still Tom Foster—and Ron had known the man for most of his adult life.

Anonymous had also tracked Foster along the tangled path of a worldwide child porn ring. And had discovered that the man had actually made two trips back to the United States since he'd disappeared. Both times for child porn activity.

Tom had a new name: Fred Waring.

Ron was given a 'heads up' by Anonymous that he was coming back again. Which he had.

Ron grabbed him out near the taxi stand at Reagan airport. A small needle in the neck and Tom looked just like a drunken traveler being helped into a car by his friend.

John was startled out of his daydream by the sound of an approaching car. He was lying face down on the road and the car would have to either stop or run him over. John held his breath. He knew it was Masterson.

The car stopped. John heard the sound of another engine approaching from farther back. He knew who that was, too.

The sound of a car door opening and closing, then heavy footsteps approaching.

He could feel his presence as the man knelt down beside him. John's face was turned in the other direction so Carl wouldn't recognize him.

Fingers were on his neck now, checking his pulse. Then both hands on his back, shaking him gently. "Hey, buddy, can you hear me? Are you okay?"

John pushed with his hands and slowly raised himself up into a kneeling position, head down. Then he heard the ominous click of a gun being cocked. He looked up. Ron was standing behind Masterson with a pistol up against the back of his head.

Then the words, "No, he's not okay, Mr. Carl Masterson of the NSA. He's dying, you son of a bitch."

CHAPTER 47

It was just a short hike through the woods to the ramshackle cabin. And it was indeed falling down around itself—it was a wonder any of it was still standing. Ron and John had driven their cars into the woods as far as they could before the tree growth got too dense. At that point, they could see the shack off in the distance, so they hauled Carl out of the trunk of Ron's car and just abandoned their cars on the crude dirt road.

Ron pushed Carl in front and pointed towards the cabin. "Walk. That's where we're going to have a little chat."

Ron glanced back at John pulling up the rear. He hadn't said very much since he'd pulled himself up off the road. "You okay, John?"

He nodded. "Yeah, doin' just fine, Ron. Let's get this over with."

Carl hadn't said a word since they'd grabbed him. Ron could tell just by the look on his face that he'd been surprised to see that the man lying on the road was John Fletcher, and it all seemed to sink in to him pretty quickly after that. Ron figured that the guy had enough training to know that sometimes silence was the best option. Ron recalled that Carl had been with the FBI before joining the NSA, and had degrees in law and criminology, too—so he wasn't just your normal, everyday hostage.

They walked up the rotting steps onto the tiny porch. Ron held his Smith and Wesson 357 Magnum in one hand pointed at the back of Carl's head and, with the other hand he shoved open the rickety old door. The hinges squeaked as the door swung ajar, revealing a lone figure slumped in a chair against the far wall.

Ron shoved Carl inside the little one-room cabin. The wooden floors were rotting and the glass in the windows had long since fallen out, evidenced by the shards of glass littering the floor. But, it was the perfect interrogation room in Ron's opinion.

He looked down at his old friend. In appearance, Tom was still Tom, despite the beard and longer hair. But he was a different Tom now in so many other ways. He was the man who had applied the Thermate and fuses to the underside of the rollercoaster track, enabling the mass murder to happen. He was also a pathetic coward and a pedophile who'd abandoned his family and fled the country. No, this wasn't the trusted friend and partner who he'd known for over twenty years. At least, he thought he'd known him—obviously, no one really knew Tom, not even his own family.

Tom's hands were duct-taped together behind the back of the chair. As well, his ankles were constrained and duct tape also ran around his thighs to the underside of the chair.

And there was a sock in his mouth.

Carl stood as still as a statue, almost military-like, and stared at the wall. With the gun still trained on him, Ron yanked the sock out of Tom's mouth and then kicked another chair over from the corner of the room into position beside Tom's. "I thought you two might like to sit side by side."

Tom's eyes looked like they were tearing up. "Ron, why...are you...doing this?"

"Shut up, Tom. You make me sick."

Ron dropped his car keys onto an old table and swiped up a roll of duct tape. He then directed his attention to Carl. "Sit down in that chair so I can make you look like your friend here." Ron handed his pistol to John. "Keep this trained on him while I tape him up."

At that instant, Carl made his move. In one swift motion, he spun around and kicked the gun out of John's inexperienced hand. Then, with one quick flick of his wrist, a gun appeared in his hand. Ron recognized it as a Derringer, a small caliber weapon that could easily be concealed inside the sleeve of a shirt and attached to a spring release mechanism. Ron cursed himself for being so careless. He'd frisked his body and checked his ankles, but hadn't considered the possibility of a Derringer up his sleeve.

John dove to the floor, hands outstretched, reaching out desperately for Ron's pistol. Too late. Carl fired at John before he had the chance to reach the gun. John yelled out as the bullet tore into him, but he continued to slither along the floor in his quest to retrieve the menacing 357 Magnum.

Carl didn't waste time. He swung the Derringer around in the other direction just as Ron dove behind an old desk. Then one last glance at John, who now had his hand on the Magnum.

Out the door he went, but first he took Ron's car keys. Ron cursed to himself—his second mistake. He'd carelessly tossed them onto the little table when he picked up the duct tape. Through the window, Ron could see Carl rushing back the way they had come, along the little dirt path towards the cars.

Ron ran over to John and took the gun out of his hand. "Apply pressure to the wound, John! I'm going after him!"

He raced out the door and headed up the path. Carl was fast and Ron remembered that the man had been an NFL fullback. So, of course he was fast. But Ron was fast, too. He crashed through the bushes and trees, branches scratching against his face. He slipped twice on the muddy path, falling backwards onto his ass, but just as quickly got himself back in the hunt again. As he ran, he caught a glimpse of the two shiny cars through the dense foliage. And he saw Carl, too, about five feet away from freedom.

Carl heard him. He whirled around, dropped to his knees, and fired off a shot. Ron dove to the ground. The bullet tore into the bark of a tree only a foot or so away from Ron's head.

But that was two shots. Ron knew that Carl's gun was now empty. Those cute little Derringers were double-barreled and after those two barrels were used, that was it. It would take him too long to reload.

Ron crawled up from the mud and put on a burst of speed. Carl had his back turned and was now fiddling with the key fob. Ron ran faster than he'd ever run in his life. The man could not get away. They'd never find out what was going on without him and they probably wouldn't get another chance at him.

As Ron came within ten feet of the car, he saw that Carl was now in the driver's seat and he heard the engine start up. At the very instant it started to move, Ron did a swan dive onto the hood and grabbed onto the windshield wiper arms. Carl glared at him through the windshield and began swerving the car violently back and forth. Then it sped up, kicking up mud along the makeshift road. Ron held on for dear life, as his body swung around in motion with the car. He wanted to reach for his gun, but he didn't dare let go.

Suddenly, the car lost its traction and slid off the road. It skidded sideways along a patch of mud, then quickly straightened itself out again. All of a sudden, the car steered to the left, seemingly taking direct aim into the forest thickness.

The impact was unexpected. The windshield wiper arms broke off in Ron's hands as he slid backwards off the hood of the car. Carl had deliberately slammed them into a tree.

Ron was lying face down in the mud and was aware of the car spinning its wheels, trying desperately to back off the tree. Only the front right fender had been crunched, so the car was still driveable.

As the car labored to reverse itself in the thick sludge, Ron staggered to his feet and wiped the mud out of his eyes. He pulled the big Magnum out of his waistband, took aim at the passenger side of the front windshield and pulled the trigger. The windshield shattered instantly and Carl's shocked face could be seen clearly, no longer disguised by tinted glass.

Ron walked up to the car, keeping the gun pointed at Carl's head. He yanked open the door and Carl thrust his hands in the air.

"Get out and start walking. You know the way."

*****

The two prisoners were sitting quietly, duct-taped to their chairs, while Ron attended to John's wound. The bullet had only grazed him in the side and he hadn't lost too much blood. The duct tape came in handy, keeping the pressure on until John could bandage it up properly back at home.

John put his jacket back on as if nothing had happened and pointed to a case sitting in the corner of the room. "Is that the stuff I asked for?"

Ron nodded. "Yep. I left it when I brought Tom here. What do you want to do with it?"

"Not yet. We'll leave that for a bit."

John walked up to Carl and knelt down in front of him. "Tell us about Operation Backwash."

Silence.

Without any warning John reared his fist back and smashed it forward into Carl's face. Ron could hear the bones of the killer's nose crunching from way back where he was standing. Blood started streaming down Carl's mouth and chin.

John continued, "Your goons killed my wife. And then you sent them after Shelby and me. In case you were wondering where they disappeared to, I buried them in my backyard."

Ron noticed Tom cringe and he thought he could see some kind of reaction in Carl's face, but he wasn't sure. The man was one cool customer.

"You two worked together." John nodded in Tom's direction. "I'm guessing you blackmailed him about his seedy little double life. Am I right?"

Carl didn't move, but Tom nodded agreeably.

John turned his attention to Tom. "Do you know what Operation Backwash is?"

"No...my role was limited. I've never even saw this guy until today."

John didn't believe a word. "Your role was limited, huh? You're absolutely useless to me."

Tom opened his mouth to say something else, but John raised his hand. "Don't say anything else. You're more pathetic than this character."

John thrust his hand up to Carl's throat and began pushing in his Adam's apple. "I'll ask you one more time. What is Operation Backwash?"

Silence again, except for a choking sound coming from his throat. The man was not going to say a thing.

John stood up and walked over to the corner where the case was standing. He brought it back and set it down on the floor in front of the two killers. Ron walked over and knelt down beside him; pulled a tiny key from his pocket, inserted it into the lock, and flipped the case open.

He took out a small plastic bottle, a brush, two magnesium fuses, and a tiny remote control unit.

John pulled a knife out of a sheath in his waistband and then with several expert swipes, turned Carl's and Tom's shirts into shards. He ripped the shredded clothing away from their bodies until they were naked from the waist up.

"One thing you probably know, Masterson, is that Thermate burns through pretty much everything, not just metal."

John opened the bottle and calmly began brushing the sticky substance onto Carl's bare abdomen. He drew a complete circle around the man's midsection, from front to back. A sinister ring. Then he repeated the process with Tom.

Ron thought that John seemed almost robotic—like he was programmed. But he was pretty sure that this little bit of theater was going to get some answers. He reached into the case and took out the fuses. He handed them to John while he cut two strips of duct tape. John stuck one fuse up against the painted-on Thermate, right near Carl's belly button. Ron applied the tape, and then they turned their attention to Tom.

"What...what are you guys...doing? Why?"

Ron glared into the eyes of his old friend. "You, of all people, know the destructive power of Thermate. You used it to heartlessly kill all those innocent people. And you even had one of our own engineers killed, too, cruelly set up to be your patsy. Do you sleep at night? So, because you're a pervert who didn't want to get found out, more than two dozen people had to die, Tom? Is that how simple the equation was for you?"

Tom just lowered his head.

They finished their artistry around Tom's abdomen, then stood back and admired their work.

John picked up the remote control. "Okay, Carl—you know how this will work. It's only fitting justice that you guys are now painted with the same substance that you used to commit mass murder. So, you tell us what we want to know or I press this remote. I don't have to describe what that sensation is going to feel like for you, do I?"

Carl sighed with resignation—the first sound out of his mouth since they'd captured him. "Okay, you win. I'll tell you. Operation Backwash is a plan to steal water from Canada. An underground tunnel has been built from the Illinois River to Lake Erie. It will punch through in a couple of days. Water will then divert through the tunnel to the Illinois River and on from there to the Mississippi. And also pour down into the High Plains aquifer."

Ron's lips started to move, but no sound came out. Then he found the words. "You killed all those people to keep that secret?"

"We needed to silence Alexei Dragunov. He became a huge liability to us. But it had to look like an accident. And the tunnel is a secret; it has to stay that way for the foreseeable future, for obvious reasons."

John took a step towards Carl. "So, you're going to steal from our neighbor, one of our closest allies? Is it your intention to make every single country in the world hate us? Is that the goal of you guys? That's what it's coming to, you know."

"America is drying up. We need that water, much more than Canada does."

Ron just shook his head in dismay. "No, there's more to this than just theft. I don't get it. Tell us the rest. Now!"

Carl just stared at him with a cold, blank look in his eyes.

John thrust the remote forward, pointing it at Carl's chest. "I don't buy it either. You'd better tell us something else right now! I'll count to three. One... Two..."

Carl wiggled in his chair, rocking the legs. His face was one of pure panic. "No! Stop! Yes, there's more! We're faking a terrorist attack on the United States. A swarm of insect-bots will be launched from the Canadian side of the border, aimed at the western shores of Lake Michigan. It's actually a brilliant plan. They're laced with hydrogen cyanide and it will look like terrorists tried to poison the water supply. We'll blame it on a terrorist cell in Canada, and blame the Canadians for their poor security against terrorism. This will justify our moving troops up to the Canadian border and protecting the Great Lakes system. As I said, it's brilliant."

John waved the remote in the air. "Christ Almighty! You call this 'brilliant'? Just how many are going to die from this deception? Tell us! How many innocent Americans are going to be poisoned to death?"

Carl swallowed hard. "A few thousand in Milwaukee and Green Bay. Just enough to get Americans and the rest of the world outraged, and supportive of our troop movement."

Even Tom looked shocked. He turned his head towards Carl. "Are you mad?"

Carl scowled. "I'm a patriot. And I, along with many others, are prepared to make tough decisions to protect the United States of America. So, no, I'm not mad—I'm a hero. A future without water is not a pretty one."

Ron laughed. "That's the same thing you clowns said about oil. And when that became a crisis you just went out and took what you needed from other countries. Always the same pattern with you guys—the military option, fake wars, and fake terrorist attacks. And now, once again, you're going to kill our own people to justify your twisted adventures."

"I've told you what you wanted to know. So, it's out in the open. Do what you have to do. It's going to happen regardless. Now, let me go. I don't care what you do with this pervert beside me, but let me go. I've cooperated with you."

Ron turned toward John, a question in his eyes. At that same instant, he saw a blur of movement. John's hand swooped down and yanked the Magnum out of

Ron's waistband. Then he backed up and pointed the gun at Ron's chest.

In as calm a voice as he could muster, Ron asked, "John...what...are you doing?"

John's face was devoid of expression. His eyes were steady and his gun hand was unwavering. "I don't want to shoot you, Ron. That's the last thing I want to do. But I will if you don't get out of here now. Get in your car, drive back to Alexandria, and send out the alarm. Tell everyone who needs to know—but most of all, tell the officials in Green Bay and Milwaukee. Do it, before it's too late. There's another 911 about to happen and this one will probably be even more deadly."

Ron wasn't sure what to do. He was afraid of what John was planning, but he also knew in his gut that what his friend was intending to do was indeed the right thing. Gruesome and cruel, but right.

Part of him wanted to talk him out of it, but the other part, the soldier in him, knew that it had to be done. Still, it horrified him and he'd been a Navy Seal. It took a lot to horrify him. And he knew that by threatening him with the gun, John was protecting him—better that he not know or be a part of what was about to happen. John wanted Ron left clean. As for John, he didn't care because he was dying anyway.

And from the look in John's eyes, Ron was convinced beyond a doubt that he would indeed shoot him if he tried to stop him. Not shoot to kill though—just enough to put him down. He knew John was a good man; he wouldn't kill one of the good guys. And, as far as Ron was concerned, he wasn't going to take a bullet for the two scum sitting against the wall.

He made his decision. Ron backed up towards the door. He made the 'sign of the cross' and whispered, "God have mercy on you, John."

Then he turned around and ran out the door towards the relative sanity of his car.

*****

John Fletcher waited until he saw the headlights of Ron's car weaving their way through the forest. Then he turned and faced his captives.

"Both of you are going to pay for what you did. All those innocent people who died. It's hard to imagine that anything would justify that. But you did justify it, Masterson, for reasons of national security and power. And you, Tom, just to save your sorry ass from humiliation.

"Once again, Masterson, you and other psychopaths just like you, will lie to the people of the world to get them to support your twisted causes. You and your predecessors did it with TWA 800; again with 911; you did it with the Gulf of

Tonkin as a prelude to Viet Nam; you did it with JFK; you spread your lies about the Ukraine, Syria, Iraq, Libya and Iran, and have demonized most of the other Middle Eastern countries. Yet, you and your types still can't seem to understand why we're so universally hated.

"And then you made it personal. You killed my wife, and you tried to kill Shelby, then tried to kill me. I feel like just ripping your face off with my bare hands, but I don't want your slimy skin on my fingers."

Tom yelled. "Hey, I didn't even know what it was all about! I didn't have a part in any of this Backwash thing! I was just following orders!"

John glared at him. "That makes you even more pathetic."

Carl was squirming in his chair. John could tell he was trying desperately to loosen the tape on his wrists and ankles.

Then he shouted out, "I can make you a rich man! What will it take? Just tell me!"

John laughed. "I think you've forgotten that I'm dying. And even if I wasn't, you couldn't buy me."

"I told you what you wanted to know! We had a deal!"

John pointed the remote. "We had no such deal. And even if we did, I'd break it. I guess I'll be seeing both of you in hell."

They yelled out in unison. "No!"

John pressed the button. Instantly, on both men, a ring of fire began swirling around their abdomens. First it was just sparks that encircled them. But the sparks quickly turned to full blown flames, piercing into their mid-sections. Both of them twitched violently in their chairs and screamed at the top of their lungs as the flames embraced them. They knew what was happening, but for some macabre reason they forced themselves to look down, watching in horror as the flames quickly sliced their bodies in half.

It didn't take long. John, being a metallurgical engineer, knew how fast Thermate worked. The ring of fire expanded fast. First, their bodies were literally sliced in half by the fast burning ring. Then the flames spread outwards and burned each half beyond recognition.

John watched in cold detachment, just long enough until they no longer resembled human beings. Because that's how he wanted to remember them.

Then, as the cabin itself became engulfed in flames, John made his exit, hiking back up the path towards his car.

Once inside the car, he reclined his seat, and just breathed deeply for a few minutes while staring back at the hypnotic yellow glow.

And he thought he heard a soft voice whispering in his ear.

"Thank you, John."

CHAPTER 48

Ron Collens had prepared himself to tell only as much of the story as his stomach would allow.

He'd rushed back from the cabin only to lay awake most of the night. And thought of phoning John Fletcher while he was tossing and turning, but didn't know why. It certainly wouldn't have helped him fall asleep. And what could he possibly ask him? Did he really want to know? John hadn't wanted Ron to see the inevitable happen, but he was also smart enough to know that Ron was tuned in. Ron knew what John was going to do, and John knew it.

Carl and Tom had died grisly deaths. The look in John's eyes when he left him in the cabin told him there would be no forgiveness, no last minute appeals. He was out for vengeance and nothing was going to stop him. It was odd to think that the only way John felt he could save his own soul was to kill those two pieces of human trash. And kill them in graphic fashion. Quick and painless would not have satisfied John—he wanted them to be horrified and in extreme pain during the last moments of their lives. Retribution.

And Ron wondered how he would have felt if his own wife had been murdered and he knew he only had months to live. And the answer he was getting from himself was that he would probably do exactly what John had done.

Every human being on the planet had the capacity for violence—it all depended on what the circumstances were. Some people were just violent by nature. And then there were others, like John, who were the gentle good guys who'd finally had enough of the bad guys. They simply reached deep within their souls to find their primal instinct. They wanted justice, and were frustrated that the only way to get that was to do it themselves. The 'system' was no longer their trusted friend.

Fighting 'fire with fire' was the method John had chosen. Violence begot violence—there was no end to the cycle once it started. It was true with wars and it was true with crime.

At that very moment, Ron was sitting in Nate's office with Nate and Robin. The less the two of them knew, the better. But, at the very least, the three of them together had to deal with the horrible story that John and Ron had extracted from

Masterson. That mind-numbing knowledge of what was about to happen around the Lake Michigan area of the United States. It couldn't be ignored. But would anyone listen? Would anyone believe them?

When he was finished telling his story, Nate and Robin just stared at Ron with shock and disbelief written all over their faces.

Nate broke the silence. "Uh, okay…we now know what this was all about. Water."

"Yes."

"You and John did this together."

"Yes."

"Where is John now?"

"I don't know—presume at home."

Robin jumped in. "How credible is all this?"

Ron folded his arms across his chest. "Very credible, Robin."

"Well, if you managed to get Masterson to talk and confirm all this, he shouldn't mind coming forward and making a statement. 'Blowing the whistle,' so to speak."

Ron winced. "No, Robin, we're going to have to blow the whistle ourselves."

"Why? Who's going to believe us? He's in a high position with the NSA—he'll be believed because he had personal involvement with this diabolical plot. If he indeed has suddenly found a conscience, we should try to convince him to go all the way."

Nate poured himself some coffee from the steaming pot on the table. "Robin, you're thinking and talking like a lawyer, which of course you are. But, I believe Ron is trying to tell us something by not saying anything at all."

Robin looked from Ron to Nate, and then back to Ron again. "Oh…I see. At least, I think I see. I guess I don't want to hear anything more about this. That would be best, wouldn't it, Ron?"

Ron nodded. "Yes, Robin, that would be best."

Nate stood and started pacing. "We have to do something. This is horrific. And I'm talking about the fake terrorist attack, not the water issue. That's bad enough, and it'll cause an international crisis, for sure—but it's just theft. The other part of the plan is, once again, mass murder, and we have a chance to try to stop it."

Ron stood as well. He was feeling sick in the pit of his stomach—a combination of what he knew had happened back at the ramshackle old cabin and what he knew was *going* to happen when the hydrogen cyanide was released. He talked as he paced. "Nate, we have to try to make contact with city officials in Green Bay and Milwaukee. And we need to do it fast. This thing could happen today for all we know."

Nate rubbed his forehead as he walked over to his computer. He typed a few keys and read what was on the screen. Then he typed again and scanned the image. "Okay, I have the names and phone numbers for the mayors of both cities. I think I should call them myself, right now."

Nate picked up the phone. Robin stood up and walked over to Nate's desk—took the phone out of his hand and rested it back in the cradle. Nate looked at her, puzzled. "What's wrong?"

"I'm the one who should make the call, Nate—not you, and especially not Ron. If what happened last night is what I think happened, you're going to bring a firestorm down upon yourselves. It might turn out that this poison gas attack won't happen at all. There might be a good chance that with Masterson... silenced, they will abandon the operation entirely. And if they evacuate these two cities, a process involving hundreds of thousands of people, you could be charged with malicious mischief. The FBI would be all over you—and we already know that they seem to be in the loop on this whole thing, so they'd love to blame you for salacious allegations."

"Okay, I understand."

Robin continued, "And one of the biggest advantages of me making the call is that I'm a lawyer and consequently have more credibility than you. Your name has been all over the news. If it doesn't happen you'll be in trouble, and if does happen you'll also be in trouble. They'll want to know how you obtained the information, and may even make a case to imply that you were involved. But, with me representing both you and Ron, we have the power of confidentiality in our favor. I don't have to disclose where I got the information—I'm only doing my citizen's duty and my duty as an officer of the court, in passing the information along."

Ron shook his head. "Jesus, all we're trying to do is save lives here! What a country—it's amazing that we have to worry about these things when we're just trying to do the right thing."

Robin nodded. "Yes, Ron—it is what it is. Sad but true." She grabbed a sheet of paper off Nate's desk and pulled a pen out of her vest pocket. Then she started to write.

Nate leaned over the desk to take a look. "What are you doing?"

"Drafting a quickie legal agreement, authorizing me to represent you and Ron privately on the matter of 'information that has come to your attention.' I already work for you, of course, but that's a master/servant relationship within Flying Machines Inc. We need to have an agreement between us within my private practice as just an ordinary lawyer. That will protect you and me with the principle of 'confidentiality.'"

"God, I'm sure glad I asked you to sit in today."

Robin smiled. "I have to look out for you boys so you don't go off half-cocked!" She turned to Ron. "Go out in the hall and grab someone, anyone, to come in here to witness this."

Ron was back in less than ten seconds, with a young lady in tow. "Guys, this is Jennifer Logan."

Robin shook her hand. "Sit down, please. I just want you to witness this little agreement. And write down your home address and phone number underneath your signature."

The three of them signed and Jennifer witnessed. The agreement was done. After Jennifer left the office, Robin walked around and sat behind Nate's desk. She scanned the mayoral information for the city of Green Bay that was still open on the screen.

Then she took a deep breath, picked up the phone and dialed. Ron sat next to Nate on the couch. He could tell that Nate was just as tense as he was, wringing his hands together and biting his lips.

"It's okay, buddy. We're doing our best to stop this. Nothing more we can do."

Nate frowned. "I can't believe that the Black Mamba has led to this—a trail to a possible national tragedy. I wonder if Tom knew what this was leading to. I sure hope I get my hands on that prick one day, Ron."

Ron patted his knee, and said in a somber tone. "Trust me, Nate, you won't be able to."

At that comment, Nate just stared into Ron's eyes, searching. Ron was sure he caught what his eyes were saying and that was confirmed when Nate nodded his head and whispered, "Okay, I get it."

Robin was talking. They both concentrated on listening to her side of the conversation.

"I already told you who I am. I'll repeat—my name is Robin Gilchrist and I'm a practicing lawyer, a member of the Bar in Alexandria, Virginia."

"Well, does he have his cell phone with him?"

"Can't you patch me through to him?"

"I'm sure he'll want to interrupt his golf game to hear what I have to say. It's an extreme emergency."

They could tell by the look on her face that Robin was getting frustrated. She impatiently tapped her pen on the desk as she waited to be connected.

"Hello? Mr. Mayor?"

"Good. Thanks for taking my call."

"I'm sure you'll want to cancel the rest of your game once you hear what I have to say."

"Okay, well, my name is Robin Gilchrist and I'm a lawyer down here in

Virginia."

"Yes, the weather here is just fine, thank you." Robin rolled her eyes. "The reason I'm calling you is that clients of mine have come into some information that was so disturbing that I had to phone you right away."

"No, I'm not at liberty to identify them. But, you need to know that a terrorist attack is pending and imminent, involving cities and communities bordering the west shore of Lake Michigan. Specifically, your city of Green Bay, and also Milwaukee."

"Yes, the information I have is solid. The attack will come from across the lake in a form that may resemble a swarm of insects; grasshoppers specifically. But that will be an illusion—in fact they will be nanobots laden with hydrogen cyanide. The cyanide will be released once the western shore is reached, and I don't think I have to tell you how deadly airborne cyanide will be to the population."

"No, this isn't a joke. I'll give you my phone number here and you can call me back if you wish to verify who I am. You can also look me up in the Virginia Bar registry. I know this sounds crazy, but, trust me, this is a real and imminent threat."

"Well, I was hoping that you'd begin evacuating the city. If you start immediately there might be just enough time to save some lives."

"No, I can't comment on why Homeland Security hasn't increased the threat level."

"Mr. Mayor, you can file a complaint against me if you wish. I don't care. Please, just take what I'm saying seriously. Something terrible is about to happen, and…"

Robin stared at the phone, and then slammed it down in the cradle. "He hung up on me! Unbelievable! He thinks I'm a nutcase!"

Ron poured Robin some coffee and took it over to her. "It does sound kinda nutsy, don't you think? Flying grasshopper robots loaded with poison? I mean, if we hadn't gone through the bizarre things we'd gone through, and we were just hearing something like that right out of the blue, what might our reaction be?"

Nate added, "Yes, and remember, you're not a government official—if it was someone in the government calling, the mayor might have listened more seriously to you."

As she picked up the phone again to make her second call, she raised her other hand in frustration. "We can't talk to anyone in the federal government— we tried, didn't we? Where did that get us? The FBI making us the villains for trying to implicate the NSA! So—who can we possibly call when the government is intent on attacking its own people? Now I can understand the frustrations of all those people who passed along tips and warnings in advance of 911. No one listened to them either."

She dialed Milwaukee. After a few minutes of similar banter, Robin was looking at another dead phone. "He hung up, too!"

Nate shook his head in disgust and walked behind the desk. He made a few clicks on the keyboard and pointed at the screen.

"Okay, Robin, make your last call. Phone Canada."

CHAPTER 49

The last two days had been total escapism for Nate and Shelby. It was the weekend and Shelby was off work, so he'd convinced her to spend most of it in bed with him. Not because he was particularly horny and not because she was either. It was just a comfort. And he needed the comfort. Desperately.

They ate in bed, drank in bed, and made love in bed…and even sometimes on the floor. Sometimes accidentally and sometimes on purpose. They did anything to make themselves forget. Had sex in imaginative ways that under normal circumstances they probably wouldn't have.

Did some *nursey* role plays—a fantasy that Nate had harbored in his mind ever since he was a teenager. When he'd suffered the concussion in football, one of his fondest memories from his hospital stay was one particular nurse. She always dressed commando, and every time she bent over, his eyes just caught the lower edge of her ass.

He confessed this fantasy to Shelby, turning beet red in the process. Her reply was, "We can play that game." And they did. It turned out better than Nate's fantasy, because even though that nurse was commando, she hadn't possessed the ass that Shelby did. So, his fantasy changed forever—now it would always be Shelby in the highlight reel. And being a nurse in real life, the role play was an easy one for her. She made the fantasy real.

But there was a price to pay. Nate had to act out, too—and in Shelby's fantasy, he had to be a masseur with wandering hands. This was an easy one for him to play-act, because his hands wandered all over her body at the best of times. But… he had to be sincere, act it out in a real way. This was the part he found difficult— because he talked too much. Lying seductively on her stomach, she turned around in frustration and told him to shut up. "I don't want you to have a conversation with me, I just want you to fuck me. It ruins the fantasy if I hear your voice, because I know your voice. So, shut up and seduce me!"

They had lots of laughs during their two days in bed. And lots of real conversations, too, which was what he loved about Shelby. She was easy to talk to about the fluff stuff, but also intelligent enough to engage in the heavy stuff, too. Lots of debates about world issues, the climate, where to go on vacation, how many kids they were going to have, where they would live…and whether they even wanted to work anymore.

They tried talking about virtually everything except what they'd gone through the past few weeks. Nate told her how Robin had tried to warn city officials in Milwaukee and Green Bay, but that she'd been ignored. And he told her that Robin had also phoned the Canadian government's ministry of natural resources and told them the whole story. They'd received a better reaction from Canada. Two follow-up phone conversations later and they were satisfied that at least someone was listening to them.

But…the most important warning, the one to the two cities in the state of Wisconsin, had been basically laughed at. Which meant people were going to die if Operation Backwash was executed.

Nate and Shelby decided before the weekend started that they just didn't want to know—that they preferred to be in denial for two days; be silly and carefree for forty-eight glorious hours.

But the end of the weekend was near—it was Sunday night and they were still in bed, trays of leftover food beside them on the night table, a half-finished bottle of wine on the floor.

Shelby gently rubbed his arm. "We should just travel. See the world before it all dries up."

Nate grimaced. "It does make you think, doesn't it? If things are so severe now that cause our own country to steal water from our friendliest ally, what's next?"

"I don't think the world has much time left, Nate. Well, maybe the world does, but I don't think the human race does."

Nate shook his head. "Not if things continue the way they're heading. And, nature might not do it to us—we might just wipe ourselves out. I mean, how insane is it to think of a country attacking itself—not it's enemies—but itself. Killing its own people just to get support for its twisted agenda. It's sick, absolutely sick. What chance does the human race have if that's something governments can get away with?"

Shelby gently stroked Nate's penis. "Maybe we could do this 'escaping from reality' thing for the rest of our lives? I mean, what a shame if we just worked and worked and then it all came to a shocking end. Life's too precious—John Fletcher is sure aware of that."

"Well, I have enough money. We could do that. I could just leave the company in Ron's good hands, while you and I roam. I'd still retain my share ownership in the company, and collect my share of the profits, but I wouldn't need to be here. We could just enjoy life the way it was meant to be enjoyed. Before it's all gone."

She stroked Nate's penis faster. "I'd love to be your roaming partner. And I have money, too, so I'd pay my way."

Nate grinned at her. "The only thing you have to do to pay your way is to just do more of what you're doing right now!"

Shelby stopped stroking. She brought her hand up from his penis and shoved him out of bed onto the floor. "You're a pig, Nathan Morrell!"

Nate lay on the floor, laughing. "I thought I'd just lighten the mood a little."

Shelby allowed a smile to cross her face. Then she slipped off the bed and climbed on top of him. "You know what?"

"What?"

"That's one of the things I adore about you."

He kissed her, and then slipped his eager penis inside her for probably the twentieth time that weekend. "I'm glad you adore me."

Shelby kissed him back and smiled in that coy way Nate loved so much. "No, I didn't say I adored *you*. I said that was just 'one of the *things*.'"

Nate rolled her over onto her back. "Well, let's see if we can change that."

*****

They were both in the kitchen preparing a late night snack. Shelby closed the fridge door, placed a package of Stilton cheese on the counter, and then just hugged Nate hard from behind.

He turned his head. "Aww...nice. But what was that for?"

"It's time, Nate."

"What do you mean?"

"I think you know what I mean. We've escaped from reality for two days, but it's time. We had good reasons to want to forget...and kinda just hide away. But we can't run away from this any longer and a lot has probably happened over the weekend. We have to face it. It's the end of a long ordeal and we have to know how it ended. Closure."

Nate turned around and hugged her back. For two days, he'd dreaded this moment. He just didn't want to know. Before they'd started their re-enactment of the John Lennon/Yoko Ono lie-in, Nate had put the phone message system on 'silent' so he wouldn't hear the messages as they were left. Just a few minutes before, he'd taken a glance at the machine's counter display—a total of forty messages were waiting for him. Something had happened, he was sure of it. He wouldn't normally get that many calls on his landline during a two-day stretch.

That phone had rung off the hook for two days, and he and Shelby had promised each other that it wouldn't be answered. And they'd turned off their cell phones, too. An equal number of messages were probably waiting for them there as well. They also promised each other that the TV and radio were off limits.

There had been at least thirty knocks on his door while they were luxuriating in bed—they just giggled and kept as quiet as mice. For a time, it had been fun playing hooky from life. They pretended to be happy, silly and giggly—it was fun, but they both knew it was just a charade. They were kidding themselves.

They had done everything possible to make sure they were shut off from everything except each other. And that had been real nice. This was something Nate had never done before and he promised himself that he would do it again really soon...with Shelby.

But she was right. It was time. The charade was over. Real life beckoned.

Shelby looked deep into Nate's eyes. "Let's find out what Carl Masterson has done. Maybe we'll get some good news and find out that he and his cronies failed."

Nate cupped her face in his hands. "If it succeeded, it won't be by his hand. He's dead."

Shelby's eyes flared. "What? Who killed him?"

"I'm not going to tell you that. Tom Foster is dead, too. All you need to know is that I didn't kill them."

Shelby swallowed hard and whispered softly as she lay her head against Nate's chest, "I'm glad it wasn't you. But...I have to admit—whoever did it deserves a medal."

Nate wrapped his arm around her waist and guided her towards the living room. "Are you ready, Shelby?"

"Yes, Nate, I'm ready. It's been a wonderful weekend, but we need to rejoin life, as ugly as it may be."

They sat down together on the couch and Nate clicked the remote for the big screen TV. It was already set to CNN and the two of them held hands as the rolling headlines scrolled across the bottom. And in giant font at the top of the screen were the words: 'Breaking News.' An anchorman named Todd Stevens was talking, seemingly half out of breath.

"...*was executed with extreme precision. For those of you who have just joined us, once again a horrific attack has been carried out by Islamic terrorists against the United States of America. Details are still sketchy, but there are reports of people dead in the streets, in their cars, in their offices and in their homes. The two cities that have been most impacted by this attack are Green Bay and Milwaukee, but almost all of the towns along the western shore of Lake Michigan have been affected in some way. The state of Wisconsin is in absolute shock, as is the entire country, and indeed the world. Casualties are estimated to be in the thousands, possibly even exceeding the number of people killed in the 911 attacks on New York and Washington.*

"*Joining me now on Skype from Washington is General Charles 'Bull' Tetford, the Pentagon spokesman. General, can you fill in the blanks for us a bit? I know you're very busy right now, but America needs to know what has happened and what will be happening going forward."*

"Yes, this is another sad day for America, Todd. We probably knew in our hearts that this would happen again, but we hoped that our security measures would work. But we failed— or should I say, our neighbor's security measures failed. We have no control over what other countries do and, in this case, it appears as if Canada's weak response to terrorism threats has brought this upon us. The attack came from the Canadian side of the border—early indications are that a swarm of insect robots flew across Lake Michigan in a brazen attempt to poison our water supply. But the terrorists apparently overestimated the distance of flight and, instead of releasing the poison gas over the lake, it went airborne over land. That's why we have the mass casualties that we're seeing in our towns and cities."

"General, do you know at this stage what type of poison was used?"

"Yes, it appears to be hydrogen cyanide."

"How were you able to determine that so fast?"

"Air sample tests and just the speed of the reactions from the victims. It has all the signatures of hydrogen cyanide."

"General, has any group claimed responsibility yet?"

"No, but we know who it is. Our intelligence community has moved fast on this. We were able to backtrack 'chatter' and it appears to be a cell based in the Toronto area. We've contacted Canadian officials and alerted them, but we have no idea of what, if anything, they've done so far."

"Is it Al Qaeda again?"

"Not exactly, although very similar radical ideologies. It appears to be a cell affiliated with ISIS—the militant group that is presently tearing apart Syria and Iraq. That group issued threats against America and England several weeks ago—we took those threats seriously, but it doesn't appear as if the Canadians shared our concerns."

Todd Stevens was suddenly handed a piece of paper by one of the producers.

"Excuse me, General—I've just been given something. I'm scanning it now."

The anchorman read the report, then took a deep breath.

"General, things are obviously happening fast. Could you comment on the report that U.S. Marines have been amassed at positions along our border with Canada?"

"Yes, that is correct. We were so alarmed by this security breakdown, and the fact that an attack against us was launched from Canada, that we felt we had no choice but to take it upon ourselves to protect the Great Lakes water supply. We can't take a chance on another attack happening. It would be disastrous for America."

"Will troops be crossing the border?"

"I can't comment on operational matters."

"Will the U.S. military be using armed drones as it does in the Middle East, to search out this terrorist group in Canada?"

"We know where they are. We've offered that help to Canada and so far they've refused. If

we feel that we are in imminent danger from Canada, we won't hesitate to use drones, which is our right under international law."

Todd was handed another sheet of paper. He read it quickly.

"General, I have a report in my hand which says that Canada has responded by posting troops on their side of border locations in the Great Lakes region."

"Well, that is certainly their right to do. It doesn't concern me at all. In fact, our two militaries can work together to protect against the next attack and secure the precious water supply that our two countries share equally."

"General, the report I have outlines something else. The troop complement on the Canadian side also includes 2,500 British Special Forces soldiers who have been in training exercises with the Canadians at Trenton, Ontario."

Skype went silent for a few seconds.

"General?"

"Yes...yes, I'm here. I'll have to get back to you on that. I see that I'm being summoned into a meeting. I'll have to sign off, Todd."

"I understand, General. One last quick question—do you have any comment on reports that are pouring in that there is an alarming drop in the water level of one of the Great Lakes, the giant Lake Erie? Is that related in any way to this terrorist attack?"

"As I said, Todd, I have to go. Sorry—I'll be pleased to join you again later. We ask all Americans to stay vigilant—we'll get through this as we have before. God bless you all and God bless the United States of America."

Nate aimed the remote at the TV and clicked off. Shelby was still holding his hand, but it felt so moist that it was almost dripping.

He leaned in and kissed her on the cheek. "Are you okay?"

She turned her head and tried to focus her eyes. But Nate could see that they were rolling. She was on the verge of another one of her fainting spells.

He grabbed her shoulders and shook them hard. Then he slapped her face, just as he had so many weeks before when they were hanging on for dear life to the trestle structure of the Black Mamba.

"Scream, Shelby! Scream your heart out!"

CHAPTER 50

The waiting room was jam packed.

With patients who looked forlorn, helpless and hopeless. No surprise there, of course, since all of them were being treated for conditions similar to what John Fletcher had.

It was the cancer clinic in downtown Washington, D.C. Several prominent oncologists worked out of the medical center and John's wannabe savior was a woman. He liked her—she was compassionate and smart as a whip. And she had truly believed early on that John might have a chance. But that faded fast as soon as she saw his first brain scan...and the second...and then the third. The thing was growing like a pumpkin on steroids.

Doctor Joyce Hatfield was an optimist by nature—John was able to sense that the first time he met her. But his condition seemed to have sucked that wonderful characteristic out of her. Perhaps it was because she was a woman. She was more sensitive and caring than a typical male doctor. He could always tell from the look in her eyes and the tone of her voice that she was sad for him. Didn't want to see him in pain—wanted so much to make his passing as comfortable as possible. Didn't want to say goodbye to him.

John didn't even understand why he still came here. What was the point? He thought he was probably doing it more for his doctor than for himself, funny as that sounded. Because John was a sensitive and compassionate person, too. He knew the good doctor was having such a hard time with this. Not being able to save him when that was her entire reason for existence. Joyce was just maintaining him now—trying to slow down the growth of the tumor as much as possible, to eke out as many more days of life for him that she could.

But what Joyce didn't know was that John didn't give a shit anymore. He would never admit that to her, because it would not only hurt her, but it would be an insult to her profession. She was doing what she thought was best and to hear that John just wanted it to be over would break her heart. And John didn't want to break any hearts. His was already broken, of course, but why pass that misery onto others? He just couldn't.

This wasn't his regular day to come in. Joyce's secretary had left a message for him, asking him to pop in for a short meeting. John figured that Joyce's 'missionary zeal' was probably causing her to re-think John's treatment. She probably wanted to step up the radiation now that time was winding down. Joyce most likely wanted to try to wind it up again, try to buy more time.

What Joyce didn't know was that John had already made a decision before he arrived for the appointment. He was going to tell her that he wanted the radiation treatments to stop. There was just no point. He wanted nature to just take its course—there was no point anymore, no point delaying the inevitable. He wasn't going to tell her he wanted to die—he would never tell her that. He would simply tell her that he just wanted to die with some dignity.

John rubbed his eyes. They were sore from lack of sleep. No wonder—who could sleep with what John had on his conscience. Curious though, he thought. While his eyes were sore, he wasn't getting the occasional blurriness anymore. And he hadn't had even one headache in at least a week. Before then, he got several a day like clockwork.

A wry smile crept across his face. *No doubt just the calm before the storm. Good. Bring it on. I'm ready.*

There was a TV hanging on the wall in the waiting room. Of course, it was tuned to CNN. As if the people in this room needed one more thing to get depressed over. Now they had to sit here and watch the news.

The non-stop coverage of the human disaster in Wisconsin was continuing. CNN had even come up with a cute little tagline for the tragedy, as they always did with wars and natural disasters. For this one, the label they had come up with was 'Deadly Air.'

Well done, CNN. Do you really think people need your stupid insensitive titles in order to stay engaged in the stories?

John shook his head slowly as he watched the story unfolding on the screen. There was footage being shown from a news helicopter circling above downtown Milwaukee. As the video camera panned down, it was easy to see bodies—hundreds of them—lying in the streets. It was a gruesome and disturbing sight, but the helicopter kept showing it. Street after street. But it was sensational, and that's what today's media outlets wanted to show. That's what got ratings.

John couldn't take it anymore. He got up, walked over to the TV, and hit the power button.

One of the patients, a grungy looking guy in a plaid shirt, yelled out, "Hey, what are you doing? I was watching that!"

John glared at him. "Well, I don't want to see it."

"Too bad for you." The guy got up and turned the TV back on. "Who made you the TV boss, buddy?"

"Okay, we'll take a vote." John looked around the room. "Who wants to see that crap? Raise your hands."

He didn't have to count. About ninety percent of the hands in the room went up. John just shook his head and sat down again. "Okay, you win. Enjoy."

Suddenly, his name was called out. John was glad he was going to be spared having to watch the very mess that he'd been involved in up to his neck. He was particularly saddened about it all knowing that Ron, Nate and Robin had tried desperately to send out warnings. Ron phoned him on the day the news of the attacks broke and told him about their gallant but fruitless efforts.

If those stupid politicians had only listened there wouldn't be a news helicopter gleefully showing film footage of what literally looked like Doomsday. And why were the bodies still there? Surely the air was safe enough by now? Was the government deliberately leaving them there for a prescribed period of time necessary for maximum shock value? To garner support for their deception?

John got up and followed the nurse who'd called out his name, making a face at 'plaid shirt man' as he walked past him.

He walked into Doctor Joyce Hatfield's office and sat down in his usual seat. She looked up from her work and smiled warmly at him. "John, it's so good to see you! How have you been?"

How can I possibly answer that question truthfully? Well, okay, I've killed four men in the most gruesome ways you can imagine, but other than that I'm doing fine, thank you.

"I'm doin' okay, Joyce. How are you?"

"I'm just wonderful, John. I'm glad you agreed to come in today."

John grimaced. "Well, I wanted to come in to see you anyway. Don't be upset with me, but I want the radiation treatments to stop. I've had it with them."

Joyce smiled. "I agree. We'll stop them right away."

John was stunned. "Oh, okay. I'm surprised you're so agreeable. Thanks, Joyce."

"You're welcome." She waved a file in the air. "I have the results of the brain scan we did on you a few days ago. John, I don't know how to tell you this—and I don't even understand it myself and neither do my colleagues. But your tumor is gone. There is no sign of it anywhere in your brain. It didn't shift, it's not hiding. It's just...gone."

John couldn't believe what he was hearing. He pinched his arm to make sure he wasn't dreaming. "How is that possible?"

"It's not possible. In fact, it's *impossible*. But it's happened; I don't know how it happened, but it did. It's a miracle, John. It's not the radiation that did this—it can't possibly achieve that kind of result in such a short period of time. And, even over a long period of time, we never see a result like this from radiation on such a large and aggressive tumor as yours was."

John stood up and headed for the door. Joyce came around from behind her desk and gave him a big hug. "I'm so happy for you, John. I know you must be in shock right now, but in a day or two it will register. You have your life back, John."

He smiled politely. "No, I really don't, Joyce. But thanks for your kind words. It's been a pleasure having you care for me."

John turned the door handle. He felt Joyce's hand on his shoulder.

"You must have a guardian angel watching over you, John."

*****

John was sitting in his living room, with a glass of scotch whiskey in one hand and a cigarette in the other. He hadn't smoked in five years, but he felt like chaining. On impulse, he had stopped at a gas station on the way home and bought a pack. Just one pack—he wouldn't need more than that.

Not one light was on in the house—darkness was preferred. The only illumination coming into the room was from the constant parade of headlights going up and down the busy street that his dingy rental home was situated on. God, he missed his old house. And, God, he missed Linda. Terribly.

John poured himself another full glass of scotch, then lit another cigarette. The ashtray was half full and the bottle was half empty. He was making progress.

As he sat there getting more and more drunk, he took stock of his new status.

He was alone without the love of his life. Linda was gone forever—all he had left were the memories they'd made together. There would never be another Linda and he might have another thirty years in front of him without her. That thought made his heart ache.

He had a son, but had no idea where he was. And Vincent wanted nothing to do with his dad anyway. He wondered how he was doing, what he looked like, who was in his life.

He had lost the job that he'd toiled at for decades—a job that for the most part he'd loved, except for the TWA 800 lies and the Black Mamba tragedy.

John had discovered that he could kill, and kill quite easily. He'd slaughtered four men in ways that would probably make even the most hardened murderers cringe. He'd discovered a rage inside him that had become insatiable.

And the end result of the Black Mamba intrigue was a faked terrorist attack on innocent Americans. The images of those poor souls lying in the streets of Milwaukee tugged at John's heart. The heart-tugging part was a good thing though—it was encouraging to John that he hadn't totally lost himself.

He took a long sip of scotch and lit another cigarette.

Poor Doctor Joyce Hatfield. She had been so happy—it was probably the highlight of her career, and John wished he could have celebrated a bit with her. She was a good person.

284

But what Joyce didn't understand was that John was shattered with the news. It was the last news he'd wanted to hear. He had been welcoming death. Wanted it to hurry up. It was the only thing that had kept him going since Linda died. He needed to join her and there was absolutely nothing on earth that was worth living for anymore.

He had no purpose, no zeal, and no passion. And that emptiness inside had helped him become a killer. It was that absence of feeling that had enabled him to exact vengeance for Linda. It allowed the rage to burn through him to the point where he became an animal—just long enough to do what needed to be done.

Because he knew at that time that he wouldn't have to live with it for very long.

But now he *would* have to live with it.

And because of the 'miracle' it would be decades before he saw Linda again.

John chugged the rest of his scotch and stubbed out his cigarette. Then he stood up, swaying a bit from the scotch, and felt his way through the dark to the basement stairway. He flicked on the light switch and held on tight to the railing as he made his way down the steep stairs.

He staggered with purpose towards the stool in the corner. Picked it up and carried it over to the center of the room, placing it underneath the noose that was still hanging from the steel beam running along the underside of the ceiling.

John Fletcher took a deep breath and climbed on top of the stool. He positioned the noose around his neck and adjusted the knot to the back and slightly to the side. Then he pulled tight on the knot until he could feel his neck bulge and his throat constrict.

John closed his eyes and thought a silent prayer.

Then she was there.

He saw Linda as clear as day, floating once again in front of his eyes. She was frowning at him and her mouth wore that cute little pout that she always put on when she didn't get her way.

Her hair was flowing down past her shoulders and her eyes had that same twinkle that he remembered and adored. God, he loved her.

Then she spoke. But not really—it was not the same as *listening* to someone speak. There was no sound—it was only in his head. The words bypassed his ears and went directly to his brain. It was a weird sensation, but weirdly wonderful.

"John, you're making me sad."

He answered her, not with the spoken word but with his brain—silent words.

"I want to be with you. There's nothing here for me."

"You're a good person, John. What you did for me was heroic. You shouldn't be ashamed of yourself. It had to be done and you did it. You did it for me, but also for so many others."

"I'm not the same person I was, Linda. The only way I can be the same is to be with you

again."

"I don't want you to do this, John. I don't want you to come to me this way."

"I have nothing to live for here."

"Yes, you do. You have reasons to live."

"No, I don't."

"I won't let you do this, John. I made you all better for a reason."

"Why did you do that? When you rubbed my head that night, it was soothing. But if I'd known what you were really trying to do, I would have chased you away. I wouldn't have to do this now if you'd left me alone."

"I couldn't leave you alone then, John. You know that. And I can't leave you alone now either. I'm going to stop you."

"There's nothing you can do to stop me, Linda dear. I'm coming to you tonight."

"No, you're not. I love you, John."

Then she was gone. John was all alone in a musty basement with a noose around his neck. The same noose that not too long ago he'd used to execute a man in cold blood.

Well, he wouldn't be long.

John raised his right foot and pulled it back behind him. He was just about to give the stool a mighty kick when the phone rang. He suspended his foot in midair. He didn't know why, but for some reason he waited until the phone rang three times after which he knew the message machine would pick up.

Then he heard a familiar voice. It still sounded the same, even though it had been more than ten years since he'd last heard it.

"Dad, it's me, Vincent. If you're there, please pick up. I know it's been a long time and maybe you don't even want to ever hear my voice again...but I hope you do. I was planning to surprise you tomorrow, but I just got this sudden urge tonight to give you a call.

"I'm flying back to the States tomorrow. That lawyer you hired tracked me down—he told me about Mom. I'm so sorry and so sad that she's gone. Dad, I want you and me to start fresh—life's too short. And I'll have a surprise for you when I come; actually two surprises. My wife is the first surprise—and guess what? Her name is Linda, just like Mom! Isn't that weird? You'll love her—she's a lot like Mom, too. And I have a son! He's five now. And I named him after you, Dad. You're a grandfather to yet another John Fletcher. Okay, just wanted to let you know. We'll see you tomorrow. And...I love you, Dad. I've missed you."

As tears poured down his face in a torrent, John concentrated on keeping his balance. It wasn't easy with the inebriated state he was in. Slowly and carefully, he brought his right foot back down to the top of the stool. Then he loosened the knot and yanked the noose from around his neck.

Before even stepping down from the stool, he began making mental notes.

He had to shop for groceries…and toys. And…he had to make up the two guest bedrooms, and…

But the first thing he was going to do was burn the noose. And then give some more water to the new grass sprouts in the backyard.

John raised his wet eyes upward and smiled through his tears. "I love you, Linda. Thank you. See you later?"

THE AUTHORS

PETER PARKIN

Peter was born in Toronto, Canada, and after studying Business Administration at Ryerson University he embarked on a thirty-four year career in the business world, primarily spent in the executive ranks. He retired in 2007 after serving as the Chief Operating Officer of a major national company. Peter has written six novels; the last four with co-author, Alison Darby, of England. When he's not writing novels, Peter is active serving as a Director on four corporate boards. He has two grown sons and two grandsons and resides near the city of Calgary, on the threshold of the Rocky Mountains of Western Canada. Find out more about Peter by visiting his website. http://www.peterparkin.com.

ALISON DARBY

Alison is a life-long resident of the West Midlands region of England. She studied psychology in college and when she's not juggling a busy work life and writing novels, she enjoys researching the wonders of astronomy. Alison has co-authored four novels with Peter Parkin, and has two grown daughters who live and work in the vibrant city of London. Alison resides in an historic home in the charming town of Tettenhall, U.K.